Mr Stink

David Walliams
Mr Stink

Illustrated by Quentin Blake

HarperCollins *Children's Books*

First published in hardback in Great Britain by HarperCollins *Children's Books* 2009
First published in paperback in Great Britain by HarperCollins *Children's Books* 2010

HarperCollins *Children's Books* is a division of HarperCollins*Publishers* Ltd,
HarperCollins Publishers 1 London Bridge Street London SE1 9GF

The HarperCollins *Children's Books* website address is
www.harpercollins.co.uk

HarperCollins*Publishers*
1st Floor, Watermarque Building, Ringsend Road
Dublin 4, Ireland

111

Text © David Walliams 2009
Illustrations © Quentin Blake 2009

David Walliams and Quentin Blake assert the moral right to be identified
as the author and illustrator of this work

ISBN 978-0-00-727906-7

Printed and bound by
CPI Group (UK) Ltd, Croydon, CR0 4YY

MIX
Paper from
responsible sources
FSC™ C007454

This book is produced from independently certified FSC™ paper
to ensure responsible forest management.

For more information visit: www.harpercollins.co.uk/green

For my mum Kathleen, the kindest person

I have ever met.

Thank-yous:

Once again Quentin Blake has honoured my writing with his sublime illustrations, and to him I am enormously grateful. I still can't quite believe I have collaborated with him, as he is such a legend. Other people who I would like to thank are Mario Santos and Ann-Janine Murtagh at HarperCollins for believing in me once again. Nick Lake, my editor, deserves a big thank you for making me work so hard and taking me out for tea and cakes. The copy editor Alex Antscherl, cover designer James Annal and text designer Elorine Grant have all done magnificent jobs on this too. Also thank you to all the people at HarperCollins who work so diligently to promote and distribute the book, particularly Sam White. My literary agent Paul Stevens at Independent is a very nice man too, and dealt brilliantly with all the important contractual things that my brain cannot process.

Finally I would also like to thank all the people who wrote to me to say they enjoyed my first book, *The Boy in the Dress*, particularly the children. It is very touching when someone takes the time to write a letter, and greatly encouraged me when working on *Mr Stink*. I hope it doesn't disappoint.

1

Scratch 'N' Sniff

Mr Stink stank. He also stunk. And if it is correct English to say he stinked, then he stinked as well. He was the stinkiest stinky stinker who ever lived.

A stink is the worst type of smell. A stink is worse than a stench. And a stench is worse than a pong. And a pong is worse than a whiff. And a whiff can be enough to make your nose wrinkle.

It wasn't Mr Stink's fault that he stank. He was a tramp, after all. He didn't have a home and so he never had the opportunity to have a proper wash like you and me. After a while the smell just got worse and worse. Here is a picture of Mr Stink.

He is quite a snappy dresser in his bow-tie and tweed jacket, isn't he? But don't be fooled. The illustration doesn't do justice to the smell. This could be a scratch 'n' sniff book, but the smell would be so bad you would have to put it in the bin. And then bury the bin. Very deep underground.

That's his little black dog with him, the Duchess. The Duchess wasn't any particular breed of dog, she was just a dog. She smelt too, but not as bad as Mr Stink. Nothing in the world really smelt as bad as him. Except his beard. His beard was full of old bits of egg and sausage and cheese that had fallen out of his mouth years before. It had never, ever been shampooed so it had its own special stink, even worse than his main one.

One morning, Mr Stink simply appeared in the town and took up residence on an old wooden bench. No one knew where he had come from, or where he might be going. The town folk were mostly nice to him. They sometimes dropped a few coins at his feet, before rushing off with their eyes watering. But no one was really *friendly* towards him. No one stopped for a chat.

At least, not till the day that a little girl finally plucked up the courage to speak to him – and that's where our story begins.

"Hello," said the girl, her voice trembling a little with nerves. The girl was called Chloe. She was only twelve and she had never spoken to a tramp before. Her mother had forbidden her to speak to 'such creatures'. Mother even disapproved of her daughter talking to kids from the local council estate. But Chloe didn't think Mr Stink *was* a creature. She thought he was a man who looked like he had a very interesting story to tell – and if there was one thing Chloe loved, it was stories.

Every day she would pass him and his dog in her parents' car on the way to her posh private school. Whether in sunshine or snow, he was always sitting on the same bench with his dog by his feet. As she luxuriated on the leather of the back seat with her poisonous little sister Annabelle, Chloe would look out of the window at him and wonder.

Millions of thoughts and questions would swim through her head. Who was he? Why did he live on the streets? Had he ever had a home? What did his dog eat? Did he have any friends or family? If so, did they know he was homeless?

Where did he go at Christmas? If you wanted to write him a letter, what address would you put on the envelope? 'The bench, you know the one – round the corner from the bus stop'? When was the last time he'd had a bath? And could his name *really* be Mr Stink?

Chloe was the kind of girl who loved being alone with her thoughts. Often she would sit on her bed and make up stories about Mr Stink. Sitting on her own in her room, she would come up with all kinds of fantastical tales. Maybe Mr Stink was a heroic old sailor who had won dozens of medals for bravery, but had found it impossible to adapt to life on dry land? Or perhaps he was a world-famous opera singer who one night, upon hitting the top note in an aria at the Royal Opera House in London, lost his voice and could never sing again? Or maybe he was really a Russian secret agent who had put on an elaborate tramp disguise to spy on the people of the town?

Chloe didn't know anything about Mr Stink. But what she did know, on that day when she stopped to talk to him for the first time, was that he looked like he needed the five-pound note she was holding *much* more than she did.

He seemed lonely too, not just alone, but lonely in his soul. That made Chloe sad. She knew full well what it was like to feel lonely.

Chloe didn't like school very much. Mother had insisted on sending her to a posh all-girls secondary school, and she hadn't made any friends there. Chloe didn't like being at home much either. Wherever she was she had the feeling that she didn't quite fit in.

What's more, it was Chloe's least favourite time of year. Christmas. Everyone is supposed to love Christmas, especially children. But Chloe hated it. She hated the tinsel, she hated the crackers, she hated the carols, she hated having to watch the Queen's speech, she hated the mince pies, she hated that it never really snowed like it's supposed to, she hated sitting down with her family to a long, long dinner, and most of all, she hated how she had to pretend to be happy just because it was December 25th.

"What can I do for you, young lady?" said Mr Stink. His voice was unexpectedly posh. As no one had ever stopped to talk to him before, he stared slightly suspiciously at this plump little girl. Chloe was suddenly a bit frightened. Maybe it wasn't such a good idea to talk to the old tramp after all. She had been working up to this moment for weeks, months even. This wasn't how it had all played out in her head.

To make matters worse, Chloe had to stop breathing through her nose. The smell was starting to get to her. It was like a living thing, creeping its way up her nostrils and burning the back of her throat.

"Erm, well, sorry to bother you…"

"Yes?" said Mr Stink, a little impatiently. Chloe was taken aback. Why was he in such a hurry? He *always* sat on his bench. It wasn't like he suddenly needed to go somewhere else.

At that moment the Duchess started barking at her. Chloe felt even more scared. Sensing this, Mr Stink pulled the Duchess's lead, which was really just a bit of old rope, to encourage her to be quiet.

"Well," Chloe went on nervously, "my auntie sent me five pounds to buy myself a Christmas present. But I don't really need anything so I thought I would give it to you."

Mr Stink smiled. Chloe smiled too. For a moment it looked as if he was going to accept Chloe's offer, then he looked down at the pavement.

"Thank you," he said. "Unimaginable kindness, but I can't take it, sorry."

Chloe was confused. "Why ever not?" she asked.

"You are but a child. Five pounds? It's too, too generous."

"I just thought—"

"It's really kind of you, but I'm afraid I can't accept. Tell me, how old are you, young lady? Ten?"

"TWELVE!" said Chloe loudly. She was a little short for her age, but liked to think she was grown-up in lots of other ways. "I'm twelve. Thirteen on January the ninth!"

"Sorry, you're twelve. Nearly thirteen. Go and buy yourself one of those new musical stereo discs. Don't you worry about an old vagabond like me." He smiled. There was a real twinkle in his eye when he smiled.

"If it's not too rude," said Chloe, "can I ask you a question?"

"Yes, of course you can."

"Well, I would love to know: why do you live on a bench and not in a house like me?"

Mr Stink shuffled slightly and looked anxious. "It's a long story, my dear," he said. "Maybe I will tell you another day."

Chloe was disappointed. She wasn't sure there would *be* another day. If her mother found out that she was even talking to this man, let alone offering him money, she would do her nut.

"Well, sorry for bothering you," said Chloe. "Have a lovely day." As the words came out she cringed. What a stupid thing to say! How could he possibly have a lovely day? He was a smelly old tramp, and the sky was growing gloomy with black clouds. She took a few paces up the street, feeling embarrassed.

"What's that on your back, child?" called out Mr Stink.

"What's what on my back?" asked Chloe, trying to look over her shoulder. She reached round and tore a piece of paper from her blazer. She peered at it.

Written on the piece of paper, in thick black letters, was a single word.

LOSER!

Chloe felt her stomach twist with humiliation. Rosamund must have sellotaped it to her when she left school. Rosamund was the head girl of the cool gang. She was always bullying Chloe, picking on her for eating too many sweets, or for being poorer than the other girls at school, or for being the girl neither team ever wanted on their side in hockey matches. As Chloe had left school today Rosamund patted her on the back several times, saying "Merry Christmas", while all the other girls laughed. Now Chloe knew why. Mr Stink rose creakily from his bench and took the paper from Chloe's hands.

"I can't believe I've been going round with that on my back all afternoon," said Chloe. Embarrassed to feel tears welling up, she looked away, blinking into the sunlight.

"What is it, child?" asked Mr Stink, kindly.

Chloe sniffed. "Well," she said, "it's true, isn't it? I really am a loser."

Mr Stink bent down to look at her. "No," he said, authoritatively. "You're not a loser. The real loser is the person who stuck it to you in the first place."

Chloe tried to believe him, but couldn't quite. For as long as she could remember she had felt like a loser. Maybe Rosamund and all those other girls in her gang were right.

"There's only one place for this," said Mr Stink. He screwed up the piece of paper and, like a professional cricketer, expertly bowled it into

the bin. Chloe clocked this and her imagination instantly started whirring; had he once been captain of the England cricket team?

Mr Stink brushed his hands together. "Good riddance to bad rubbish," he said.

"Thanks," murmured Chloe.

"Not at all," said Mr Stink. "You mustn't let bullies get you down."

"I'll try," said Chloe. "Nice to meet you Mr… um…" she began. Everyone called him Mr Stink, but she didn't know if he knew that. It felt rude to say it to his face.

"Stink," he said. "They call me Mr Stink."

"Oh. Nice to meet you, Mr Stink. I'm Chloe."

"Hello, Chloe," said Mr Stink.

"You know, Mr Stink," said Chloe, "I still might go the shops. Do you need anything? Like a bar of soap or something?"

"Thank you, my dear," he replied. "But I have

no use for soap. You see, I had a bath only last year. But I would *love* some sausages. I do adore a nice meaty sausage…"

2

Icy Silence

"Mother?" said Annabelle.

Mother finished chewing her food completely, then swallowed it, before finally replying.

"Yes, my darling child?"

"Chloe just took one of her sausages off her plate and hid it in her napkin."

It was Saturday evening, and the Crumb family sat at the dining room table, missing *Strictly Come Dancing* and *The X-Factor* as they ate their dinner. Mother had banned watching television and eating at the same time. She had decided that it was 'awfully common'. Instead the family had to sit in icy silence and eat their dinner staring at the walls. Or sometimes Mother would choose a subject for discussion, normally what she would do if she ran the country. That was her absolute favourite. Mother had given up running a beauty salon to stand for Parliament, and had no doubt in her mind that one day she would be Prime Minister.

Mother had named the white Persian family cat Elizabeth, after the Queen. She was obsessed with Being Posh. There was a downstairs loo that was kept locked for 'very important guests', as if a member of the royal family was going to swing by for a waz. There was a china tea set in the cupboard that was 'for best', and had never once been used. Mother even sprayed air freshener in the garden. Mother would never go out, and not even answer the door, unless immaculately groomed, with her beloved pearls around her neck and her hair made stiff with enough hairspray to create its own hole in the ozone layer. She was so used to turning up her nose at everybody and everything, it was in danger of staying that way. Here's a picture of her.

My word, she looks posh, doesn't she?

Unsurprisingly Father, or Dad as he preferred to be called when Mother wasn't around, opted for a quiet life and usually didn't speak unless spoken to. He was a big powerful man, but his wife made him feel small inside. Dad was only forty, but he was already going bald and starting to stoop. He worked long hours at a car factory on the edge of the town.

"Did you hide a sausage in your napkin, Chloe?" demanded Mother.

"You are always trying to get me into trouble!" snapped Chloe.

This was true. Annabelle was two years younger than Chloe, and one of those children adults think are perfect, but other children don't like because they are snotty little goody-goodies. Annabelle loved getting Chloe into trouble. She would lie on her bed in her bright pink room upstairs and roll around crying, shouting "CHLOE, GET OFF ME! YOU ARE HURTING ME!" even though Chloe was quietly writing away in her room next door. You *could* say that Annabelle was evil. She was certainly evil to her older sister.

"Oh, sorry Mother, it just slipped into my lap," said Chloe guiltily. Her plan had been to smuggle the sausage out for Mr Stink. She had been thinking about him all evening, imagining him shivering out there in the cold dark December night as they sat in the warm, eating away.

"Well then Chloe, unroll it from your napkin and put it back on your plate," ordered Mother. "I am so ashamed that we are even eating sausages for dinner. I gave your father strict instructions to dispatch himself to the supermarket and purchase four wild sea-bass fillets. And he comes home with a packet of sausages. If anyone called around and saw us eating food like this it would be hideously embarrassing. They'd think we were savages!"

"I am sorry, my darling wife," protested Dad. "They were all out of wild sea-bass fillets." He gave Chloe the tiniest wink as he said this, confirming her suspicion that he had deliberately disobeyed Mother's orders. Chloe smiled at him discreetly. She and her dad both loved sausages and lots of other food that Mother didn't approve of, like burgers, fish-fingers, fizzy drinks, and especially Mr Whippy ice-cream ('the devil's spume', Mother called it). "I have never eaten anything from a van," she would say. "I'd rather die."

"Right now, all hands on deck as we clear up," said Mother when they had finished eating. "Annabelle, my precious angel, you clear the table, Chloe, you can wash up and Husband, you can dry." When she said "all hands on deck", what she really meant was everybody's hands except hers. As the rest of the family all went about their duties Mother reclined on the sofa and started unwrapping a wafer-thin chocolate mint. She allowed herself one chocolate mint a day. She nibbled so infuriatingly slowly she made each one last an hour.

"One of my Bendicks luxury chocolate mints has gone walkies again!" she called out.

Annabelle shot Chloe an accusing look before returning to the dining room to collect some more plates. "I bet it was you, fatty!" she hissed.

"Be nice, Annabelle," chided Dad.

Chloe felt guilty, even though it wasn't her who had been scoffing her mother's chocolates. She and Dad assumed their familiar positions at the sink.

"Chloe, why were you trying to hide one of your sausages?" he asked. "If you didn't like it, you could have just said."

"I wasn't trying to hide it, Dad."

"Then what were you doing with it?"

Suddenly Annabelle appeared with another stack of dirty plates and the pair fell silent. They waited a moment until she had gone.

"Well, Dad, you know that tramp who always sits on the same bench every—"

"Mr Stink?"

"Yes. Well, I thought his dog looked hungry and I wanted to bring her a sausage or two."

It was a lie, but not a big one.

"Well, I suppose there isn't any harm in giving his poor dog a bit of food," said Dad. "Just this once though, you understand?"

"But—"

"Just this once, Chloe. Or Mr Stink will expect you to feed his dog every day. Now, I hid another packet of sausages behind the crème fraîche, whatever that is. I'll cook them up for you before your mother gets up tomorrow morning and you can give them—"

"WHAT ARE YOU TWO CONSPIRING ABOUT?" demanded Mother from the sitting room.

"Oh, erm, we were just debating which of the Queen's four children we most admire," said Dad. "I am putting forward Anne for her equestrian skills, though Chloe is making a strong case for Prince Charles and his unrivalled range of organic biscuits."

"Very good. Carry on!" boomed the voice from next door.

Dad smiled at Chloe cheekily.

3

The Wanderer

Mr Stink ate the sausages in an unexpectedly elegant manner. First he took out a little linen napkin and tucked it under his chin. Next he took an antique silver knife and fork out of his breast pocket. Finally he produced a dirty gold-rimmed china plate, which he gave to the Duchess to lick clean before he set down the sausages neatly upon it.

Chloe stared at his cutlery and plate. This seemed like another clue to his past. Had he perhaps been a gentleman thief who crept into country houses at midnight and made off with the family silver?

"Do you have any more sausages?" asked Mr Stink, his mouth still full of sausage.

"No, just those eight I'm afraid," replied Chloe.

She stood at a safe distance from the tramp, so that her eyes wouldn't start weeping at the smell. The Duchess looked up at Mr Stink as he ate the sausages, with a heartbreaking longing that suggested that all love and all beauty was contained in those tubes of meat.

"There you go, Duchess," said Mr Stink, slowly lowering half a sausage into his dog's mouth. The Duchess was so hungry she didn't even chew; instead she swallowed it in half a millisecond before returning to her expression of sausage-longing. Had any man or beast ever eaten a sausage so quickly? Chloe was half-expecting a gentleman in a blazer and slacks with a clipboard and stopwatch to appear and declare that the little black dog had set a new sausage-eating international world record!

"So, young Chloe, is everything fine at home?" asked Mr Stink, as he let the Duchess lick his fingers clean of any remnants of sausage juice.

"I'm sorry?" replied a befuddled Chloe.

"I asked if everything was fine at home. If things were tickety-boo I am not sure you would be spending your Sunday talking to an old vagabond like me."

"Vagabond?"

"I don't like the word 'tramp'. It makes you think of someone who smells."

Chloe tried to conceal her surprise. Even the Duchess looked puzzled and she didn't speak English, only Dog.

"I prefer vagabond, or wanderer," continued Mr Stink.

The way he put it, thought Chloe, it sounded almost poetic. Especially 'wanderer'. She would love to be a wanderer. She would wander all around the world if she could. Not stay in this boring little town where nothing happened that hadn't happened the day before.

"There's nothing wrong at home. Everything is fine," said Chloe adamantly.

"Are you *sure*?" enquired Mr Stink, with the wisdom some people have that cuts right through you like a knife through butter.

Things were, in fact, not at all fine at home for Chloe. She was often ignored. Her mother doted on Annabelle – probably because her youngest daughter was like a miniature version of her. Every inch of every wall in the house was covered with celebrations of Annabelle's infinite achievements.

Photographs of her standing smugly on winner's podiums, certificates bearing her name emblazoned in italic gold, trophies and statuettes and medals engraved with 'winner', 'first place' or 'little creep'. (I made up that last one.)

The more Annabelle achieved, the more Chloe felt like a failure. Her parents spent most of their lives providing a chauffeur service for Annabelle's out of school activities. Her schedule was exhausting even to *look* at.

Monday

5am Swimming training

6am Clarinet lesson

7am Dance lesson, tap and contemporary jazz

8am Dance lesson, ballet

9am to 4pm School

4pm Drama lesson, improvisation and movement

5pm Piano lesson

6pm Brownies

7pm Girls' Brigade

8pm Javelin practice

Tuesday

4am Violin lesson

5am Stilt-walking practice

6am Chess Society

7am Learning Japanese

8am Flower-arranging class

9am to 4pm School

4pm Creative writing workshop

5pm Porcelain frog painting class

6pm Harp practice

7pm Watercolour painting class

8pm Dance class, ballroom

Wednesday

3am Choir practice

4am Long-jump training

5am High-jump training

6am Long-jump training again

7am Trombone lesson

8am Scuba-diving

9am to 4pm School

4pm Chef training

5pm Mountain climbing

6pm Tennis

7pm Drama workshop, Shakespeare and his contemporaries

8pm Show jumping

Thursday

2am Learning Arabic

3am Dance lesson, break-dance, hip-hop, krumping

4am Oboe lesson

5am Tour de France cycle training

6am Bible studies

7am Gymnastics training

8am Calligraphy class

9am to 4pm School

4pm Work experience shadowing a brain surgeon

5pm Opera singing lesson

6pm NASA space exploration workshop

7pm Cake baking class, level 5

8pm Attend lecture on 'A History of Victorian Moustaches'

Friday

1am Triangle lesson, grade 5

2am Badminton

3am Archery

4am Fly to Switzerland for ski-jump practice. Learn about eggs from an expert on eggs (TBC) on outbound flight.

6am Do quick ski-jump, and then board inbound flight. Take pottery class on flight.

8am Thai kick-boxing (remember to take skis off before class).

9am to 4pm School

4pm Channel swimming training

5pm Motorbike maintenance workshop

6pm Candle making

7pm Otter rearing class

8pm Television viewing. A choice between either a documentary about carpet manufacturing in Belgium, or a Polish cartoon from the 1920s about a depressed owl.

And that was just the weekdays. The weekends were when things *really* got busy for Annabelle. No wonder Chloe felt ignored.

"Well, I suppose things at home are… are…" stammered Chloe. She wanted to talk to him about it all, but she wasn't sure how.

Bong! Bong! Bong! Bong!

No, I haven't lost my mind, readers. That was meant to be the church clock striking four.

Chloe gasped and looked at her watch. Four o'clock! Mother made her do her homework from four until six every day, even in the school holidays when she didn't have any to do.

"Sorry Mr Stink, I have to go," she said. Secretly Chloe was relieved. No one had ever asked her how she felt before, and she was beginning to panic...

"Really, child?" said the old man, looking disappointed.

"Yes, yes, I need to get home. Mother will be furious if I don't get at least a C in Maths next term. She sets me extra tests during the holidays."

"That doesn't sound much like a holiday to me," said Mr Stink.

Chloe shrugged. "Mother doesn't believe in holidays." She stood up. "I hope you liked the sausages," she said.

"They were scrumptious," said Mr Stink. "Thank you. Unimaginable kindness."

Chloe nodded and turned to run off towards home. If she took a short-cut she'd be back before Mother.

"Farewell!" Mr Stink called after her softly.

4

Drivel

Terrified of being late for homework hour, Chloe began to quicken her pace. She didn't want her mother to ask questions about where she'd been or who she'd been talking to. Mrs Crumb would be horrified to find out her daughter had been sitting on a bench with someone she would describe as a 'soap-dodger'. Grown-ups always have a way of ruining everything.

Chloe stopped hurrying, though, when she saw that she was about to pass Raj's shop. *Just one chocolate bar*, she thought.

Chloe's love of chocolate made her one of

Raj's best customers. Raj ran the local newsagent shop. He was a big jolly jelly of a man, as sweet and colourful as his slightly over-priced confectionery. Today, though, what Chloe really needed was some advice.

And maybe some chocolate. Just one bar, of course. Maybe two.

"Ah, Miss Chloe!" said Raj, as she entered the shop. "What can I tempt you with today?"

"Hello, Raj," said Chloe smiling. She always smiled when she saw Raj. It was partly because he was such a lovely man, and partly because he sold sweets.

"I have some Rolos on special offer!" announced Raj. "They have gone out of date and hardened. You may lose a tooth as you chew into one, but at 10p off you can't really argue!"

"Mmm, let me think," said Chloe scouring the racks and racks of confectionery.

"I had half a Lion bar earlier, you are welcome to make me an offer on the other half. I'll take anything upwards of 15p."

"I think I'll just take a Crunchie, thanks Raj."

"Buy seven Crunchie bars you get an eighth Crunchie bar absolutely free!"

"No thanks, Raj. I only want one." She put the money down on the counter. 35p. Money well spent considering the nice feeling the chocolate would give her as it slipped down her throat and into her tummy.

"But Chloe, don't you understand? This is a unique opportunity to enjoy the popular chocolate-covered honeycomb bar at a dramatic saving!"

"I don't need eight Crunchie bars, Raj," said Chloe. "I need some advice."

"I don't think I am really responsible enough to give out advice," replied Raj without a hint of irony. "But I'll try."

Chloe loved talking to Raj. He wasn't a parent or a teacher, and whatever you said to him, he would never judge you. However, Chloe still gulped slightly, because she was about to attempt another little lie. "Well, there's this girl I know at school…" she began.

"Yes? A girl at school. Not you?"

"No, somebody else."

"Right," said Raj.

Chloe gulped again and looked down, unable to meet his gaze. "Well, this friend of mine, she's started to talk to this tramp, and she really likes talking to him, but her mother would blow a fuse if she knew, so I – I mean, my friend – doesn't know what to do."

Raj looked at Chloe expectantly. "Yes?" he said. "And what is your question exactly?"

"Well Raj," said Chloe. "Do you think it's

wrong to talk to tramps?"

"Well, it's not good to talk to strangers," said
Raj. "And you should never let anyone give you
a lift in a car!"

"Right," said Chloe, disappointed.

"But a tramp is just somebody without a
home," continued Raj. "Too many people walk
on by and pretend they're not there."

"Yes!" said Chloe. "That's what I think too."

Raj smiled. "Any of us could become homeless
one day. I can see nothing wrong with talking to
a tramp, just like you would anyone else."

"Thanks Raj, I will… I mean, I'll tell her. This
girl at school, I mean."

"What's this girl's name?"

"Umm… Stephen! I mean Susan… no, Sarah.
Her name is Sarah, definitely Sarah."

"It's you, isn't it?" said Raj smiling.

"Yes," admitted Chloe after a millisecond.

"You are a very sweet girl, Chloe. It's lovely that you would take the time to talk to a tramp. There but for the grace of God go you and I."

"Thanks, Raj." Chloe went a little red, embarrassed by his compliment.

"Now what can you buy your homeless friend for Christmas?" said Raj as he scoured around his disorganised shop. "I have a box full of Teenage Mutant Ninja Turtles stationery sets I can't seem to shift. Yours for only £3.99. In fact buy one set, get ten free."

"I'm not sure a tramp really has any need for a Teenage Mutant Ninja Turtles stationery set, thanks anyway Raj."

"We all have use of a Teenage Mutant Ninja Turtles stationery set, Chloe. You have your Teenage Mutant Ninja Turtles pencil, your Teenage Mutant Ninja Turtles eraser, your Teenage Mutant Ninja Turtles ruler, your

Teenage Mutant Ninja Turtles pencil case, your Teenage Mutant—"

"I get the idea, thanks, Raj, but I'm sorry, I'm not going to buy one. I've got to go," said Chloe, edging out of the shop as she unwrapped her Crunchie.

"I haven't finished, Chloe. Please, I haven't sold one! You also have your Teenage Mutant Ninja Turtles pencil sharpener, your Teenage Mutant Ninja Turtles notepad, your Teenage Mutant... oh, she's gone."

"And what's this, young lady?" demanded Mother. She was standing waiting in Chloe's room. Between her thumb and index finger was one of Chloe's exercise books from school. Mother held it as if it were an exhibit in a court case.

"It's just my maths book, Mother," said Chloe, gulping as she edged into the room.

You might think that Chloe was worried because her maths work wasn't up to scratch. But that wasn't quite it. The problem was, Chloe's maths book didn't have any maths in it! The book was supposed to be full of boring numbers and equations, but instead it was positively overflowing with colourful words and pictures.

Spending so much time alone had turned Chloe's imagination into a deep dark forest. It was a magical place to escape to, and so much more thrilling than real life. Chloe had used the exercise book to write a story about a girl who is sent to a school (loosely based on her own) where all the teachers are secretly vampires. She thought it was much more exciting than boring equations, but Mother clearly didn't agree.

"If it is your mathematics book, why does it contain this repulsive horror story?" said Mother. This was one of those questions when you aren't supposed to give an answer. "No wonder you did so poorly in your mathematics exam. I imagine you have spent the time in class writing this… this *drivel*. I am so disappointed in you, Chloe."

Chloe felt her cheeks smarting with shame

and hung her head. She didn't think her story was drivel. But she couldn't imagine telling her Mother that.

"Don't you have anything to say for yourself?" shouted Mother.

Chloe shook her head. For the second time in one day she wanted to just disappear.

"Well, this is what I think of your story," said Mother, as she started trying to rip up the exercise book.

"P-p-please… don't…" stammered Chloe.

"No, no, no! I'm not paying your school fees for you to waste your time on this rubbish! It's going in the bin!"

The book was obviously harder to rip than Mother had expected, and it took a few attempts to make the first tear. However, soon the book was nothing more than confetti. Chloe bowed her head, tears welling up in her eyes, as her mother dropped all the pieces in the bin.

"Do you want to end up like your father? Working in a car factory? If you concentrate on your maths and don't get distracted by silly stories, you have a chance of making a better life for yourself! Otherwise you'll end up wasting your life, like your father. Is that what you want?"

"Well, I—"

"How dare you interrupt me!" shouted Mother. Chloe hadn't realised this was another one of those questions you're not actually meant to answer. "You'd better buck your ideas up, young lady!"

Chloe wasn't quite sure what that meant, but it didn't seem like the best time to ask. Mother left the room, dramatically slamming the door behind her. Chloe slowly sat down on the edge of her bed. As she buried her face in her hands, she thought of Mr Stink, sitting on his bench with only the Duchess for company. She wasn't homeless like him, but she *felt* homeless in her heart.

5

Abandon Starbucks!

Monday morning. The first proper day of the Christmas holidays. A day Chloe had been dreading. She didn't have any friends she could text or email or SMS or Facebook or Twitter or whatever, but there was *one* person she wanted to see...

By the time Chloe got to the bench it was raining heavily, and she wished she'd at least paused to pick up an umbrella.

"The Duchess and I weren't expecting to see you again, Chloe," said Mr Stink. His eyes twinkled at the surprise, despite the rain.

"I am sorry I ran off like that," said Chloe,

"Don't worry, you are forgiven," he chuckled.

Chloe sat down next to him. She gave the Duchess a stroke, and then noticed that the palm of her hand was black. She surreptitiously wiped it on her trousers. Then she shivered, as a raindrop ran down the back of her neck.

"Oh, no, you're cold!" said Mr Stink. "Shall we take shelter from the rain in a coffee shop establishment?"

"Err... yes, good idea," said Chloe, not sure if taking someone quite so stinky into an enclosed space really *was* a good idea. As they walked into the town centre, the rain felt icy, almost becoming hail.

When they arrived at the coffee shop, Chloe peered through the steamed-up glass window. "I don't think there's anywhere to sit down," she said. Unfortunately, the coffee shop was full to bursting with Christmas shoppers, trying to avoid the cruel British weather.

"We can but try," said Mr Stink, picking up the Duchess and attempting to conceal her under his tweed jacket.

The tramp opened the door for Chloe and she squeezed herself inside. As Mr Stink entered, the pleasing aroma of freshly-brewed coffee keeled over and died. His own special smell replaced it. There was silence for a moment.

Then panic.

People started running towards the door, clutching serviettes to their mouths as makeshift gas masks.

"Abandon Starbucks!" screamed a member of staff, and his colleagues immediately stopped making coffees or bagging muffins and ran for their lives.

"It seems to be thinning out a little," announced Mr Stink.

Soon they were the only ones left in the shop. *Maybe smelling this bad has its advantages*, thought Chloe. If Mr Stink's super-smell could empty a coffee shop, what else could it do? Maybe he could clear the local ice rink of skaters so she could have it all to herself? Or they could go to Alton Towers together and not have to queue for a single ride? Better still, she could take him and his smell into school one day, and if he was particularly stinky the headmistress would have to send everyone home and she could have the day off!

"You take a seat here, child," said Mr Stink. "Now, what would you like to drink?"

"Er... a cappuccino, please," replied Chloe, trying to sound grown-up.

"I think I'll have one too." Mr Stink shuffled behind the counter and started opening tins. "Righty-ho, two cappuccinos coming right up."

The machines hissed and spat for a few moments, and then Mr Stink pottered back over to the table with two mugs of a dark, unidentifiable liquid. On closer inspection, it appeared to be some kind of black slime, but Chloe was too well brought up to complain and pretended to sip whatever it was that he had concocted for her. She even managed an almost convincing, "Mmm... lovely!"

Mr Stink stirred his solid liquid with a dainty little silver spoon he pulled out from his breast pocket. Chloe stole a glance at it and noticed it was monogrammed, with three little letters delicately engraved on the handle. She tried to get a better look, but he put it away before she could see what the letters were. What could they mean? Or was this simply another item Mr Stink had purloined during his career as a gentleman thief?

"So, Miss Chloe," said Mr Stink, breaking her train of thought. "It's the Christmas holidays, isn't it?" He took a sip from his coffee, holding his mug elegantly between his fingers. "Why aren't you at home decorating the tree with your family or wrapping presents?"

"Well, I don't know how to explain…" No one in Chloe's family was good at expressing their feelings. To her mother, feelings were at best an embarrassment, at worst a sign of weakness.

"Just take your time, young lady."

Chloe took a deep breath and it all came flooding out. What started off as a stream soon became a rushing river of emotion. She told him how her parents argued most of the time and how once she was sitting on the stairs when she heard her Mother shout, "I am only staying with you for the sake of the girls!"

How her little sister made her life a misery. How nothing she did was ever good enough. How if she brought home some little bowl she had made in pottery class her Mother would put it at the back of a cupboard, never to be seen again. However, if her little sister brought any piece of artwork home, however awful, it was put in pride of place behind bulletproof glass as if it was the *Mona Lisa*.

Chloe told Mr Stink how her mother was

always trying to force her to lose weight. Up until recently, Mother had described her as having "puppy fat". But once she turned twelve, Mother rather cruelly started calling it "flab" or even worse "blubber", as if she was some species of whale. Perhaps Mother was trying to shame her into losing weight. In truth, it only 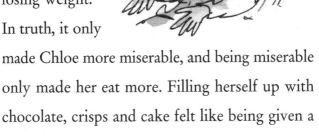 made Chloe more miserable, and being miserable only made her eat more. Filling herself up with chocolate, crisps and cake felt like being given a much-needed hug.

She told Mr Stink how she wished her dad would stand up to her mother sometimes. How she didn't find it easy to make friends, as she was so shy. How she only really liked making up stories, but it made her mother so angry. And how Rosamund ensured that every day at school was an absolute misery.

It was a long, long list, but Mr Stink listened intently to everything she said as jolly Christmas songs played incongruously in the background. For someone who spent every day with only a little black dog for company, he was surprisingly full of wisdom. In fact, he seemed to relish the opportunity to listen and talk and help. People didn't really stop to talk to Mr Stink – and he seemed pleased to be having a proper conversation for once.

He told Chloe, "Tell your Mother how you feel, I am sure she loves you and would hate you to be unhappy." And, "...try and find something fun you can do with your sister." And, "...why not talk to your dad about how you feel?"

Finally, Chloe told Mr Stink about how

Mother had ripped her vampire story to shreds. She had to try very hard not to cry.

"That's terrible, child," said Mr Stink. "You must have been devastated."

"I hate her," said Chloe. "I hate my mother."

"You shouldn't say that," said Mr Stink.

"But I do."

"You are very angry with her, of course, but she loves you, even if she finds it hard to show it."

"Maybe." Chloe shrugged, unconvinced. But having talked everything through she felt a little calmer now. "Thank you so much for listening to me," she said.

"I just hate to see a young girl like you looking sad," said Mr Stink. "I may be old, but I can remember what it was like to be young. I just hope I helped a little."

"You helped a lot."

Mr Stink smiled, before letting the last sludge of his volcanic gloop slip down his throat. "Delicious! Now, we'd better leave some money for our beverages." He searched around in his pockets for some change. "Oh, bother, I can't read the board without my spectacles. I'll leave six pence. That should be enough. And a tuppence tip. They will be pleased with that. They can treat themselves to one of those new-fangled video cassettes. Right, I think you'd better be heading home now, young lady."

The rain had stopped when they left the coffee shop. They sauntered down the road as cars hummed past.

"Let's swap places," said Mr Stink.

"Why?"

"Because a lady should always walk on the inside of the pavement and a gentleman on the outside."

"Really?" said Chloe. "Why?"

"Well," replied Mr Stink, "the outside is more dangerous because that's where the cars are. But I believe it was originally because in the olden days people used to throw the contents of their chamber pots out of their windows and into the gutter. The person on the outside was more likely to get splattered!"

"What's a chamber pot?" said Chloe.

"Well I don't wish to be crude, but it's a kind of portable toilet."

"Ugh! That's gross. Did people do that when you were a boy?"

Mr Stink chuckled. "No, that was a little before my time, child. In the sixteenth century, in fact! Now, Miss Chloe, etiquette demands we swap places."

His old-world gallantry was so charming it made Chloe smile, and they changed places.

They strolled side by side, passing high-street shop after high-street shop, all trying to herald the approach of Christmas louder than the next. After a few moments Chloe saw Rosamund walking towards them with a small flotilla of shopping bags.

"Can we cross the road, please? Quickly," whispered Chloe anxiously.

"Why, child? Whatever is the matter?"

"It's that girl from school I just told you about, Rosamund."

"The one who stuck that sign to your back?"

"Yes, that's her."

"You need to stand up to her," pronounced Mr Stink. "Let her be the one to cross the road!"

"No... please don't say anything," pleaded Chloe.

"Who is this? Your new boyfriend?" laughed Rosamund. It wasn't a real laugh, like people do when they find something funny. That's a lovely sound. This was a cruel laugh. An ugly sound.

Chloe didn't say anything, just looked down.

"My daddy just gave me £500 to buy myself whatever I wanted for Christmas," said Rosamund. "I blew the lot at Topshop. Shame you're too fat to get into any of their clothes."

Chloe merely sighed. She was used to being hounded by Rosamund.

"Why are you letting her talk to you like that, Chloe?" said Mr Stink.

"What's it to you, Grandad?" said Rosamund mockingly. "Hanging around with smelly old tramps now, are you Chloe? You *are* tragic! How long did it take you to find that sign on your back then?"

"She didn't find it," said Mr Stink, slowly and deliberately. "I did. And I didn't find it amusing."

"Didn't you?" said Rosamund. "All the other girls found it really funny!"

"Well, then they are as vile as you," said Mr Stink.

"*What*?" said Rosamund. She wasn't used to being talked to like that.

"I said 'then they are as vile as you'," he repeated, even louder this time. "*You* are a nasty little bully." Chloe looked on anxiously. She hated confrontation.

To make matters worse, Rosamund took a pace forward and stood eye to eye with Mr Stink. "Say that to my face, you old stinker!"

For a moment Mr Stink fell silent. Then he opened his mouth and let out the deepest darkest dirtiest burp.

"BBBBBBBBBBBBBBBBBB BBBBBBBBBBBBBBBBBBBB BBBBBBBBBBBBBBBBBBBB BBBBBBUUUUUUUUU UUUUUUUUUUUUUUU UUUUUUUUUUUUUUUU

UUUUUUUUUUUUUR
RRRRRRRRRRRRRRRR
RRRRRRRRRRRRRRRR
RRRRRRRRRRRRRRRR
RRRRRRRRRRRRRRRR
PPPPPPPPPPPPPPPP
PPPPPPPPPPPPPPPP
PPPPPPPPPPPPPPPP
PPPPPPPPPPPPPPP!!
!!!!!!!!!!!!!!!!!!!!!!!!!!!!!!!
!!!!!!!!!!!!!!!!!!!!!!!!!!!!!
!!!!!!!!!!!!!!!!!! "

Rosamund's face turned green. It was as if a putrid tornado had engulfed her. It was the smell of coffee and sausages and rotten vegetables recovered from bins all rolled into one. Rosamund turned and ran, hurtling down the high street in such a panic that she dropped her TopShop bags on the way.

"That was so funny!" laughed Chloe.

"I didn't mean to belch. Most impolite. It was just that coffee repeating on me. Dear me! Now next time I want to see you stand up for yourself, Miss Chloe. A bully can only make you feel bad about yourself if you *let* them."

"OK... I'll try," said Chloe. "So... see you tomorrow?"

"If you really want to," he replied.

"I would love to."

"And I would love to too!" he said, his eyes twinkling and twinkling as the last golden glow of the sunlight splintered through the sky.

At that moment a 4x4 thundered past. Its giant tyres sloshed through a huge puddle by the bus stop, sending up a wave that soaked Mr Stink from dirty head to dirty foot.

Water dripping from his glasses, he gave Chloe a little bow. "And that," he said, "is why a gentleman always walks on the outside."

"At least it wasn't a chamber pot!" chuckled Chloe.

6

Soap-Dodgers

The next morning Chloe pulled open her curtains. Why was there a giant 'O' and a giant 'V' stuck to her window? She went outside in her dressing gown to investigate.

'VOTE CRUMB!' was spelled out in giant letters across the windows of the house. Elizabeth the cat pattered out with a rosette emblazoned with the words 'Crumb for MP' attached to her jewel-encrusted collar.

Then Annabelle came skipping out of the house with an air of self-congratulatory joy that was instantly annoying.

"Where are you going?" asked Chloe.

"As her favourite daughter, Mother has entrusted *me* with the responsibility of putting these leaflets through every door in the street. She's standing to be a Member of Parliament, remember?"

"Let me see that," said Chloe, reaching out to grab one of the leaflets. The two warring sisters had long since dispensed with 'please' and 'thank you'.

Annabelle snatched it back. "I am not wasting one on you!" she snarled.

"Let me see!" Chloe pulled the leaflet out of Annabelle's hand. There were some advantages to being the older sister; sometimes you could use brute force. Annabelle huffed off with the rest of the leaflets. Chloe walked back into the house studying it, her slippers moistening with the dew. Mother was always going on and on about how she should run the country, but Chloe found the whole subject so dreary and dull that her imagination would float away into la-la land whenever the subject came up.

On the front of the leaflet was a photograph of Mother looking incredibly serious, with her finest pearls around her neck, her hair so waxy with spray that it would become a fireball if you put a lit match to it. Inside was a long list of her policies.

1) A curfew to be introduced to ensure all children under 30 are not allowed out after 8pm and are preferably in bed with lights out by 9pm.

2) The police to be given new powers to arrest people for talking too loudly in public.

3) Litterbugs to be deported.

4) The wearing of leggings to be outlawed in public areas, as they are 'extremely common'.

5) The national anthem to be played in the town square every hour on the hour. Everyone must be upstanding for this. Being in a wheelchair is no excuse for not paying your respects to Her Majesty.

6) All dogs to be kept on leads at all times. Even indoors.

7) Verruca socks to be worn by everyone attending the local swimming pool whether they have a verruca or not. This should cut down the chance of verruca infection to less than zero.

8) The Christmas pantomime to be discontinued due to the consistent lewdness of the humour (jokes about bottoms, for example. There is nothing funny about a bottom. We all have a bottom and we all know full well what comes out of a bottom and what sound a bottom can make of its own accord).

9) Church-going on Sunday morning to be compulsory. And when you do go you have

to sing the hymns properly, not just open and close your mouth when the organ plays.

10) Mobile telephonic devices to have only classical music ringtones from now on, like Mozart and Beethoven and one of the other ones, not the latest pop songs from the hit parade.

11) Unemployed people not to be allowed to claim benefit any more. Dole scum only have themselves to blame and are just plain idle. Why should we pay for them to sit at home all day watching or appearing on *The Jeremy Kyle Show*?

12) Giant bronze statues of royals Prince Edward and his fragrant wife Sophie, Countess of Wessex, to be erected in the local park.

13) Tattoos on anyone but visiting sailors to be banned. Tattoos can to be dropped off anonymously at police stations without prosecution.

14) Fast food burger restaurants to introduce plates, cutlery and table service. And stop serving burgers. And French fries. And nuggets. And those apple pies that are always too hot in the middle.

15) The local library to stock only the works of Beatrix Potter. Apart from *The Tale of Mr Jeremy Fisher*, as the sequence when the frog, Mr Fisher, is swallowed by a trout is far too violent even for adults.

16) Football games in the local park are a nuisance. From now on only imaginary balls to be used.

17) Only nice films to be offered for rental in Blockbuster. That is to say films about posh people from the olden days who are too shy even to hold hands.

18) To combat the growing problem of 'hoodies' all hooded tops to have the hoods cut off.

19) Video games rot the brain. Any video games (or computer games or console games or whatever the stupid things are called) to be played only between 4pm and 4:01pm daily.

20) Finally, all homeless people, or 'soap-dodgers', are to be banned from our streets. They are a menace to society. And, more importantly, they smell.

Chloe slumped down on the sofa when she read these last sentences. There was a loud squeak as she did so. Mother had insisted on keeping on the plastic covers the sofa and armchair had arrived in, so as to keep them immaculate. They were indeed still immaculate, but it meant your bum got really hot and sweaty.

What about my new friend Mr Stink? Chloe thought. *What's going to happen to him? And what about the Duchess? If he is banned from the streets where on earth is he going to go?*

And then, a moment later, *Wow, my bum is getting incredibly hot and sweaty.*

She chaffed her way sadly back up the stairs to her room. Sitting on her bed, she stared out of the window. Because she was shy and awkward, Chloe didn't make friends easily. Now her newest friend Mr Stink was going to have to leave the town. Maybe for ever. She stared out through the glass at the deep blue endless air. Then, just before her eyes lost focus in the infinite sky of nothing, she looked down. The answer was at the end of the garden staring back at her.

The shed.

7

A Bucket in the Corner

This operation had to be top-secret. Chloe waited until darkness fell, and then led Mr Stink and the Duchess silently down her street, before slipping through the side gate to her garden.

"It's just a shed..." said Chloe apologetically as they entered his new abode. "I'm sorry there's no ensuite bathroom, but there is a bucket in the corner there just behind the lawnmower. You can use that if you need to go in the night..."

"Well, this is unimaginably kind, young

Miss Chloe, thank you," said Mr Stink, smiling broadly. Even the Duchess seemed to bark 'thank you', or at least 'cheers'. "Now," continued Mr Stink, "are you sure your mother and father don't mind me being here? I would hate to be an unwelcome guest."

Chloe gulped, nervous about the lie that was about to come out of her mouth. "No... no... they don't mind at all. They're just both very busy people and they apologise that they weren't able to be here right now to meet you in person."

Chloe had carefully picked the right time to settle Mr Stink in. She knew Mother was out campaigning for election, and Dad was picking up Annabelle from her sumo-wrestling class.

"Well I would love to meet them both," said Mr Stink, "and see what people turned out such a wonderfully generous and thoughtful daughter. This will be so much warmer than my bench."

Chloe smiled shyly at the compliment. "Sorry there are all these old cardboard boxes in here," she said. She started to move them out of the way, to give him room to lie down. Mr Stink gave her a hand, lifting some of the boxes on top of each other. When she got to the bottom box, Chloe paused. Poking out of the top was a charred electric guitar. She examined it for a moment, puzzled, then rummaged through the box and found a pile of old CDs. They were all the same, stacks and stacks of an album entitled *Hell For Leather* by The Serpents of Doom.

"Have you ever heard of this band?" she asked.

"I don't really know any music past 1958, I'm afraid."

Chloe studied the picture on the cover for a moment. Super-imposed in front of a drawing of a giant snake stood four long-haired, leather-jacketed types. Chloe's eyes fixed on the guitar player, who looked an *awful* lot like her dad, only with a mess of curly black hair.

"I don't believe it!" said Chloe. "That's my dad."

She hadn't had any idea her dad had ever had a perm, let alone that he'd been in a rock band! She didn't know which was more shocking – the idea of him not being bald, or the idea of him playing electric guitar.

"Really?" said Mr Stink.

"I think so," said Chloe. "It looks like him anyway." She was still studying the album cover with a curious combination of pride and embarrassment.

"Well, we all have secrets, Miss Chloe. Now what should I do if I require a pot of tea or a round of sausage sandwiches on white bread please with HP sauce on the side? Is there a bell I should ring?"

Chloe looked at him, a little surprised. She hadn't realised she was going to have to feed him as well as shelter him.

"No, there's no bell," she said. "Erm, you see that window up there? That's my bedroom."

"Ah yes?"

"Well if you need something, why don't you flash this old bicycle light up at my window? Then I can come down and... erm... take your order."

"Perfection!" exclaimed Mr Stink.

Being in the confined space of the shed with Mr Stink was beginning to make it difficult for Chloe to breathe. The smell was especially bad today. It was stinky even by Mr Stink's stinky standards. "Would you like to have a bath before my family get back?" Chloe said hopefully. The Duchess looked up at her master with a look of desperate hope in her blinking eyes. It was the stink that made her blink.

"Let me think…"

Chloe smiled at him expectantly.

"Actually, I'll leave it for this month, thank you."

"Oh," said Chloe, disappointed. "Is there anything I can get you right now?"

"Is there an afternoon tea menu perhaps?" asked Mr Stink. "A choice of scones, cakes and French pastries?"

"Erm… no," said Chloe. "But I could bring you a cup of tea and biscuits. And we should have some cat food that I could bring for the Duchess."

"I am pretty sure the Duchess is a dog not a cat," pronounced Mr Stink.

"I know, but we only have a cat, so we've only got cat food."

"Well, maybe you could pop into Raj's shop tomorrow and buy the Duchess some tins of dog food. Raj knows the brand she likes." Mr Stink rummaged in his pockets. "Here's a ten pence piece. You can keep the change."

Chloe looked in her hand. Mr Stink had actually placed an old brass button there.

"Thank you so much, young lady," he continued. "And please don't forget to knock when you return in case I am getting changed into my pyjamas."

What have I done? thought Chloe, as she made her way across the lawn back to the house. Her head was buzzing with more imaginary life-stories for her new friend, but none of them seemed quite right. Was he an astronaut who had fallen to earth and, in the shock, lost his memory? Or perhaps he was a convict who had escaped from prison after serving thirty years for a crime he didn't commit? Or, even better, a modern-day pirate who had been forced by his comrades to walk the plank into shark-infested waters, but against all the odds had swum to safety?

One thing she knew for sure was that he did really whiff. Indeed she could still smell him as she reached the back door. The plants and flowers in the garden seemed to have wilted with the smell. They were all now leaning away from the shed as if they were trying to avert their stamens. *At least he's safe*, thought Chloe. *And warm, and dry, if only for tonight.*

When she got up to her room and looked out of the window, the light was flashing already.

"All-butter highland shortbread biscuits if you have them, please!" called up Mr Stink. "Thank you so much!"

8

Maybe It's the Drains

"What's that smell?" demanded Mother as she entered the kitchen. She had been out all day campaigning and looked stiffly immaculate as ever in a royal blue twin-set – except for her nose, which was twitching uncontrollably in disgust.

"What smell?" said Chloe, with a short delay as she gulped.

"You must be able to smell it too, Chloe. That smell of... Well, I'm not going to say what it reminds me of, that would be impolite and unbecoming of a woman of my class and distinction, but it's a bad smell." She breathed in and the smell seemed to take her by surprise all over again. "My goodness, it's a very bad smell."

Like a malevolent cloud of darkest brown, the smell had seeped through the timber of the shed, no doubt peeling off the creosote as it travelled. Then it had crept its way across the lawn, before opening the cat flap and starting its aggressive occupation of the kitchen. Have you ever wondered what a bad smell looks like? It looks like this...

Oh, that's a nasty one. If you put your nose right up against the page you can almost smell it.

"Maybe it's the drains?" offered Chloe.

"Yes, it must be the drains leaking again. Even more reason why I need to be elected as an MP. Now, I have a journalist from *The Times* coming to interview me at breakfast this week. So you must be on your best behaviour. I want him to see what a nice normal family we are."

Normal?! thought Chloe.

"Voters like to see that one has a happy home life. I just pray that this foul stench will be gone by then."

"Yes…" said Chloe. "I'm sure it will. Mother, was Dad – I mean, Father – ever in a rock band?"

Mother stared at her. "What on earth are you talking about, young lady? Where would you get such a ridiculous idea?"

Chloe swallowed. "It's just I saw this picture

of this band called The Serpents of Doom and one of them looked a lot like — "

Mother went a little pale. "Preposterous!" she said. "I don't know what's got into you!" She fiddled with her bouffant, almost as if she was nervous. "Your father, in a rock band of all things! First that exercise book full of outrageous stories, and now this!"

"But — "

"No buts, young lady. Honestly, I don't know what to do with you any more."

Mother looked really furious now. Chloe couldn't understand what she'd done wrong. "Well, pardon me for asking," she sulked.

"That's it!" shouted Mother. "Go to bed, right now!"

"It's twenty past six!" Chloe protested.

"I don't care! Bed!"

Chloe found it hard to get to sleep. Not only because she had been sent to bed so ridiculously early, but also and more importantly because she had moved a tramp into the shed. She noticed the light of the torch bouncing off her bedroom window and looked at her alarm clock. It was 2:11am. What on earth could he want at this time of night?

Mr Stink had made the shed quite homely. He had fashioned a bed out of some piles of old newspapers. An old piece of tarpaulin was his duvet, with a grow bag for a pillow. It looked almost comfy. An old hosepipe had been arranged in the shape of a dog-basket for the Duchess. A plant-pot full of water sat beside for a bowl. In chalk he'd expertly drawn some old-fashioned portraits on the dark wooden creosoted walls, like the ones you see in museums or old country houses, depicting people from history. On one side he'd even drawn a window, complete with curtains and a sea view.

"You seem to be settling in then," said Chloe.

"Oh, yes, I can't thank you enough, child. I love it. I feel like I finally have a home again."

"I'm so pleased."

"Now," said Mr Stink. "Miss Chloe, I called you down here because I can't sleep. I would like you to read me a story."

"A story? What kind of story?"

"You choose, my dear. But I implore you, nothing too girly please…"

Chloe tiptoed up the stairs back to her room. Sometimes she liked to move around the house without making a sound, and so could remember where all the creaks were on the stairs. If she put her foot right in the middle of *this* step, or the left side of *this* one, she knew she wouldn't be heard. If she woke Annabelle up, she knew her little sister would relish the chance of getting her into deep deep trouble. And this wouldn't be normal everyday trouble like not eating your cabbage or 'forgetting' to do your homework. This would be 'inviting a tramp to live in the shed' trouble. It would be off the scale. As this simple graph shows:

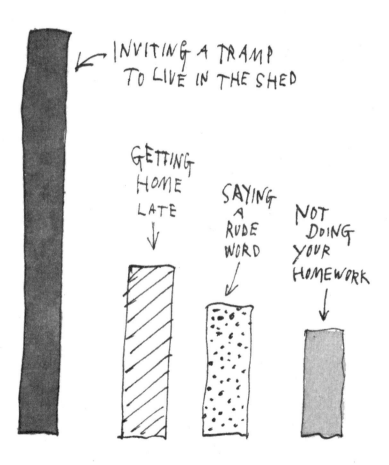

INVITING A TRAMP TO LIVE IN THE SHED

GETTING HOME LATE

SAYING A RUDE WORD

NOT DOING YOUR HOMEWORK

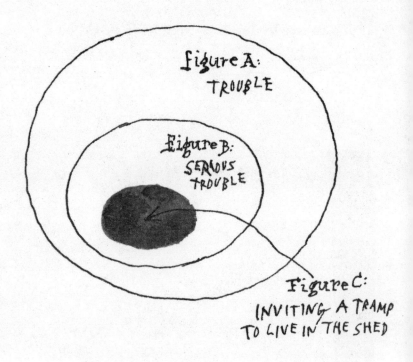

Alternatively, if you look at this simple Venn diagram you can see that if figure A is 'trouble' and figure B is 'serious trouble', then this shaded area here, representing inviting a tramp to live in the shed, is a sub-section of figure B.

I hope that makes things clear.

Chloe looked on her bookshelf, behind the little ornamental owls she collected even if she wasn't sure why. (Did she even *like* owls? Some distant aunt buys you a porcelain owl one day, some other aunt assumes you're collecting them, and by the end of your childhood you've got hundreds of the stupid things. Owls, not aunts.)

Chloe studied the spines of her books. They were quite girly. Lots of pinky-coloured books that matched her stupid pinky-coloured room that she hated. She hadn't chosen the colour of her walls. Hadn't even been asked. Why couldn't her room be painted black? Now *that* would be cool. Her mother only bought her books about ponies, princesses, ballet schools and brainless bleach-blonde teenagers in America whose only worry was what to wear to the prom. Chloe wasn't the least bit interested in any of them, and she was pretty sure Mr Stink wouldn't be either.

The one story she had written had been torn to shreds by her mother. This wasn't going to be easy.

Chloe tiptoed back down the stairs and shut the kitchen door behind her incredibly slowly so it wouldn't make a noise, and then knocked gently on the shed door.

"Who is it?" came a suspicious voice.

"It's me, Chloe, of course."

"I was fast asleep! What do you want?"

"You asked me to read you a story."

"Oh well, now you've woken me up you better come in…"

Chloe took a last deep breath of the fresh night air and entered his den.

"Goody!" said Mr Stink. "I used to love a bed-time story."

"Well, actually I'm sorry, but I couldn't really find anything," said Chloe. "All my books are horribly girly. Most of them are pink, in fact."

"Oh dear," said Mr Stink. He looked disappointed for a moment, then he smiled at a thought. "But what about one of your stories?"

"My stories?"

"Yes. You told me you like to make them up."

"But I couldn't just... I mean... what if you don't like it?" Chloe's stomach fizzed with a peculiar mix of excitement and fear. No one had ever asked to hear one of her stories before.

"I'm sure I'll love it," said Mr Stink. "And anyhow, you'll never know until you try."

"That's true," said Chloe, nodding. She hesitated for a moment, then took a deep breath. "Do you like vampires?" she asked.

"Well, I don't know any socially."

"No, I mean, would you like to hear a story about vampires? These are vampires who are teachers in a school. Who suck the blood out of their poor unsuspecting pupils..."

"Is this the story your mother tore up?"

"Erm... yes," replied Chloe sadly. "But I think I can remember most of it."

"Well, I would love to hear it!"

"Really?"

"Of course!"

"All right," said Chloe. "Please can you pass me the torch?"

Mr Stink passed it to her and she turned it on and put it under her face to look scary.

"Once upon a time..." she began, before losing her nerve.

"Yes?"

"Once upon a time... no, I can't do it! Sorry."

Chloe hated reading out loud in class. She was

so shy she would even try and hide under her desk to avoid it. This was even *more* terrifying. These were her words. It was much more private, more personal, and she suddenly felt like she wasn't ready to share it with anyone.

"Please, Miss Chloe," said Mr Stink encouragingly. "I really want to hear your story. It sounds top banana! Now you were saying, once upon a time…"

She took a deep breath. "Once upon a time, there was a little girl called Lily who hated going to school. It wasn't because the lessons were hard, it was because all her teachers were vampires…"

"Wonderful opening!"

Chloe smiled, and continued. Soon she was really getting into it, and putting on voices for her heroine Lily, Lily's best friend Justin who was bitten by the music teacher in a piano lesson and became a bloodsucker too, and Mrs Murk, the evil headmistress, who was in fact empress of vampires.

The tale unravelled all night. Chloe finished the story just before dawn as Lily finally drove her hockey stick through the headmistress's heart.

"… Mrs Murk's blood spurted out of her like newly struck oil, redecorating the sports hall a dark shade of crimson. The end."

Chloe turned off the torch, her voice hoarse and her eyes barely still open.

"What an absolutely gripping yarn," announced Mr Stink. "I can't wait to find out what happens in book two."

"Book *two*?"

"Yes," said Mr Stink. "Surely after killing the headmistress Lily is moved to another school. And all the teachers there could be flesh-eating zombies!"

That, thought Chloe, *is a very good idea*.

9

A Little Bit of Drool

Chloe looked at her alarm-clock radio when she finally dropped into bed. 6:44am. She had never been to bed that late, ever. *Adults* didn't even go to bed that late. Maybe very naughty rock-star ones, but not many. She closed her eyes for a second.

"Chloe? *Chloeee*? Wake up! *Chloeeeee*?" shouted Mother from outside the door. She knocked on the door three times. Then paused and knocked one more time which was especially annoying, as Chloe hadn't expected her to. She looked at the alarm-clock radio thing again.

6:45am. She had either been asleep for a whole day or a whole minute. As she couldn't open her eyes, Chloe guessed it must have been a minute.

"*Whaaaat…?*" she said, and was shocked by how deep and gravelly she sounded. Telling stories all night had turned Chloe's voice into that of a sixty-year-old ex-coal miner who smoked a hundred roll-ups a day.

"Don't 'what' me, young lady! It's time you stopped lazing in bed. Your sister has already completed a triathlon this morning. Now get up. I need your help today on the campaign trail!"

Chloe was so tired she felt like she had grown into her bed. In fact, she wasn't sure where her body ended and the bed began. She slid out from under her duvet and crawled to the bathroom. Blinking in the mirror, Chloe thought for a moment that she was looking at her own nana. Then, sighing, she made her way downstairs and to the kitchen table.

"We are going campaigning today," said Mother as she sipped her grapefruit juice and swallowed the motorway tailback of vitamin pills and food supplements she had lined up neatly on the table.

"It sounds *booorrrring*," said Chloe. She made the word 'boring' sound even more boring by making it longer than it really needed to be. On Sunday mornings, Mother would allow the television to be switched on so she could watch programmes about politics. Chloe liked watching television. In a house where viewing was rationed, even an advert for a Stannah stair lift was a treat. However, these political discussion shows – which for no apparent reason were broadcast on Sunday mornings – were bum-numbingly boring. They made Chloe think that she wanted to be a kid forever if this was what the grown-up world was like.

Chloe always suspected that her mother had another motive for watching: she had a crush on the Prime Minister. Chloe couldn't see it herself, but lots of women her mother's age seemed to find him dishy. To Dad's amusement, Mother would always stop whatever she was doing to watch the PM if he came on the news. Once, Chloe had even spotted a little bit of drool ooze out of her mother's mouth when there was some footage of the Prime Minister in denim shorts playing Frisbee on a beach.

Of course, even the sight of her mother drooling didn't make those politics shows any less boring. But Chloe would have watched a hundred of them if it meant not having to spend the day campaigning with Mother. *That* was how boring it was going to be.

"Well, you are coming whether you like it or not," said Mother. "And put on that frilly yellow dress that I bought you for your birthday. You look almost pretty in that."

Chloe did not look anywhere near pretty in it. She looked like a Quality Street. If that wasn't bad enough, she looked like one of the unpopular flavours that get left in the tin until way into the New Year. The only colour she really liked wearing was black. She thought black was cool, and even better it made her look less chubby. Chloe desperately wanted to be a Goth, but she didn't know where to start. You couldn't buy Goth clothes in Marks & Spencer's. And anyway, you also needed the white make-up and the black hair-dye, and most importantly the skill of looking down at your shoes at all times.

How would she go about becoming a Goth? Was there an application form to fill out? A committee of super-Goths who would vet you for Gothness, or was it Gothnicity? Chloe had once seen a real-life Goth hanging around by a bin in the high street and become incredibly excited. She really wanted to go over and ask her how to get started in the Goth world, but she was too shy. Which was ironic, since shyness is something you need if you want to be a successful Goth.

In the unlikely event of Elizabeth the cat becoming a Goth, she would look like this.

Fig A.

Fig B.

Let's get back to the story…

"It's cold outside, Chloe," said Mother, when Chloe came downstairs in the horrible Quality Street dress. "You'll need a coat. How about that tangerine-coloured coat your grandmother made you last Christmas?"

Chloe reached into the room under the stairs. This was where everyone in the family kept their coats and wellington boots. She heard a rustle in the darkness. Had Elizabeth the cat got shut in there by mistake? Or had Mr Stink moved indoors? She switched on the light. Peeking out from behind the bottom of an old fur coat was a frightened face.

"Dad?"

"Shush!"

"What are you hiding in here for?" Chloe whispered. "You are meant to be at work."

"No, I'm not. I lost my job at the factory,"

said Dad sorrowfully.

"*What*?"

"A whole load of us got made redundant two weeks ago. No one is buying new cars right now. It's the recession, I suppose."

"Yes, but why are you hiding?"

"I'm too frightened to tell your mother. She'll divorce me if she finds out. Please, I beg you, don't tell her."

"I'm not sure she'd div—"

"Please, Chloe. I'll sort all this out soon. It's not going to be easy, but I'll get another job if I can."

He leaned forward so that the hem of the fur coat was draped over his head, the thick fur looking like a mess of curly hair.

"So that's what you look like with hair!" Chloe whispered.

"What?"

It was *definitely* Dad on that CD cover. With the fur over his head, he looked just like he did in the photo, with that astonishing perm!

"If you need a job, you could always go back to playing guitar with the Serpents of Doom," said Chloe.

Dad looked startled. "Who told you I was in a band?"

"I saw your CD and I asked Mother, but she—"

"Shh!" said Dad. "Keep it down. Wait... where did you see this CD?"

"Er... I was... um... looking for my old hamster cage in the shed and it was in a box with a load of old junk. There was a burnt guitar with it."

Dad opened his mouth to say something, but just at that moment, a door slammed upstairs.

"Come along, Chloe!" boomed Mother.

"Promise you won't say anything about me losing my job," whispered Dad.

"I promise."

Chloe shut the door, leaving her dad on all fours in the darkness. Now she had two fully grown men hiding around the house. *What's next?* she thought. *Am I going to find Grandad in the tumble dryer?!*

10

Slightly Chewed

Being on the political campaign trail meant Chloe knocking on what seemed like everybody's front door in the town and Mother asking people if she could "rely on their vote". Those who said they were going to vote for Mother were instantly rewarded with a big smile and an even bigger sticker to put in their window proclaiming 'Vote Crumb'. Those who said they *weren't* voting for her were going to miss an awful lot of daytime telly. Mother was the kind of person who wouldn't give up without a fight.

They passed the newsagent's shop. "I wonder if Raj would put one of my posters up in his window," said Mother, as she strode towards the store. Chloe clomped behind in her uncomfortable Sunday-best shoes, struggling to keep up. Her mind had been elsewhere all day. Now she was carrying around *two* hot-air balloon-sized secrets in her head – Mr Stink hiding in the garden shed and her dad hiding in the cupboard under the stairs!

"Ah, my two favourite customers!" exclaimed Raj as they entered the shop. "The beautiful Mrs Crumb and her charming daughter, Chloe!"

"It's Croooome!" corrected Mother. "So, Raj, can I rely on your vote?"

"Are you on *The X-Factor*?!" said Raj excitedly. "Yes, yes, of course I will vote for you. What are you singing on Saturday?"

"No, she's not doing *The X-Factor*, Raj," interjected Chloe, trying not to laugh at the thought.

"*Britain's Got Talent* perhaps? You are maybe doing a ventriloquist act with a naughty otter puppet called Jeremy? That would be most amusing!"

"No, she's not doing *Britain's Got Talent* either." Chloe smirked.

"*How do you solve any dream will I'd do*

anything or whatever it's called with Graham thingy?"

"It's the election, Raj," interrupted Mother. "You know, the local election? I am standing to be our local MP."

"And when is this election thing happening then?"

"Next Friday. I can't believe you've missed it! It's all over these newspapers, Raj!" Mother gestured at the piles and piles of newspapers in the shop.

"Oh, I only read *Nuts* and *Zoo*," said Raj. "I get all the news I need from them."

Mother looked at him disapprovingly, even though Chloe suspected she wasn't sure what either *Nuts* or *Zoo* were. Chloe had once seen a copy of *Nuts* that one of the older boys had brought into school, and knew it was rude.

"What do you think are the important issues

facing Britain today, Raj?" asked Mother, delighted with the cleverocity and inteligentness of her own question.

Raj pondered for a moment, then shouted over at some boys who were loitering by the pick 'n' mix. "Don't put the liquorice in your mouth unless you are going to buy it, young man! Oh dear, I will have to put that liquorice on special offer now!"

Raj grabbed a pen and a piece of card. He wrote 'slightly chewed', and put it on the liquorice box. "Sorry, what was the question again?"

Note to self, thought Chloe. *Never buy liquorice from this shop again.*

"Erm... Now where was I?" said Mother to Raj. "Ah yes, what do you think are the most — ?"

" — important issues affecting Britain today, Raj?" chimed in Raj. "Oh, I didn't need to say

'Raj'. I am Raj. Well, I think it would be a great advance if Cadbury's Creme Eggs were available not just at Easter but all year round. They are one of my most popular items. I also strongly believe that Quavers should diversify from cheese flavours to incorporate Asian Chicken and Lamb Rogan Josh varieties. And most importantly, and I know this may be controversial, but I think that coffee Revels should be banned as they spoil an otherwise wonderfully enjoyable confectionery. There, I've said it!"

"Right," said Mother.

"And if you promise to change the government policy on those issues you can rely on my vote, Mrs Crumb!"

Mother had had a mixed response to her campaigning so far, and was eager to secure this potentially crucial vote.

"Yes, I will certainly try, Raj!" she said.

"Thank you so much," said Raj. "Please help yourself to something from the shop."

"No, I couldn't possibly, Raj!"

"Please, Mrs Crumb. Have a nice box of Terry's All Gold, I have only taken out the caramel squares. Mmm, they are delicious. And perhaps Chloe would like this Finger of Fudge? It's a bit squashed as my wife sat on it, but it's perfectly fine to eat."

"We couldn't possibly accept these kind gifts, Raj," said Mother.

"Well, why not buy them then? One box of Terry's All Gold, £4.29, and a Finger of Fudge, 20p. That's £4.49. Let's call it £4.50. Easier if I just take £5. Thank you so much."

Chloe and Mother exited the shop holding their confectionery. Mother held her partially eaten box of chocolates with barely disguised disdain.

"Now, don't forget, Raj. The election is next Friday!" said Mother as she opened the door.

"Oh, I can't do next Friday, Mrs Crumb. I have to stay here as I am expecting a large shipment of Smarties! But good luck to you!"

"Ah… Thank you," replied Mother, looking crestfallen.

"Mrs Crumb," said Raj. "May I interest you in something incredibly special that will certainly become something of a family heirloom to be passed down through the generations? Something your grandchildren will one day take proudly to have valued on *The Antiques Road Show*?"

"Yes?" said Mother expectantly.

"It's a Teenage Mutant Ninja Turtles stationery set…"

11

Hair Pulling

"What are you hiding in the shed?" said Annabelle with accusatory glee.

It was midnight and Chloe was once again tiptoeing past her sister's room, this time to tell Mr Stink about Lily's newest adventure with her flesh-eating zombie teachers. Annabelle stood in her doorway in her pink pony pyjamas. Her hair was in bunches. And in case of fire she slept in lip-gloss. She looked sickeningly cute.

"Nothing," said Chloe, gulping.

"I know when you're lying, Chloe."

"How?"

"You gulp when you tell a lie."

"No I don't!" said Chloe, trying very hard not to gulp. She gulped.

"You just did! What's in there anyway? Have you got a boyfriend hiding in there or something?"

"No, I haven't got a boyfriend, Annabelle."

"No, of course not. You would need to lose some weight first."

"Just go back to bed," said Chloe.

"I am not going to bed until you tell me what you've got in the shed," announced Annabelle.

"Keep your voice down. You are going to wake everyone up!"

"No I won't keep my voice down! In fact it is going to get louder and louder. La la la la la la la la la la la la la la la la!"

"*Shush*!" hissed Chloe.

"La la la la la la la la la la la la la la la

la la la la la la la la la la la la la la la la
la la la la la la la la la la la la la la la la
la la la la la la la la la la la la la la la
la...!"

Chloe pulled her little sister's hair sharply.
There was a pause for a moment, as Annabelle
stared at Chloe in shock. Then she opened her
mouth.

"AAAAAAAAAAAAAAAAAAA
AAAAAAAAAAAAAAAAAAA
AAAAAAAAAAAAAAAAAAA
AAAAAAAAAAAAAAAAAAA
AAAAAAAAAAAAAAAAAAA
AAAAAAAAAAAAAAAAAAA
AHHHHHHHHHHHHHHHHH
HHHHH!" wailed Annabelle.

"Girls! What on earth is all this noise?" said
Mother as she sailed out of her bedroom in her
silk nightgown.

Annabelle tried to speak, but hyperventilated through her tears.

"Ugh… eh… ah… eh… ah… ughhhh… ah… eh… ugh…"

"What on earth have you done to her, Chloe?" demanded Mother.

"She's putting it on! I didn't pull her stupid hair that hard!" Chloe protested.

"You pulled her *hair*? Annabelle is down to the last thousand for a model casting tomorrow for George at Asda and she has to look perfect!"

"Ugh… ah… eh… ah. She's ah eh got ugh ugh ugh hiding ugh ugh something eh ah ugh in the ugh ugh ughu shed," said Annabelle as she squeezed out some more tears.

"Father," ordered Mother. "Come out here this instant!"

"I'm asleep!" came the muffled cry from their bedroom.

"THIS INSTANT!"

Chloe looked down at the carpet so Mother couldn't read her face. There was a pause. The three ladies of the house listened as Dad got out of bed. Next they heard the sound of someone passing water into a toilet bowl. Mother's face turned red with fury.

"I SAID THIS INSTANT!"

The sound abruptly stopped and Dad scurried out of the bedroom in his Arsenal FC pyjamas.

"Annabelle said Chloe is hiding something in the shed. Chocolate, most likely. I need you to go down there and take a look."

"Me?" protested Dad.

"Yes you!"

"Can't it wait until the morning?"

"No it can't."

"There's nothing down there," pleaded Chloe.

"SILENCE!" demanded Mother.

"I'll just get a torch," sighed Dad.

He made his way slowly downstairs, and Mother, Chloe and Annabelle rushed to the window of the master bedroom to watch him walk to the end of the garden. The moon was full, and it bathed the garden in an eerie glow. The torchlight danced around the trees and shrubs as he walked. They looked on breathlessly as Dad slowly opened the shed door. It creaked like a muffled scream.

Chloe could hear her heart beating. Was this the moment that would seal her doom forever? Would she be made to eat only cabbage for every meal from now on? Or get sent to bed before she'd even got up? Or be grounded for the rest of her life? Chloe gulped louder than she had ever gulped before. Mother heard this and shot her a look of dark, burning suspicion.

The silence was like thunder. A few seconds passed, or was it a few hours or even years? Then Dad emerged slowly from the shed. He looked up at the window and shouted, "There's nothing here!"

12

Pongy Pong

Did I dream the whole thing? thought Chloe as she lay in bed. She was in that place between asleep and awake. That place where you can still remember dreaming. It was 4:48am, and now she was beginning to wonder if Mr Stink even really existed.

At dawn her curiosity got the better of her. Chloe edged down the stairs, and tiptoed across the cold wet grass to the shed door. She lingered outside for a moment, before opening it.

"Ah, there you are!" said Mr Stink. "I am very hungry this morning. Poached eggs please, if it's not too much trouble. Runny in the middle. Sausages. Mushrooms. Grilled tomatoes. Sausages. Baked beans. Sausages. Bread and butter. Brown sauce on the side. Don't forget the sausages. English breakfast tea. And a glass of orange juice. Thank you so much."

Chloe obviously hadn't dreamed the whole thing, but she was beginning to wish she had. It was all thrillingly, terrifyingly real.

"Freshly-squeezed orange juice to your liking, sir?" she asked sarcastically.

"Actually, have you got any that's very slightly off? I prefer that. Perhaps that was squeezed a month or so ago?"

Just then, Chloe spotted an old dog-eared black-and-white photograph that Mr Stink had placed on a shelf. It showed a beautiful young couple standing proudly next to an immaculate and perfectly rounded Rolls

Royce, parked in the driveway of a magnificent stately home.

"Who's that?" she asked, pointing to the photo.

"Oh, nobody, n-n-n-nothing…" he stammered. "Just a sentimental old photograph, Miss Chloe."

"Can I see?"

"No, no, no, it's just a foolish picture. Please, pay it no heed." Mr Stink was becoming increasingly flustered. He snatched the photograph from the shelf, and put it in his pyjama pocket. Chloe was disappointed. The photograph had seemed like another clue to Mr Stink's past, like his little silver spoon, or the way he'd bowled that piece of paper into the bin. This one had seemed like the best clue yet. But now Mr Stink was shoo-ing her out of the shed. "Don't forget the sausages!" he said.

How on earth did Dad miss him? thought Chloe, as she went back to the house. Even if he hadn't seen Mr Stink in the shed, he surely must have smelled him.

Chloe tiptoed into the kitchen and opened the fridge door as quietly as possible. She stared into the fridge, and began carefully moving jars of mustard and pickle so they wouldn't clink. She hoped to find some out of date orange juice that might appeal to Mr Stink's tainted palate.

"What are you doing?" said a voice.

Chloe startled. It was only Dad, but she wasn't expecting to see him up this early. She gathered herself for a moment.

"Nothing, Dad. I'm just hungry that's all."

"I know who's in the shed, Chloe," he said.

Chloe looked at him, panicked, unable to think, let alone speak.

"I opened the shed door last night to see an old tramp snoring next to my lawnmower," Dad went on. "The pong was… well… pongy. It was an extremely pongy pong…"

"I wanted to tell you, honestly I did," said Chloe. "He needs a home, Dad. Mother wants all homeless people driven off the streets!"

"I know, I know, but I'm sorry Chloe, he can't stay. Your mother will go nuts if she finds out."

"Dad, I'm sorry."

"It's OK, love. I am not going to say anything to your mother. You've kept your promise not to tell anyone about me losing my job, haven't you?"

"Yes, of course."

"Good girl," said Dad.

"So," said Chloe, glad to have Dad to herself for a while. "How did your guitar get all burned?"

"Your mother put it on the bonfire."

"No!"

"Yes," said Dad sorrowfully. "She wanted me to move on with my life. She was doing me a favour, I suppose."

"A *favour*?"

"Well, The Serpents of Doom were never going to make it. I got the job at the car factory and that was that."

"But you had an album! You must have been

dead famous," chirped Chloe excitedly.

"No, we weren't at all!" chuckled Dad. "The album only sold twelve copies."

"*Twelve*?" said Chloe.

"Yes, and your grandma bought most of those. We were pretty good, though. And one of our singles got into the charts."

"What, the top forty?"

"No, we peaked at 98."

"Wow," said Chloe. "Top 100! That's pretty good, isn't it?"

"No, it isn't," said Dad. "But you're very sweet to say so." He kissed her on the forehead and opened his arms to give her a hug.

"There's no time for cuddles!" said Mother as she strode into the kitchen. "The man from *The Times* will be here soon. Father, you make the scrambled eggs. Chloe, you can lay the table."

"Yes, of course, Mother," said Chloe, with at least half her brain worrying about when Mr Stink was going to get his breakfast.

"So how important is your family to you, Mrs Crumb?" asked the serious-looking journalist. He wore thick glasses and was old. In fact he had probably been born an old man. Plopped out of his mother, wearing glasses and a three-piece suit. He was called Mr Stern, which Chloe thought was pretty fitting. He didn't look like he smiled a lot. Or indeed ever.

"Actually, it's pronounced Croombe," corrected Mother.

"No, it's not," said Dad before his wife shot him a look of utter fury. The Crumb family was sitting around the dining table and not enjoying their posh breakfast. It was all such a lie. They didn't normally sit round the dining room table

eating smoked salmon and scrambled eggs. They
would be round the *kitchen* table eating Rice
Krispies or Marmite on toast.

"Very important, Mr Stern," said Mother.

"The most important thing in my life. I don't know what I'd do without my husband, Mr Crooome, my darling daughter, Annabelle and the other one... whatshername? Chloe."

"Well, then I ask you this Mrs... Croooooome. Is your family more important to you than the future of this country?"

That was a toughie. There was a pause during which a civilization could rise and fall.

"Well, Mr. Stern..." Mother said.

"Yes, Mrs Crooooooooome...?"

"Well, Mr Stern..."

"Yes, Mrs Crooooooooooooooooooooooooooo ooome...?"

At that moment there was a little rat-tat-tat on the window. "Excuse me for interrupting," said Mr Stink with a smile, "but please could I have my breakfast now?"

13

Shut your Face!

"Who on earth is *he*?" enquired Mr Stern as Mr Stink trudged around in his filthy striped pyjamas to the backdoor.

There was silence for a moment. Mother's eyes bulged out of their sockets and Annabelle looked like she was about to shriek or vomit or both.

"Oh, he's the tramp who lives in our shed," said Chloe.

"The tramp who lives in our shed?" repeated Mother incredulously. She looked at her husband with black fire in her eyes.

He gulped.

"I told you she was hiding something in there, Mother!" exclaimed Annabelle.

"He wasn't there when I looked!" protested Dad. "He must have concealed himself behind a trowel!"

"What a wonderful woman you are, Mrs Croooooooooooome," said Mr Stern. "I read about your policies on the homeless. About driving them off the streets. I had no idea you meant we should drive them into our homes and let them come and *live* with us."

"Well I…" spluttered Mother, lost for words.

"I can assure you I am going to write an absolutely glowing piece about you now. This will make the front page. You could be the next Prime Minister of the country!"

"My sausages?" said Mr Stink, as he entered the dining room.

"Excuse me?" said Mother, before putting her hand over her mouth in horror at the smell.

"Forgive me," said Mr Stink. "It's just that I asked your daughter Chloe for some sausages two hours ago, and my sincerest apologies, but I am getting rather peckish!"

"You say I could be the next Prime Minister of the country, Mr Stern?" said Mother, thoughtfully.

"Yes. It's so kind of you. Allowing a dirty old smelly tramp like this – I mean, no offence—"

"None taken," replied Mr Stink without hesitation.

"—to come and live with you. How could you *not* be elected as an MP now?"

Mother smiled. "In that case," she said, turning to Mr Stink, "how many sausages would you like my very good friend who lives in my shed and hardly stinks at all?"

"No more than nine, please," replied Mr Stink.

"Nine sausages coming right up!"

"With poached eggs, bacon, mushrooms, grilled tomatoes, bread and butter and brown sauce on the side, please."

"Certainly, my extremely close and beloved friend!" came the voice from the kitchen.

"You smell so rank I think I'm going to die," said Annabelle.

"That's not nice, Annabelle," said Mother breezily from the kitchen. "Now come and help me in here, darling, there's a good girl!"

Annabelle ran to the sanctuary of the kitchen. "It stinks in here now as well!" she screamed.

"Shut your face!" snapped Mother.

"So, tell me… tramp," said Mr Stern, leaning in towards Mr Stink before the smell got to him and he leaned back. "Is it just you living in the shed?"

"Yes, just me. And of course my dog, the Duchess…"

"HE'S GOT A DOG?" cried Mother anxiously from next door.

"And how do you find living here?" continued Mr Stern.

"Nice," said Mr Stink. "But I warn you, the service is painfully slow…"

14

Lady and the Tramp

'LADY AND THE TRAMP' was the headline.

Mr Stern had been true to his word and the story had made the front page of *The Times*. A large photograph of Mother and Mr Stink accompanied the piece. Mr Stink was smiling broadly, showing his blackened teeth. Mother was trying to smile, but because of the smell she had to keep her mouth firmly closed. As soon as the paperboy put the paper through the letterbox, the Crumbs pounced upon it and devoured it in a frenzy. Mother was famous! She read the article out loud with pride.

Mrs Crumb may not look like a political revolutionary in her smart blue suits and pearls, but she could well change the way we live our lives. She is standing for MP in her local town and, although her policies read as very hard line, she has taken the extraordinary step of inviting a tramp to live with her family.

"It was all my idea," said Mrs Crumb (pronounced 'Crooooooooooooooome'). "At first my family was dead against it, but I just had to give this poor filthy flea-ridden dirt-encrusted stomach-turningly smelly beggar-man and his abhorrent hound a home. I love them both dearly. They're part of the family now. I couldn't imagine life without them. If only other people were as beautifully kind-hearted as me. A modern day saint, some people are saying. If every family in this country was to let a tramp

live with them it could solve the problem of homelessness forever. Oh, and don't forget to vote for me in the forthcoming election."

It's a genius idea, and could put Mrs Crumb in line to be the next Prime Minister.

The tramp, known only as 'Mr Stink' had this to say. "Please could I trouble you for another sausage?"

"It wasn't your idea, Mother," snapped Chloe, too angry to merely sulk.

"Not strictly speaking, dearest, no…"

Chloe glared at her, but at that moment the telephone tinkled.

"Get that will you, someone? It's probably for me," said Mother, grandly.

Annabelle dutifully picked up the phone. "Crooombe residence. Who is speaking please?" she asked, just as her mother had instructed her to. Mother even had a special telephone voice, a note posher than her usual one.

"Who is it, dear?" said Mother.

"It's the Prime Minister," replied Annabelle, putting her hand over the mouthpiece.

"The *Prime Minister*?" squealed Mother.

She hurled herself towards the telephone.

"Mrs Croooombe speaking!" said Mother in a truly ridiculous voice, a good note posher than even her usual telephone one. "Yes, thank you, Prime Minister. It was a super piece in the newspaper, Prime Minister."

Mother was drooling again. Dad rolled his eyes.

"I would be delighted to be a guest on *Question Time* tonight, Prime Minister," said Mother.

Then she went quiet. Chloe could hear a murmur from the other end of the line, followed by silence.

Mother's jaw dropped open.

"*What*?" she growled into the phone, losing her poise and dignity for an instant.

Chloe looked at Dad questioningly and he shrugged.

"What do you mean, you want the tramp to go on as well?" said Mother, incredulous.

Dad grinned. *Question Time* was a serious political discussion programme hosted by a Sir. It was Mother's big chance to shine, and she obviously didn't want it ruined by a malodorous old tramp.

"Well, yes," went on Mother, "I know it makes a good story, but does he really have to be on too? He reeks!"

There was another pause while the Prime Minister spoke, the murmur getting a little bit louder. Chloe was impressed with the man. Anyone who could get Mother to stop talking for a moment *deserved* to run the country.

"Yes, yes, well, if that's what you really want Prime Minister, then yes, of course I will bring Mr Stink along. Thank you so much for calling. By the way I make a very moist Lemon Drizzle Cake. If you are ever passing by on your battle bus I would be delighted to offer you a slice or two. No? Well, goodbye... Goodbye... Goodbye..." She checked one last time that he had definitely gone. "Goodbye."

Chloe rushed into the garden to tell Mr Stink the news. She heard a "Grrrrrr" and assumed it must be the Duchess. However, it was actually Elizabeth the cat who was growling. She was looking up at the roof of the shed, where a trembling Duchess was hiding. The little black dog was yelping softly. Chloe chased Elizabeth away, and eventually coaxed the Duchess down. She patted her.

"There, there," she said. "That nasty puss has gone now."

Elizabeth flew out of the bushes and through the air like a kung-fu kitten. A terrified Duchess rocketed up the apple tree to safety. Elizabeth prowled around the trunk, hissing malevolently.

Chloe knocked on the shed door. "Hello?"

"Is that you, Duchess?" came Mr Stink's voice from inside.

"No, it's Chloe," said Chloe. *He's nuts!* she thought.

"Oh, lovely Chloe! Do come in, dear heart."

Mr Stink upturned a bucket. "Please, please take a seat. So did your mother and I make the newspaper?"

"You're on the front page. Look!"

She held up the paper and he let out a little chuckle. "Fame at last!"

"And that's not all. We just had a call from the Prime Minister."

"Winston Churchill?"

"No, we've got a new one now, and he wants you and mother to go on this programme called *Question Time* tonight."

"On the televisual box?"

"The TV? Yes. And I was thinking, before you go on..." Chloe looked at Mr Stink hopefully.

"It might be a good idea if you had a…"

"Yes, child?"

"Well a…"

"Yes…?"

"A…" She finally plucked up the courage to say it, "…bath?"

Mr Stink looked at her suspiciously for a few seconds.

"Chloe?" he asked at last.

"Yes, Mr Stink?"

"I don't smell, do I?"

How could she answer that? She didn't want to hurt Mr Stink's feelings, but then again it would be much easier to be around him if he were introduced to Mr Soap and his charming wife, Mrs Water…

"No, no, no, of course you don't smell," said Chloe, gulping the biggest gulp that had ever been gulped.

"Thank you, my dear," said Mr Stink, seeming almost convinced. "Then why do people call me Mr Stink?"

In her head, Chloe heard the intensely dramatic music from *Who Wants to be a Millionaire?* This could in fact have been the million pound question. But Chloe had no '50/50', no 'ask the audience' and not even a 'phone a friend' at her disposal. After a long pause, in which you could have watched all three *Lord of the Rings* films in their specially extended director's cuts, words started to form in Chloe's mouth.

"It's a joke," she heard herself saying.

"A joke?" asked Mr Stink.

"Yes, because you actually smell really nice so everyone calls you Mr Stink as a joke."

"Really?" His suspicion seemed to be thawing a little.

"Yes, like calling a really small man 'Mr Big' or a very thin person 'Fatso'."

"Oh, yes, I understand, most amusing!" chuckled Mr Stink.

The Duchess looked at Chloe with a look that said, *You had the chance to tell him, but you chose to carry on the lie.*

How do I know that the Duchess's look said this? Because there is an excellent book in my local library entitled *One Thousand Doggy Expressions Explained* by Professor L. Stone.

I digress.

"But," said Chloe, "you might like to have a bath, well, just for fun..."

15

Bath time

This was no ordinary bath time. Chloe realised this had to be run like a military operation.

Hot water? Check.

Towels? Check.

Bubble bath? Check.

Rubber duck or similar animal-based bath toy? Check.

Soap? Was there enough soap in the house? Or in the town? Or indeed in the whole of Europe, to make Mr Stink clean? He hadn't had a bath since – well, he claimed last year, but it might as well have been since dinosaurs ruled the earth.

Chloe turned on the taps, running them both together so the temperature would be just right. If it was too hot or too cold it might scare Mr Stink off baths for ever. She poured in some bubble bath, and gave it a swirl. Then she laid out some neatly folded towels, pleasingly warm from the airing cupboard, on a little stool by the bath. In the cabinet she found a multi-pack of soaps. It was all going perfectly according to plan, until…

"He's escaped!" said Dad, poking his head around the bathroom door.

"What do you mean, 'escaped'?" said Chloe.

"He's not in the shed, he's not in the house, I couldn't see him in the garden. I don't know where he is."

"Start the car!" said Chloe.

They sped off out of their street. This was exciting. Dad was driving faster than usual, although still one mile an hour less than the speed limit, and Chloe sat in the front seat, which she hardly ever did. All they needed were some doughnuts and coffee to go, and they could be two mismatched cops in a Hollywood action movie. Chloe had a hunch that if Mr Stink was anywhere he would be back sat on his bench where she had first talked to him.

"Stop the car!" she said, as they passed the bench.

"But it's a double yellow line," pleaded Dad.

"I said, stop the car!"

Dad stamped on the brake. The tyres screeched as the car stopped. They were both propelled forward a little in their seats. They smiled at each other at the excitement of it all – it was as if they had just ridden a rollercoaster. Chloe sprang out of the car and slammed the door shut, something she would never dare do if her mother were around.

But the bench was empty. Mr Stink wasn't there. Chloe sniffed the air. There was a faint whiff of him, but she couldn't really tell if this was a recent one or a lingering odour from a week or so ago.

Dad drove around the town for another hour. Chloe checked all the places she thought her tramp friend might be – under bridges, in the park, in the coffee shop, even behind bins. But it seemed as though he really had disappeared. Chloe felt like crying. Maybe he had left the town – he was a wanderer, after all.

"We'd better head home now, darling," said Dad softly.

"Yep," said Chloe, trying to be brave.

"I'll put the kettle on," said Dad as they walked indoors.

In Britain, a cup of tea is the answer to every problem.

Fallen off your bicycle? Nice cup of tea.

Your house has been destroyed by a meteorite? Nice cup of tea and a biscuit.

Your entire family has been eaten by a Tyrannosaurus Rex that has travelled through a space/time portal? Nice cup of tea and a piece of cake. Possibly a savoury option would be welcome here too, for example a Scotch egg or a sausage roll.

Chloe picked up the kettle and went to the sink to fill it. She looked out of the window.

Just then, Mr Stink's head popped up from the pond. He gave her a little wave. Chloe screamed.

When they'd got over their shock, Chloe and Dad walked slowly towards the pond. Mr Stink was humming the song 'Row row row your boat' to himself. As he sang, he rubbed algae into himself with a water lily. A number of goldfish floated upside down on the water's surface.

"Good afternoon, Miss Chloe, good afternoon, Mr Crumb," said Mr Stink brightly. "I won't be too long. I don't want to get too wrinkled in here!"

"What… what… what are you doing?" asked Dad.

"The Duchess and I are having a bath of course, as young Chloe suggested."

At that moment the Duchess appeared out of the murky depths, covered in weeds. As if it wasn't enough that he was having a bath in a pond, Mr Stink had to share it with his dog too. After a few moments the Duchess clambered out of the pond, leaving behind a large black scum layer floating on the water. She shook herself dry and Chloe stared at her in surprise. It turned out she wasn't a little black dog after all, but a little white one.

"Mr Crumb, sir?" said Mr Stink. "Would you mind awfully passing me a towel? Thank you so much. Ah! I am as clean as a whistle now!"

16

Rule Britannia

Mother sniffed. And sniffed again. Her nose wrinkled with disgust.

"Are you sure you had a bath, Mr Stink?" she enquired, as Dad drove all the family and Mr Stink to the television studio.

"Yes, I did, Madam."

"Well, there is a funny smell of pond in this car. And dog," pronounced Mother from the front seat.

"I think I'm going to puke," pronounced Annabelle from the back seat.

"I've told you before, darling. We don't say

'puke' in this family," corrected Mother. "We say we are feeling very slightly nauseous."

Chloe opened the window discreetly, so as not to hurt Mr Stink's feelings.

"Do you mind if we keep the window closed?" asked Mr Stink. "I am a little chilly."

The window went up again.

"Thank you so much," said Mr Stink. "Such unimaginable kindness."

They stopped at some traffic lights and Dad reached for one of his hard rock CDs. Mother slapped his hand, and he put it back on the steering wheel. She then put her favourite CD on the car stereo, and the old couple in the next car looked at the Crumb family strangely as 'Rule Britannia, Britannia rules the waves' came blaring out of their car.

"Mmm, no no no, that won't do at all…" said the

TV producer as he studied Mr Stink. "Can we put some dirt on him? He doesn't look trampy enough. Make-up? Where's make-up?"

A lady with far too much make-up on appeared from around a corridor, scoffing a croissant and holding a powder-puff.

"Darling, have you got any grime?" asked the producer.

"Come this way, Mr…?" said the make-up lady.

"Stink," said Mr Stink proudly. "Mr Stink. And I am going to star on the television tonight."

Mother scowled.

Chloe, Annabelle and Dad were led to a little room with a television, half a bottle of warm white wine and some stale crisps, to watch the show being broadcast live.

The thunderous title music started, there was polite applause from the audience and the pompous-looking presenter, Sir David Squirt addressed the camera. "Tonight on *Question Time* it's an election special. We have representatives from all the major political parties, and also a tramp who goes by the name of Mr Stink. Welcome to the programme, everyone."

Everyone around the table nodded, apart from Mr Stink who proclaimed loudly, "May I say what a delight it is for me to be on your show tonight?"

"Thank you," said the presenter uncertainly.

"Being homeless I have never seen it," said Mr Stink. "In fact, I have absolutely no idea who you are. But I am sure you are wildly famous. Please continue, Sir Donald."

The audience laughed uncertainly. Mother looked displeased. The presenter coughed nervously and tried to continue.

"So the first question tonight…"

"Are you wearing make-up, Sir Declan?" enquired Mr Stink innocently.

"A little, yes. For the lights of course."

"Of course," agreed Mr Stink. "Foundation?"

"Yes."

"Eye liner?"

"A little."

"Lip-gloss?"

"A smidge."

"Looks nice. I wish I'd had some now. Blusher?"

The audience chuckled throughout this exchange. Sir David moved on rapidly. "I should explain that Mr Stink is here tonight as he has been invited to live with Mrs Crumb…"

"Crooommmbe," corrected Mother.

"Oh," said Sir David. "I do apologise. We checked the pronunciation with your husband, and he said it was Crumb."

Mother went red with embarrassment. Sir David turned his attention back to his notes. "Later on in the programme," he said, "we will be discussing the difficult topic of homelessness."

Mr Stink put his hand up.

"Yes, Mr Stink?" asked the presenter.

"May I just pop to the lavatory, Sir Duncan?"

The audience laughed louder this time.

"I should have gone before we started, but I asked the make-up lady to do my hair and it took forever. Don't get me wrong, I am thrilled with the results; she gave me a wash and blow-dry. They even put something called gel in it, but I didn't get a chance to go to the little boy's room."

"Of course, if you need to go, go…"

"Thank you so, so much," said Mr Stink. He rose to his feet and started to potter off the set. "I shouldn't be too long, I think it's just a number one."

The audience howled again with laughter. In the little room with the stale crisps and the television Chloe and Dad were laughing too. Chloe looked at Annabelle. She was trying not to laugh, but a smile was definitely creeping up her face.

"My apologies!" exclaimed Mr Stink as he crossed the stage again in the opposite direction. "I am told the lavatory is this way…!"

17

Collapsed Bouffant

"And that's why I feel that there should be a curfew on all people under thirty." Mother was in full flow now, and she smiled as she received a smattering of applause for this comment from the people over thirty in the audience. "They should all be in bed by eight o'clock at the latest…"

"Sorry I was a while," said Mr Stink as he ambled back on to the set. "I thought it was just a number one, but while I was standing there I suddenly got the urge to have a number two." The audience erupted into laughter, some even applauding in delight as this serious show descended into a discussion of an old tramp's toilet habits. "I mean, I usually do my number twos in the mornings, between 9:07 and 9:08, but I had an egg sandwich backstage before I came on the show tonight. I don't know if you made the sandwiches, Sir Derek?"

"No, I don't make the sandwiches, Mr Stink. Now please can we get back to the question of curfews for young—"

"Well, it was a delicious sandwich, don't get me wrong," said Mr Stink. "But egg can sometimes make me want to go. And I don't always get that much of a warning, especially at my age. Do you ever have that problem, Sir Doris? Or do you have the bum of a much younger man?"

Another massive wave of laughter crashed on to the stage. In the stale crisps room even Annabelle was laughing now.

"We are here to discuss the serious topics of the day, Mr Stink," continued Sir David. His face was redder than red with anger as his serious political programme, a programme he had presented for forty tedious years, was rapidly turning into a comedy show starring an old tramp. The audience was enjoying it immensely though, and booed Sir David a little as he tried to steer the show back to politics. He shot them a steely stare before turning to the new star of the show. "And my name is Sir David. Not Sir Derek, or Sir Doris. *Sir David*. Now, let's move on to the question of homelessness, Mr Stink. I have a statistic here which says that there are over 100,000 homeless people in the UK today. Why do you think so many people are living on the streets?"

Mr Stink cleared his throat a little. "Well, if I may be so bold, I would venture that part of the problem stems from the fact that we are seen as statistics rather than people." The audience applauded and Sir David leaned forward with interest. Perhaps Mr Stink wasn't the clown he had taken him for.

"We all have different reasons for being homeless," continued Mr Stink. "Each homeless person has a different story to tell. Perhaps if people in the audience tonight, or out there watching at home, stopped to *talk* to the homeless people in their town, they would realise that."

The audience were applauding even louder now, but Mrs Crumb leaped in. "That's what I did!" she exclaimed. "I just stopped to talk to this tramp one day and then asked him to come and live with my family. I've always put others before myself. I suppose that's always been my downfall," she said, tilting her head to the side and smiling at the audience as if she were an angel sent down from heaven.

"Well, that's not really true is it, Mrs Crumb?" said Mr Stink.

There was silence. Mother stared at Mr Stink in horror. The audience shifted excitedly in their seats. Dad, Annabelle and Chloe all leaned forward closer to the television. Even Sir David's moustache twitched in anticipation.

"I don't know what you mean, my very close friend…" squirmed Mrs Crumb.

"I think you do," said Mr Stink. "The fact is, it wasn't *you* who invited me in, was it?"

Sir David's eyes gleamed. "Then who *did* invite you to stay with the Crumb family, Mr Stink?" he enquired, back in his stride now.

"Mrs Crumb's daughter, Chloe. She's only twelve but she's an absolutely fantastic girl. One of the sweetest, kindest people I have ever met."

These words fell on Chloe like an enormous YES. Then everyone in the stale crisps room looked towards her and she was overcome by embarrassment. She hid her face in her hands. Dad stroked her back proudly. Annabelle pretended not to be interested, and helped herself to another stale crisp.

"She should really come out here and take a bow," announced Mr Stink.

"No, no, no," snapped Mother.

"No, Mrs Crumb," said Sir David. "I think we'd all like to meet this extraordinary little girl."

The audience applauded his suggestion. But Chloe felt glued to her seat. She couldn't even speak out loud in front of the class. She didn't want to be on television in front of millions of people!

What would she say? What would she do? She

didn't know any tricks. This was going to be the most embarrassing moment of her life, even worse than when she threw up her macaroni cheese all over Miss Spratt in the language lab. But the applause was getting louder and louder, and eventually Dad took her hand and gently pulled her to her feet.

"You're feeling shy, aren't you?" whispered Dad.

Chloe nodded.

"Well you shouldn't. You're a fantastic girl. You should be proud of what you've done. Now come on. Enjoy your moment in the limelight!"

Hand in hand they raced down the corridor towards the set. Just out of sight of the cameras Dad let her hand go, and smiled supportively as she stepped out into the light. The audience applauded wildly. Mr Stink beamed over at her, and she tried to beam back. Mother was the only person not applauding, so Chloe's eyes were drawn towards her. Chloe tried to meet her gaze, but Mother turned her head sharply to look the other way. This made Chloe even more uncomfortable, and she tried to do a curtsy but didn't really know how to, and then ran off the stage, back into the safety of the stale crisps room.

"What a charming child," said Sir David. He turned to Mother. "Now I have to ask you, Mrs Crumb. Why did you lie? Was it purely to further your own political ambitions?"

The other guests from rival political parties looked at Mrs Crumb and tutted. As if *they* would ever dream of doing anything so immoral! Mother started to perspire. Her hair lacquer began to melt and her make-up ran slowly down her face. Dad, Chloe and Annabelle sat and watched her squirm, unable to help.

"Well, as if anyone would want that old tramp in their house," she shouted finally. "Look at him! You lot watching this at home can't smell him, but take it from me, he stinks! He stinks of dirt and sweat and poo and pond and dog. I wish that great stinky stinker would just stink off out of my home for ever!"

There was shocked silence for a moment. Then the boos started, getting louder and louder. Mother looked at the audience in panic. At that moment her bouffant collapsed.

18

Rabbit Droppings

"WE WANT STINK! WE WANT STINK!"

Chloe peeked through a gap in the curtains. There was a huge crowd of people outside their house. News reporters, camera crews, and hundreds and hundreds of local people waving large pieces of cardboard emblazoned with slogans.

Mr Stink's appearance on television the previous night had obviously had an enormous effect on people. Overnight he had gone from being an unknown smelly tramp to a hugely famous smelly tramp.

Chloe put on her dressing gown and raced down to the shed.

"Is it time for Lily to meet the flesh-eating zombie teachers?" enquired Mr Stink as she entered.

"No, no, no, Mr Stink! Can't you hear the crowds outside?!"

"I'm sorry, I can't hear you properly," he said. "I found these rabbit droppings in the garden. They make excellent earplugs." He popped out the two little brown pellets as Chloe looked on with a curious mixture of disgust and admiration at his ingenuity. For those of you who may find yourself out in the wild and in need of earplugs, just follow this easy step-by-step guide.

Fig A

Fig B

First find a friendly rabbit.

Wait patiently for it to deposit some droppings for you.

Fig C

Fig D

Insert one in each ear. Larger ears will require bigger droppings and possibly even a bigger rabbit.

Enjoy a great night's sleep only slightly marred by the smell of rabbit poo.

The Duchess sniffed at the droppings in the vain hope that they might be a couple of rogue Maltesers or at the very worst some of Raj's despised coffee Revels, but quickly turned up her nose when she realised they were poo, and went back to her makeshift basket.

"That's better," said Mr Stink. "You know, I had the strangest dream last night, Miss Chloe. I was on television discussing all the important issues of the day! Your mother was there too! It was hilarious!"

"That was no dream, Mr Stink. That really happened."

"Oh, dear," said the tramp. "Maybe it wasn't so funny after all."

"It was *hilarious*, Mr Stink. You were the star of the show. And now there's hundreds of people camped outside the house."

"What on earth do they want, child?"

"You!" said Chloe. "They want to interview you I think. And some people want you to be the Prime Minister!"

The crowd was getting louder and louder now. "WE WANT STINK! WE WANT STINK! WE WANT STINK!"

"Oh my word, yes I can hear them. They want me as Prime Minister, you say? Ha ha! I must remember to appear on television more often! Maybe I can be king next too!"

"You'd better get up, Mr Stink. Now!"

"Yes, of course, Miss Chloe. Right, I want to look smart for my fans."

He bumbled around the shed sniffing his clothes and grimacing. *If even he thinks they're smelly*, thought Chloe, *they must be really bad.*

"I could put some clothes on a quick wash and dry for you," she offered hopefully.

"No, thank you, my dear. I don't think washing machines are hygienic. I'll just get the Duchess to chew some of the particularly nasty stains out."

He dug through a pile of his clothes and pulled out a pair of spectacularly dirt-encrusted brown trousers. Whether they had been brown when they started their life was now anybody's guess. He passed them to the Duchess, who began her task of a reluctant dry cleaner and started munching on the stains.

Chloe cleared her throat. "Um… Mr Stink. You said on the TV show how every homeless person has a different story to tell. Well, can you tell me your story? I mean, why did you end up on the streets?"

"Why do you think, my dear?"

"I don't know. I've got millions of theories. Maybe you were abandoned in a forest as a baby and raised by a pack of wolves?"

"No!" he chuckled.

"Or I reckon you were a world-famous rock star who faked your own death as you couldn't handle all the adulation."

"I wish I was!"

"All right then, you were a top scientist who invented the most powerful bomb in the world and then, realising its dangers, went on the run from the military."

"Well, those are all very imaginative guesses," he said. "But I am sorry, none of them are right. You're not even close, I'm afraid."

"I thought not."

"I will tell you when the time is right, Chloe."

"Promise?"

"I promise. Now please give me a few minutes, my dear. I must get ready to greet my public!"

19

Supertramp

"I AM NOT APOLOGISING TO HIM!"

"YOU HAVE TO!"

Mr Stink sat at the head of the kitchen table reading all about himself in the newspapers as Chloe stood at the stove frying some sausages for him. Her parents were arguing again in the next room. It wasn't a conversation that their house guest was meant to hear, but they were so angry their voices were becoming louder and louder.

"BUT HE DOES SMELL!"

"I KNOW HE SMELLS BUT YOU DIDN'T NEED TO SAY IT ON THE TELEVISION."

Chloe smiled over at Mr Stink. He looked so engrossed in all the headlines, 'Supertramp!', 'Stinky Superstar Steals Show!', 'Homeless Man Saves Boring Election', that he appeared not to be listening. Or maybe he'd put his rabbit dropping earplugs back in.

"OBVIOUSLY NOT!" shouted Mother. "LAST NIGHT I HAD ANOTHER CALL FROM THE PRIME MINISTER TELLING ME I HAVE EMBARRASSED THE PARTY AND HE WANTS ME TO WITHDRAW AS A CANDIDATE!"

"GOOD!"

"WHAT DO YOU MEAN 'GOOD'?!"

"THIS WHOLE THING HAS TURNED YOU INTO A MONSTER!" shouted Dad.

"WHAT?! I AM NOT A MONSTER!"

"YES, YOU ARE! MONSTER! MONSTER! MONSTER!"

"HOW DARE YOU?!" screamed Mother.

"GO AND APOLOGISE TO HIM!"

"NO!"

"APOLOGISE!"

For a moment all you could hear was the sizzle of sausage fat and lard in the frying pan. Then, slowly, the door opened and Mother oozed like slime into the room. Her bouffant was still not what it was. She hesitated for a moment. Her husband appeared in the doorway and gave her a stern look. She did a little theatrical cough.

"Her-hum. Mr Stink?" she ventured.

"Yes, Mrs Crumb?" replied Mr Stink without looking up, still engrossed in the papers.

"I would like to say… sorry."

"What on earth for?" he enquired.

"For what I said about you on *Question Time* last night. About you smelling of all those things. It was impolite."

"Thank you so much, Mrs…"

"Call me Janet."

"Thank you so much, Mrs Janet. It *was* rather hurtful as I do pride myself on my personal hygiene. Indeed I had a bath just before I went on the show."

"Well, you didn't really have a *bath*, did you? You had a *pond*."

"Yes, I suppose you're right. I did have a pond. And if you so wish I will have another 'pond' next year, so I remain perfectly clean."

"But you're not clean you sti—" began Mother.

"Be nice!" interrupted Dad forcibly.

"You don't know this," said Mother to Mr Stink. "But after what I said on *Question Time* last night I have been asked by the Prime Minister to pull out of the election."

"Yes, I do know actually. I heard you and

your husband arguing just a moment ago in the living room."

"Oh," said Mother, uncharacteristically lost for words.

"Sausages are ready!" said Chloe, trying to save her Mother from further humiliation.

"I'd better be off to work now, love," said Dad. "I don't want to be late."

"Yes, yes," said Mother waving him away distractedly. He discreetly picked up a couple of slices of bread and slipped them in his pocket on the way out. Chloe heard the front door loudly open and close, and then the door to the room under the stairs very quietly do the same.

"Just seven sausages today please, Miss Chloe," said Mr Stink. "I don't want to put on weight. I have to think of my fan base."

"Fan base?!" said Mother in a barely disguised jealous rage.

The telephone, which had been crouching on the table doing very little, suddenly sang its little song. Chloe picked it up. "Crooombe residence. Who is speaking please...? It's the Prime Minister!"

Mother's face lit up with hope, and even her bouffant seemed to perk up a bit. "Ah yes! I knew my darling Dave would change his mind!"

"He wants to talk to Mr Stink, actually," continued Chloe. Mother's smile turned upside down.

Mr Stink picked up the receiver with a nonchalance that suggested he often received calls from world leaders. "Stink here. Yes? Yes? Oh yes...?"

Mum and Chloe studied his face like a map,

trying to read from his reactions what the Prime Minister was saying.

"Yes, yes, yes. Well, yes, thank you Prime Minister."

Mr Stink put the receiver down and sat back at the table to resume his now daily task of reading about himself in the newspapers.

"*Well*?" asked Chloe.

"Yes, well?" chimed in Mother.

"The Prime Minister has invited me to go for tea at Number Ten Downing Street today," said Mr Stink matter-of-factly. "He wants me to take over from you, Mrs Crumb, as the local candidate. May I have those sausages now please, Chloe?"

20

Grubby Toilet Roll

"Hoooorrraaaayyyyy!" There was a huge cheer as Mr Stink appeared at the upstairs window. All he had to do was stand and wave for the crowd to roar their approval. The cameras all zoomed in and the microphones leaned forward. One lady even held her baby up so the infant could catch sight of this new star. Chloe

stood a few paces behind Mr Stink, watching like a proud parent. She hadn't enjoyed being on the television that much and preferred to let Mr Stink take centre stage. He gestured for everyone to be quiet. And there was quiet.

"I have written a short speech," he announced, before unrolling a very long, grubby toilet roll and reading from it.

"First of all, may I say how very honoured I am that you have all turned out to see me today."

The crowd cheered again.

"I am but a humble wanderer. A vagrant maybe, certainly a vagabond, a street dreamer if you will…"

"Oh, get on with it!" hissed Mother from behind Chloe.

"Shussshh!" shushed Chloe.

"As such, I had no idea that simply appearing on the electric televisual apparatus would have quite such an astonishing effect. All I can say at this time is that I am meeting with the Prime Minister today at Number Ten to discuss my political future."

The crowd went wild.

"Thank you all for your incredible kindness," he concluded, before rolling his toilet roll back up and disappearing from view.

"Miss Chloe?" he said.

"Yes?" she answered.

"If I am meeting the Prime Minister I think I need a make over."

Chloe wasn't sure exactly what a 'make over' was. She knew there were lots of shows on TV that did make overs, but Mother didn't allow her to watch them. Feeling like the ugly duckling of the family she didn't own any make-up either, so tentatively she knocked on her little sister's door to see if she could borrow some. Annabelle had drawers full of make-up. She always asked for it for her birthday and Christmas, as she liked nothing better than painting it all on and performing her own little beauty pageants in front of her bedroom mirror.

"Has he gone yet?" asked Annabelle.

"No, he hasn't. Maybe if you bothered to talk to him you would see how nice he is."

"He smells."

"So do you," said Chloe. "Now, I need to borrow some of your make-up."

"Why? You don't wear make-up. You're not pretty, so there's no point."

For a moment Chloe entertained a number of

fantasies where her little sister met horrific ends. Plunged into a pool of piranhas perhaps? Abandoned in the Arctic wastes in her underwear? Force-fed marshmallows until she exploded?

"It's for Mr Stink," she said, filing away all those fantasies in her brain for a later date.

"No way."

"I'll tell Mother you're the one who's been secretly scoffing her Bendicks chocolate mints."

"What do you need?" replied Annabelle in a heartbeat.

Later, Mr Stink sat on an upturned plant pot in the shed as the two girls fussed around him.

"It's not too much, is it?" he enquired.

Unexpectedly enjoying herself, Annabelle had gone a little over the top. Did Mr Stink really need pink glittery blusher, electric-blue eyeliner,

purple eye shadow and orange nail varnish to go
and meet the Prime Minister?

"Erm…" said Chloe.

"No, you look great, Mr Stink!" said
Annabelle, as she attached a butterfly hair-clip to
his head. "This is so much fun! It's the best
Christmas Eve ever!"

"Aren't you supposed to be singing carols in

church or something?" asked Chloe knowingly.

"Yes, but I hate it. It's so boring. This is way more cool." Annabelle looked thoughtful. "You know, it's so tedious sometimes doing all those stupid hobbies and sports and stuff."

"Why do them then?" enquired Chloe.

"Yes, why do them, dear?" chimed in Mr Stink.

Annabelle looked confused. "I don't know really. I suppose to make Mother happy," she said.

"Your Mother won't be truly happy if you aren't. You need to find the things that make *you* happy," said Mr Stink with authority. It was hard to take him seriously though, what with his multi-coloured eye make-up.

"Well... this afternoon has made me happy," said Annabelle. She smiled at Chloe for the first time in years. "Hanging out with *you* has made me happy."

Chloe smiled back, and they nervously held each other's gaze for a moment.

"What about me?" demanded Mr Stink.

"You too of course!" laughed Annabelle. "You actually get used to the smell after a while," she whispered to Chloe, who shushed her and smiled.

All of a sudden the shed shook violently. Chloe rushed to the door and opened it to see a helicopter hovering overhead. Engine whirring, it slowly came down to land in their garden.

"Ah, yes. The Prime Minister said he would be sending that to pick us up," announced Mr Stink.

"Us?" said Chloe.

"You don't think I was going to go without you, do you?"

21

Wet Wipe

"Why don't you come too?" shouted Chloe to Annabelle over the thunderous noise of the blades.

"No, this is your day, Chloe," her little sister hollered back. "This is all because of you. And besides, that helicopter's tiny. It'll absolutely *whiff* in there…"

Chloe grinned and waved goodbye as the helicopter slowly ascended, flattening most of the plants and flowers in the garden as it did so. Mother's bouffant danced around her head like candyfloss on a windy day at the seafront as she attempted to hold it down. Elizabeth the cat got blown across the lawn. She tried desperately to cling on to the grass with her claws. But despite meowing for mercy the wind from the blades was just too strong and she shot across the garden like a furry cannonball and into the pond.

Plop!

The Duchess looked down from the helicopter window, smirking.

As they glided up and up and up Chloe saw her house, and her street, and her town get smaller and smaller. Soon the postal districts were packed below her like squares on a chessboard. It was unutterably thrilling. For the first time in her life, Chloe felt like she was at the centre of the world. She looked over at Mr Stink. He was getting re-acquainted with a toffee bon-bon that, from the looks of it, had been in his trouser pocket since the late 1950s. Apart from his jaw working desperately to chew the ancient confectionery he looked perfectly relaxed, as if taking a helicopter ride to see the Prime Minister was something he did most days.

Chloe smiled over at him, and he smiled back with that special twinkle in his eye that almost made you forget how bad he smelled.

Mr Stink tapped on the pilot's shoulder. "Are you going to be coming round with a trolley service at any point?" he asked.

"It's just a short flight, sir."

"Any chance of a cup of tea and a bun then?"

"I am very sorry, sir," replied the pilot with a firmness that suggested this conversation was about to be over.

"Very disappointing," said Mr Stink.

Chloe recognised the door of Number Ten Downing Street, because it was always on those boring political shows she was allowed to watch on Sunday mornings. It was big and black and always had a policeman standing outside. She thought, *If I joined the police I would want to be chasing baddies all day, not standing outside a door thinking about whether or not I should have spaghetti hoops for my tea.* However, she wisely kept that thought to herself as the policeman opened the door for them with a smile.

"Please take a seat," said an immaculately dressed butler haughtily. The staff were used to playing host to royalty and world leaders at 10 Downing Street, not a little girl, a transvestite tramp and his dog. "The Prime Minister will be with you shortly."

They were standing in a big oak-panelled room with dozens of gold-framed oil paintings of serious-looking old men staring out at you from the walls. The tinsel round the frames did little to counter their severe looks. Suddenly, the double doors flew open and a herd of men in suits approached them.

"Good afternoon, Mr Stinky!" said the Prime Minister. You could tell he was in charge as he was walking at the front of the herd.

"It's just Stink, Prime Minister," corrected one of his advisors.

"How are you doing, mate?" said the Prime Minister, trying to downplay his poshness. He offered out his perfectly manicured and moisturized little hand for Mr Stink to shake. The tramp offered his own big dirty gnarled hand and, looking at it, the Prime Minister quickly withdrew his, preferring to give his new best friend a mock punch on the shoulder. He then examined his knuckles and noticed they had some grime on them.

"Wet wipe!" he demanded. "Now!"

A man at the back of the herd hurriedly

produced a wet wipe and it was passed forward to the Prime Minister. He quickly wiped his hand with it before passing it back to the man at the back.

"A pleasure to meet you too, Mr Prime Minister," said Mr Stink without conviction.

"Call me Dave," said the Prime Minister. "Gosh, he does smell like a toilet," he whispered to one of his advisors.

Mr Stink looked at Chloe, hurt, but the Prime Minister didn't notice. "So, you made quite a splash on *Question Time*, my homeless pal," he continued. "Ruddy hilarious. Ha ha ha!" He wiped away a non-existent tear of laughter from his eye. "I think we could use you."

"*Use* him?" asked Chloe suspiciously.

"Yeah, yeah. It's no secret it's not looking good for me in the election. My approval rating with the public right now is…"

One of the herd hastily opened a folder and there was a long pause as he flicked through pages and pages of information.

"Bad."

"Bad. Right. *Thanks*, Perkins," said the Prime Minister, sarcastically.

"It's Brownlow."

"Whatever." The Prime Minister turned back to Mr Stink. "I think if we had you, a real life tramp, take over from Mrs Crumb as candidate it could be brilliant. It's far too late to rope anyone else in now, and you would be the ideal last-minute replacement. You're just so *funny*. I mean, to laugh *at*, not really with."

"Excuse me?" said Chloe, feeling very protective of her friend now.

The Prime Minister ignored her. "It's genius! It really is. If you joined the party it would fool the public into thinking we *cared* about the homeless! Maybe one day I could even make you Minister for Soap-Dodgers."

"Soap-Dodgers?" said Mr Stink.

"Yeah, you know, the homeless."

"Right," said Mr Stink. "And as Minister

for the Homeless, I would be able to help other homeless people?"

"Well, no," said the Prime Minister. "It wouldn't *mean* anything, just make me look like a fantastic tramp-loving guy. Well, wadda you say, Mr Stinky-poo?"

Mr Stink looked very ill at ease. "I don't... I mean... I'm not sure—"

"Are you *kidding* me?" laughed the Prime Minister. "You're a tramp! You can't have anything better to do!"

The suited herd laughed too. Suddenly Chloe had a flashback to her school. The Prime Minister and his aides were behaving exactly like the gang of mean girls in her year. Still stumbling for words, Mr Stink looked over to her for help.

"Prime Minister...?" said Chloe.

"Yes?" he answered with an expectant smile.

"Why don't you stick it up your fat bum!"

"You took the words right out of my mouth, child!" chuckled Mr Stink. "Goodbye, Prime Minister, and Merry Christmas to you all!"

22

Long Lion Days

Chloe and Mr Stink weren't invited to take the helicopter home. They had to get the bus.

As it was Christmas Eve, the bus was chock-a-block with people, most of them barely visible under their mountains of shopping bags. As Chloe and Mr Stink sat side by side on the top deck, bare branches dragged against the grimy windows.

"Did you see the look on his face when you told him to stick it up his…?" exclaimed Mr Stink.

"I can't believe I did it!" said Chloe.

"I'm so glad you did," said Mr Stink. "Thank

you so much for sticking up for me."

"Well, you stuck up for me with that awful Rosamund!"

"'Stick it up your bum!' So naughty! Though I might have said something far ruder! Ha ha!"

They laughed together. Mr Stink reached into his trouser pocket to pull out a dirty old handkerchief to dry his tears of joy. As he raised the handkerchief to his face, Chloe spotted that a label had been sewn on to it. Peering closer, she saw that the label was made of silk, and a name was embroidered delicately on it…

"Lord… Darlington?" she read.

There was silence for a moment.

"Is that *you*?" said Chloe. "Are you a lord?"

"No… no…" said Mr Stink. "I'm just a humble vagabond. I got this handkerchief… from a jumble sale."

"May I see your silver spoon then?" said Chloe, gently.

Mr Stink gave a resigned smile. He reached into his jacket pocket and slowly withdrew the spoon, then handed it to her. Chloe turned it over in her hands. Looking at it close up, she realised she'd been wrong. It wasn't three letters engraved on it. It was a single letter on a crest, held on each side by a lion.

A single, capital letter D.

"You *are* Lord Darlington," said Chloe. "Let me see that old photograph again."

Mr Stink carefully pulled out his old black and white photograph.

Chloe studied it for a few seconds. It was just as she'd remembered. The beautiful young couple, the Rolls Royce, the stately home. Only now, when she looked at it, she could see the resemblance between the young man in the photo and the old tramp beside her. "And that's you in the picture."

Chloe held the photograph delicately, knowing she was handling something very precious. Mr Stink looked much younger, especially without his beard and dirt. But the eyes were sparkling. It was unmistakably him.

"The game's up," said Mr Stink. "That *is* me, Chloe. A lifetime ago."

"And who's this lady with you?"

"My wife."

"Your wife? I didn't know you were married."

"You didn't know I was a lord, either," said Mr Stink.

"And that must be your house then, Lord Darlington," said Chloe, indicating the stately home standing behind the couple in the photograph. Mr Stink nodded. "Well then, how come you're homeless now?"

"It's a long story, my dear," said Mr Stink, evasively.

"But I want to hear it," said Chloe. "Please? I've told you so much about my life. And I've always wanted to know your story, Mr Stink, ever since I first saw you. I always knew you must have a fascinating tale to tell."

Mr Stink took a breath. "Well, I had it all, child. More money than I could ever spend, a beautiful house with its own lake. My life was like an endless summer. Croquet, tea on the lawn, long lion days spent playing cricket. And to make things even more perfect I married this beautiful, clever, funny, adorable woman, my childhood sweetheart. Violet."

"She is beautiful."

"Yes, yes, she is. She was. Unutterably so. We were deliriously happy, you know."

It was all so obvious now to Chloe. The way Mr Stink had expertly bowled the screwed up piece of paper into the bin, his silver monogrammed cutlery and his impeccable table manners, his insistence on walking on the outside of the pavement, the way he had decorated the shed. It was all true. He was *super*-posh.

"Soon after that photograph was taken Violet became pregnant," continued Mr Stink. "I couldn't have been more thrilled. But one night, when my wife was eight months pregnant, my chauffeur drove me to London to have dinner with a group of my old school friends at a gentlemen's club. It was just before Christmas, actually. I stayed late into the night, selfishly drinking and talking and smoking cigars…"

"What do you mean, selfishly?" said Chloe.

"Because I should never have gone. We were caught in a blizzard on the way home. I didn't get back until just before dawn, and found that the house was ablaze…"

"Oh no!" cried Chloe, not sure if she could bear to hear the rest of the story.

"A piece of coal must have fallen out of the fireplace in our bedroom, and set the carpet alight as she slept. I ran out of the Rolls and waded through the deep snow. Desperately I tried to fight my way into the house, but the fire brigade wouldn't let me. It took five of them to hold me back. They tried their best to save her but it was too late. The roof fell in. Violet didn't stand a chance."

"Oh my God!" Chloe gasped.

Tears filled the old tramp's eyes. Chloe didn't know what to do. Dealing with emotions was a new thing to her, but tentatively she reached out her hand to comfort him. Time seemed to slow down as her hand reached his. This made the tears really flow, and he shook with half a century of pain.

"If only I hadn't been at the club that night, I could have saved her. I could have held her all night, made her feel safe and warm. She wouldn't have needed the fire. My darling, darling Violet." Chloe squeezed his dirty hand tight.

"You can't blame yourself for the fire."

"I should have been there for her. I should have been there…"

"It was an accident," said Chloe. "You have to forgive yourself."

"I can't. I never can."

"You are a good man, Mr Stink. What happened was a terrible accident. You must believe that."

"Thank you, child. I shouldn't really cry. Not on public transport." He sniffed, and gathered himself together a little.

"So," said Chloe, "how did you end up living on the streets?"

"Well, I was heartbroken. Utterly inconsolable. I had lost my unborn child and the woman I loved. After the funeral I tried to return to the house. Lived alone in a wing that hadn't been so badly damaged by the blaze. But the house carried so many painful memories, I couldn't sleep. Being there gave me terrible nightmares. I kept seeing her face in the flames. I had to get away. So one day I started walking and I never came back."

"I am so sorry," said Chloe. "If people only knew that…"

"Like I said on the televisual apparatus, every homeless person has a story to tell," said Mr Stink. "That's mine. I am sorry it didn't involve spies or pirates or what have you. Real life isn't like that, I'm afraid. And I didn't mean to upset you."

"Christmas must be the hardest time for you," said Chloe.

"Yes, yes, of course. Christmas is an emblem of perfect happiness I find very hard to bear. It's a time when families come together. For me it's a reminder of who's not there."

The bus reached their stop, and Chloe's arm found a home in Mr Stink's as they walked towards the family house. She was relieved to see that all the reporters and camera crews had moved on. The funny old tramp must be old news by now.

"I just wish I could make everything right," said Chloe.

"But you are making everything right, Miss Chloe. Ever since you came and talked to me. You've made me smile again. You've been so kind to me. You know, if my child had ended up like you, I would have been very proud."

Chloe was so touched she could hardly think what to say. "Well," she said, "I know you would have made a great dad."

"Thank you, child. Unimaginable kindness."

Nearing the house, Chloe looked at it and realised something. She didn't *want* to go home. She didn't want to live with her awful Mother and have to go to that horrible posh school any more. They walked in silence for a moment, then Chloe took a deep breath and turned to Mr Stink.

"I don't want to go back there," she said. "I want to go wandering with you."

23

Plastic Snowman

"I'm sorry Miss Chloe, but you can't possibly come with me," said Mr Stink as they stood in the driveway.

"Why not?" protested Chloe.

"For a million different reasons!"

"Name one!"

"It's too cold."

"I don't mind the cold."

"Well," said Mr Stink, "living on the streets is far too dangerous for a young girl like you."

"I'm nearly thirteen!"

"It's very important you don't miss school."

"I hate school," said Chloe. "Please please please, Mr Stink. Let me come with you and the Duchess. I want to be a wanderer like you."

"You must think about this properly for a moment, child," said Mr Stink. "What on earth is your mother going to say?"

"I don't care," snapped Chloe. "I hate her anyway."

"I've told you before, you mustn't say that."

"But it's true."

Mr Stink sighed. "Your mind is made up is it?"

"One hundred percent!"

"Well, in that case, I'd better go and talk to your mother for you."

Chloe grinned. This was superbrilliantamazing! It was really going to happen. She was going to be free at last! No more being sent to bed early. No more maths homework. No more wearing yellow frilly dresses that made her look like a Quality Street. Chloe was a hundred times more excited than she had ever been in her life. She and Mr Stink were going to wander the world together, eating sausages for breakfast, lunch and dinner, having baths in ponds, and emptying Starbucks wherever they went...

"Thanks so much, Mr Stink," she said, as she put her key in the lock for the last time.

As Chloe raced excitedly around her room throwing clothes and the chocolate bars she had hidden under her bed into her bag, she could hear faint voices in the kitchen downstairs. *Mother won't care*, thought Chloe. *She'll hardly miss me anyway! The only person she cares about is Annabelle.*

Chloe looked around her little pink room. Strangely, she felt a tingle of fondness for it now that she was leaving. And she was going to miss Dad, and of course Annabelle, and even Elizabeth the cat, but a new life was calling her. A life of mystery and adventure. A life of making up bed-time stories about vampires and zombies. A life of burping in the faces of bullies!

Just then, there was a gentle knock on the door. "I'm just coming, Mr Stink!" Chloe called out, as she threw the last ornamental owl into her bag.

The door opened slowly. Chloe turned around and gasped.

It wasn't Mr Stink.

It was Mother. She stood in the corridor, her eyes red from crying. A tear was running down her cheek and a little plastic snowman dangled incongruously above her head.

"My darling Chloe," she spluttered. "Mr Stink

just told me you wanted to leave home. Please. I beg you, don't go."

Chloe had never seen Mother looking so sad. Suddenly, she felt a little guilty. "I, er, just thought you wouldn't mind," she said.

"Mind? I couldn't bear it if you left." Mother started sobbing now. This was so unlike her. It was as if Chloe was looking at another person entirely.

"What did Mr Stink say to you?" she asked.

"The old man gave me a good talking to," said Mother. "Said how unhappy you've been at home. How I had to work at being a better mother. He told me how he'd lost his own family, and if I wasn't careful, I was going to lose you. I felt so ashamed. I know we haven't always seen eye to eye on things Chloe, but I do love you. I really do."

Chloe was horrified. She'd thought Mr Stink was just going to ask if she could go with him, but instead he'd made Mother cry. She was furious with him. This wasn't the plan at all!

And just then, Mr Stink appeared solemnly in

the doorway. He stood a pace behind Mother.

"I'm sorry Chloe," he ventured. "I hope you can forgive me."

"Why did you say what you did?" she asked angrily. "I thought we were going to wander the world together."

Mr Stink smiled kindly. "Maybe one day you'll wander the world on your own," he said. "But for now, trust me, you need your family. I would give anything to have mine back. Anything."

Mother's legs looked like they were going to give way, and she stumbled towards Chloe's bed. She sat there and wept, hiding her face in shame at her tears. Chloe looked at Mr Stink silently for a long time. Deep down, she knew he was right.

"Of course I forgive you," she said to him finally, and he smiled that eye-twinkling smile of his.

Then she softly sat down next to her mother and put an arm around her.

"And I love you too, Mum. Very much."

24

Yuckety Yuck Yuck

It was well into the night on Christmas Eve now, and down in the living room, Dad waved a large festive assortment tin under Mr Stink's nose. "Would you like a biscuit?" he asked.

Dad had already scoffed quite a few, having been hiding in the room under the stairs again all day with only a couple of slices of dry bread to keep him going. Mr Stink eyed the contents of the tin with disgust.

"Have you any stale ones?" he asked. "Maybe with just a hint of mould?"

"I don't think so, sorry," replied Dad.

"No thank you then," said Mr Stink. He patted the Duchess, who was sitting on his lap, trading evil looks across the coffee table with Elizabeth. The family cat was bundled up in a towel on Annabelle's lap, still recovering from her 'swim'.

"Never mind about the biscuits," said Annabelle. "I want to know what you said to the Prime Minister's offer?"

"Chloe told him to stick it up his—"

"We told him he wasn't interested," interjected Chloe hastily. "So maybe you can still stand to be the local MP, Mum."

"Oh no, I don't want to," said Mum. "Not after I humiliated myself on television."

"But now you've met Mr Stink and seen how other people live their lives you could try to make things *better* for people," suggested Chloe.

"Well, perhaps I could try and stand again at the next election," said Mother. "Though I will have to change my policies. Especially the one about the homeless. I am sorry I got it so wrong."

"And the one about the unemployed, eh, Dad?" said Chloe.

"What's this?" said Mother.

"Thank you, Chloe," said Dad sarcastically. "Well, I didn't want to tell you, but the car factory looks like it's going to close soon and it had to let most of us go."

"So you are…?" asked Mother incredulous.

"Unemployed, yes. Or 'dole scum' as you might say. I was too scared to tell you so I've been hiding in the room under the stairs for the last month."

"What do you mean, you were too scared to tell me? I love you, and I always will, whether you've got a job at the stupid car factory or not."

Dad put his arm around her and she nuzzled up her head to meet his lips with hers. Their kiss lingered for a few moments, as Chloe and Annabelle looked on with a mixture of pride and embarrassment. Your parents kissing. Nice but somehow yuck. Them snogging is even worse. Yuckety yuck yuck.

"I *would* go back to being in a rock band, but you put my guitar on the bonfire!" said Dad with a chuckle.

"Don't!" said Mum. "I still feel so bad about that. I fell for you like a ton of bricks when I first saw you on stage with the band. That's why I married you. But when the album didn't sell I could see how upset you were, and I couldn't bear it. I thought I was trying to help you move on with your life, but now I realise all I did was crush your dreams. And that's why I don't want to make the same mistake twice."

She got up and started searching in the bottom drawer of the sideboard where she kept her secret stash of Bendicks chocolate mints. "I am so sorry I tore up your story, Chloe." Mum pulled out the maths exercise book of Chloe's that she had ripped to pieces. She had painstakingly sellotaped the whole thing back together, and her eyes still shining with tears she handed it back to Chloe. "After *Question Time* I had a lot of time to think," she said. "I fished this out of the bin and I read it to the end, Chloe. It's brilliant."

Chloe took back the book with a smile. "I promise to try harder in my maths lessons from now on, Mum."

"Thank you, Chloe. And I have something

for you too, my darling," said Mum to Dad. From under the tree she pulled out a beautifully wrapped present that was exactly the shape of an electric guitar.

25

Black Leather Mistletoe

"I've got some black leather mistletoe this Christmas,

I'm gonna kiss you and give you a bad shaving rash..."

Dad had plugged his shiny new electric guitar into its amp and was strutting up and down the living room exuberantly singing one of his old band's songs. He was clearly having the time of his life. It was almost as if his perm had grown back too. Mum, Chloe, Annabelle and Mr Stink sat on the sofa and clapped along. Even Elizabeth

and the Duchess were curled up together nodding their heads in time with the music. The heavy rock wasn't quite to Mr Stink's taste, and to combat the noise he had discreetly re-inserted his rabbit-dropping earplugs.

"Yeah baby I'm gonna feast on your mince pies,

And give you a real good yuletide surprise…!"

The song ended with a huge flourish on Dad's guitar, and his tiny stadium of fans cheered and clapped him excitedly.

"Thank you, Wembley. Thank you so much. That was, of course, The Serpents of Doom's Christmas single, 'Black Leather Mistletoe', which rocketed to number 98 in the charts. Now for my next song…"

"I think that's enough heavy rock music just for now, dear," said Mum, as if she might already be regretting giving him that present. She turned to Chloe and said, "You don't want to leave any more, do you?"

"No Mum, not in a million years. This is the

best Christmas ever."

"Oh, wonderful!" said Mum. "It's super that we are all together having fun like this."

"But..." said Chloe. "There is one thing I would like."

"Name it," said Mum.

"I would like Mr Stink to move in properly."

"What?" asked Mum with a gasp.

"That's a great idea," said Dad. "We've all loved having you around, Mr Stink."

"Yes, you feel like part of the family now," said Annabelle.

"Well, I suppose he could stay for a little while longer in the shed..." said Mum reluctantly.

"I didn't mean in the shed. I meant in our house," said Chloe.

"Of course," said Dad.

"That would be great!" chimed in Annabelle.

"Well, erm, oh, um..." Mum looked

increasingly flustered. "I do really appreciate what Mr Stink has done for us, but I'm not sure he would feel at home here. I don't imagine he has ever lived in a house as nice as this…"

"Actually, Mr Stink used to live in a stately home," corrected Chloe gleefully.

"What? As a servant?" said Mum.

"No, it was *his* stately home. Mr Stink is really a lord."

"A lord? Is this true, Mr Stink?"

"Yes, Mrs Crooooooombe."

"A stately hobo! Well, that changes everything!" announced Mum, beaming with pride that she finally had someone truly posh in the house. "Husband, take the plastic covers off the sofa. Annabelle, get out the best china! And if you would like to use the downstairs lavatory at any time Lord Stink, I have the key right here."

"Thank you, but I don't need to go right now. Oh, hang on a moment…"

They all looked at Mr Stink expectantly. Chloe, Annabelle and Dad were just curious to finally see what the downstairs loo actually looked like from the inside, since none of them had ever been allowed in there.

"No… no, false alarm."

Mum continued babbling breathlessly. "And… and… and you can have our bedroom, your lordship! I can sleep on the sofa bed and my husband would be more than happy to move into the shed."

"What the—?" said Dad.

"Please… please… please stay here with us," interjected Chloe.

Mr Stink sat in silence for a moment. The cup and saucer in his hands started rattling, then a little tear formed in his eye. It travelled slowly down his cheek, creating a little streak of white on his grimy face. The Duchess looked up at him and tenderly licked it off her master's face. Chloe's hand tiptoed its way across the sofa to comfort him.

He held it tight. He held it so tight that she knew this was goodbye.

"Such unimaginable kindness. Thank you. Thank you all, so much. However, I am going to have to say no."

"Stay with us for Christmas Day and Boxing Day at least," pleaded Annabelle. "Please...?" said Chloe.

"Thank you," said Mr Stink. "But I am afraid I have to refuse."

"But why?" demanded Chloe.

"My work here is done. And I'm a wanderer," said Mr Stink. "It's time for me to wander on."

"But we want you to be safe and warm here with us," said Chloe. Tears were rolling down her cheeks now. Annabelle wiped away her sister's tears with her sleeve.

"I am sorry, Miss Chloe. I have to go. No tears please. No fuss. Farewell to you all and thank you for all your kindness." Mr Stink put down his cup and saucer, and headed for the door. "Come on, Duchess," he said. "It's time to go."

26

Little Star

He walked off into the moonlight. The moon was full and bright that night, and it looked so perfect that it couldn't be real. It was as if it had been painted, and hung there on a hook, it was so impossibly beautiful. There wasn't any snow, there never is at Christmas these days, except on the cards. Instead the streets were damp from a storm, and the moon was reflected in hundreds of little puddles. Most of the houses were adorned with Christmas decorations of one sort or another, with fairy-lit trees glinting through the double-glazing. The decorations looked almost beautiful too, competing with the moon and the stars in their own feeble way. All you could hear was the rhythmic scuff of Mr Stink's battered brogues as he walked slowly along the road, the Duchess following dutifully a pace behind, her head bowed.

Chloe watched him unseen from an upstairs window. Her hand touched the cold glass, trying to reach out to him. She watched him disappear out of sight, before sloping back to her room.

Then, sitting there on her bed, she remembered a reason to see him one last time.

"*Lily and the Flesh-Eating Zombie Teachers!*" she shouted, as she ran down the street.

"Miss Chloe?" said Mr Stink turning round.

"I have been thinking and thinking about Lily's second adventure. I would love to tell it to you now!"

"Write it down for me, child."

"Write it down?" asked Chloe.

"Yes," said Mr Stink. "One day I want to walk into a bookshop and see your name on one of the covers. You have a talent for telling stories, Chloe."

"*Do* I?" Chloe had never felt she had a talent for anything.

"Yes. All that time spent alone in your room will pay off one day. You have an extraordinary imagination, young lady. A real gift. You should share it with the world."

"Thank you, Mr Stink," said Chloe shyly.

"I'm glad you came running after me though," said Mr Stink. "I just remembered I have something for you."

"For me?"

"Yes, I saved up all my loose change and bought you a Christmas present. I think it's something rather special."

Mr Stink rummaged in his bag and pulled out a package wrapped in brown paper and tied up with string. He handed it to Chloe, who unwrapped it excitedly. Inside was a Teenage Mutant Ninja Turtles stationery set.

"It is a Teenybopper Mucus Karate Tortoise thing. I thought you'd like it. Mr Raj told me it was the very last one he had in his shop."

"Did he now?" Chloe smiled. "This is the best present I have ever had." She wasn't lying. That Mr Stink had saved up all his pennies to buy her something meant the whole world to her. "I will treasure this for ever, I promise."

"Thank you," said Mr Stink.

"And you've just given my whole family the best Christmas present ever. You brought us together."

"Well, I'm not sure I can take all the credit for that!" he smiled. "Now, you should really go home now, young Chloe. It's cold, and it feels like it's going to rain."

"I don't like the thought of you sleeping outside," she said. "Especially on a cold damp night like this."

Mr Stink smiled. "I like being outside, you know. On our wedding night my darling Violet showed me the brightest star in the sky. Do you see? That one there?"

He pointed it out. It twinkled brightly like his eyes.

"I see it," said Chloe.

"Well, that night we stood on the balcony of our bedroom and she said she would love me for as long as that star kept shining. So every night, before I go to sleep, I like to gaze at that star and think about her, and the great love we shared. I see the star, and it's her I see."

"That's beautiful," said Chloe, trembling and

trying hard not to cry.

"My wife isn't gone. Every night she meets me in my dreams. Now go home. And don't worry about me, Miss Chloe. I have the Duchess and my star."

"But I'll miss you," said Chloe.

Mr Stink smiled, then pointed up at the sky. "Do you see Violet's star?" he asked.

Chloe nodded.

"Do you see how there's another little star just under it?"

"Yes," said Chloe. Up in the night sky, Violet's star burned brightly. Below it a smaller star twinkled in the blackness.

"Well, you are a very special young lady," said Mr Stink. "And when I look at *that* star I am going to think about you."

Chloe felt overwhelmed. "Thank you," she said. "And I'll look at it and think about you."

She gave him a big hug and didn't want to let go. He stood still and held her for a moment before rocking a little to set himself free. "I have to go now. My soul is restless and I need to wander. Goodbye, Miss Chloe."

"Goodbye, Mr Stink."

The wanderer wandered off down the road as night slinked like a panther down the sky. She watched him disappear out of sight, until all that could be heard was silence echoing around the streets.

Later that night, Chloe sat alone on her bed. Mr Stink was gone. Perhaps for ever. But she could still smell him. She would always be able to smell him.

She opened her maths exercise book and began to write the first words of her new story.

Mr Stink stank...

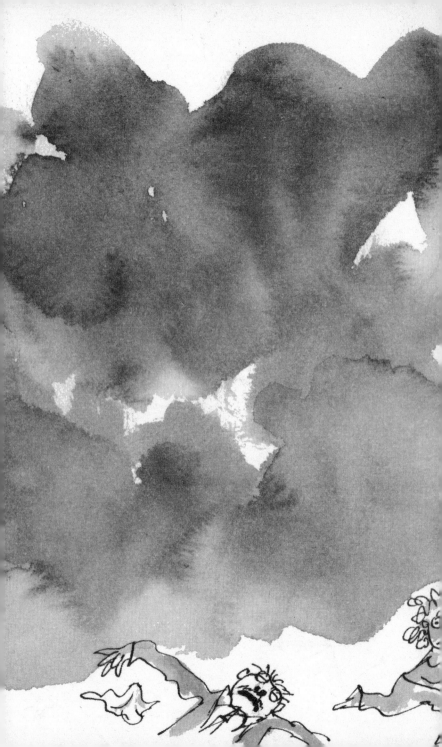

Frank's dad was a champion banger racer, King of the Track. Gilbert the Great! But, when a terrible accident sees him go from hero to zero, Frank and Gilbert are left with nothing – and in the grips of a wicked crime boss and his henchmen.

Then, when Gilbert is thrown in prison, only Frank can come to his rescue . . .

Have you got them all?

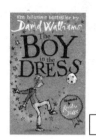

Illustrated in glorious colour!

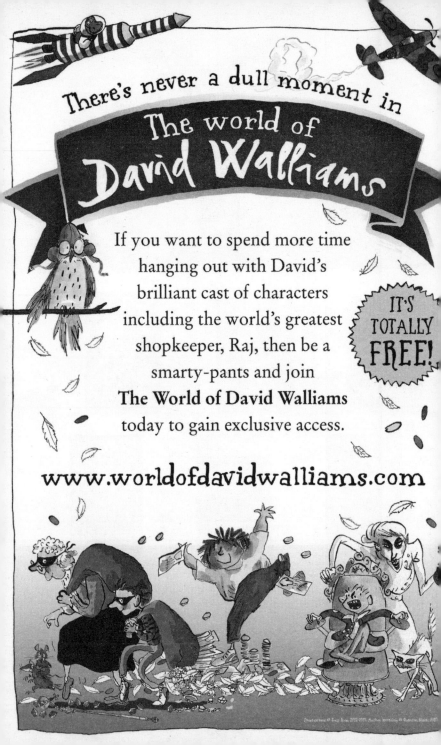

RATBURGER

David Walliams
RATBURGER

Illustrated by Tony Ross

HarperCollins *Children's Books*

First published in hardback and paperback in Great Britain
in 2012 by HarperCollins *Children's Books*
HarperCollins *Children's Books* is a division of
HarperCollins*Publishers* Ltd,
HarperCollins Publishers
1 London Bridge Street
London SE1 9GF

The HarperCollins *Children's Books* website address is
www.harpercollins.co.uk

HarperCollins*Publishers*
1st Floor, Watermarque Building, Ringsend Road
Dublin 4, Ireland

77

ISBN 978-0-00-745354-2

Printed and bound by
CPI Group (UK) Ltd, Croydon, CR0 4YY

MIX
Paper from
responsible sources
FSC™ C007454

For Frankie, the boy with the beautiful smile.

Thank-yous:

I would like to thank the following people, in order of importance:

Ann-Janine Murtagh, my boss at HarperCollins. I love you, I adore you. Thank you so much for believing in me, but most of all, thank you for being you.

Nick Lake, my editor. You know I think you are the absolute best in the business, but also thank you so much for helping me NOT ONLY grow as a writer, but also as a man.

Paul Stevens, my literary agent. I wouldn't pay you 10% plus VAT for making a few phone calls if I didn't feel completely blessed to be represented by you.

Tony Ross. You are the most talented illustrator in the price range we had available. Thank you.

James Stevens and Elorine Grant, the designers. Thanks.

Lily Morgan, the copy editor. Cheers.

Sam White, the publicity manager. Geraldine Stroud, the publicity director. Ta.

Meet the characters in this story:

Dad, a dad

Burt, a burger-van man

Sheila,
Zoe's stepmother

Zoe, a little girl

Mr Grave, the
headmaster

The Ogre,
a terrifying
teacher

Raj, a large
newsagent

Tina Trotts,
the local bully

Gingernut,
a dead
hamster

Armitage,
a live rat

1

Prawn-Cocktail-Crisp Breath

The hamster was dead.

On his back.

Legs in the air.

Dead.

With tears running down her cheeks, Zoe opened the cage. Her hands were shaking and her heart was breaking. As she laid Gingernut's little furry body down on the worn carpet, she thought she would never smile again.

"Sheila!" called Zoe, as loudly as she could. Despite her father's repeated pleas, Zoe refused to call her stepmother 'Mum'. She never had, and she vowed to herself that she never would. No one could replace Zoe's mum – not that her stepmother ever even tried.

"Shut ya face. I'm watchin' TV and stuffin' meself!" came the woman's gruff voice from the lounge.

"It's Gingernut!" called Zoe. "He's not well!"

This was an understatement.

Zoe had once seen a hospital drama on the telly where a nurse tried to revive a dying old man, so she desperately attempted to give her hamster mouth-to-mouth resuscitation by blowing very gently into his open mouth. That didn't work. Neither did connecting the rodent's little heart to an AA battery with a paper clip. It was just too late.

The hamster was cold to the touch, and he was stiff.

"Sheila! Please help…!" shouted the little girl.

At first Zoe's tears came silently, before she let out a gigantic cry. Finally she heard her stepmother trudge reluctantly down the hall of the little flat, which was situated high up on the 37th floor of a leaning tower block. The woman made huge effort noises whenever she had to do anything. She was so lazy she would order Zoe to pick her nose for her, though of course Zoe always said 'no'. Sheila could even let out a groan while changing channels with the TV remote.

"Eurgh, eurgh, eurgh, eurgh…" huffed Sheila as she thundered down the hall. Zoe's stepmother was quite short, but she made up for it by being as wide as she was tall.

She was, in a word, spherical.

Soon Zoe could sense the woman standing

Ratburger

in the doorway, blocking out the light from the hall like a lunar eclipse. What's more, Zoe could smell the sickly sweet aroma of prawn cocktail crisps. Her stepmother loved them. In fact, she boasted that from when she was a toddler she had refused to eat anything else, and spat any other food back in her mum's face. Zoe thought the crisps stank, and not even of prawns. Of course the woman's breath absolutely reeked of them too.

Even now, as she stood in the doorway, Zoe's stepmother was holding a packet of the noxious snack with one hand and feeding her face with the other while she surveyed the scene. As always, she was wearing a long grubby white T-shirt, black leggings and furry pink slippers. The bits of skin that were exposed were covered in tattoos. Her arms bore the names of her ex-husbands, all since crossed out:

"Oh dear," the woman spat, her mouth full of crisps. "Oh dear, oh dear, how very very sad. It's 'eartbreakin'. The poor little fing has snuffed it!" She leaned over her little stepdaughter and peered down at the dead hamster. She sprayed the carpet with half-chewed pieces of crisp as she spoke.

"Dear oh dear oh dear and all dat stuff," she added, in a tone that did not sound even remotely sad.

Just then a large piece of half-chewed crisp sprayed from Sheila's mouth on to the poor thing's little fluffy face. It was a mixture of crisps and spit[1]. Zoe wiped it away gently, as a tear dropped from her eye on to his cold pink nose.

"'Ere, I got a great idea!" said Zoe's stepmother. "I'll just finish dese crisps and ya can shove the little fing in de bag. I won't touch it meself. I don't wanna catch summink."

Sheila lifted the bag above her mouth and poured the last of the prawn cocktail crisp crumbles down her greedy throat. The woman then offered her stepdaughter the empty bag. "Dere ya go. Bung it in 'ere, quick. Before it stinks de whole flat out."

Zoe almost gasped at the unfairness of what the woman had just said. It was her fat stepmother's

---

[1] *The technical name for this is a 'spisp'.*

prawn-cocktail-crisp breath that stank the place out! Her breath could strip paint. It could shear the feathers off a bird and make it bald. If the wind changed direction, you would get a nasty waft of her breath in a town ten miles away.

"I am not burying my poor Gingernut in a crisp packet," snapped Zoe. "I don't know why I called for you in the first place. Please just go!"

"For goodness' sake, girl!" shouted the woman. "I was only trying to 'elp. Ungrateful little wretch!"

"Well, you're not helping!" shouted Zoe, without turning round. "Just go away! Please!"

Sheila thundered out of the room and slammed the door so hard that plaster fell from the ceiling.

Zoe listened as the woman she refused to call 'Mum' trudged back to the kitchen, no doubt to rip open another family-sized bag of prawn cocktail crisps to fill her face with. The little girl was left alone in her tiny bedroom, cradling her dead hamster.

But how had he died? Zoe knew that Gingernut was very young, even in hamster years.

Could this be a hamster murder? she wondered.

But what kind of person would want to murder a defenceless little hamster?

Well, before this story is over, you will know. And you will also know that there are people capable of doing much, much worse. The most evil man in the world is lurking somewhere in this very book. Read on, if you dare...

2

A Very Special Little Girl

Before we meet this deeply wicked individual, we need to go back to the beginning.

Zoe's real mum died when she was a baby, but Zoe had still had a very happy life. Dad and Zoe had always been a little team, and he showered her with love. While Zoe was at school, Dad went out to work at the local ice-cream factory. He had adored ice cream ever since he was a boy and loved working in the factory, even though his job involved long hours, not much money and very hard work.

What kept Zoe's dad going was making

brand new ice-cream flavours. At the end of every shift at the factory he would rush home excitedly, laden with samples of some weird and wonderful new flavour for Zoe to be the first to try. Then he would report back what she liked to the boss. These were Zoe's favourites:

Sherbert Bang
Bubblicious Bubblegum
Triple Choco-Nut-Fudge Swirl
Candyfloss Supreme

Caramel & Custard

Mango Surprise

Cola Cube & Jelly

Peanut Butter & Banana Foam

Pineapple & Liquorice

Whizz Fizz Spacedust Explosion

Her least favourite was Snail & Broccoli. Not even Zoe's dad could make snail and broccoli ice cream taste good.

Not all of the flavours made it to the shops (especially not Snail & Broccoli) but Zoe tried them all! Sometimes she ate so much ice cream she thought she would explode. Best of all, she would often be the only child in the world to try them, and that made Zoe feel like a very special little girl indeed.

There was one problem.

Being an only child, Zoe had no one at home

to play with, apart
from her dad, who
worked long hours
at the factory. So by
the time she reached
the age of nine, like
many kids, she
wanted a pet with
all her heart and soul.
It didn't have to be
a hamster, she just
needed something,
anything, to love.
Something that she
hoped would love
her back. However,
living on the 37th
floor of a leaning
tower block, it had

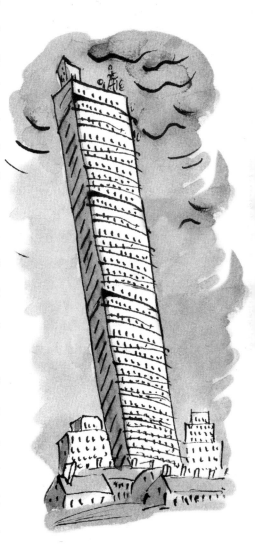

to be something small.

So, on Zoe's tenth birthday, as a surprise, Dad left work early and met his daughter at the school gates. He carried her on his shoulders – she had always loved that ever since she was a baby – and took her to the local pet shop. There, he bought her a hamster.

Zoe picked out the fluffiest, cutest baby one, and named him Gingernut.

Gingernut lived in a cage in the little girl's bedroom. Zoe didn't mind that Gingernut would go round and round on his wheel at night keeping her awake. She didn't mind that he nipped her finger a couple of times when she fed him biscuits as a special treat. She even didn't mind that his cage smelled of hamster wee.

In short, Zoe loved Gingernut. And Gingernut loved Zoe.

Zoe didn't have many friends at school.

What's more, the other kids bullied her for being short and ginger and having to wear braces on her teeth. Just one of those things would have been enough for her to have a hard time. She had hit the jackpot with all three.

Gingernut was small and ginger too, though of course he didn't wear braces. That smallness and gingerness was probably, deep down, why Zoe chose him out of the dozens of little balls of fluff snuggled up together behind the glass at the pet shop. She must have sensed a kindred spirit.

Over the weeks and months that followed, Zoe taught Gingernut some mind-boggling tricks. For a sunflower seed, he would stand on his back legs and do a little dance. For a walnut, Gingernut would do a back-flip. And for a lump of sugar, he would spin around on his back.

Zoe's dream was to make her little pet world famous as the very first breakdancing hamster!

She planned to put on a little show at Christmas for all the other children on the estate. She even made a poster to advertise it.

Then one day, Dad came home from work with some very sad news, which would tear their happy little life apart...

3

Nuffink

"I lost my job," said Dad.

"No!" said Zoe.

"They are shutting down the factory – moving the whole operation to China."

"But you will find another job, won't you?"

"I will try," said Dad. "But it won't be easy. There'll be loads of us all looking for the same ones."

And as it turned out, it wasn't easy. It was, in fact, impossible. With so many people losing their jobs all at once, Dad was forced to claim benefit money from the government. It was a pittance, barely enough to live on. With nothing to do all day, Dad became more and more down. To begin with he went to the Job Centre every day. But there were never any jobs within a hundred miles and eventually he started going to the pub instead – Zoe could tell because she was fairly sure that Job Centres didn't stay open till late at night.

Zoe became more and more worried about her father. Sometimes she wondered if he had given up on life altogether. Losing first his wife, and then his job, seemed like just too much for him to bear.

Little did he know, things were about to get much much worse…

Dad met Zoe's stepmother when he was at his saddest. He was lonely and she was on her own, her last husband having died in a mysterious prawn-cocktail-crisp-related incident. Sheila seemed to think that husband number ten's benefit money would provide her with an easy life, with fags on tap and all the prawn cocktail crisps she could eat.

As Zoe's real mum had died when Zoe was a baby, as much as she tried, and she tried and tried, Zoe could not remember her. There used to be photographs of Mum up all over the flat. Mum had a kind smile. Zoe would stare at the photographs, and try and smile just like her. They certainly looked alike. Especially when they were smiling.

However, one day when everyone was out, Zoe's new stepmother took all the photographs down. Now they were conveniently 'lost'. Probably burned. Dad didn't like talking about Mum because it would just make him cry. However, she lived on in Zoe's heart. The little girl knew that her real mum had loved her very much. She just knew it.

Zoe also knew her stepmother did *not* love her. Or even like her very much. In truth, Zoe was pretty sure her stepmother hated her. Sheila treated her at worst as an irritant, at best as if she were invisible. Zoe often overheard her stepmother saying she wanted her out of the house as soon as she was old enough.

"De little brat can stop spongin' off me!" The woman never gave her a penny, not even on her birthday. That Christmas, Sheila had given Zoe a used tissue as a present, and then laughed in her face when the little girl unwrapped it. It was full of snot.

Soon after Zoe's stepmother moved into the flat, she demanded that the hamster move out.

"It stinks!" she shrieked.

However, after a great deal of shouting and slamming of doors, Zoe was finally allowed to keep her little pet.

Sheila carried on despising Gingernut, though. She moaned and moaned that the little hamster chewed holes in the sofa, even though it was burning hot ash falling from her fags that had really created them! Over and over again she warned her stepdaughter she would "stamp on de nasty little beast if I ever catch it out of its cage".

Sheila also mocked Zoe's attempts to teach her hamster to breakdance.

"You're wastin' your time with dat nonsense. You and dat little beast will amount to nuffink. Ya 'ear me? Nuffink!"

Zoe heard, but chose not to listen. She knew she had a special way with animals, and Dad had always told her so.

In fact, Zoe dreamed of travelling the world with a huge menagerie of animal stars. One day, she would train animals to do extraordinary feats that she believed would delight the world. She even made a list of what these madcap acts could be:

A frog who is a superstar DJ

A rapping terrapin

Two gerbils who ballroom dance together

An elephant who
sings opera

A donkey who does
magic tricks

A tap-dancing
centipede

A boy band comprised entirely of guinea pigs

A street-dance group of tortoises

A cat who does impressions
(of famous cartoon cats)

A ballet-dancing pig

A worm hypnotist

A high-wire acrobatics
act with cows

An ant who does
ventriloquism

A daredevil mole who does incredible stunts like being shot out of a cannon

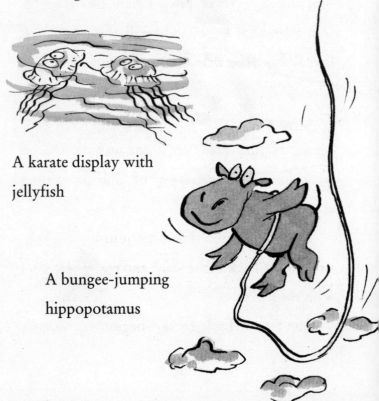

A karate display with jellyfish

A bungee-jumping hippopotamus

Zoe had it all planned out. With the money the animals earned, she and her father could both escape the leaning, crumbling tower block for ever. Zoe could buy Dad a much bigger flat, and she could retire to a huge country house and set up a sanctuary for unwanted pets. The animals could run around in the grounds all day, and sleep together in a giant bed at night. 'No animal too big or too small, they will all be loved' was to be written over the entrance gates.

Then on that fateful day, Zoe came home from school to find that Gingernut was dead. And with him, Zoe's dreams of animal-training stardom died too.

So, reader, after that little journey back in time, we're back at the start, and ready to get on with the story.

Don't turn back to the beginning though,

that would be really stupid and you would go round and round in circles reading the same few pages. No, move on to the next page, and I will continue with the story. Quickly. Stop reading this and move on. Now!

4

Dirty Business

"Flush it down de bog!" shouted Sheila.

Zoe was sitting on her bed listening through the wall to her dad and stepmother arguing.

"No!" replied Dad.

"Give it 'ere ya useless git! I'll bung it in de bin!"

Zoe often sat on her bed in her too-small pyjamas, listening through the paper-thin wall to her father and stepmother arguing way past her bedtime. Tonight they were of course shouting and screaming about Gingernut, who had died that day.

As they lived in a flat on the 37th floor of a dilapidated council block (which leaned heavily and should have been demolished decades ago), the family didn't have a garden. There *was* an old adventure playground in the central concrete square shared by all the blocks in the estate. However, the local gang made it too dangerous to venture near.

"Wot you lookin' at?" Tina Trotts would shout at anyone passing by. Tina was the local bully, and her gang of teenage hoodlums ruled the estate. She was only fourteen but she could make a grown man cry, and often did. Every day she would flob on Zoe's head from the flats as the little girl walked to school. And every day Tina would laugh, as if it was the funniest thing in the world.

If the family had owned an allotment or even the smallest patch of grass anywhere on the estate they could call their own, Zoe would have dug a little grave with a spoon, lowered her little friend into the hole and made a headstone with a lolly stick.

> *Gingernut,*
> *Much loved Hamster,*
> *Expert breakdancer,*
> *And sometime bodypopper.*
> *Sadly missed by his owner and friend Zoe,*
> *RIP*[2]

But of course they didn't have a garden. No one did. Instead, Zoe had wrapped her hamster carefully in a page from her History exercise book. When her dad finally returned home from the pub, Zoe gave him the precious little package.

---

[2] *It would have had to be quite a big lolly stick.*

My dad will know what to do with him, she thought.

But Zoe hadn't reckoned on her horrible stepmother getting involved.

Unlike his new wife, Dad was tall and thin. If she was a bowling ball, he was the skittle, and of course bowling balls often knock over skittles.

So now Dad and Sheila were arguing in the kitchen about what to do with the little package Zoe had given to Dad. It was always awful hearing the two of them shouting at each other, but tonight was proving particularly unbearable.

"I suppose I could get the poor girl another hamster," ventured Dad. "She was so good with it…"

Zoe's face lit up for a moment.

"Are ya crazy?" sneered her stepmother. "Another 'amster! You are so useless, ya can't even get a job to pay for one!"

"There *are* no jobs," pleaded Dad.

"You're just too lazy to get one. Ya useless git."

"I could find a way, for Zoe. I love my girl so much. I could try to save up some of my benefit money—"

"Dat's hardly enuff to keep me in prawn cocktail crisps, let alone feed a beast like dat."

"We could feed it leftovers," protested Dad.

"I am not havin' another one of dose disgusting creatures in me flat!" said the woman.

"It's not a disgusting creature. It's a hamster!"

"'Amsters are no better dan rats," Sheila continued. "Worse! I work all day on me 'ands and knees keepin' dis flat spick and span."

She does no such thing, thought Zoe. *The flat is an absolute tip!*

"And den the nasty little fing comes along and does its dirty business everywhere!" continued

Sheila. "And while I am on the subject, your aim in de bog could be better!"

"Sorry."

"Wot do ya do? Put a sprinkler on de end of it?"

"Keep your voice down, woman!"

The little girl was once again finding out the hard way that secretly listening to your parents talk could be a very dangerous game. You always ended up hearing things you wished you never had. Besides, Gingernut *didn't* do his dirty business everywhere. Zoe always made sure she picked up any rogue droppings from his secret runs around her room with some loo paper and flushed them safely down the toilet.

"I'll take the cage down the pawn shop then," said Dad. "I might get a few quid for it."

"*I* will take it down de pawn shop," said his wife aggressively. "You'll just spend the money down de pub."

"But—"

"Now put de nasty little fing in de bin."

"I promised Zoe I would give him a proper burial in the park. She loved Gingernut. Taught him tricks and everything."

"Dey were pathetic. PATHETIC! A breakdancin' 'amster?! Absolute rubbish!"

"That's not fair!"

"And you're not going out again tonight. I don't trust ya. You'll be back down de pub."

"It's shut now."

"Knowing you, you'll just wait outside until it opens tomorrow morning... Now come on, give it 'ere!"

Zoe heard the pedal bin open with the stamp of her stepmother's chubby foot and the faint sound of a thud.

With tears streaming down her face, Zoe lay

down in bed, and covered herself with her duvet. She turned to her right side. In the half-light she stared at the cage as she did every night.

It was agonising to see it empty. The little girl closed her eyes but couldn't sleep. Her heart was aching, her brain was spinning. She was sad, she was angry, she was sad, she was angry, she was sad. She turned on to her left side. Maybe it would be easier to sleep facing the grimy wall rather than staring at the empty cage. She closed her eyes again, but all she could think about was Gingernut.

Not that it was easy to think, what with the noise coming from the neighbouring flat. Zoe didn't know who lived there – people in the tower block weren't exactly close – but most evenings she heard shouting. It seemed like a man screaming at his daughter, who would often cry, and Zoe felt sorry for her, whoever she was. However bad Zoe thought her life was, this girl's sounded worse.

But Zoe blocked out the shouting, and soon fell asleep, dreaming of Gingernut, breakdancing in heaven…

5

Droppings

Zoe trudged even more reluctantly than usual to school the next morning. Gingernut was dead, and with that her dreams had died too. As Zoe walked out of the estate, Tina flobbed on the little girl's head as she always did. As she was wiping the flob out of her frizzy hair with a page ripped from one of her exercise books, Zoe saw Dad crouched over by the tiniest patch of grass.

He appeared to be digging with his hands.

He turned around quickly, as if in shock. "Oh, hello, my love…"

"What are you doing?" said Zoe. She leaned

over him, to see what he was up to, and saw that the little package containing Gingernut was laid on the ground, next to a small mound of earth.

"Don't tell your mum…"

"Stepmum!"

"Don't tell your stepmum, but I fished the little fella out of the bin…"

"Oh, Dad!"

"Sheila's still asleep, snoring away. I don't think she heard anything. Gingernut meant so much to you and I just wanted to give him, you know, a proper burial."

Zoe smiled for a moment, but somehow she found herself crying too.

"Oh, Dad, thank you so much…"

"No word of this to her though, or she'll murder me."

"Of course not."

Zoe knelt down beside him, picked up the

little package and lowered Gingernut into the small hole her father had dug.

"I even got one of these for a headstone. One of the old lolly sticks from the factory."

Zoe took out her chewed biro from her pocket, and scribbled 'Gingernut' on the stick, though there wasn't really room for the 't', so it just read:

GINGERNU

Dad filled in the hole, and they stood back and looked at the little grave.

"Thanks, Dad. You are the best…"

Now Dad was crying.

"What's the matter?" asked Zoe.

"I am not the best. I am so sorry, Zoe. But I will get another job one day. I know I will…"

"Dad, a job doesn't matter. I just want you to be happy."

"I don't want you to see me like this…"

Dad started walking away. Zoe pulled on his arm, but he shook it out of her grasp, and walked off back to the tower block.

"Come and meet me at the school gates later, Dad. We can go to the park, and you can put me on your shoulders. I used to love that. It don't cost a thing."

"Sorry, I'll be in the pub. Have a good day at school," he shouted, without looking back. He was hiding his sadness from his daughter, like he always did.

Zoe could feel her stomach screaming in hunger. There had been no dinner last night as Sheila had spent all the benefit money on fags, and there was no food in the house. Zoe hadn't eaten for a very long time. So she stopped off at Raj's Newsagent.

All the kids from school went to his shop before or after school. As Zoe never received pocket money, she would only come in to the shop and gaze longingly at the sweets. Being exceptionally kind-hearted, Raj often took pity on the girl and gave her free ones. Only the out-of-date ones though, or those with a hint of mould, but she was still grateful. Sometimes she would be allowed a quick suck on a mint before Raj asked her to spit it out so he could put it back in the packet to sell it to another customer.

This morning Zoe was especially hungry, and

was hoping Raj would help…

TING went the bell as the door opened.

"Aaah! Miss Zoe. My favourite customer." Raj was a big jolly man, who always had a smile on his face, even if you told him his shop was on fire.

"Hello, Raj," said Zoe sheepishly. "I don't have any money again today I am afraid."

"Not a penny?"

"Nothing. Sorry."

"Oh dear. But you do look hungry. A quick nibble on one of these chocolate bars perhaps?"

He picked up a bar and unwrapped it for her.

"Just try and eat around the edge please. Then I can put it in the wrapper and back on sale. The next customer will never know!"

Zoe nibbled greedily on the chocolate bar, her front teeth munching off the edges like a little rodent.

"You look very sad, child," said Raj. He was always good at spotting when things were wrong, and could be a lot more caring than some parents or teachers. "Have you been crying?"

Zoe looked up from her nibbling for a moment. Her eyes still stung with tears.

"No, I'm fine, Raj. Just hungry."

"No, Miss Zoe, I can see something is wrong." He leaned on the counter, and smiled supportively at her.

Zoe took a deep breath. "My hamster died."

"Oh, Miss Zoe, I am so so sorry."

"Thank you."

"You poor thing. A few years ago I had a pet tadpole and it died, so I know how you feel."

Zoe looked surprised. "A pet tadpole?" She had never heard of anyone having one as a pet.

"Yes, I called him Poppadom. One night I left him swimming around in his little fish bowl, and when I woke up in the morning there was this naughty frog there. He must have eaten Poppadom!"

Zoe couldn't quite believe what she was hearing.

"Raj…"

"Yes…?" The newsagent wiped a tear from his eye with the sleeve of his cardigan. "Sorry, I always get quite emotional when I think about Poppadom."

"Raj, tadpoles turn into frogs."

"Don't be so stupid, child!"

"They do. So that frog *was* Poppadom."

"I know you are just making me feel better, but I know it's not true."

Zoe rolled her eyes.

"Now tell me about your hamster…"

"He is, I mean, was, so special. I trained him to breakdance."

"Wow! What was his name?"

"Gingernut," said Zoe sadly. "My dream was that one day he would be on the TV…"

Raj thought for a moment, and then looked Zoe straight in the eyes. "You must never give up on your dreams, young lady…"

"But Gingernut is dead…"

"But your *dream* doesn't need to die. Dreams never die. If you can train a hamster to breakdance, Miss Zoe, just imagine what you could do…"

"I suppose…"

Raj looked at his watch. "But as much as I would like to, we can't stand here chatting all day."

"No?" Zoe loved Raj, even if he didn't know a tadpole turned into a frog, and never wanted to leave his messy little shop.

"You better be off to school now, young lady.

You don't want to be late…"

"I suppose so," mumbled Zoe. Sometimes she wondered why she didn't just bunk off like so many of the others.

Raj beckoned with his big hands. "Now, Miss Zoe, give me the chocolate bar please, so I can put it back on sale…"

Zoe looked at her hands. It had gone. She was so hungry she had devoured every last morsel, save for one tiny square.

"I am so sorry, Raj. I didn't mean to. I really didn't!"

"I know, I know," said the kindly man. "Just put it back in the wrapper. I can sell it as a special diet chocolate to someone fat like me!"

"Good idea!" said the little girl.

Zoe went over to the door, and turned around to face the newsagent.

"Thank you, by the way. Not just for the

chocolate. But for the advice…"

"Both are free of charge for you any time, Miss Zoe. Now run along…"

Raj's words went round and round in Zoe's mind all day at school, but when she returned home to the flat she felt the same sense of absence. Gingernut was gone. For ever.

Days went by, then weeks, then months. She could never forget about Gingernut. He was such a special little hamster. And he brought her so much joy in a world of pain. From the moment he died, Zoe felt as if she was walking through a storm. Very slowly, as the days and weeks passed, the rain became a little lighter. Though the sun had still not shone.

Until one night, months later, when something completely unexpected happened.

Zoe was lying in bed after another insufferable

day at school at the hands of the bullies, and the dreaded Tina Trotts in particular. There was shouting from next door as usual. Then, out of a brief moment of quiet in the night, came a tiny sound. It was so soft at first it was almost imperceptible. Then it became louder. And louder.

It sounded like nibbling.

Am I dreaming? thought Zoe. *Am I having one of those strange dreams that I am lying in bed awake?*

She opened her eyes. No, she wasn't dreaming.

Something small was moving in her bedroom.

For a mad moment, Zoe wondered if it could be the ghost of Gingernut. Lately she'd found a couple of what seemed like droppings in her room. *No, don't be crazy*, she told herself. *Must be funny-shaped clumps of dust, that's all.*

At first all she could see was a tiny shadowy

shape in the corner by the door. She tiptoed out of bed to have a closer look. It was little and dirty and a tad smelly. The dusty floorboards creaked a little under her weight.

The tiny thing turned around.

It was a rat.

6

Rat-a-tat-tat

When you think of the word 'rat', what is the next thing to come into your head?

Rat... vermin?

Rat... sewer?

Rat... disease?

Rat... bite?

Rat... plague?

Rat... catcher?

Rat... a-tat-tat?

Rats are the most unloved living things on the planet.

Kittens

Puppies

Bunnies

Hamsters

Gerbils

Guinea pigs

Baby elephants

Koala bears

Piglets

Penguins

Butterflies

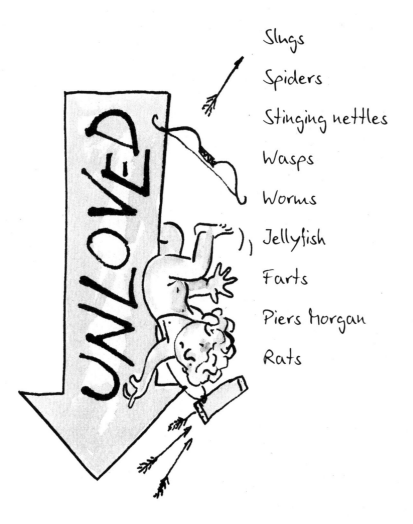

Slugs

Spiders

Stinging nettles

Wasps

Worms

Jellyfish

Farts

Piers Morgan

Rats

However, what if I told you that what Zoe found in her room that night was a *baby* rat?

Yes, this was the cutest, sweetest, littlest baby rat you can imagine, and it was crouching in the corner of her room, nibbling on one of her dirty hole-ridden socks.

With a tiny pink twitching nose, furry ears and huge, deep, hopeful eyes, this was a rat that could win first prize in a vermin beauty pageant. This explained the mysterious droppings that Zoe had recently found in her room: it must have been this little mite.

Well, it certainly wasn't me.

Zoe had always thought she would be terrified if she ever saw a rat. Her stepmother even kept rat poison in the kitchen, as there was always talk of an infestation in the crumbling block of flats.

However, this rat didn't seem very terrifying.

In fact, if anything, the rat appeared to be terrified of *Zoe*. When the floorboard creaked as she approached, it skirted the wall and hid under her bed.

"Don't be scared, little one," whispered Zoe. Slowly she put her hand under the bed to try and stroke the rat. It shivered in fear at first, its fur standing up on end.

"Shush, shush," said Zoe, comfortingly.

Little by little, the rat made its way through the garden of dust and dirt under Zoe's creaky little bed and approached her hand. It sniffed her fingers, before licking one, then another. Sheila was too idle to cook, and Zoe was so starving she had stolen a bag of her stepmother's dreaded prawn cocktail crisps for her dinner. The rat must have been able to smell them on her fingers, and despite Zoe's grave misgivings about the snack, which bore no relation to prawns or indeed cocktails, the rat didn't seem to mind.

Zoe let out a little giggle. The nibbling tickled her. She lifted her hand to stroke the rat, and it ducked underneath and raced to the far corner of the room.

"Shush, shush, come on. I only want to give you a stroke," implored Zoe.

The rat peeked at her with uncertainty, before tentatively, paw by paw, making its way over to her hand. She brushed its fur with her little finger as lightly as she could. The fur was a lot softer than she imagined. Not as soft as Gingernut's, nothing was. But surprisingly soft nonetheless.

One by one, Zoe's fingers lowered and soon she was stroking the top of the rat's head. Zoe let her fingers trickle down its neck and back. The rat arched its back to meet her hand.

Most likely it had never been shown such tenderness before. Certainly not by a human. Not only was there enough rat poison in the world to kill every rat ten times over, but when people saw a rat, they would generally either scream or reach for a broom to whack it with.

Looking at this little tiddler now, though, it was hard for Zoe to understand why anyone would want to harm him.

Suddenly, the rat's little ears shot up and Zoe quickly turned her head. Her parents' bedroom door was opening, and she could hear her stepmother thundering along the hallway, huffing with each step. Hurriedly, Zoe snatched up the rat, cupped it in her hands, and jumped back into bed. Sheila would go crazy if she knew her stepdaughter was in bed cuddling a rodent. Zoe took the duvet between her teeth and hid under the covers. She waited and listened. The bathroom door creaked open and closed, and Zoe could hear the muffled sound of her stepmother thudding down on to the cracked toilet seat.

Zoe sighed and opened her hands. The baby rat was safe. For now. She let the little rodent scamper over her hands and on to her torn pyjama top.

"Kiss kiss kiss kiss." She made a little kissing

noise just like the one she used to do with Gingernut. And just like her hamster used to do, the rat approached her face.

Zoe planted a little kiss on its nose. She pushed a dent in the pillow next to her head, and gently laid the rat down into it. It fitted perfectly, and soon she could hear it snoring very quietly next to her.

If you have never heard a rat snoring before, this is what it sounds like:

Zzzzzzzzzzzzzzzzzzzzzzzzzzz ZZZZZZZZZzzzz z z z z z z z z z z zzzzzzzzzzzzzzzzz.

"Now, how on earth am I going to keep you a secret?" Zoe whispered.

7

Animal Smuggling

It isn't easy to smuggle a rat into school.

The hardest animal to sneak into school is of course the blue whale. Just too big and wet.

Hippopotamuses are also hard to slip in unnoticed, as are giraffes. Too fat and tall respectively.

Lions are inadvisable. All that roaring gives them away.

Seals bark too much. As do walruses.

Skunks smell really bad – even worse than some teachers.

Kangaroos just don't stop hopping.

Boobies[3] sound too rude.

Elephants tend to break the chairs.

An ostrich will get you to school quickly, but is too big to hide in your school bag.

Polar bears blend into arctic wastes very well, but can be spotted instantly in a school dinner queue.

Smuggling a shark into school would lead to instant expulsion, especially if you had

---

[3] *A booby is a type of seabird closely related to the gannet. In case you thought I had made it up for a cheap laugh. As if I would do that!*

swimming lessons that day. They have a tendency to eat the children.

Orang-utans are also a no-no. They can be very disruptive in class.

Gorillas are even worse, especially in Maths. Gorillas are not good with numbers, and hate doing sums, although they are surprisingly good at French.

A herd of wildebeest is almost impossible to take into school without a teacher noticing.

Nits, on the other hand, are ludicrously easy. Some children smuggle thousands of nits into school every day.

A rat is still a difficult animal to smuggle into school. Somewhere between a blue whale and a nit on the 'hard to smuggle into school' scale.

The problem was that it was impossible for Zoe to leave the little thing at home. Gingernut's old battered cage was long gone, as her stepmother had taken it to the pawnbrokers. The ghastly woman had swapped it for a few coins, which she promptly spent on a bumper-box of prawn cocktail crisps. Thirty-six bags that she had demolished before breakfast.

If Zoe had just left the rat running around the flat, she knew that Sheila would have poisoned it or stamped on it or both. Her stepmother made no secret of hating all rodents. And even if Zoe had hidden the rat in a bedroom drawer, or in a box under her bed, there was a very good chance Sheila would have found it. Zoe knew that her stepmother always rummaged through her possessions the moment she left for school. Sheila was looking for things she could sell or swap for a fag or two, or some more prawn cocktail crisps.

One day, all of Zoe's toys had gone, another day it was her beloved books. It was just too risky to leave the rat alone in the flat with that woman.

Zoe considered putting the rat in her school bag, but because she was so poor she had to take her books to school in a beaten-up plastic carrier bag, held together with strips of sticky tape. It was too much of a risk that the little rodent might nibble its way out. So Zoe hid it in the breast pocket of her two-sizes-too-large blazer. Yes, she could feel it constantly wriggling around, but at least she knew it was safe.

As Zoe came out of the stairwell of the tower block and into the concreted communal area, she heard a shout from above her. "Zoe!"

She looked up.

Big mistake.

A huge flobbet of flob flobbed square on to her face. Zoe saw Tina Trotts standing at the railings several floors up.

"HA HAH HA!" Tina shouted down.

Zoe refused to cry. She just wiped her face with her sleeve and turned away, Tina's laughter still echoing behind her. She probably *would* have cried, but then she felt the little rat move in her pocket, and she instantly felt better.

Now I've got a little pet again, she thought. *It might just be a rat, but it's only the beginning...*

Perhaps Raj was right: her dream of training an animal to entertain the nation wasn't dead after all.

The rat's presence remained a comfort when Zoe arrived at school. This was Zoe's first year at big school and she hadn't made a single friend there yet. Most of the kids were poor, but Zoe was the poorest. It was embarrassing for her to have to go to school in unwashed clothes from charity shops. Clothes which were either far too big or far too small for her, and most of which had gaping holes in them. The rubber sole had all but fallen off her left shoe, and flapped against the ground every time she took a step.

FLIP FLAP FLIP FLAP FLIP FLAP went her shoes every time she walked anywhere.

FLIPITY FLAP FLIPITY FLAP FLIPITY FLAP if she ran.

In assembly, after an announcement about an end-of-term talent show, the pale headmaster Mr Grave stepped up to speak. He stood in the centre of the stage, unblinkingly staring at the hundreds of pupils gathered in the school hall. All the children were a little bit scared of him. With his staring eyes and pale skin, wild rumours abounded among the younger pupils that he was secretly a vampire.

Mr Grave proceeded to give a stern warning to those "errant pupils" who, against the rules, had been smuggling their mobile phones into school. This was just about everyone, though Zoe was far too skint to even dream of ever owning one.

Great, thought Zoe. *Even when we're being told off I get left out.*

"Needless to say, I'm not just talking about phones!" boomed Mr Grave, as if reading Zoe's mind. His voice could carry across a crowded playground at break-time and make every pupil fall silent in a heartbeat. "*Anything* that beeps or vibrates is strictly forbidden! Did you hear me?" he boomed again.

"Forbidden! That is all. Dismissed."

The bell rang and the kids plodded off to their lessons. Sitting on the uncomfortable little grey plastic chair on her own lonely row at the back of the assembly hall, Zoe wondered nervously if her rat came under Mr Grave's description. It certainly vibrated. And sometimes it beeped. Or at least squeaked.

"Don't make a sound today, little rat," she said.

The rat squeaked.

Oh no! thought Zoe.

8

Bread Sandwich

So as not to be jostled at the door, Zoe waited a few moments before ambling off to her first lesson. Amazingly, Maths, which she always found cataclysmically boring, passed without incident. As did Geography, where she wondered if her new-found knowledge of oxbow lakes might come in useful in adult life. During the lessons, Zoe stole an occasional glance into her blazer inside pocket, and saw that the little rat was sleeping. It must really enjoy a nice lie-in.

At break-time, Zoe locked herself in a cubicle in the girls' toilets and fed the rat some of the bread she was meant to be saving for her lunch. She made her own packed lunch whenever there were scraps of food still in the house. However, this morning there was absolutely nothing in the fridge other than a few cans of very strong lager, so she made herself a bread sandwich out of some stale slices left out on the side…

The recipe was simple:

BREAD SANDWICH

You will need: *three slices of bread.*

Instructions: take one slice of bread, and put it between the other two slices of bread.

The end.[4]

---

[4] My new cookbook, *101 Ways to Make a Bread Sandwich*, is out next year.

Unsurprisingly, the rat liked bread. Rats like most food we like.

Zoe sat on the toilet seat, and the rat perched on her left hand while she fed it with her right. It gobbled up every last mouthful.

"There you go, little—"

At that moment Zoe realised she had yet to name her tiny friend. Unless she wanted to give it a name suitable for a boy or a girl like 'Pat' or

'Les' or 'Viv', she would first have to find out if it was indeed a boy or a girl. So Zoe carefully picked the rat up to have a closer look. Just as she was trying to undertake a more thorough investigation, a thin arch of yellow liquid sprayed from just underneath the rat's tummy, narrowly missing Zoe, and decorating the wall.

The girl now had a definitive answer. She was convinced that the wee had come from a tiny little spout, though it was impossible to look again, with the rat now wriggling in her hands.

But she was sure it was a boy.

Zoe looked up for inspiration. On the toilet door, some older girls had scratched obscene sentences with a compass.

'Destiny is a complete @**$$$$&!%^!%!!!!' Zoe read, which I think we can all agree is very rude, even if she is.

Destiny would have been a stupid name for

a rat. Especially a boy rat, thought the little girl.
Zoe continued searching the names on the door
for inspiration.

Rochelle... no.

Darius... no.

Busta... no.

Tupac... no.

Jammaall... no.

Snoop... no.

Meredith... no.

Kylie... no.

Beyonce...no.

Tyrone... no.

Chantelle... no.

Despite being crowded with words (and some
rude drawings), the toilet door wasn't providing
as much inspiration as Zoe had hoped. She sat

up from the toilet seat and turned around to flush, so as not to alert the suspicion of the girl she could hear in the next cubicle. At that moment, she spied some posh writing amidst all the ingrained stains in the toilet bowl.

"Armitage Shanks," she read out loud. It was only the name of the toilet manufacturer, but the little rat's ears twitched when she said it, as if in recognition.

"Armitage! That's it!" she exclaimed. It was a suitably upper-class-sounding name for this special little fellow.

Suddenly there was a loud thud on the toilet door.

BOOM
BOOOM
BOOOOM.

Ratburger

"Who have you got in there, you little squirt?" came a guttural voice from outside.

No! thought Zoe. *It's Tina Trotts.* The spit from today's flob had still not entirely come off Zoe's little freckled face.

Tina was only fourteen but built like a trucker. She had big hands that could punch, big feet that could kick, a big head that could butt, and a big butt that could squash.

Even the teachers were scared of her. Inside the cubicle, Zoe was quaking with fear.

"There's no one in here," said Zoe.

Why did I say that? she instantly thought. The mere act of saying that there was no one in there meant there was definitely, without doubt, one hundred per cent, someone in there.

Zoe was in terrible danger, but only if she opened the door. For now, she was safe inside the—

"Get out of the bog right now before I smash the door in!" threatened Tina.

Oh dear.

9

One Shoe

Zoe quickly put Armitage back in her blazer pocket.

"I am just having a wee!" said Zoe. Then she made a rather pitiful sound that she hoped would sound like water gushing into a bowl by pursing her lips and blowing. It ended up sounding more like a snake hissing.

"Ppppppppppppppppppsssssssssssssssssss ssssssssssssssssssssssssssssssssssssssssss. . . . ."

Of course, Zoe's hope was that this would convince Tina Trotts that she was using the toilet for legitimate purposes only, and not for feeding a bread sandwich to a long-tailed rodent.

Zoe then took a deep breath and opened the toilet door. Tina stared down at Zoe, two of her usual goons flanking her.

"Hello, Tina," said Zoe in a voice quite a few octaves higher than her usual one. In attempting to play the innocent, she felt like she was giving the appearance of someone who was in fact exceedingly guilty.

"Oh, it's you! Who were you talking to, Braceface?" demanded Tina, leaning into the cubicle now.

"Myself," said Zoe. "I often actually talk to myself whenever I am passing water…"

"Passing wot?!"

"Um… having a wee? So if you will excuse me I have to be off to my History class…" With that, the little ginger girl tried to ease past Tina and her foot soldiers.

"Not so fast," said Tina. "Me and my gang own these bogs. We sell stolen gear from in 'ere. So unless you want to buy a trainer we nicked, sod off!"

"Don't you mean a pair of trainers?" enquired Zoe.

"No. I mean a trainer. They only put one out on the shelves so it's much easier to steal one than two."

"Mmmm," mused Zoe, not sure why anyone with two feet would want to buy just the one shoe.

"Listen, Ginge," continued the bully. "We don't want you in our bogs. You hear? Puttin' off all the customers by talking to yerself like some nutter…"

"Understood," muttered Zoe. "Very sorry, Tina."

"Now give us yer money," demanded Tina.

"I don't have any," replied Zoe. She wasn't lying. Her dad had been on benefits for years so she never ever received pocket money. When she walked to school she would scour the pavements for coins. One particularly lucky day she had found a five-pound note in a gutter! It was wet, it was dirty, but it was hers. Skipping home in delight, she stopped off at Raj's Newsagent and bought a whole box of chocolates to share with her family. However, before Zoe's dad had got home, her stepmother had scoffed every single one, even the dreaded cherry liqueurs, before gobbling down the box too.

"No money? Likely story," splattered Tina. Splattering is a bit like spluttering but the person being talked to ends up covered in spit.

"What do you mean?" said Zoe. "We both

live on the same estate. You know I don't have any cash."

Tina scoffed. "I bet you get pocket money. Always walking around like you own the place. Girls – grab her."

Like clockwork, the bullies circled our little heroine. The two goons seized her arms tightly.

"Aaah!" screamed Zoe in pain. Their fingernails were digging into her little arms as Tina's large dirty hands started rooting in Zoe's pockets.

Zoe's heart started pounding. Armitage the rat was lying asleep in the breast pocket of her blazer. Tina's chubby fingers were prodding and poking everywhere. Within seconds they would come into contact with a small rodent, and Zoe's life at school would change for ever.

Bringing a rat into school was not something you would ever live down.

Once, a boy a few years above had mooned out of the coach window on a school trip to the railway museum and ever since then he had only ever been called 'Hairy Bum' by everyone in the school, even the teachers.

Time slowed down and then speeded up as Tina's search for money led inevitably to Zoe's breast pocket. Her fingers thrust in and poked poor little Armitage on the nose.

"What's this?" said Tina. "The little ginge has got something living in there."

Now, Armitage must have not taken kindly to being prodded by a big dirty finger on the nose, because he bit into it.

"Aaaaaaaaaaaaaaaaaaaaaaaar rrrrrrrrrrrrrrrgggggggg gggggggggggggggghh hhhhhhhhhhhh!!!!!!!!!!! !!!!!!!!!!!!!!!!!!!!!!!!" screamed Tina.

Her hand shot out of Zoe's pocket, but Armitage was still attached, clinging on with his little sharp teeth, dangling from her finger.

"EEEEEeeeeeeeuuu UUUUUUUURRRRRRRR RRRGGGGGGGGGGGG HHHHHHHHHH!!!!!!!!!!!!!!! !!!!!!!!!!!!!!!!!!!!!" squealed the bully. "It's a rat!"

10

The Ogre

"It's only a baby rat," reasoned Zoe, trying to calm Tina down. She was afraid she might smack Armitage against something and hurt him.

Tina started shaking her hand violently as she ran around the girls' toilets in utter panic. However, the baby rat would not let go. The goons stood as still as statues, searching their tiny brains for the appropriate response to 'rat attached to finger'.

Unsurprisingly, nothing seemed to come to mind.

"Hold still," said Zoe.

Tina kept running around.

"I said *hold still*."

Seemingly shocked by this authoritative tone from the small ginger girl, Tina stopped moving.

Carefully, as if dealing with an angry bear, Zoe took Tina's hand in hers. "Come on, Armitage…"

Carefully she prised the rat's sharp front teeth off the large girl's finger.

"There you go," said Zoe in the manner of a dentist who had just given a child a mildly painful filling. "Come on now. Tut-tut. It wasn't too bad."

"The little @**$$$$&!%^!%!!!! bit me!" protested Tina, revealing herself as the likely author of the insulting message on the toilet door. The bully examined her finger, two tiny drops of blood oozing out of the tip.

"Tina, they are nothing more than pin pricks," replied Zoe.

The two goons craned their long necks to get a closer look, and nodded their heads in agreement with Zoe. This infuriated Tina and her face went fiery red like a volcano about to explode.

There was an eerie silence for a moment.

I am about to die, thought Zoe. *She is actually going to kill me.*

Then the bell rang for the end of break.

"Well, if you'll excuse us," said Zoe, more calmly than she felt, "Armitage and I don't want to be late for our History class."

"Why is 'e called dat?" grunted one goon.

"Erm, it's a long story," said Zoe, who wasn't about to tell them he was named after a toilet. "Another time perhaps. Goodbye!"

The three bullies were too shocked to stop

her. Cupping her little friend in her hand, she strolled out of the toilets. Just clear of the door, she realised she wasn't actually breathing, and that she should probably start again. Then she gave Armitage a little kiss on the head.

"You are my guardian angel!" she whispered before placing him carefully back in her breast pocket.

Zoe suddenly realised Tina and her gang might be following her, so without looking back, she quickened her pace. The stroll became a stride and the stride became a sprint and before she knew it she was sitting breathless in her History class, which was presided over by Miss Ogden. As the History teacher was so ferocious, she had been given the nickname 'The Ogre'.

The teacher always wore knee-high leather boots with heels that made her look even shorter than she actually was. However, what Miss Ogden lacked in height she made up

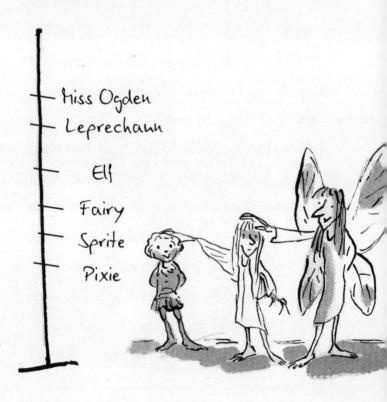

Miss Ogden
Leprechaun
Elf
Fairy
Sprite
Pixie

for in ferocity. Her teeth would not have
been out of place in the mouth of a crocodile.
She bared these teeth whenever a pupil
displeased her, which was often. Kids didn't
have to do much to infuriate her, even an

involuntary sneeze or a cough could result in a monstrous snarl from the terrifying teacher.

"You are late," growled Miss Ogden.

"Sorry, Miss Ogre," said Zoe, without thinking.

Oh no.

There were a few chuckles from her classmates, but mainly gasps. Zoe was so used to calling the History teacher 'Miss Ogre' behind her back that she had done it to her face by mistake!

"What did you say?" demanded Miss Ogden.

"I said 'sorry, Miss Ogden'," spluttered Zoe. The sweat that had sprung up on her run from the girls' toilets was now teeming out of her pores. Zoe looked like she had been caught in a vicious thunderstorm. Armitage was squirming too, probably because the blazer pocket that had become his home was suddenly damp with warm sweat. It must be like a sauna in there! Surreptitiously, Zoe reached a hand up to her breast and patted gently to calm her little friend.

"One more piece of misconduct from you," said Miss Ogden, "and you will not just be out of this classroom, you will be out of the school."

Zoe gulped. She had only just started at big school, and she wasn't used to getting into trouble. She had never done anything wrong at her little school, and even the *thought* of doing something wrong frightened her.

"Now, back to the lesson. Today you are going to learn more about... the Black Death!" pronounced Miss Ogden, as she scrawled the words as high as she could reach on the board, which was actually the bottom.

Writing on the board was a real problem for Miss Ogden, in fact. Sometimes she would order a child to get down on the classroom floor on their hands and knees.

The miniature teacher would then climb on top of them, so she could reach high enough to wipe the board clean of the previous teacher's scribbling. For very high scribblings from very tall teachers you simply stacked up more children.

The Black Death was not on the school history syllabus, but Miss Ogden taught it anyway. Legend had it that one year all of her class failed their exam because instead of teaching them about Queen Victoria she spent a whole year relishing the gruesome details of the medieval torture of being hanged, drawn and quartered. Miss Ogden would refuse to teach anything but the most grisly passages of history: beheadings, flogging, burning at the stake. The teacher would grin and bare her crocodile teeth at the mention of anything cruel and brutal and barbaric.

In fact, this term Miss Ogden had been going on non-stop about the Black Death. It was her absolute obsession. Unsurprising really, as this was one of the darkest periods in human history, when in the fourteenth century 100 million people died from a terrifying infectious disease.

Victims would be covered in giant boils, vomit blood, and die. The cause, they had learned in the previous lesson, was nothing more than a fleabite.

"Boils the size of apples! Imagine that. Vomiting until all that was left to sick up was your own blood! They couldn't dig the graves fast enough! Wonderful stuff!"

The children stared at Miss Ogden, open-mouthed with terror. At that moment the headmaster Mr Grave entered the classroom without knocking, his long coat flapping behind him like a cape. The naughty kids at the back of the class who had been texting throughout the lesson quickly hid their mobile phones under the desk.

"Ah, Mr Grave, to what do I owe the pleasure?" said Miss Ogden, smiling. "Is it about the talent show?"

Zoe had long since suspected that Miss Ogden had a soft spot for the headmaster. Only that morning, Zoe had passed a poster in the corridor for the end-of-term talent show that Miss Ogden was putting on. The poster was of course placed very low down on the wall, really at knee height for most pupils. It seemed very out of character for Miss Ogden to organise something so fun, and Zoe wondered if she had only done it to impress the headmaster. It was well known that Mr Grave, despite his scary vampire appearance, was a great lover of school plays and the like.

"Good morning, Miss Ogre, I mean Miss Ogden..." Even Mr Grave couldn't stop himself!

The History teacher's smile dropped.

"I am afraid it isn't about the talent show, though I am grateful to you for putting it on."

Miss Ogden beamed again.

"No," boomed Mr Grave. "It's something

much more serious I'm afraid."

Miss Ogden's smile dropped once more.

"You see," said the headmaster, "the caretaker has found a... a... dropping in the girls' toilets."

11

The Black Death

All the kids in the class started sniggering when the headmaster used the word 'dropping', except Zoe.

"Someone did a poo on the toilet floor, sir?!" asked one of the boys, laughing.

"Not a human dropping! An animal one!" shouted the headmaster. "Mr Bunsen, the head of Science, is studying it now to find out what animal it is from. But we suspect it to be some kind of rodent…"

Armitage wriggled, and Zoe gulped. A rogue dropping must have plopped out unnoticed on to the toilet floor.

Stay very, very still, Armitage, thought Zoe.

Unfortunately, Armitage was not a mind-reader.

"If any pupil considers it acceptable to bring a pet into this school, let me tell you it is forbidden. Strictly forbidden!" pronounced the headmaster from the front of the class.

It was funny seeing the two teachers stand next to each other for a moment, such was the height difference.

"Any pupil found smuggling an animal of any kind into school will be instantly suspended. That is all!" With that, he turned and left the room.

"Masterful! Goodbye, Mr Grave…!" called Miss Ogden after him. She watched him go, wistfully. Then she turned back to her pupils. "Right, you heard Colin, I mean Mr Grave. It is forbidden to bring pets into school."

The kids all looked around at each other and started whispering.

"Bring a pet into school?" Zoe could hear them saying to each other. "Who would be so stupid?"

Zoe sat as still as she could, staring forward in silence.

"SILENCE!" snarled Miss Ogden, and there was silence. "It is not an opportunity to talk! Now let's get back to the lesson. The Black Death." She underlined those three words on the board.

"So, how did the incredibly deadly disease travel all the way from China to Europe? Anybody?" asked the teacher without turning around. She was one of those teachers who asked questions but didn't wait for answers. So, a millisecond after posing the question, she herself answered it.

"Nobody? *Rats* brought the fatal disease. Rats, on board merchant ships."

Zoe couldn't feel Armitage squirming around any more, and breathed a sigh of relief. He must have gone to sleep.

"But it wasn't the rats' fault, was it?" blurted out Zoe, without putting her hand up. She couldn't believe her little friend's great great great great great great great grandparents could be responsible for such incredible suffering. Armitage was far too sweet to hurt a soul.

Miss Ogden spun round on her heels (which despite being high still didn't make her even of medium height). "Did you speak, child?" she whispered, as if she was a witch incanting a spell.

"Yes, yes…" spluttered Zoe, now beginning to wish she had kept her mouth shut after all. "Forgive me, but I just wanted to say, Miss

Ogden that you shouldn't really blame the rats for this terrible disease, as it wasn't their fault. It was the fleas catching a free ride on their backs that are really to blame…"

All the kids in the class were now looking at Zoe in disbelief. Despite this being a rough school, and teachers often having to leave with nervous breakdowns, no one *ever* interrupted Miss Ogden, especially not to spring to the defence of rats.

The classroom fell deathly silent. Zoe looked around. Every pair of eyes in the room was now glaring at her. Most of the girls looked disgusted, and most of the boys were laughing.

Then, suddenly, Zoe felt like she had a tremendous itchy itch on her head. Quite the itchiest itchy itch that had ever itched. It was, in a word, itchtastic.

What on earth is that…? she wondered.

"Zoe?" sneered Miss Ogden, now staring intently at exactly the place where Zoe had the itch on her head.

"Yes, Miss?" asked Zoe, perfectly innocently.

"You have a rat on your head..."

12

Instant Suspension

What is the worst thing that could ever happen to you at school?

When you arrive in the morning, you walk through the playground and realise you forgot to put on any clothes except your school tie?

In an exam you become so nervous about getting the answers right and your stomach churns up so badly that your bum explodes?

During a football match you run around kissing all your team-mates after you have scored a goal, only to be told by the PE teacher that it was, in fact, an own goal?

You trace your family tree in a History class and you find out you are related to your headmaster?

You have a sneezing fit in front of the head teacher and cover them head to toe in snot?

It's fancy dress day at school but you get the date wrong and you spend the entire day dressed up as Lady Gaga?

You are playing Hamlet in William Shakespeare's play at school and halfway through the 'To be or not to be...' speech your Auntie rushes up from the audience, spits on a tissue and wipes your face with it?

You take off your trainers after games and the smell of mouldy cheese is so bad the entire school has to be closed down for a week to be de-fumigated?

At lunchtime in the dining hall you overdose on baked beans and you do a blow-off that lasts all afternoon?

You smuggle a rat into school in your blazer and it climbs up and sits on your head during a lesson?

Any of those would be enough to get you added to the list of infamous pupils – those famous for all the wrong reasons. With the 'rat on head' incident, Zoe was about to be on the list of shame for ever.

"You have a rat on your head," repeated Miss Ogden.

"Oh, do I, Miss?" said Zoe, mock-innocently.

"Don't worry," said Miss Ogden. "Sit very still, and we'll call for the caretaker. I'm sure he can kill it."

"Kill it! No!" Zoe reached on to her head and lifted the rodent over her now-even-more-wiry mess of red hair and held it in front of her. Children around her got up from their seats and backed away from her.

"Zoe... do you *know* this rat?" said Miss Ogden, suspiciously.

"Um... no," said Zoe.

At this point, Armitage ran up her arm and climbed into her breast pocket.

Zoe looked down at him. "Er..."

"Did that rat just climb into your pocket?"

"No," said Zoe, ridiculously.

"It is clear," said Miss Ogden, "that this filthy beast is your pet."

"Armitage is not a filthy beast!"

"Armitage?" said Miss Ogden. "Why on earth is he called that?!"

"Oh, it's a long story, Miss. Look, he's safely in my pocket now. Please continue."

The teacher and the rest of the class were so gobsmacked by her casual response, for a moment no one knew what to say or do. The silence was deafening, but it didn't last.

"You heard what the headmaster said," roared Miss Ogden. "Instant suspension!"

"But but but I can explain…"

"GET OUT! GET OUT OF MY CLASSROOM YOU VILE LITTLE GIRL! AND TAKE THAT DISGUSTING CREATURE WITH YOU!" snarled the teacher.

Without making eye contact with anyone, Zoe quietly gathered her books and pens and put them in her plastic bag. She pushed her chair back and it squealed against the shiny floor.

"Excuse me," said Zoe to no one in particular. As quietly as she could, she made her way to the door. She put her hand on the handle —

"I SAID 'INSTANT SUSPENSION'!"

yelled Miss Ogden. "I DON'T WANT TO SEE YOU UNTIL THE END OF TERM!"

"Um... Bub-bye then," said Zoe, not sure of what else to say.

She opened the classroom door slowly, and closed it quietly behind her. Behind the frosted glass in the corridor she could see thirty distorted little faces press themselves up against it to watch her go.

There was a pause.

Then there was an enormous eruption of laughter, as the little girl made her way along the hall. Miss Ogden yelled at them,

"SILENCE!"

With everyone still in class, the school felt strangely tranquil. All Zoe could hear were her own little footsteps echoing along the corridor, and the flapping of the rogue sole of her shoe. For a moment the drama of what had only just taken place seemed extremely distant, as if it had all happened in someone else's lifetime. School had never felt so eerily empty before, it was like this was a dream.

Yet if this was the calm after the storm, it wasn't to last long. The bell rang for lunch break, and like a dam bursting the classroom doors in the long corridor flung open and a blast of schoolchildren spurted out. Zoe quickened her pace. She knew the news of her having a rat on her head in History class would spread like the plague itself. Zoe had to get out of school, and fast...

13

Burt's Burgers

Soon Zoe noticed she was running, but her short little legs were no match for the older, taller kids, who were soon barging past her so they could be first in the queue at the burger van to stuff their faces at lunch.

Zoe shielded Armitage with her hand. She had been knocked to the ground in the school corridor so many times before. At last she made it out into the relative safety of the playground. She kept her head down, hoping not to be recognised.

However, there was only one way out of

the playground on to the main road. Every day there was the same grimy beaten-up burger van parked outside, which had 'Burt's Burgers' emblazoned across it. Even though the food from the van was horrible, the school dinners were even more nauseating, so most of the kids took the least worst option and queued up outside the van for their lunch.

Burt was as unsavoury as the burgers he served. The self-styled 'chef' always wore the same filthy striped top and grease-encrusted jeans, which he wore low below his giant belly. Over the top hung a bloody overall. The man's hands were always filthy, and his thick mop of hair was covered in flakes of dandruff the size of Rice Krispies. Even his dandruff had dandruff. The flakes would drop into the deep-fat fryer causing it to hiss and spurt whenever he leaned over it. Burt would

sniff constantly, like a pig snuffling in mud. No one had ever seen his eyes, as he always wore the same pitch-black, wraparound sunglasses. His false teeth rattled in his mouth whenever he spoke, causing him to whistle involuntarily. School legend had it that they had once fallen out of his mouth into a bap.

Burt's burger van didn't offer much of a menu:

BURGER IN A BAP 79P
BURGER ONLY 49P
BAP ONLY 39P

And there were no restaurant stars awarded as yet. The food was just about edible if you were absolutely starving. You had to pay an extra 5p for a squirt of ketchup, though it didn't look or taste much like ketchup; it was brown and had little black bits in it. If you complained, Burt would shrug and mutter breathlessly, "It's my own special recipe, my dears."

To Zoe's horror, Tina Trotts was already there, right at the front of the queue. If she hadn't been bunking off her lesson anyway, she would surely have intimidated her way to the front.

Spotting her, Zoe put her head down even

further, so that all she could see was the tarmac. But her head wasn't far enough down to go unrecognised.

"RAT-GIRL!" shouted Tina. Zoe popped her head up to see the long line of kids all looking at her. Some of her classmates were now in the queue as well, and all started pointing and laughing.

Soon it seemed like the whole of the school was laughing at her.

"HA HA HA HA HA HA HA HA HA HA HA HA HA HA HA HA HA HA HA HA HA HA HA HA HA HA HA HA HA HA HA HA HA HA HA HA HA HA !!!!!!!!! !! !! !! !!!!!!!!!!!!!!!!!!!!!!!!!!!"

Never had laughter sounded so cold. Zoe looked up for a moment. Hundreds of little eyes stared at her, but it was the figure of Burt, hunched over in his van, whose face she was drawn to. His nose was twitching, and a large gloop of slobbering saliva fell from the corner of his mouth into Tina's bap...

Zoe couldn't go home.

Her stepmother would be at the flat watching daytime TV, smoking fags and stuffing her face with prawn cocktail crisps. If Zoe told her why she had been suspended, there was no way she would be able to keep Armitage. Most likely Sheila would instantly exterminate him. With her big heavy foot. Zoe would have to peel him off the sole of her stepmother's furry pink slipper.

Quickly, Zoe considered her options:

1) Go on the run with Armitage and hold up banks like Bonnie & Clyde and go out in a blaze of glory.

2) Both have plastic surgery and then go and live in South America where no one would know them.

3) Tell her dad and stepmother that it was 'Adopt-a-Rodent' week at school and there was absolutely nothing to worry about.

4) Claim that Armitage was not a real rat but an animatronics one that she had made in Science class.

5) Say that she was training the rodent for some top-secret spy work for the Intelligence Service.

6) Give Armitage a white hat and paint him blue and pretend he was a toy Smurf.

7) Make two hot air balloons out of her stepmother's gigantic bra, one large and one small, and fly off the roof to another county.

8) Hijack a mobility scooter and speed off to safety.

9) Invent and build a dematerialisation machine and beam herself and Armitage to safety[5].

10) Just go to Raj's shop and have some sweets...

Unsurprisingly, Zoe chose the last option.

"Aah, Miss Zoe!" proclaimed Raj, as she opened the door to his shop. The bell rang as she entered.

TING.

"Shouldn't you still be in school, Miss Zoe?"

---

[5] *This may have been a teeny bit too complicated to achieve.*

Raj asked.

"Yes, I should," muttered Zoe, downcast. She felt as if she was about to burst into tears.

Raj rushed out from behind his counter and gave the little ginger girl a hug.

"What's the matter, young lady?" he asked, pressing her head to his big comfy belly. It was so long since anyone had given Zoe a hug. Unfortunately though, her braces got caught on his woollen cardigan, and for a moment she was stuck to him.

"Oh dear," said Raj. "Let me just detangle myself." He gently prised his cardigan from out of the metal.

"Sorry, Raj."

"No problem, Miss Zoe. Now, tell me," he began again, "what on earth has happened?"

Zoe took a deep breath and then told him. "I have been suspended."

"No?! You are such a well-behaved child. I don't believe it!"

"It's true."

"Whatever for?"

Zoe thought it might be easier to show him, so she reached into her breast pocket, and pulled out her rat.

" Aaaaaaaaaarrrrrrrrrrr
rrggggggggggggggg

gggghhhhhhhhhhhh hhhhhhhh!!" screamed Raj.

He scuttled away and clambered up on top of the counter. There he stood for quite a while screaming.

"Aaaaaaaarrrrrrrrrr rggggggggggggggg ggghhhh!!

"Aaaaaaaaarrrrrrrrrr rrgggggggggghhh!!

"I don't like mice, Miss Zoe. Please please please, Miss Zoe. Please. I beg you. Put it away."

"Don't worry, Raj, it's not a mouse."

"No?"

"No, it's a rat."

Then Raj's eyes bulged and he let out a deafening scream.

"AAAAAAAAAA
AAAAAAAAAAAAAAAAAAAA
AAAAAAAAAAAA
AAAAAAAAAAAAAAAAAAAA
AAAAAAAAAAAA
AAAAAAAAAAAAAAARRRR
RRRRRRRRRRRRRR
RRRRRRRRRRRRRR
RRRRRRRRRRRRRR
RRRRRRRRRRRRRR
RRRRRRRRRRRRRRRRRR
RRRRRRRRRRRRRRRRRRRR
RRRRRRRRRRRRRRRR
RRRRRRRRRRRRRRRRRRRR
RRRRRRRRRRRRRRRRRRRR
RRGGGGGGGGGGGGGGGGGG
GGGGGGGGGGGG
GGGGGGGGGGGGGG
GGGGGGGGGGGGGGGGGG

GGGGGGGGGGG
GGGGGGGGGGGGGG
GGGGGGGGGGGGGGGGGGG
GGGGGGGGGGGG
GGGGGGGGGGGGGGGGGG
HHHHHHHHHHHH
H H H H H H H H H H H H H
HHHHHHHHHHHH
H H H H H H H H H H H H H
HHHHHHHHHHHH
H H H H H H H H H H H H H
HHHHHHHHHHHH
HHHHHHHHHHHH!!!!!!!!!!!!!!!!!!!!!!!!!!
!!
!!!!!!!!!!!!!!!!!!!!!!!!!!!!!!!!!!!!
!!!!!!!!!!!!!!!!!!!!!!!!!!!!!!!!!!!!!
!!!!!!!!!!!!!!!!!!!!!!!!!!!!!!!!!!!"

14

A Bogie on the Ceiling

"No, no, please," pleaded the newsagent. "I don't like it! I don't like it!"

TING!

An old lady entered the shop, and looked up bemused at the newsagent perched on top of his counter. Raj was clutching his trouser legs, what little hair he had on his head standing on end, and he was trampling all the newspapers in terror with his big clumsy feet.

"Ah, hello, Mrs Bennett," said Raj, his voice shaking. "Your *Knitting Weekly* is on the shelf, you can pay me next time."

"What on earth are you doing up there?" enquired the old lady, quite reasonably.

Raj looked over at Zoe. Surreptitiously, she put her finger to her mouth, imploring him not to tell. She didn't want everyone to know she had a rat, or soon the news would spread to the estate and her dreaded stepmother. Unfortunately, though, Raj was not a natural liar.

"Erm, um, well…"

"I just bought some Spacedust," said Zoe, stepping in. "You know, the popping sweets? It had been left out in the sun and became highly explosive and when I opened the bag it sprayed all over the shop."

"Yes, yes, Miss Zoe," chimed in Raj. "A most regrettable incident because it's only been fifteen years since I had the shop repainted. I am just trying to pick the Spacedust off the ceiling."

Raj came across a particularly ingrained piece of dirt on the ceiling and scratched at it. "Spacedust everywhere, Mrs Bennett. Please pay me next week..."

The old lady shot him an unconvinced look and peered up at the ceiling. "That's not Spacedust, that's just a piece of snot."

"No, no, no, Mrs Bennett, that's where you are wrong. Look..."

Reluctantly Raj used his fingernail to prise away the bogie he had long since sneezed up there and popped it in his mouth.

"Pop!" he added unconvincingly. "Oh, I love Spacedust!"

Mrs Bennett looked at the newsagent as if he was quite mad. "It looked more like a big piece of snot to me," she muttered before leaving the shop.

TING.

Raj quickly spat out the ancient bogie.

"Look, the little thing is not going to hurt you," said Zoe. She gently took him out of her pocket. Cautiously Raj clambered down, and slowly approached his worst nightmare.

"He's only a baby," said Zoe encouragingly.

Soon Raj was at eye level with the rodent.

"Ooh, well, he is a particularly pretty one. Look at his dinky little nose," said Raj with a sweet smile. "What's his name?"

"Armitage," answered Zoe confidently.

"Why is he called that?" asked Raj.

Zoe was embarrassed she had named her pet after a make of toilet and simply said, "Oh, it's a long story. Give him a stroke."

"No!"

"He won't hurt you."

"If you are sure…"

"I promise."

"Come here, little Armitage," whispered the newsagent.

The rat squirmed closer to Raj to be stroked by this frightened-looking man.

"AAAAAAHHHHH! HE MADE A LUNGE AT ME!" shouted Raj, and with that he ran out of the shop waving his arms in the air…

TING.

Zoe followed him out, and saw he was halfway down the street, running so fast he would give the Olympic-gold-winning sprinters a run for their money.

"COME BACK!" she shouted.

Raj stopped and turned round, and reluctantly plodded back past the row of shops to his one. When he finally tiptoed the last few paces towards the girl and her pet, Zoe said, "He was just trying to say hello."

"No, no, no, sorry, but he got quite close."

"Don't be a baby, Raj."

"I know, sorry. He's lovely really."

Raj took a deep breath, and reached out to give Armitage the gentlest little stroke. "It's nippy out. Let's take him inside."

TING.

"What am I going to do with him, Raj? My stepmother won't let me keep him at home, especially as the little fella got me suspended from school. That woman hated my hamster,

146

she is never in a million years going to let me keep a rat."

Raj thought for a moment. To aid concentration he popped an extra strong mint in his mouth.

"Maybe you should set him free," said the newsagent finally.

"Free?" said Zoe, a single tear welling in her eye.

"Yes. Rats are not meant to be pets…"

"But this little one is so cute…"

"Perhaps, but he is going to grow. He can't spend his whole life in your blazer pocket."

"But I love him, Raj, I really do."

"No doubt, Miss Zoe," said Raj, crunching on his extra strong mint. "And if you love him, you should set him free."

15

Ten-Tonne Truck

So this was goodbye. Zoe knew deep down she would never be able to keep Armitage for long. There were a hundred reasons, but the most important one was:

HE WAS A RAT.

Children don't have rats as pets. They have cats and dogs and hamsters and gerbils and guinea pigs and mice and rabbits and terrapins and tortoises, posh ones even sometimes have ponies, but never rats. Rats live in sewers, not in little girls' bedrooms.

Zoe trudged miserably out of Raj's shop.

The newsagent may sometimes try and sell his customers a half-eaten chocolate bar, or put a partially sucked toffee bonbon back in the sweet jar, but all the local kids knew that when it came to advice he was the best.

And that meant she had to say goodbye to Armitage.

So Zoe took the long way back to her flats, through the park. She thought this would be the perfect place to set little Armitage free. There would be crusts of bread left out for the ducks for him to eat, a pond for him to drink from and maybe even take the occasional bath in, and perhaps there was a squirrel or two whom he could befriend, or at least one day be on nodding terms with.

The little girl carried the little rat in her hand for the last part of the journey. As it was the middle of the afternoon, the park was all but empty save for a few old ladies being walked by their dogs. Armitage wrapped his tail around her thumb. It was almost as if he sensed something was amiss, and he clung on to her little fingers as tightly as he could.

Trudging along as slowly as possible, Zoe eventually reached the middle of the park. She stopped a good distance from the yapping dogs and hissing swans and barking park-keeper. Slowly she crouched down to the ground and unclosed her hand. Armitage didn't move. It was as if he didn't want to be parted from his new friend. He cuddled up to her hand, breaking Zoe's heart as he did it.

Zoe shook her hand a little, but this only made him grip tighter with his tail and toes. Fighting back tears she picked the rat up gently by the fur on the back of his neck and placed him carefully on the grass. Once again Armitage didn't move.

Instead he just looked up at her longingly. Zoe knelt down and kissed him gently on his little pink nose.

"Goodbye, little fellow," she whispered. "I am going to miss you."

A tear dropped from her eye. It landed on Armitage's whiskers and his tiny pink tongue slipped out to catch it.

The little rat tilted his little head to one side, as if trying to understand her, which just made it harder for Zoe.

In fact, saying goodbye was so unbearably sad, she just couldn't take it any more. Zoe took a big breath and stood up, and promised herself she would not look back. That promise lasted only a dozen steps, as she couldn't help stealing a glance one last time to the spot where she left him. To Zoe's surprise, Armitage was already gone.

He must have already scampered off to the safety of the bushes, she thought. She scoured the nearby grass for signs of movement, but it was tall and he was short, and apart from a light breeze blowing the tips, the grass didn't move. Zoe turned round and reluctantly headed home.

Leaving the park, she crossed the road. For a moment it was free of the hum of cars, and in the silence, Zoe thought she heard a tiny 'eek'. She spun round, and in the middle of the road was Armitage.

He had been following her all along.

"Armitage!" she exclaimed excitedly. He didn't want to be free; he wanted to be with her! She was so glad. She had been imagining all kinds of awful scenarios from the moment she left him behind – like Armitage being gobbled up by a vicious swan, or wandering into the road and being hit by a ten-tonne truck.

At that moment something came thundering along the road towards Armitage, who was still scampering slowly across to join Zoe.

It was... a ten-tonne truck.

Zoe stood frozen, watching the truck speeding closer and closer towards Armitage. The driver would never spot a baby rat in the road, and Armitage would be flattened, and be nothing more than a splat on the tarmac...

"**NNNNNNNNNOOO OOOOOOOOOOOOOOO OO!!!!**" cried Zoe, but the truck thundered on. There was nothing she could do.

Armitage looked in the direction of the truck and, realising he was in trouble, started scampering back and forth across the road. The little rat was in a terrible panic. But if Zoe ran into the road she would be flattened too!

It was too late. The truck roared over him

and Zoe covered her eyes with her hands.

RRRRrrrrrrrrr RRUUUUUUUUUUUU UUUUUUMMммммм MMMMMMMMMB BBBBBBBBBBB BBBBBBBBBLL LLLLLLLLLL LLLLLLEEEE EEEEEEEE!!!!!! !!!!!!!!!!!!!!!!!!!!!!

Only when she could hear the truck's engine fading into the distance did Zoe dare open her eyes again.

She looked for the splat on the road.

But it wasn't there.

What was there... was Armitage! A little

shaken perhaps, but alive. The lorry's giant tyres must have just missed him.

Looking right and left and right again to check there were no cars, Zoe ran into the road and scooped him up.

"I am not letting go of you, ever," said Zoe, as she held him close. Armitage let out a little loving 'eek'…

16

The Blackberry Bush

Nature finds a way to create life everywhere. In a smelly alleyway that connected the road to Zoe's estate, among all the crisp wrappers and empty beer cans, stood a proud little blackberry bush. Zoe loved the blackberries – they were like free sweets. She was pretty sure Armitage would like them too. She picked a large one for herself, and a little one for her furry friend.

Carefully, she placed the baby rat on to the wall. As Armitage watched, Zoe put the blackberry into her mouth and started chewing enthusiastically and making appreciative noises.

Then she took the smaller blackberry between her thumb and forefinger and held it out towards him. Armitage must have been hungry because slowly he stood up on his hind legs to greet it.

Zoe was delighted. The rat took the blackberry between his front paws and nibbled it greedily. It was gone in seconds. Soon he was looking longingly up at Zoe for another one. She picked another off the bush and held it up just above his nose. Without hesitation, Armitage stood up on his hind legs again. Zoe moved the blackberry around, and he followed it around on his back legs. It was as if he was doing a little dance.

"What a talented fellow you are!" said Zoe, as she gave him the blackberry. Once again he ate it greedily, and Zoe stroked the back of his neck. "Good boy!"

Inside, she was buzzing with excitement. Armitage could be trained! Better still, it was like he *wanted* to be. He'd got the idea of standing up even quicker than Gingernut had…

Soon Zoe was plucking as many blackberries as she could off the bush. Just as she had with her hamster, she began teaching Armitage some tricks. There was:

The walk.   The jump.

The hop on one leg.   The wave.

The dance.

Soon the bush was bare, and Armitage looked rather stuffed and tired. Zoe knew it was time to stop. She whisked him up in her arms and gave him a kiss on his nose.

"You are amazing, Armitage. That's what I will call you when we perform together on stage. The Amazing Armitage!"

Zoe skipped down the alleyway. Her heart was dancing, as were her feet.

It was only when Zoe reached her estate that the spring in her step vanished. Not only would she have to tell her stepmother that she was suspended, she'd have to come up with some explanation as to why.

The whole episode would give her stepmother a reason to make Zoe's life even more of a living hell. And what was a million times worse, a reason to end the little rat's life. A life that had only just begun.

As Zoe approached the great leaning tower block, she noticed something peculiar. Burt's burger van was parked right outside her towering block of flats. In the many years she had lived there since her mother died, she had never ever seen the van there before. It was only *ever* parked outside her school.

What on earth is that doing there? she thought.

Even from a distance, the smell of fried meat was stomach-churning. However hungry Zoe was, she had never bought a burger from Burt's van. The stench alone was enough to make her want to projectile-vomit. The ketchup was decidedly iffy too. Passing the van, she noticed how disgustingly grimy it was – even the dirt was dirty. Zoe ran her index finger along the chassis, and a splodge of sludge an inch thick came off in her hand.

Perhaps Burt has just moved into the block

of flats, she thought. She hoped not though, as he was seriously creepy. Burt was the sort of man your nightmares had nightmares about.

The tiny flat was high up on the 37th floor, but the lift always stank. You had to hold your breath in there, which wasn't easy over thirty-seven floors. So Zoe would always take the stairs. Armitage was safely lying in her blazer pocket, and she could feel the weight of his tiny body bounce against her heart with every step. Her breathing grew louder and louder as she ascended the building. The stairs were littered with all kinds of rubbish, from cigarette butts to empty bottles. The steps stank too, but not as much as the lift, and of course you weren't so closed in.

As usual, by the time Zoe reached the 37th floor, she was completely breathless and panting like a dog. Zoe stood outside the front door for a moment, pausing to catch her breath before she put her key in the lock. The headmaster Mr Grave would no doubt have called her parents to tell them their daughter had been suspended. Within seconds, Zoe was sure to let loose her stepmother's fury, a fury no doubt more rabid even than the hounds of hell.

Zoe silently twisted the key, and reluctantly pushed the rotting door open. Even though her stepmother rarely went out, the TV was off and Zoe couldn't hear anyone in the house, so she tiptoed across the hall to her bedroom, being careful to avoid the squeakiest floorboards. She turned the door handle to her room and stepped inside.

A strange man was standing in her bedroom facing the window.

"Aaaaaahhhhhh!!!!!!!!" Zoe screamed, startled.

Then the man turned round.

It was Burt.

17

"I Smell a Rat!"

"I smell a rat!" wheezed Burt.

Except it wasn't Burt. Well, it *was* Burt, but he had drawn a moustache on his face very poorly with a marker pen.

"What on earth are *you* doing here?" said Zoe. "And why have you got a moustache drawn on your face?"

"It is a real moustache, my dear," said Burt. He breathed heavily when he spoke. His voice matched his face: they had both stepped out of a horror film.

"No, it's not. You've drawn it on."

"No, I haven't."

"Yes, you have, Burt."

"My name is not Burt, child. I am Burt's twin brother."

"What's your name then?"

Burt thought for a moment. "Burt."

"Your mum had twins and called them both 'Burt'?"

"We were very poor and we couldn't afford a name each."

"Just get out of my room, you creep!"

All of a sudden Zoe heard her stepmother pound along the corridor. "Don't ya dare speak to the nice pest control man like dat!" she screeched, as she waddled into the room.

"He's not the pest control man. He sells burgers!" protested Zoe.

Burt stood between them with a smirk on his face. It was impossible to see what his eyes were doing because his wraparound sunglasses were black as the deepest, darkest oil.

"Wot are ya talkin' about, ya stupid girl? He catches rats," shouted Zoe's stepmother. "Don't ya?"

Burt nodded silently and smiled, flashing his ill-fitting false teeth.

The little girl grabbed her stepmother by her thick tattooed forearm, and led her to the window.

"Look at his van!" she declared. "Tell me

what's written on the side!"

Sheila looked out of the grimy window, to the vehicles parked down below. "Burt's Pest Control," she read.

"What?" said Zoe.

She wiped some of the smudges off the window, and peered out. The woman was right. It did say that. How was it possible? It looked like the same van. Zoe looked over at Burt. His smirk had widened. As she watched, he took a dirty little brown paper bag out of his pocket, and picked something out of it. Zoe could have sworn whatever he put in his mouth was moving. Could it have been a cockroach? Was that this depraved man's idea of a snack?!

"See?" said Burt. "I'm a rat catcher."

"Whatever," said Zoe. She turned to her stepmother. "Even if he is, which he isn't because he's a burger-van man, why is he in my *bedroom*?" she demanded.

"He is 'ere coz he 'eard at school dat ya brought a rat into ya lessons," replied her stepmother.

"It's a lie!" said Zoe, lying.

"Den why did I get a call from your 'eadmaster today? Eh? EH? ANSWER ME! 'E told me everyfink. Ya disgusting little girl."

"I don't want any trouble, my dear," said Burt. "Just hand the little creature over." He held out his grubby and gnarled hand. Burt had a dirty old cage on the floor by his feet that looked like it was made from a metal basket from a deep-fat fryer. Only instead of using it to fry chips, he had squashed hundreds and hundreds of rats into it.

At first glance, Zoe thought the rats were dead, as they weren't moving. On closer inspection, she realised they were alive, it was just they were packed in so tight they could hardly move. Many looked like they could hardly breathe either, they were all so squashed in together. It was a sickening sight, and Zoe wanted to cry at the shocking cruelty of it.

Just then Zoe felt Armitage wriggling in her breast pocket. Perhaps he could smell fear. The little girl discreetly brought her hand up to her breast to hide the wriggles. Her mind was racing with potential lies, before she arrived at one.

"I set him free," she said. "The headmaster is right, I did bring a rat into school, but I set him free in the park. Just ask Raj – he told me to do it. You should go and look for the rat in the park," she added, suddenly cupping Armitage through her blazer pocket, as the little rodent was squirming like crazy now.

There was a deathly pause. Then Burt sneered, "You are lying, my dear."

"I'm not!" said Zoe, a little too quickly.

"Don't lie to the nice man," bellowed Sheila. "We can't 'ave another filthy disease-ridden creature runnin' around the flat."

"I'm not lying," protested Zoe.

"I can smell it," said the vile man, his vile nose twitching. "I can smell a rat from miles away."

Burt sniffed the air, then wheezed. "Baby ones smell especially sweet..." He licked his lips, and Zoe shuddered.

"There's no rat here," said Zoe.

"Hand it over," said Burt. "Then I give it a quick whack with this special high-tech rodent stunner." He produced a bloody mallet from his back pocket. "It's painless really, they don't feel a thing. Then he can join his friends for a nice play in here." Burt indicated the cage, by kicking it hard with the heel of his dirty boot.

Zoe was horrified, but composed herself before she spoke. "You are quite wrong, I am afraid. There is no rat here. If it comes back we will of course call you immediately. Thank you."

"Hand it over. Now," wheezed the sinister man.

Meanwhile, Sheila was studying the step-daughter she loathed intently, and noticed the awkward positioning of her left hand.

"Ya vile creature!" accused the woman, as she yanked her stepdaughter's hand away. "It's in her blazer."

"Madam, you hold her down," directed Burt. "I can whack the rat through the cloth. There will be less blood on the carpet that way."

"Noooooooooooooooo!" screamed Zoe. She tried to wrestle her arm away from her stepmother, but the woman was a lot bigger and stronger than her stepdaughter. The little girl lost her balance and crashed to the floor. Armitage wriggled out of her pocket and started scurrying across the carpet.

"Aaaaaaaaaaaaaaaaaaaa aaahhhhhhhhhhhhhhh hhhhhhhh!!!!!!!!!!!!!!! !!!!" screamed her stepmother. "Get it away from me!"

"Trust me, he won't feel a thing," wheezed Burt, as he got down on his hands and knees, brandishing the bloody mallet. His nose twitched as he chased the rat around the room, whacking the implement on to the floor, missing Armitage by millimetres.

"Stop!" screamed Zoe. "You'll kill him!"

She tried to make a charge at the man, but her stepmother held her back by her arms.

"Come here, you little beauty!" whispered Burt, as he brought the mallet crashing down repeatedly on to the dusty carpet, plumes of ingrained dirt now exploding into the air with every thwack.

Armitage scurried this way and that, trying desperately to avoid being whacked. The mallet walloped down, just catching his tail.

"Eeeeeeekkkkkkkk!" squealed the rat in pain, and he dashed off to hide under Zoe's bed. This did not deter Burt, who, without taking off his dark glasses, got down on to his belly and slithered under the bed like a snake, flailing his mallet wildly from side to side.

Zoe writhed out of her stepmother's grasp and launched herself on to the man's back as soon as he appeared from under the bed. The little girl had never hit anyone before, and now she had leaped astride his back like a cowboy on a bull at an American rodeo, thumping his shoulders with all her might.

Within seconds her stepmother yanked her off by her hair and pinned her against the wall, before Burt disappeared under the bed again.

"Zoe, no! You're an animal. Ya 'ear me? An animal!" screamed the woman. Zoe had never seen her stepmother so uncontrollably angry.

Muffled under the bed, Zoe could hear thud

after thud of the mallet crashing down on the carpet. Tears were streaming down the girl's face. She couldn't believe her beloved little friend was going to meet such a violent end.

THWACK!

And then there was silence. Burt wriggled out from under the bed. Exhausted, he sat on the floor. In one hand he held the bloody mallet. Between the fingers of his other hand he held a lifeless Armitage, dangling by his tail, before announcing triumphantly…

"Gotcha!"

18

"Pulverisation"

"Prawn cocktail crisp?" offered Sheila to the man.

"Mmm, don't mind if I do," Burt replied.

"Just one."

"Sorry."

"So, er, wot 'appens to all these rats?" continued Sheila in her poshest voice as she showed Burt to the door. Zoe was sitting crying on her bed. Her stepmother was so appalled by Zoe's behaviour she had locked her in her room. As much as Zoe rattled the handle and banged on the door, it wouldn't move. The little girl was utterly broken. There was nothing to do but weep. She listened to her stepmother show the repulsive man out.

"Well I tell the kiddies…" replied Burt in a tone that was meant to be reassuring but actually sounded disturbing, "…that they all go to a special hotel for rats."

Sheila laughed. "And they believe ya?"

"Yes, the little fools think they all get to frolic outdoors in the sunshine, before relaxing in a spa area, having massages and facials and the like!"

"But really…?" whispered Sheila.

"I pulverise them! In my special pulverisation machine!"

Sheila let out a gurgling laugh. "Is it painful?"

"Very!"

"Ha ha! Good. Do ya stamp on 'em?"

"No."

"Oh, I would stamp on 'em and then pulverise them. Then they would suffer twice as much!"

"I must try that, Mrs…?"

"Oh, just call me Sheila. Another prawn cocktail crisp?"

"Ooh, yes please."

"Just one."

"Sorry. Such a delicate flavour," mused Burt.

"Exactly like a real prawn cocktail, I dunno how they do it."

"Have you ever had a real prawn cocktail?"

"Nah," replied the woman. "But I don't need to. They taste just the same as the crisps."

"But of course. Madam, if you don't mind me saying, you are an extremely beautiful woman. I would love to take you out for dinner tonight."

"Oh, ya naughty man!" flirted Zoe's stepmother.

"Then I can treat you to one of my very special burgers."

"Ooh, yeah please!" The horrific woman added another sickeningly girly little laugh at the end. Zoe couldn't believe her stepmother was actually flirting so outrageously with this loathsome individual.

"Just me, you and all the burgers we can stuff down our gobs…" mused Burt.

"How romantic…" whispered Sheila.

"Until later, my Princess…"

Zoe heard the door close, and her stepmother thunder back along the corridor to her daughter's bedroom, before unlocking the door.

"You're in so much trouble, young lady!" said Sheila. She must have kissed Burt goodbye because she now had black marker pen above her lip.

"I don't care!" said Zoe. "All I care about is Armitage. I have to save him."

"Who's Armitage?!"

"He's the rat."

"Why would ya call a rat that?" asked the woman, incredulous.

"It's a long story."

"Well it's a completely stupid name for a rat."

"What would you call him?"

Sheila thought for a long while.

"Well?" asked Zoe.

"I'm finkin'."

A long silence followed during which Sheila looked like she was concentrating very hard. Finally she said, "Ratty!"

"A bit unoriginal," muttered Zoe.

That made her stepmother even more furious.

"You're evil. Ya know that, young lady. Evil! I've got a good mind to throw ya out on to the street! How could ya attack dat lovely man?"

"Lovely?! The man is a rat murderer!"

"No, no, no. They all go to a special rat sanctuary and have spa treatments…"

"Do you think I am completely stupid? He kills them."

"He doesn't stamp on 'em though. They are just pulverised. Shame, really."

"That's monstrous!"

"Who cares? One less rat."

"No. I have to save my little Armitage. I have to—"

Zoe stood up and headed for the door. Her stepmother pressed her firmly back down on to the bed with her considerable weight.

"You're not goin' anywhere," said the woman. "Yer grounded. Ya hear me? G-R-O-N-D-E-D! Grounded!"

"There's a 'U' in grounded," said Zoe.

"No dere isn't!" Sheila was really angry now. "Ya aint leaving dis room until I say so. Ya can sit in 'ere, fink about what ya 'ave done. And rot!"

"Wait until my dad gets home!"

"What's dat useless git gonna do?"

Zoe's eyes stung. Dad might have fallen on hard times, but he was still her father. "Don't you dare talk about him like that!"

"All he's good for is benefit money and a roof over me 'ead."

"I'll tell him you said that."

"He knows it already. I tell 'im every night," snorted the gruesome lady, with a guttural laugh.

"He loves me. He won't let you treat me like this!" protested Zoe.

"If 'e loves ya so much, why does he spend his whole life down de boozer?"

Zoe fell silent. She didn't have an answer to that. The words broke her heart into millions of tiny pieces.

"Ha!" said the woman. With that Sheila slammed the door shut and locked it behind her.

Zoe rushed to the window and peered down at the road. She had a pretty good view of it, what with being thirty-seven floors up in the crumbling tower block. In the distance, she could see Burt speeding off in his van. He wasn't much of a driver: she watched as he knocked off a few car wing mirrors and nearly ran over an old lady, before the van zoomed off out of view.

Outside, the sky grew dark, but the thousands of streetlights in the town lit up the outside world. They bathed her room in an ugly orange glow that could never be turned off.

Late into the evening, Dad finally returned from the pub. There was shouting between him and Sheila as there always was, and the slamming of doors. Dad never came into Zoe's bedroom to see her; most likely he had fallen asleep on the sofa before he had the chance.

Night came and went without sleep for Zoe. Her head was spinning and her heart was aching. In the morning she heard her dad go out, presumably to wait for the pub to open, and her stepmother turn on the TV. Zoe banged and banged on the door, but her stepmother would not let her out.

I am a prisoner, thought Zoe. She lay back down on her bed in despair, thirsty, hungry and desperately needing a wee.

Now what do prisoners do? she said to herself. *They try to escape…!*

19

The Great Escape

Armitage was in terrible danger. Zoe needed to save him. And fast.

She remembered that Burt parked his filthy burger van outside her school every day, so if she could just break out of her room she could follow him. Then she could find where he imprisoned all the rats before they were 'pulverised'.

Zoe pondered all the different ways in which she might try to escape:

1. She could tie all her bed sheets together, then try and abseil to safety.

Though, as she lived on the 37th floor, she wasn't sure the sheets would get her much further down than the 24th. Chance of death – high.

2. There was always the birdman option. Make some kind of glider from coat-hangers and knickers and fly down to freedom. Chance of death – high; and more importantly Zoe didn't have enough pairs of clean knickers.

3. Dig. Tunnels had been a favourite method of escape for soldiers in prisoner of war camps. Chance of death – low.

The problem with number three was that below Zoe's room was the flat of a moany old lady who, despite having the yappiest dogs herself, always went on and on about the noise from above. She would turn Zoe in to her stepmother in no time.

I could always tunnel sideways! thought Zoe.

She unstuck a poster of the latest boy band, and gently tapped the wall behind it with her fingernails. The tapping echoed into the next flat, which meant the wall must be thin. Over the years she had heard a great deal of shouting coming from next door, but it was too muffled to deduce what kind of people lived there – a girl and her parents, Zoe thought, but maybe others too. Whoever they were though, their lives sounded every bit as miserable as Zoe's, if not more so.

The plan itself was simple. The poster could be replaced at any time to hide what was going on. All she needed now was something to tunnel through the wall with. Something metal and sharp. *A key*, she thought, and ran excitedly to the door, only to remember that the key was on the other side. That was the whole reason she had to escape!

Duh! she said to herself.

Zoe rummaged through her belongings, but her ruler, her comb, her pen and her hangers were all made of plastic. Anything plastic would snap instantly if she tried to hollow out a wall with it.

Zoe caught sight of herself in the mirror and realised the answer was staring her in the face. Her braces. The blasted things would at last be of some use[6]. Zoe pulled them out with her fingers, and dashed to the wall. Without even pausing to wipe the spit off them she scratched at the wall. No wonder the braces were painful and rubbed against her gums, and got stuck in Raj's cardigan – the metal was sharp! Quickly the plaster from the wall was flaking on to the

---

[6] *Other than straightening teeth, of course. (I have to write that, as otherwise any orthodontists reading might make a complaint, even though they are all nothing more than blood-thirsty torturers.)*

floor. Soon Zoe had scratched through the plaster to the bricks behind it, and the braces became thick with all the paint and plaster and dust from the wall.

Suddenly Zoe heard the key in the lock turn in her bedroom door and she leaped up and stuck the poster back on the wall. Just in time, she remembered to shove her braces back in her mouth, though there wasn't time to wipe them first.

Sheila looked at her stepdaughter suspiciously. She looked like she knew Zoe was up to something, but she didn't know what. Yet.

"Do ya want some grub? I suppose I betta feed ya," said the vile woman. "If ya starve to death I'll have social services all over me like a bleedin' rash." Sheila's beady little eyes circled the room. Something was definitely different. She just couldn't quite put her chubby finger on it.

Zoe shook her head. She didn't dare speak with her mouth full of dust. In truth she was starving, but she had to get on with her escape plan, and didn't want any more interruptions.

"Ya must need to use the bog?" said the big lady.

Zoe spotted her stepmother's gaze searching the room. The little girl shook her head again. She thought she was going to choke, the dust now seeping right down the back of her throat. In truth she was bursting and she kept on having to cross her legs, but if she went to the loo and her stepmother searched her room she might just find the beginnings of the tunnel.

"'Ave ya got ya braces in?"

Zoe nodded vigorously, and then attempted a closed-mouth smile.

"Show me," pressed her stepmother.

Zoe slowly opened her mouth a little bit, to show a little bit of metal.

"I can't see. Wider!"

Reluctantly the girl opened her mouth, displaying the braces caked in dust. The woman peered to have a closer look.

"Ya need to clean your teef, they're disgustin'. Nasty creature you are."

Zoe closed her mouth and nodded in agreement. Sheila looked at her stepdaughter one last time and shook her head in revulsion, before turning to leave.

Zoe smiled. She had got away with it. For now.

She waited to hear the key turn in the door, and then turned towards the wall. Her boy-band poster was upside down! She prayed the one with the back to front hair would never find out she had put the poster upside down – he was Zoe's favourite and they were going to get married. He just didn't know it yet.

And on a slightly more urgent note: thank goodness her stepmother had missed the fact that the poster was no longer the right way up. Zoe spat out her braces and wiped her dry-as-a-desert tongue on her sleeve to try and remove the dust, then went back to work.

All through the night she scratched and scratched through the wall until finally she broke through. Her braces were now a misshapen mess, and she tossed them aside. So happy to be nearly there, Zoe excitedly let her fingers take over now. Scratching away to make the hole bigger, crumbling bits of plaster off in her hands as fast as she possibly could.

Zoe wiped her eyes and peered through the hole. She had no idea what would be on the other side. Taking a closer look she realised she could see a face.

A face she knew.

It was Tina Trotts.

20

Tug of War

Of course, Zoe had always known that the bully lived somewhere in her block of flats. Her gang permanently occupied the adventure playground. What's more, every day Tina spat on Zoe's head from a stairwell, but Zoe had no idea the horrible girl lived this close!

Then Zoe had a thought that made her feel confused: this meant it was Tina's family who shouted at each other and slammed doors more than even her own. It was Tina who got screamed at by her dad. And whom Zoe had felt sorry for, as she lay trying to get to sleep at night.

Zoe shook her head, to get rid of this strange new sensation of feeling *sorry* for Tina Trotts. Then she reminded herself of another sensation – flob on her face – and she stopped.

It was now mid-morning. Zoe had been scratching away at the wall all through the night. On the other side of the hole was Tina's big ugly face, snoring. She was lying on her bed, which, as if in a mirror image, was placed in exactly the same place as Zoe's was in her room. The room was bare of possessions though; it looked more like a prison cell than a girl's bedroom.

Tina was wrapped up in her grubby duvet. For a young girl she snored like a camel, loud and low, and her lips wobbled when she exhaled.

If you have ever wondered what a snoring camel sounds like, it goes something like this:

ZZZZZZZZZZZZZZZ
zzzzZZZZzzzzZzzzzzzzzzzz!

HH**HHHH**MM
MMMMMMMPPPP
PPPPPPPPPHHH
HHHHHHHHHHHH!
ZZZZZZZZZZZZZ
ZZZ**ZZZ**ZzzZZZ
zzzz**ZZZZ**zzz**ZZZ**
ZZZzzzzzz!

It was a school day and Tina should be in lessons by now, but Zoe knew that most days she bunked off and when she didn't, she came and went as she pleased.

Now Zoe was face to face with her worst enemy. Yet there was no turning back. Everything in Zoe's room was covered in a thick dust as a result of her excavations. As soon as her stepmother unlocked the door to come in to check up on her, it would be game over, and she would never ever see Armitage again…

Right now, though, Tina's big scary face was right on the other side of the hole. Zoe peered at the bully's surprisingly thick nostril hair wondering what on earth to do next.

Suddenly Zoe thought of a plan. If only she could grab a corner of Tina's duvet, she could tug it sharply through the hole. Then, as Tina rolled on to the floor, Zoe could climb through the hole, jump over her, and bolt out through Tina's flat to safety.

It now occurred to her that she should revise the chance of death for the digging plan to 'high'.

At that moment, she heard her stepmother's footsteps thundering down the corridor.

Zoe had to act, and fast. She reached her hand through the hole, took a deep breath, and tugged as hard as she could on the duvet, which was rather greasy to the touch. It was as if it had never been washed. The yank was hard enough to send Tina rolling on to the floor...

THUD
THUD
THUD!

Just as Zoe heard the key turning in her bedroom door, she clambered through the hole. Unlike a rat, though, Zoe didn't have whiskers, and even though she was an unusually small girl she had rather underestimated her size. When her body was halfway through the hole, she became completely and utterly stuck. Try as she might to wriggle, she could not move an inch. Tina had now of course woken up, and it would be an understatement to say she did not look in a good mood. She was angrier than a great white shark that had been called a rude name.

The bully rose slowly to her feet, looked at

Zoe and started pulling violently at the small girl's arms, doubtless so she could get her whole body through to her room and beat her up more thoroughly.

"I am going to get you, you little runt," she growled.

"Oh, good morning, Tina," said Zoe, her tone imploring a non-violent response to this unusual situation. Meanwhile, no doubt hearing all the commotion, Sheila had rushed into the bedroom behind her and grabbed hold of her stepdaughter's legs. The odious woman was pulling as hard as she could on them.

"Come 'ere! When I get me 'ands on ya!" screamed the big lady.

"Good morning, stepmother," called Zoe over her shoulder. Again the chirpy tone did nothing to pacify the woman holding on to her ankles.

Soon Zoe was buffeting back and forward through the hole.

"Oooh!" she cried as she was pulled one way.

"Aaah!" she cried as she was pulled the other.

Soon it was like she was singing a rather repetitive pop song.

"Oooh! Aaah! Oooh! Aaah! Oooh! Aaaah! Oooh! Aaah! Oooh! Aaaah! Oooh! Aaah!"

Backward. Forward. Backward. Forward.

Soon after that the wall started crumbling around her as she was yanked back and forth.

Tina was strong, but Zoe's stepmother had weight on her side. It was a surprisingly even tug of war, which as a result felt like it would never end. Both were pulling so hard on Zoe's limbs that as she screamed she was aware of one positive to the situation: whoever won, Zoe would at least be taller by the end of it.

She felt like a particularly prized Christmas
cracker. However, just like a Christmas cracker,
she was sure to explode. Larger bits of plaster

were now crumbling off the wall, and dropping
on to her head.

"AAAAAAAAA
AAAAAAAAAA
AAAAARRRRR
RRRRRGGG
GGGGGHH
HHHHH!!!!"

cried Zoe.

A massive crack blasted across the wall.

CCCCCCCCC
CCCCCRRRR

RRRRRRR
RRRAAAAA
AAAAACCCC
KKKKKKK!!!!!!!

All of a sudden Zoe could feel the whole wall giving way. Soon it all came crashing down to the floor in a blizzard of dust.

BBBBBBB

BBBBBBB

OOOOOOO

MMMMMMM

|||||||||||||||||||||||||||||||

•••••••••••••••••••••••••••••••

OOOOOO
OOOOOOOO
MMMMM!!!!!!!!!!
!!
❙❙

The noise was deafening, and soon all Zoe could see was white. It looked a bit like this:

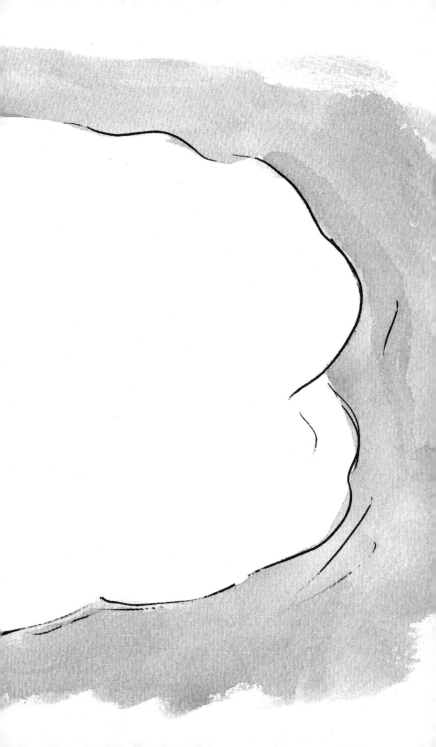

21

Sizzling Bottom

It was as if there had been an earthquake, but at least Zoe's arms and legs were now free.

Somewhere in the dust cloud in her now-shared bedroom she could hear Tina and her stepmother coughing. Zoe knew she now had a split second to make her escape, and rushed forward. Unable to see anything, she used her hands to desperately find a door handle. Zoe opened the door and hurled herself into the corridor.

Completely disorientated by the explosion of dust, it was only now she realised she was running through Tina's flat. It was even grottier than Zoe's. There was no furniture or carpet to speak of. The wallpaper was peeling off the walls and there was a smell of damp everywhere. It was as if they were living like squatters in their own flat.

However, this was no time for a makeover, even a fifteen-minute one like on TV, and after a few moments Zoe found the front door. Her little heart beating faster than ever before, she tried desperately to unlock it. Her hands were trembling, and she was unable to turn the bolt.

Then, out of the dust cloud behind her, stumbled two monstrous ghostly figures, huge and looming, all white but with open, screaming mouths and eyes bulging out red in fury. It was like something out of a horror film.

"AAAAAAAR RRRRGGGGHH!"

screamed Zoe.

Then she realised it was Tina and her stepmother, both covered head to toe in white dust.

"AAAAAAA ARRRGGGGHH!"

screamed Zoe.

"COME 'ERE!" shouted Sheila.

"I AM GOING TO GET YOU!"

bellowed Tina.

Zoe's hands shook even more, but she just managed to open the door in time. As Zoe slid out, four chubby hands caked in white dust grabbed at her clothes, ripping strips off her blazer. Somehow Zoe managed to slip away and slammed the door behind her. Running down the communal corridor Zoe realised that both ways out of the great leaning tower block, the stairs and the lift, were sure to result in capture.

Then Zoe remembered there was scaffolding on the far side of the flats.

Thinking there might be a way down somehow, she raced over. She opened a window and climbed out on to the scaffold, before closing the window behind her. A wicked wind shook the thin boards beneath her feet. She looked down. Thirty-seven floors! Even the buses on the street looked tiny, like little toys. Zoe's head spun. This was beginning to seem like a terrible idea.

But behind her, Tina and Sheila's furious faces were pressed up against the glass, and they were banging on the window.

Without thinking, Zoe ran along the outside of the building, as her stepmother and Tina fought to be first out on to the scaffold to give chase. At the end of the wooden walkway there was a large plastic tube that went all the way down thirty-seven floors to a skip. Zoe had thought it looked like a waterslide, though it was designed to pass all the unwanted bits of debris from the building repairs down to the ground safely.

It was just big enough for a little girl.

Turning round, Zoe saw Tina and her stepmother a few paces behind her. She took a deep breath and leaped into the tube. Red plastic surrounded her, and she slid faster than she could have imagined, screaming as she went. Down, down, down. Would it never come to an end? Down and down she swirled, travelling faster and faster as she neared the ground. The little girl had never been on a waterslide, and for a moment the sensation of travelling so fast on her bottom was fun. As there was no water though, her bottom became hotter and hotter as it rubbed against the plastic.

Then, without warning, the ride finished and the little girl flew out of the tube into the skip. Fortunately there was an old mattress someone had illegally dumped in there, and it cushioned her fall. Her sizzling bottom now cooling, Zoe looked up at the scaffold.

She could see her over-sized stepmother stuck in the mouth of the tube, with Tina vigorously trying to push her down by putting all her weight on the woman's huge bum. Push and push as much as she might, Sheila's body just wouldn't fit. Zoe couldn't help but smile. She was safe, for the moment at least. But she knew someone she loved was in the most terrible danger. If she didn't find Armitage fast, he would be pulverised!

22

Free Spit

It was only when she looked at her reflection in a shop window that Zoe realised that, like Tina and Sheila, she was also covered from head to toe in dust. She had wondered why passers-by had been giving her funny looks, and why children in pushchairs burst into tears when they saw her and were wheeled by their pregnant mothers from her path.

Wiping the dust off her little plastic watch, she saw it was nearly lunchtime. Burt's van would be parked outside the school playground as it always was, frying up his noxious burgers.

The dust had gone right down the back of her throat, and Zoe was desperately in need of a drink, so she made a short pit-stop.

TING!

"Aaah! Miss Zoe!" exclaimed Raj. "Is it Halloween already?"

"Erm, no…" spluttered Zoe. "It's, er, mufti day at school, you know, where you can wear whatever you like."

Raj studied the small dusty girl. "So forgive me, but what have you dressed as?"

"Dustgirl."

"Dustgirl?"

"Yes, Dustgirl. She is a superhero, you know."

"I have never heard of her."

"She is very popular."

"Dustgirl, eh? So what is her superpower?" enquired Raj, genuinely curious.

"She is very good at dusting," replied Zoe,

now desperate for the exchange to come to an end.

"Well, I must look out for her."

"Yes, I think they are bringing out a *Dustgirl* movie next year."

"It is sure to be a blockbuster," replied Raj, clearly not a hundred per cent convinced. "People do love to watch someone doing the dusting. I know I do."

"Raj, please can I have a drink?"

"Of course, Miss Zoe. Anything for you. I have got some bottles of water there."

"Just tap water would be fine."

"No, I insist, take a bottle from the chill cabinet."

"Well, thank you."

"My pleasure," smiled Raj.

Zoe made her way from the counter and selected a small bottle of water. She downed most of it, then washed her face clean with the remainder. Instantly she felt a whole lot better.

"Thank you, Raj, you are so good to me."

"You are a very special little girl, Miss Zoe. And not just because you are ginger. Please can you pass me the empty bottle, Miss Zoe?"

Trampling dust through his little shop, Zoe returned the bottle to Raj, and he took it off behind the multicoloured plastic curtains to the back. Zoe could hear a tap running, and a few moments later he reappeared to pass the bottle back to her.

"If you could pop it back in the cabinet, please," he said with a smile.

"But it's covered in dust, and it's got my spit all around the top."

"And the beauty of the scheme, my friend, is there is no extra charge for the spit!" said Raj triumphantly.

Zoe looked at the newsagent, and then dutifully returned the bottle to where she had taken it from.

"Goodbye, Raj."

"Goodbye, er, Dustgirl. And good luck!"

TING!

Now Zoe felt a tiny little bit like she *was* a superhero, albeit one whose special power was dusting. However, just like a superhero, she was fighting evil.

Powering down the street, a trail of dust behind her, Zoe soon spotted Burt's van. It was parked where it always was outside the school playground, and there was a line of eager children queuing down the road. Approaching from the road side, she saw that the van was emblazoned with 'BURT'S PEST CONTROL'.

That's curious, she thought. Zoe hid behind the defaced and battered school sign, and waited

222

until the bell rang for the end of lunch break. She couldn't risk being seen back at school since she was suspended. That could lead to instant expulsion.

DDDRRRRRRIIIIIINNNNNNN NNNGGGGGGGG. The bell finally rang

and Burt served his final customer, squirting the peculiar dark ketchup on to the distinctly unappetising-looking burger. Zoe scuttled across the road, and hid on the other side of the van, where it faced on to the pavement. Looking up at the writing this side she saw that it read 'BURT'S BURGERS'.

"This is so strange," whispered Zoe to herself. The van said 'BURT'S BURGERS' on one side and 'BURT'S PEST CONTROL' on the other.

Zoe stared at the van. The creepy man was only using the same vehicle for catching rats that he did for frying burgers! Zoe was no expert, but was pretty sure the government's Food Standard Agency would take a very dim view of this. It was going to result in an angry letter at least.

The van's engine started, and Zoe scampered around to the back, silently opened the door and leaped inside. She closed it as quietly as she could behind her, and lay down on the cold metal floor.

Then the engine started up, and the van drove off.

With Zoe hiding inside it.

23

The Pulverisation Machine!

At eye level, Zoe could see huge bags of rotting burgers with maggots crawling out of them. She put her hand over her mouth, for fear she might scream or throw up, or both.

The van hurtled through the town. She could hear it scraping against other cars, and the horns of other vehicles hooting as it sped through red lights. Zoe popped her head up to watch in terror through a little window, as they spread chaos and carnage in their wake, not to mention quite a few broken-off wing mirrors. Burt was driving so recklessly, she was frightened he would kill them both.

The van was travelling so fast that in no time they were on the outskirts of town in a large, deserted industrial estate. Enormous empty warehouses that looked like they were falling down blotted out the sky, and soon the van stopped outside a particularly dilapidated one. Zoe looked up, out of the fat-splattered window. This warehouse was like a gigantic aircraft hangar.

Zoe took a deep breath, and everything turned dark as Burt drove the van inside. As soon as it lurched to a halt, she climbed out of the back and hid under the van. Trying to breathe as quietly as possible she looked around the giant space. There were cages and cages of rats all piled up on top of each other. It looked like there were thousands of them in here, waiting to be pulverised.

Beside the cages was a tank of cockroaches, with a sticker that simply read 'Ketchup'.

I'm so glad I never ate one of Burt's burgers, thought Zoe. Even so, she still felt really sick.

In the middle of the warehouse was a dirty old stepladder that led up to a massive machine. *This must be his pulverisation machine!* thought Zoe. It was old and rusty, and looked like it had been made out of bits from cars that had fallen apart, pieces of old freezers and microwave ovens. The whole thing was held together with sticky tape.

As Zoe watched from underneath the van, Burt approached the machine.

The main part of the contraption was a massive metal funnel, with a long conveyor belt leading from underneath it. A huge wooden rolling pin hovered over the belt. Next, metal arms that could have been parts of old food mixers stood ready at the side. On the end of the arms were round metal tubes that looked like sawn-down sections of old piping, or perhaps even parts of a lorry exhaust pipe.

If the noise of the squeaking rats was deafening, it was nothing compared to the sound of the machine.

As soon as Burt walked over and pulled the lever on the side to turn it on (which was actually an arm from a shop window dummy), the metal grinding noise easily drowned out the squeaks. The whole machine rattled as if it was about to fall to pieces.

Zoe spied on Burt as he trundled over to a cage of rats. Bending down, he picked it up – there must have been a hundred rats inside, could Armitage be one of them? – and plodded over to the stepladder, moving gingerly because of the weight. Slowly but surely he climbed up the ladder, one step at a time. At the top he paused for a moment, wobbled slightly and then smiled a sickening smile. Zoe wanted to call out to stop him, but didn't dare reveal herself.

Then Burt lifted the cage above his head and tipped the rats into the machine!

They tumbled through the air to their certain death. One little rat, not much bigger than Armitage, clung on to the cage for dear life. With a sickening laugh the evil man prised its little claws off the metal, and it plunged down and down into the machine. There was then a hideous crunching sound. He really did pulverise them! Out of the bottom of the machine poured some minced meat. The meat was then flattened by a huge wooden roller, before the arms plunged down repeatedly on to the conveyor belt and chopped the meat into patties. The patties then trundled along the belt before falling into a filthy cardboard box.

Now Zoe really did want to vomit.

Burt's terrible secret was out.

Can you guess what Burt's secret was, reader?

I should hope so: there is quite a big clue in the title of this book.

Yes. He was turning rats into burgers!

Maybe, reader, you have even eaten one yourself without even knowing…

"Noooooooooooooooo!" screamed Zoe. The little girl couldn't help it, but disastrously she had given herself away…

24

Childburger

"Ha ha ha!" said Burt, not laughing.

He paced towards Zoe, his nose twitching in her direction. Now Zoe was afraid that, like the rats, she too was in mortal danger.

"Come out, little girl!" shouted the man. "I could smell you in the van. I have an extremely strong sense of smell. For rats, but also for children!"

Zoe rolled out from under the van and ran to the door of the warehouse, which she could see even from here was shut and locked. Burt must have closed it after driving in. The cruel man walked slowly behind her. That Burt didn't bother to run made him all the more terrifying – he knew she was trapped.

Zoe looked over at the cages of rats. There must be thousands of the poor creatures stacked up in there. How on earth would she find little Armitage among them? She would just have to set them *all* free. However, right now the prodigious rat killer was striding towards her, his nose twitching more and more feverishly with every step.

Not taking her eyes off him, Zoe felt her way along the wall to the huge sliding door, and started fumbling with the padlock, desperate to escape.

"Get away from me!" she shouted, her fingers fumbling ever more frantically to open the door.

"Or what?" wheezed Burt, edging closer and closer. He was so close now she could smell him.

"Or I will tell everyone about what you are doing here. Turning rats into burgers!"

"No, you won't."

"Yes, I will."

"No, you won't."

"Yes, I will."

"Yes, you will," said Burt.

"No, I won't!"

"Ha!" said Burt. "Got you! I knew you were trouble that day in your flat. That's why I *let* you climb into the back of my van and come into my secret lair."

"You knew I was there all along?"

"Oh yes, I could smell you! And now I am going to turn you into a burger. That's what evil children get for sticking their little noses in other people's business."

"Noooooo!" Zoe screamed, still desperately trying to open the old rusty padlock. The key was still in it, but it was so stiff that, try and try as she might, it just wouldn't turn.

"Ha ha," Burt wheezed. "My very first childburger!!!"

He reached out to grab her – she dodged out of the way but his big hairy hand grasped a clump of her frizzy ginger hair. Zoe flailed her arms around, trying to get the rat catcher to release his grip. Now his other hand had slammed down on to her shoulder, and was holding it tight.

Zoe slapped him hard across the face, and his dark glasses flew into the air and on to the ground.

"NO!" shouted Burt.

Zoe looked up at his eyes, but they weren't there.

Where his eyes should be, Burt had only two empty, blacker-than-black sockets in his face.

"AAAAAAAA RRRRGGGGHH!"

screamed Zoe in terror. "You have no *eyes*?!"

"Yes, child, I am completely blind."

"But… you don't have a dog or a white stick or anything."

"Don't need them," said Burt proudly. "I've this." He tapped his nose. "This is why I am the greatest rat catcher in the world, even of all time."

Zoe stopped struggling for a moment. She was frozen in terror. "What? Why?"

"Because I have no eyes, my dear, I have developed an acute sense of smell. I can smell a rat from miles away. Especially a cute little baby one like yours."

"But… but… but… you drive a van!" spluttered Zoe. "You can't drive if you are blind!"

Burt smiled, showing off his filthy false teeth. "It is perfectly easy to drive with no eyes. I just follow my nose."

"You'll kill someone!"

"In the whole twenty-five years since I have been driving, I have only run over fifty-nine people."

"Fifty-nine?!"

"I know, it's nothing. Some I had to reverse over to finish them off, of course."

"Murderer!"

"Yes, but if you don't declare them, the insurance company lets you keep your no-claims bonus."

Zoe stared into the deep dark pools in his face. "What on earth happened to your eyes?" She knew that some people were born blind, of course, but Burt *actually had no eyes at all*.

"Many years ago, I used to work in an animal laboratory," began Burt.

"A what?" interrupted Zoe.

"Doing experiments on animals and that for medical research. But I used to stay late and do my own little experiments!"

"Like what?" asked Zoe, feeling sure the answer would be something grisly.

"Pulling wings off daddy-longlegs, stapling cats' tails to the floor, hanging bunny rabbits on a clothes line by their ears, just a bit of fun."

"Fun?"

"Yes, fun."

"You are sick."

"I know," replied Burt proudly.

"But that still doesn't explain why you have no eyes."

"Be patient, child. One night I stayed very

late at the laboratory; it was my birthday and as a special treat I had planned to dunk a rat in a bath of acid."

"No!"

"But before I could dip the little thing in the liquid, the vile creature bit my hand. Hard. The same hand I was using to hold the dish of acid. The bite made me flick up my hand in pain and the acid flew up into my eyes, burning them out of their sockets."

Zoe was speechless at the horror of it all.

"Ever since then," continued Burt, "I have pulverised every rat I could get my hands on. And now I will have to do the same to you, since you have stuck your nose into my business, like a little rat yourself."

Zoe thought for a moment. "Well," she said defiantly, "it seems to me like you got your just desserts."

"No, no, no, my dear," said Burt. "On the contrary. I am going to get my dessert just now. When I eat you!"

25

Roadkill

With one hand still on the padlock, Zoe finally managed to turn the key. She yanked her head over her shoulder and, taking her cue from the rat in the laboratory, she sank her teeth into Burt's arm as hard as she could.

"OOOOOOOWWWWWW!!!!!!!" shouted the malevolent man, and in a reflex reaction his huge hand jumped off her tiny shoulder, yanking out a large clump of her ginger hair. Zoe flung the huge metal door of the warehouse open and ran out into the industrial estate.

The place was deserted, with sickly streetlights illuminating a wide street of empty, cracked concrete. Weeds grew out of the cracks.

Not sure of where to go, Zoe just ran. Ran and ran and ran. She was running so fast she thought she would trip over her own legs. All she thought about was putting as much distance between her and Burt as she could. The estate was so huge though, that she was still not outside of it yet.

Without daring to look back she could hear the van's engine starting up, and Burt grinding it into gear. Now Zoe was being pursued by a blind man driving a van. Finally she turned around and saw the van completely miss the open door, and crash out of the wall of the warehouse...

C C C C C C C C C C
C C C C C C C C C C C C

CCCRRRRRR RRAAAAAASSSSS SSHHHHHHHH!!!!!!!!!!

The impact didn't stop it. Instead the van sped faster and faster towards her.

Squinting, Zoe could just see the dark holes where Burt's eyes had once been behind the windscreen. Just below them his nose was twitching feverishly, his smell radar clearly tuned to its 'SMALL GINGER GIRL' setting.

The van was heading straight for her and travelling faster and faster by the second. Zoe had to do something or she would be roadkill.

And fast.

She darted to the left, and the van lurched to the left too. She rushed to the right, and the van careered to the right. Behind the steering wheel, Burt's evil grin widened. He was speeding closer

and closer to making his first Small-ginger-girl-burger.

Soon, the van lurched into a high gear and started gaining on Zoe, who was running as fast as her little legs would carry her. Ahead, she spotted some bins, with a pile of long forgotten rubbish bags piled up beside them. Her mind was racing faster than her legs, and she came up with a plan...

Zoe jumped over to the bins, and picked up a particularly heavy sack. As the van hurtled towards her, she threw the bag at the bonnet of the van. As it struck, she let out a blood-curdling scream, as if she had been run over.

"AAAAARRR GGGGHHHH!!!!!!"

Burt then slammed the van into reverse, no doubt thinking he would run her over one more time to make sure she was dead.

As the engine screamed, so did Zoe. The van reversed over the sack.

Then Burt leaped out of his van, and his nose twitched as he tried to locate what he believed was the small girl's body. Meanwhile, the small girl in question tiptoed off and crawled under a wire fence into a wasteland, and kept running and didn't turn back.

After her body could run no more, Zoe jogged, and after it could jog no more, she walked. As she walked she thought long and hard about what she should do next. Zoe had witnessed a blind man who drove a van making burgers out of rats. Who would believe her? Who would help her? She *needed* someone to help her. There was no way she could take on Burt on her own.

A teacher? No. After all, she was suspended

from school and forbidden to return. The headmaster would expel her on the spot if she returned.

Raj? No. He was terrified of rats. He ran down the street in panic when he saw a baby one. There was no way she could get him to step one foot inside the warehouse, with thousands of rats inside.

The police? No. They would never believe Zoe's incredible story. She would be just another girl from the rough estate, suspended from school, and now lying to get herself out of trouble. Since Zoe was so young, the police would march her straight home to her wicked stepmother.

There was just one person who could help her right now.

Dad.

It was a long time since he had been a proper

father to her, since he had come home and given her extraordinary ice creams to taste, or played with her in the park. But Sheila was wrong, Dad did love her, he always did. He just became so sad he couldn't show it any more.

Zoe knew where to find him.

The pub.

There was a massive problem. It is against the law for children to go into pubs.

26

The Executioner & Axe

Zoe's dad went to the same boozer every day, a flat-roofed pub on the edge of the estate, with the cross of St George hanging above the door and a ferocious-looking Rottweiler tied up outside. It was not a place for little girls. Indeed, the law said that only those over sixteen were allowed inside.

Zoe was twelve. Even worse, she was small for her age, and looked younger.

'The Executioner & Axe' was the name of the pub, and it was even less welcoming than it sounded.

Carefully stepping round the Rottweiler outside, Zoe peered in through the cracked window of the pub. She saw a man who looked like her dad sitting alone, slumped over a table, a half-full pint glass in his hand. He must have simply fallen asleep in the pub. She banged on the cracked window, but he didn't budge. Zoe knocked harder this time, but Dad did not rise from his slumber.

Now, Zoe had no choice but to break the law and go in. She took a deep breath, and stood up on her tiptoes to make herself a bit taller, though there was zero chance anyone would think she was old enough to be in there.

As the door swung open, several fat bald blokes wearing England football shirts looked round, and then down to Zoe's height. The pub was barely a place for women, let alone girls.

"Get out of 'ere!" shouted the ruddy-faced

landlord. He also had a bald head, framed by some wisps of hair at the side and a ponytail. There was a tattoo on his head that said WEST HAM. Actually it didn't – it said MAH TSEW. He had obviously done it himself in front of a mirror because it was all backwards.

"No," said Zoe. "I need to get my dad."

"I don't care," barked the landlord. "Out! Out of my pub!"

"If you chuck me out I will report you to the police for allowing underage drinkers in here!"

"What the blazes do you mean? Who?"

Zoe took a sip of an old toothless man's pint from a nearby table. "Me!" she said triumphantly, before the disgusting taste of the alcohol permeated her tongue and she felt suddenly more than a little sick.

The ruddy-faced man with the ponytail was evidently quite befuddled by this logic, and fell silent for a moment. Zoe approached her dad's table.

"DAD!" she shouted. "DAD!!!"

"What? What's going on?" he said, waking up with a start.

Zoe smiled at him.

"Zoe? What on earth are you doing here? Don't tell me your mum sent you?"

"She's not my mum and no she didn't."

"So why are you here?"

"I need your help."

"With what?"

Zoe took a deep breath. "There is a man in a warehouse on the edge of town who, if we don't stop him right now, is about to turn my pet rat into a burger."

Dad looked entirely unconvinced, and pulled a face suggesting his daughter had gone more than a little loopy. "Pet rat? Burgers? Zoe, please." Dad rolled his eyes. "You're pulling my leg!"

Zoe looked her father in the eye. "Have I ever lied to you, Dad?" she said.

"Well, I, er…"

"This is important, Dad. Think. Have I ever lied to you?"

Dad thought for a moment. "Well, you did say I would find another job…"

"You will, Dad, trust me. You just have to never give up."

"I have given up," said Dad sadly.

Zoe looked at her father, so beaten by life. "You don't have to. Do you think *I* should just give up on my dream of having my own performing animal show?"

Dad frowned. "No, of course not."

"Well, let's make a deal that neither of us will forget our dreams then," said Zoe. Dad nodded uncertainly. Then she pressed the advantage. "And that's exactly why I need my rat back. I've been training him – he can do so many tricks already. He's going to be amazing."

"But... a warehouse? Burgers? It all sounds a bit far-fetched."

Zoe stared deep into her father's large sad eyes. "I am not lying to you, Dad. I promise."

"Well, no, but— " he spluttered.

"There are no buts, Dad. I need your help. Now. This man threatened to turn me into a burger."

A look of horror crossed her father's face. "What? You?"

"Yes."

"Not just the rats?"

"No."

"My little girl? Into a burger?"

Zoe nodded, slowly.

Dad rose from his chair. "The evil man. I'll make him pay for that. Now... let me just have just one more pint and then we'll go."

"No, Dad, you need to come now."

Just then Dad's phone rang. The caller's name flashed up on the screen. It read 'Dragon'.

"Who's Dragon?"

"It's your mum. I mean Sheila."

So Dad had Sheila in his phone as Dragon. Zoe smiled for the first time in ages.

Then Zoe had a horrible thought. Burt could be with her!

"Don't answer it!" she implored.

"What do you mean 'don't answer it'? I will be in so much trouble if I don't!" He pressed the answer button on his phone.

"Yes, love?" said Dad in an unconvincingly affectionate tone. "Your stepdaughter?"

The little girl shook her head violently at her dad.

"No, no, I haven't seen her…" lied Dad. Zoe breathed a sigh of relief.

"Why?" he asked.

Dad listened for a moment, and then put his hand over the receiver so what he was about to say could not be heard. "There's a pest control man there at the flat, he is looking for you. Said he is returning your pet rat to you unharmed. Wants to give it to you personally. Just to be safe."

"It's a trap," whispered Zoe. "He's the one who tried to kill me."

"If I see her, I will call you straight away, my love. Bub-bye!"

Zoe could hear her stepmother screaming on the other end of the phone as Dad ended the call.

"Dad, we need to go to his warehouse right

now. If we run we might just beat him to it, and save Armitage."

"Armitage?"

"He is my pet rat."

"Oh, right." Dad thought for a minute. "Why is he called that?"

"It's a long story. Come on, Dad, let's go. There is no time to lose…"

27

A Hole in the Fence

Zoe led her father out of the pub, round the Rottweiler and on to the street. Dad stood there swaying under the orange streetlight for a moment. He looked into his daughter's eyes. There was a long stretch of silence. Then: "I'm frightened, love," said Dad.

"I am too." Zoe reached out her hand and held her father's tenderly. It was the first time they had held hands in months, maybe years. Dad used to give her the best cuddles, but after Mum died he had retreated to the back of his eyes, and never came out any more.

"But we can do this together," said Zoe. "I know we can."

Dad looked down at his daughter's hand, so small in his, and a tear formed in his eye. Zoe smiled supportively at her dad.

"Come on…" she said.

Soon they were running through the lit streets, the intervals of dark and light going by faster and faster.

"So this nutter makes rats out of burgers?" Dad said breathlessly.

"No, Dad, it's the other way round."

"Oh yes, of course. Sorry."

"And he has this enormous warehouse on this industrial estate on the outskirts of town," panted Zoe, tugging her father along by his hand.

"That's where I used to work in the ice-cream factory!" exclaimed Dad.

"It's miles away."

"It's not. I used to take a short cut when I was late, we just need to cut through here. Follow me."

Dad took his daughter by the hand and led her through a hole in a fence. Zoe couldn't help but smile at the excitement of it all.

Then her excitement faded a bit when she realised they were entering a rubbish dump.

Soon, Dad was knee-deep and Zoe was waist-deep, wading through trash. Zoe stumbled, so Dad lifted up his daughter and put her on his shoulders like he used to when they went for a walk in the park when she was very little. His hands held her legs tight.

Together they made their way through the sea of bin bags. Soon the warehouses were in sight. A titanic graveyard of empty buildings, bathed in the harshest of light.

"That's the one I used to work at," said Dad, pointing to one of the warehouses. A beaten old sign on the side of it read 'THE DELICIOUS ICE CREAM COM ANY'.

"Comany?" asked Zoe.

"Someone's taken the 'P'!" replied Dad, and they both chuckled. "Gosh, it's been years since I have been down here," said Dad.

Zoe pointed out the warehouse that now had a van-shaped hole in the wall. "That's Burt's one!"

"Right."

"Come on. We need to save Armitage."

Father and daughter skirted around the outside edge towards the giant hole in the wall. They stepped inside, and peered at the cavernous warehouse. The huge building appeared empty, except for the thousands of rats. The poor creatures were all still piled up in cages, awaiting their grisly fate as a fast-food snack.

Burt was nowhere to be seen – he must still be at the flat with Zoe's wicked stepmother, waiting to trap Zoe when she came home. No doubt salivating at the idea of turning her into a burger, albeit a particularly large one.

With trepidation, Zoe and Dad stepped inside, and Zoe showed her father the terrifying pulverisation machine.

"He goes up this ladder and drops the rats into this giant funnel, and the poor little things are rolled flat here before being formed into patties."

"Oh my word!" said Dad. "So it *is* true."

"What did I tell you?" replied Zoe.

"Which one of these poor little blighters is Armitage?" asked Dad, gazing at the thousands of terrified rodents squashed high into the mountain of cages.

"I don't know," she said, scouring all the little frightened faces, peering out from the cages, which had been stacked on top of each other. Seeing them all there, squashed in together in a big tower of rats, made her think of the block she and Dad and Sheila lived in.

Still, thought Zoe. *The rats had it worse. What with the getting minced up into burgers.*

"Now where is he?" she said. "He's got a very cute little pink nose."

"Sorry, love, they all look the same to me," said Dad, desperately trying to spot one with a particularly pink nose.

"Armitage? ARMITAGE!" called Zoe.

All the rats eeked. Every single one of them wanted to escape.

"We'll just have to set them all free," said Zoe.

"Good plan," replied Dad. "Right, you climb on my shoulders, and unlock the top one."

Dad lifted his little daughter up and sat her on his shoulders. She then held on to his head, and slowly stood up.

Zoe started unwinding the pieces of metal

wire that kept the cages locked. I say cages –
they were really old deep-fat fryers.

"How are you getting on?" said Dad.

"I'm trying, Dad, nearly got the first one
open."

"Good girl!" called up Dad encouragingly.

However, before Zoe could open the first cage, Burt's van, looking decidedly the worse for wear, came thundering into the warehouse, smashing the huge metal sliding door into the air as it did so...

CCCCRRRRR RRAAAAAASSSSSSSS SSHHHHHHHH!!!!!!!!!!

...before screeching to a halt.

RRRRRRRRRrrrrr
RRRRRRRRRRRRR
RRRRRRRRRRRRRR
RRRRRRRRRRRRRR
RRRRRRRRRRRRRR
RRRRRRRRRRRRRR
RRRRRRRRRRRRRR
RRRRRRRRRRRRR
!!!!!!!!!!!!!!!!!!!!!!!!!!!!!!!!
!!!!!!!!!!!!!!!!!!!!!!

Dad and Zoe were in deep deep trouble...

28

Rat Poison

"Now I've got you!" wheezed Burt, as he leaped down from the driving seat. "Who's that with you, little girl?"

Dad looked up at his daughter nervously. "No one!" he said.

"It's me useless git of a husband!" announced Sheila, as she plopped down from the other side of the van.

"Sheila?" said Dad, aghast. "What are you doing here?"

"I didn't want to tell you, Dad," said Zoe, stepping down from her father's shoulders to

269

the ground. "But I heard him and Sheila being all lovey-dovey...!"

"No!" said Dad.

Sheila smiled smugly at the pair. "Yeah, the little weasel's right. I am goin' to run away wiv Burt in 'is van."

The woman strutted over to the rat catcher, and took his hand. "We share a deep love of each other."

"And pulverising rats," added Burt.

"Oh yeah, we love to kill a rodent or two!"

With that the pair shared a stomach-churning kiss. It was enough to make Zoe want to hurl.

"I fancied ya more with the moustache though, Burt," said the stupendously thick woman. "Will you grow it back?"

"You two are disgusting!" shouted Dad. "How could you enjoy killing all those poor creatures!"

"Oh, shut yer face, ya idiot!" hollered Sheila. "Those rats deserve to die, disgustin' little fings!" Then she paused for a moment and looked at her stepdaughter. "That's why I murdered your 'amster."

"You killed Gingernut?" screamed Zoe, tears in her eyes. "I knew it!"

"You evil cow!" shouted Dad.

Sheila and Burt shared a sickening laugh, united by cruelty.

"Yes, I didn't want that dirty little fing in me flat. So I mixed some rat poison in wiv his food. Ha ha!" added the repulsive woman.

"How could you do that?" shouted Dad.

"Oh, shut ya face. It was only an 'amster. I always 'ated it!" replied Sheila.

"Rat poison. Mmm. A nice lingering death!" added Burt with a breathy laugh. "They just taste a bit funny afterwards, is all."

Zoe hurled herself at the pair – she wanted to tear them both to pieces. Dad pulled her back.

"Zoe, no! You don't know what they'll do." Dad had to use all his strength to stop his daughter from attacking them. "Look, we don't want any trouble," he pleaded. "Just hand over my Zoe's pet rat. Now. And we'll go."

"Never!" wheezed Burt. "The baby ones are the most succulent. I was saving him for our little date, Sheila. Mmm…"

Slowly, Burt reached towards the filthy pocket of his apron.

"In fact," he said, "I have your precious Armitage right here…"

Then he pulled the little rat out by the tail. Zoe's pet rat had been in there all along, and not in the cages after all! Burt had tied Armitage's little hands and feet tightly together with metal wire so he could not escape. He looked like a little rat escapologist.

"Nooooo!" shouted Zoe when she saw him like that.

"He is going to make a very tasty little burger!" said Burt, licking his lips.

Sheila studied the poor little thing dangling in the air, and then turned to Burt. "Ya can eat him, my one true love," she said. "I might just stick to the prawn cocktail crisps, if ya don't mind."

"Whatever you like, my angel sent from heaven."

The blind man stumbled towards the pulverisation machine, and turned the lever. A terrible grinding sound echoed through the warehouse. Slowly Burt began to climb the stepladder to the top of the funnel.

"Put down that rat!" shouted Dad.

"As if anyone ever paid the least bit of attention to ya! You're a joke!" laughed Sheila.

Zoe struggled free of her father's grip, and ran after Burt. She had to save Armitage! However, by this time the malevolent man was halfway up the stepladder, and poor little Armitage was wriggling his little body as much as he could and squeaking in terror. Zoe grabbed at Burt's leg, but he shook his foot violently to shake her off. Burt then kicked her in the nose with the heel of his boot. She was knocked down hard on to the concrete floor below.

"AAAAAAHHHHHHHHH!!!!!!!!!!!!!" screamed Zoe.

Dad sprinted over to the ladder and pursued the rat killer up on to it. Soon the two men were standing precariously on the top step, the ladder swaying side to side under their combined weight. Dad grabbed Burt's wrist, and pushed it down to force him to release his grip on the little rat.

"Drop me husband in the burger machine while you're at it!" jeered Sheila.

Dad's elbow brushed up against Burt's face and knocked the rat catcher's glasses off his head. Coming face to face with the dark pools where the man's eyes should have been, Dad was so horrified he stepped back and lost his footing. His foot slipped backwards off the top of the stepladder towards the funnel.

He began to slide down into the pulverisation machine. Dad desperately grabbed on to Burt's apron for survival, but it was so greasy he was instantly losing his grip.

"Please please," said Dad. "Help me up."

"No. I am going to feed you to the children," rasped Burt, his laugh rattling around his throat, prising Dad's fingers one by one off his apron.

"And your daughter is next!"

"Yeah! Throw her in as well!" cheered on Sheila.

Badly winded, Zoe rose unsteadily to her hands and feet, and crawled over to the stepladder to help her father. Sheila desperately tried to stop her, grabbing the little girl brutally by the hair and yanking her back. Then she swung her stepdaughter around by the hair and flung her into the air.

Up, up, up…

And then down.

Hard.

Zoe screamed in agony as she hit the ground for the second time.

"Aaaaaaaah hhhhhhhhhhhhhh!!!!! !!!!!!!!"

Despite her thick frizzy hair, the impact dazed Zoe for a moment.

"Burt? Stay there and I'll 'elp ya finish 'im off!" called Sheila to the two men still fighting over the top of the burger machine. Slowly, the grotesquely large lady made her way up the steps, the ladder creaking under her considerable weight.

Still dizzy, Zoe opened her eyes, to see her stepmother wobbling at the top of the ladder. The woman was trying to prise Dad's fingers off Burt's greasy apron. One by one she was bending them back, laughing as she forced her husband closer and closer to being turned into a burger.

However, Sheila was so heavy that as she bent to one side to prise off the poor man's final little finger, her weight made the whole ladder topple over to the side.

CCCCRRRRA AAAAAASSSSSSSSSSS HHHHHHHHHH!!!!!!

Burt and Sheila fell forwards, headfirst into the pulverisation machine...

...Dad just managed to grab on to the side of the funnel with one hand...

...Armitage was falling into the machine with the cruel rat catcher. Nothing could stop the baby rat being pulverised...

29

Pink Furry Slippers

Just then, as Burt tumbled through the air, Armitage bit the monster's finger and, squealing, Burt flicked the rat off his hand and up into the air.

Up, up, up…

…and into Dad's outstretched hand.

"Got him!" called Dad. Now he was hanging on by one hand to the lip of the funnel, and clutching Armitage with the other. Armitage was squeaking like crazy.

At that moment there was a gurgling sound and the gruesome twosome passed through the machine.

It clunked and groaned like never before, as they passed through the rollers. Finally two very large burgers trundled out.

In one, Burt's shattered wraparound shades poked out. In another, Sheila's pink furry slippers were clearly visible. They were two distinctly unappetising-looking burgers.

SHEILA BURGER

BURT BURGER

"HELP!"

yelled Dad. He was moments from being a burger himself...

Zoe's attention shot back to the funnel.

Her father was still holding on to the side of the pulverisation machine with one greasy hand, gripping Armitage in the other.

Dad's feet were still dangling over the grinders below, scuffing the tips of his shoes with a noise like a piece of paper being lowered into a desk fan.

Zoe could see that he was sliding. The grease on his hand from Burt's apron meant that slowly but surely he was losing his grip.

Any moment now, he was going to breathe his last breath.

And then come out of the machine as another rather large burger.

Her head still spinning from its collision with the floor, Zoe crawled over the cold wet concrete floor of the warehouse to the machine.

"Turn it off!" shouted Dad.

Zoe rushed over to the lever on the side. But try as she might, she couldn't get it to budge.

"It's stuck!" she called up.

"Grab the ladder, then!" called Dad.

Zoe looked: the stepladder was lying on its side on the ground where it had fallen.

"QUICK!" shouted Dad.

"EEK!" shouted Armitage, wrapping his little tail as tight as he could round Dad's free hand.

"OK, OK, I'm coming!" said Zoe.

With all her strength, the little girl righted the ladder, and ran up the steps. At the top she peered down into the huge machine. It was like looking down into the mouth of a monster. The metal grinders were like giant teeth that would chomp you to bits.

"Here!" said Dad. "Take Armitage."

Zoe reached down to take the little rat from her father's hand. Dad passed Armitage up, his legs and feet still bound together by metal wire. She hugged him close to her chest, and kissed him on the nose. "Armitage? Armitage?

Are you all right?"

Dad looked up at this moving reunion and rolled his eyes.

"Never mind about him. What about me?" he yelled.

"Oh, yes, sorry, Dad!" said Zoe. She put Armitage into her inside breast pocket and then crouched down on the ladder and offered her hands to help pull her father out. However, Dad was heavy and Zoe wobbled precariously at the top of the ladder, nearly falling headfirst into the machine.

"Careful, Zoe!" said Dad. "I don't want to drag you in too!"

Zoe took a couple of steps back down the ladder, and curled her feet around a step to form an anchor. Then she reached out her arms, and Dad held on to them, and finally pulled himself up to safety.

After climbing down the ladder, Dad yanked on the lever, turned off the machine, and lay exhausted on the floor.

"Are you OK, Dad?" asked Zoe, standing over him.

"A few cuts and bruises," he said, "but I will live. Come here. Your old dad needs a cuddle. I do love you, you know…"

"I always knew, and I love you too…"

Zoe lay down next to her father, and he put his long arms around her. As he did so, she took Armitage out of her pocket, and carefully untied his legs. Together, they had a big family cuddle.

Just then Armitage interrupted. "Eek eek!" he said, before doing a little dance to draw Zoe's gaze up – up to the tower of rats still squashed so cruelly into cages.

"I think Armitage is trying to tell us something, Dad."

"What?"

"I think he wants us to set his friends free."

Dad looked up at the towering wall of cages, which all but reached the ceiling of the warehouse. Every cage was squashed full of poor starving rats. "Yes, of course. I quite forgot!"

Dad moved the ladder over to the cages, then stood on top of it, and with Armitage safely back in her pocket, Zoe climbed on to his shoulders to reach the top cage.

"Steady!" said Dad.

"Make sure you hold on to my feet!"

"Don't worry, I've got you!"

Finally, Zoe managed to open the first of the cages. The rats clambered out as fast as they could, then used the little girl and her dad as a ladder to climb down to the safety of the ground. Soon Zoe had opened all the cages and thousands of rats were running excitedly around the warehouse floor, enjoying their new-found freedom. Then Zoe and her dad broke open the tank of cockroaches, which had narrowly escaped being ground into 'ketchup'!

"Look," said Dad. "Or, actually, don't look. You're too young to see this."

Of course, as you must know, reader, there is nothing more guaranteed to make a child look than this.

Sure enough, Zoe looked.

It was the freshly made Burt and Sheila burgers. The rats were devouring them greedily and finally having their revenge!

"Oh dear," said Zoe.

"At least they are getting rid of the evidence," said Dad. "Now come on, we'd better get out of here…"

Dad took his daughter's hand, and led her out of the warehouse. Zoe looked back at the battered van.

"What about the burger van? Burt won't need it any more," she said.

"Yes, but what on earth are we going to do with it?" asked Dad, looking at his daughter quizzically.

"Well," said Zoe. "I have an idea…"

30

Room-mates

Winter turned to spring, as the van was redecorated. Just removing the grease that had built up on every surface of the vehicle, inside and outside, took a week. Even the steering wheel was thick with slime. However, the work didn't seem like work, because Zoe and her dad did most of it together, and it was surprisingly fun. Because he was so happy, Dad didn't go to the pub once, and that made Zoe happy too.

There was a snag of course; being unemployed, Dad only received a small amount of benefit money. It was a pittance and was barely enough to feed him and his daughter, let alone refurbish a van.

Fortunately, Dad was an ingenious sort.

He had found lots of the bits and pieces he needed for the van from the rubbish dump. He rescued an old discarded little freezer and repaired it. He used that to keep the lollies cold in. An old sink was just the right size to fit in the back of the van for rinsing the scoops. Zoe found an old funnel from a skip, which with a bit of paint and papier mâché, the father and daughter managed to fashion into an ice-cream cone to stick on the front of the van.

And so it was finally done.

Their very own ice-cream van.

Zoe's suspension from school was being lifted tomorrow. However, there was still one final decision. One major, crucial thing they had to make their minds up about. One really important outstanding matter.

What to write on the side of the van.

"You should name it after you," said Zoe, as they stepped back to admire their handiwork. The van stood gleaming in the afternoon sun in the car park of the estate. Dad held a brush and a pot of paint in his hand.

"No, I have a better idea," he said with a smile. Dad lifted his hand up to the side of the van and started painting on the letters. Zoe looked on, intrigued.

'A' was the first letter.

"Dad, what are you writing?" asked Zoe impatiently.

"Shush," replied her father. "You'll see."

Then 'R', and then 'M'.

Soon Zoe had it too, and couldn't resist shouting out. "*Armitage!*"

"Yes, ha ha!" laughed Dad. "Armitage's Ices."

"I love it!" said Zoe, jumping up and down
on the pavement with excitement.

Dad added the 'I', then the 'T', then the 'A', 'G', 'E', the apostrophe, because everyone knows apostrophes are very important, then the 'S', and then the word 'ICES'.

"Are you sure you want to name it after him?" asked Zoe. "He is just a little rat, after all."

"I know, but without him, none of this would ever have happened."

"You're right, Dad. He is a very special little fellow."

"You never did tell me why you called him Armitage, by the way," said Dad.

Zoe gulped. This was absolutely not the time to tell her father he had written the name of a toilet on the side of his gleaming ice-cream van.

"Er… it's a long story, Dad."

"I've got all day."

"Right. Well, another day. I promise. In fact I had better just go and get him. I want him to see what we have done to the van…"

Armitage was all grown up now, and didn't fit in her blazer pocket any more. So Zoe had left him in the flat.

Zoe excitedly ran up the stairs of the tower block, and rushed into her bedroom. Armitage was scuttling around Gingernut's old cage. Dad had liberated the cage from the pawn shop by exchanging it for a bumper box of prawn cocktail crisps his ex-wife had amazingly left uneaten.

Of course, the room wasn't just Zoe's bedroom any more.

No: since the wall had fallen down it was now a room twice the size that she shared with someone else.

That someone else being Tina Trotts.

The council were meant to have repaired the wall ages ago, but it was still down. To Zoe's surprise, when she entered the room, Tina was kneeling beside the cage and tenderly feeding the little rat little crusts of bread through the bars.

"What are you doing?" asked Zoe.

"Oh, I thought he might be a little peckish…" said Tina. "I hope you don't mind."

"I will take over, thank you," replied Zoe, snatching the food out of Tina's hand. She was still suspicious of everything the big girl did. After all, Tina was the one who flobbed on Zoe's hair every day on the way to school. The misery she had caused would not be easily forgotten.

"Do you still not trust me?" asked Tina.

Zoe thought for a moment. "Let's just hope the council gets that wall up soon," she said, eventually.

"I don't mind," said Tina. "I have enjoyed sharing a room with you, actually."

Zoe said nothing. The silence hung in the air for a moment, and Tina started to fidget.

Aargh, thought Zoe. *Stop feeling sorry for Tina Trotts!*

The thing was, though, that in the past few weeks Zoe had come to understand a lot more about Tina's life. How her horrible father screamed at her most nights. Tina's father was a great bear of a man. He enjoyed making his daughter feel worthless, and more and more Zoe was wondering if that was why Tina did the same to others. Not just to Zoe, but to *anyone* weaker than her. A great grinding wheel of cruelty, that could go round and round for ever if someone didn't stop it.

Yet as much as Zoe now understood Tina, she still didn't like the girl.

"There is something I need to say to you, Zoe," said Tina suddenly, her eyes filling with tears. "Something I've never said to anyone. Ever. Ever ever ever. And if you repeat it, I'll kill you."

Goodness, thought Zoe. *What on earth could*

it be? Is it some terrible secret? Does Tina have
a second head that she keeps hidden under her
jumper? Or is she really a boy called Bob?

But no, reader. It was none of these things.

It was something much more shocking…

31

Rich and Famous Rat

"Sorry," said Tina, eventually.

"Sorry? That's the thing you've never told anyone, ever?"

"Er... yes."

"Oh," said Zoe. "Oh, OK."

"Oh, OK, you forgive me?"

Zoe looked at the big girl. She sighed. "Yes, Tina. I forgive you," she said.

"I am *so* sorry for being so cruel to you," said Tina. "I just... I get so angry. Especially when my dad's... you know. It just makes me want to squash something small."

"Like me."

"I know, I am so so sorry." Tina was actually crying now. It was making Zoe a bit uncomfortable – she almost wished Tina would flob on her instead. Zoe put her arms around the girl, and hugged her tightly.

"I know. I know," said the little girl softly. "All our lives are hard in one way or another. But listen to me..." Zoe rubbed away Tina's tears tenderly with her thumbs. "We need to be kind to each other, and stick together, OK? This place is tough enough without you making my life a misery."

"So no more flobbing on your head?" said Tina.

"No."

"Not even on Tuesdays?"

"Not even on Tuesdays."

Tina smiled. "OK."

Zoe passed the crusts of bread back to Tina. "I don't mind you feeding my little boy. Carry on."

"Thank you," said Tina. "Have you taught him any new tricks?" she asked, her face brightening in anticipation.

"Take him out of his cage and I'll show you," said Zoe.

Tina gently opened the door to the cage, and Armitage tentatively crawled on to her hand. This time he didn't bite her: instead he nuzzled his soft fur against her fingers.

Zoe took a peanut from a bag on the shelf, as her new friend gently lifted Armitage out on to the still dust-encrusted carpet. She showed him the peanut.

Armitage promptly stood on his hind legs and did a very entertaining backwards dance, before Zoe gave him the nut. He took the nut between his paws and nibbled at it greedily.

Tina started applauding wildly. "That's amazing!" she said.

"That's nothing!" replied Zoe, proudly. "Watch this!"

With the promise of a few more peanuts, Armitage did a forward roll, a back-flip, even spun around on his back as if he was breakdancing!

Tina couldn't believe her eyes.

"You should take him on that TV talent show," said Tina.

"I would love to!" said Zoe. "He could be the world's very first rich and famous rat. And you could be my assistant."

"Me?!" asked Tina, incredulous.

"Yes, you, in fact I need your help with a new trick I have been dreaming up."

"Well, well, I'd love to!" spluttered Tina. Then

she said, "Oh!" as if she had just remembered something.

"What is it?" said Zoe.

"The end-of-term talent show!"

Zoe still hadn't been back at school since her three-week suspension started, so she had completely forgotten about the show.

"Oh, yes, the one Miss Ogden is organising."

"The Ogre, yes. We should totally enter Armitage."

"She is *never* going to allow me to bring Armitage back into school. He was the whole reason I got chucked out in the first place!"

"No, no, no, they talked about it in assembly. As it is in the evenin', the 'eadmaster has made a special rule. Pets are allowed."

"Well, he's not a dog or a cat, but I suppose he is my pet," reasoned Zoe.

"Of course he is! And get this. The Ogre plays

the tuba, I heard her practisin'. It's awful! All the kids reckon she is only doin' it because she wants to get off wiv the 'eadmaster."

"She so fancies him!" said Zoe.

The two girls laughed. The idea of the unusually small teacher playing the unusually large instrument already seemed hilarious, let alone using the low-noted tuba as a method of seduction!

"I have to see her do that!" said Zoe.

"Me too," laughed Tina.

"I just need to show Armitage something downstairs quickly, then we can spend this evening working together on the new trick!"

"I can't wait!" replied Tina, excitedly.

32

Actually Too Much Fudge

Running down the stairs was easier than going up, and before the paint was dry on the side of the van, Zoe was breathlessly showing Armitage the results of her and her father's hard work. Dad climbed into the van and opened the sliding hatch. Zoe had never seen her father looking so happy.

"Right, so, you're my first customer. What would you like, Madam?"

"Mmm…" Zoe surveyed the flavours. It was a very long time since she had tasted the delicious frozen dessert – she wasn't even sure if she'd ever had ice cream since those evenings when her dad would rush home from the factory with some crazy new flavour for her to try.

"Cone or cup, Madam?" asked Dad, already relishing his new job.

"Cone, please," replied Zoe.

"Any particular flavour take your fancy?" asked Dad with a smile.

Zoe leaned over the counter and studied the long line of mouth-watering flavours. After all those years in the factory, Dad really did know how to make some truly scrumptious ice cream. There was:

Triple Chocolate Sundae
Strawberry & Hazelnut Swirl
Fudge, Fudge & more Fudge
Toffee Popcorn Explosion
Caramel & Honeycomb Crunch

Fudgetastic Surprise

Tutti-Frutti-Lutti

Raspberry Ripple with Dark Chocolate Chunks

Double Fudge & Coconut Cream

Cookie & Caramel Crunch

Fudge, Fudge, Fudge & more Fudge

Toffee & Peanut Butter Swirl

Pistachio & White Chocolate

Banoffi Pie with Mega Fudge Chunks

Butterscotch Bonbon Boom

Marshmallow Milkshake Supreme

Quadruple Choc Chip with Honey Swirls

Mini Chocolate Eggs & Fruits of the Forest

Snail & Broccoli

Fudge, Fudge, Fudge, Fudge, Fudge, Fudge,
Fudge, actually now too much Fudge.

It was the most magnificent collection of ice-cream flavours in the world. Apart from the

Snail and Broccoli, obviously.

"Mmm... They all look delicious, Dad. It's just too hard to make a decision..."

Father peered down at his array of ice creams. "Then I will just have to give you one of each then!"

"OK," said Zoe. "But maybe leave out the snail and broccoli?"

Her dad bowed. "As you wish, Madam."

As his daughter giggled, he piled up her cone with flavour after flavour until it was nearly as tall as she was. With Armitage in one hand, she balanced the impossibly tall ice-cream cone in the other.

"I can't eat all this on my own!" laughed Zoe. She looked up at the tower block, and saw Tina looking down at her from the 37th floor window.

"TINA! COME DOWN!" shouted Zoe at

the very top of her voice.

Soon lots of children were poking their faces out of the windows of their flats, wondering what all the noise was about.

"ALL OF YOU!" shouted Zoe up at them. She recognised a few of them, but most of them she didn't know. Some of them she had never seen before in her life, even though they were all so closely crammed into this huge ugly leaning building together. "Come on down, everyone, and help me finish my ice cream."

Within seconds, hundreds of kids with dirty but eager little faces were rushing down to the car park to take their turn to have a bite of Zoe's ridiculously tall ice cream. After a few moments, the little girl entrusted the tower of ice cream to Tina, who made sure all the kids received their fair share, especially

the tiny ones whose little mouths couldn't reach that high.

As the sound of laughter rose and the sun went down, smiling Zoe broke away from the laughing children and sat alone on a nearby wall. She brushed the litter off the wall and brought Armitage up to her face. Then she gave him a tender little kiss on the top of his head.

"Thank you," she whispered to him. "I love you."

Armitage tilted his head and looked up at her, with the sweetest little smile on his face. "Eek eek eeek eeeeeek," he said. Which, of course, from rat to English translates as:

"Thank you. I love you too."

Epilogue

"Thank you, Miss Ogre, I mean Ogden, for that beautiful tuba playing," lied Mr Grave. It had been truly awful. Like a hippopotamus farting.

Miss Ogden tottered off the stage at the school talent show, unseen behind her huge, heavy instrument.

"That way, Miss Ogden," called Mr Grave, in a concerned voice.

"Thank you, headmaster," came a muffled voice, just before Miss Ogden crashed into the wings. The tuba sounded better hitting the wall than when she had played it.

"I'm all right!" called Miss Ogden from beneath her ridiculously large tuba.

"Er… right," said Mr Grave.

"Might need the kiss of life though!"

Mr Grave, impossibly, went even more pale. "Next," he said, ignoring the teacher struggling beneath her ridiculous brass instrument, "please welcome the final act to the stage – Zoe!"

There was a cough from the side of the stage.

Mr Grave looked down at his sheet of paper. "Oh, um, Zoe and Tina!"

The audience all applauded, none louder than Dad, who was sitting proudly in the front row. Raj was sat next to him, clapping excitedly.

Zoe and Tina ran on, in matching tracksuits, and took a bow. Then Tina lay down on the stage, as Zoe set up what looked like little ramps either side, which they had made from cereal boxes.

"Ladies and gentlemen, boys and girls, please welcome: 'The Amazing Armitage'!" said the little ginger girl.

At that moment, Armitage sped across the stage, riding a wind-up toy motorbike that Dad had bought from a charity shop and repaired, and wearing a tiny crash helmet.

The crowd went wild just at the sight of him, apart from Raj, who covered his eyes in fear. He was still scared of rodents.

"You can do it, Armitage," whispered Zoe. When they had practised, he had sometimes missed the ramp and just drove past it, which didn't make for a very exciting show.

Armitage whizzed faster and faster as he reached the ramp.

Come on, come on, come on, thought Zoe.

The little rat hit the ramp perfectly.

Yes!

Armitage took off —

Armitage flew through the air —

Oh no! thought Zoe.

He was coming down too soon. He was going
to miss the ramp on the other side.

Down, down, down Armitage fell—

Zoe held her breath—

And then he landed on Tina's ample tummy.

Bounced back up in the air.

And landed on the ramp on the other side.

It was a moment of pure and utter joy. It probably even looked deliberate.

"Oof," said Tina.

"Eek," said Armitage, bringing his motorbike to a perfect stop.

The audience instantly rose to their feet and gave them a standing ovation that went on for ages – Raj even peeked out from behind his hands.

Zoe looked at Armitage, then Tina, then her dad, who was clapping like a mad man.

She couldn't help but smile.

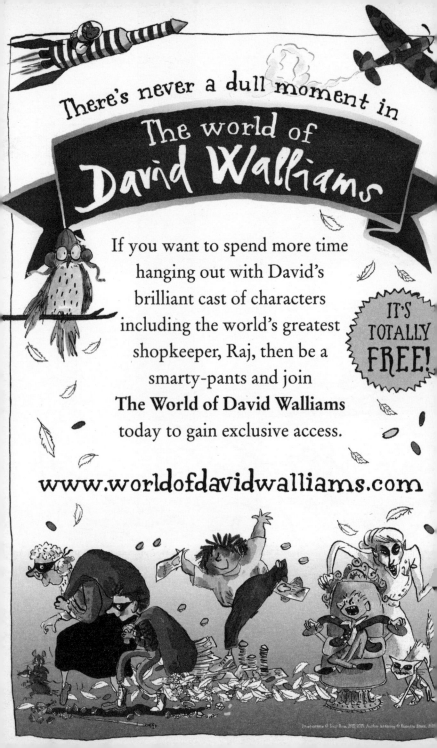

BILLIONAIRE BOY

David Walliams

BILLIONAIRE BOY

Illustrated by Tony Ross

HarperCollins *Children's Books*

First published in paperback in Great Britain by HarperCollins *Children's Books* 2011
HarperCollins *Children's Books* is a division of HarperCollins*Publishers* Ltd
1 London Bridge Street, London, SE1 9GF

The HarperCollins *Children's Books* website address is
www.harpercollins.co.uk

HarperCollins*Publishers*
1st Floor, Watermarque Building, Ringsend Road
Dublin 4, Ireland

84

ISBN 978-0-00-737108-2

Printed and bound by
CPI Group (UK) Ltd, Croydon, CR0 4YY

MIX
Paper from
responsible sources
FSC™ C007454

Voor Lara,

Ik hou meer van je, dan ik met woorden kan zeggen

Thank-yous:

I would like to thank a few people who helped make this book possible. I did most of the hard work, but I have to mention them. First, Tony Ross, for his illustrations. He could have coloured them in, but apparently you have to pay him extra. Next, I would like to thank Ann-Janine Murtagh. She is in charge of all HarperCollins children's books and is very nice and always has great suggestions. I have to say that, she is the boss. Then there is Nick Lake who is my editor. His job is to help me with the characters and story, and I couldn't do it without him. Well, I could actually, but he would cry if he wasn't mentioned here.

The cover was designed by James Stevens, and the interior was designed by Elorine Grant. I could say that 'Elorine' is a silly name, but I won't, that would be cruel. The publicist is Sam White. If you see me on *Loose Women* trying to flog this book, don't blame me, blame her. Sarah Benton, thank you so much for being the most wonderful marketing manager, whatever that is. The sales directors Kate Manning and Victoria Boodle did something too, though I am not sure what. Thank you also to the copyeditor Lily Morgan and the proofreader Rosalind Turner. If there are any spelling mistakes it's their fault. And thank you to my agent Paul Stevens at Independent for taking 10% plus VAT of my fee for sitting in his office all day drinking tea and eating biscuits.

Of course, a big thank you to *you* for buying this book. Really you shouldn't be bothering reading this bit though. It's boring. You need to get on with reading the story. It has already been called 'one of the greatest stories ever written'. Thanks for that, Mum.

1

Meet Joe Spud

Have you ever wondered what it would be like to have a million pounds?

Or a billion?

How about a trillion?

Or even a gazillion?

Meet Joe Spud.

Joe didn't *have* to imagine what it would be like to have loads and loads and loads of money. He was only twelve, but he was ridiculously, preposterously rich.

Joe had everything he could ever want.

- 100-inch plasma widescreen flat-screen high-definition TV in every room in the house ✓
- 500 pairs of Nike trainers ✓
- A grand-prix race track in the back garden ✓
- A robot dog from Japan ✓
- A golf buggy with the number plate 'SPUD 2' to drive around the grounds of his house ✓
- A waterslide which went from his

bedroom into an indoor Olympic-sized swimming pool ✔

- Every computer game in the world ✔
- 3-D IMAX cinema in the basement ✔
- A crocodile ✔
- 24-hour personal masseuse ✔
- Underground 10-lane bowling alley ✔
- Snooker table ✔
- Popcorn dispenser ✔
- Skateboard park ✔
- Another crocodile ✔
- £100,000 a week pocket money ✔
- A rollercoaster in the back garden ✔
- A professional recording studio in the attic ✔
- Personalised football coaching from the England team ✔
- A real-life shark in a tank ✔

In short, Joe was one horribly spoilt kid. He went to a ridiculously posh school. He flew on private planes whenever he went on holiday. Once, he even had Disneyworld closed for the day, just so he wouldn't have to queue for any rides.

Here's Joe. Speeding around his own private racetrack in his own Formula One racing car.

Some very rich children have miniature

versions of cars specially built for them. Joe wasn't one of those children. Joe needed his Formula One car made a bit *bigger*. He was quite fat, you see. Well, you would be, wouldn't you? If you could buy all the chocolate in the world.

You will have noticed that Joe is on his own in that picture. To tell the truth, speeding around a racetrack isn't that much fun when you are on

your own, even if you do have a squillion pounds. You really need someone to race against. The problem was Joe didn't have any friends. Not one.

- Friends ✕

Now, driving a Formula One car and unwrapping a king-size Mars Bar are two things you shouldn't try and do at the same time. But it had been a few moments since Joe had last eaten and he was hungry. As he entered the chicane, he tore open the wrapper with his teeth and took a bite of the delicious chocolate-coated nougat and caramel. Unfortunately, Joe only had one hand on the steering wheel, and as the wheels of the car hit the verge, he lost control.

The multi-million-pound Formula One car careered off the track, span around, and hit a tree.

SSSSSSSSSccccccc CCCCCCCCRRRRRRRRR RRRRRREEEeeeeeeeEEEEEECC cccccccccHHHHH HHHHHH!!!!!!!!!!!!! !!!!!!!!!!!!!!!!!!!!!!!!!!!!

The tree was unharmed. But the car was a write-off. Joe squeezed himself out of the cockpit. Luckily Joe wasn't hurt, but he was a little dazed, and he tottered back to the house.

"Dad, I crashed the car," said Joe as he entered the palatial living room.

Mr Spud was short and fat, just like his son. Hairier in a lot of places too, apart from his head – which was bald and shiny. Joe's dad was sitting on a hundred-seater crocodile skin sofa and didn't look up from reading that day's copy of the *Sun*.

"Don't worry Joe," he said. "I'll buy you another one."

Joe slumped down on the sofa next to his dad.

"Oh, happy birthday, by the way, Joe." Mr Spud handed an envelope to his son, without taking his eyes off of the magazine he was leafing through.

Joe opened the envelope eagerly. How much money was he going to receive this year? The card, which read 'Happy 12th Birthday Son', was quickly discarded in favour of the cheque inside.

Joe could barely disguise his disappointment. "One million pounds?" he scoffed. "Is that all?"

"What's the matter, son?" Mr Spud put down his newspaper for a moment.

"You gave me a million *last* year," whined Joe. "When I turned eleven. Surely I should get more now I'm twelve?"

Mr Spud reached into the pocket of his shiny grey designer suit and pulled out his chequebook. His suit was horrible, and horribly expensive. "I'm so sorry son," he said. "Let's make it two million."

Now, it's important you realise that Mr Spud had not always been this rich.

Not so long ago the Spud family had lived a very humble life. From the age of sixteen, Mr Spud worked in a vast loo-roll factory on the outskirts of town. Mr Spud's job at the factory was *sooooo* boring. He had to roll the paper around the cardboard inner tube.

Roll after roll.

Day after day.

Year after year.

Decade after decade.

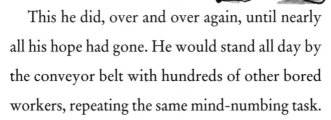

This he did, over and over again, until nearly all his hope had gone. He would stand all day by the conveyor belt with hundreds of other bored workers, repeating the same mind-numbing task.

Every time the paper was rolled onto one cardboard tube, the whole thing started again. And every loo roll was the same. Because the family was so poor, Mr Spud used to make birthday and Christmas presents for his son from the loo roll inner tubes. Mr Spud never had enough money to buy Joe all the latest toys, but would make him something like a loo-roll racing car, or a loo-roll fort complete with dozens of loo-roll soldiers. Most of them got broken and ended up in the bin. Joe did manage to save a sad looking little loo-roll space rocket, though he wasn't sure why.

The only good thing about working in a factory was that Mr Spud had lots of time to daydream. One day he had a daydream that was to revolutionise bottom wiping forever.

Why not invent a loo roll that is moist on one side and dry on the other? he thought, as he

rolled paper around his thousandth roll of the day. Mr Spud kept his idea top-secret and toiled for hours locked in the bathroom of their little council flat getting his new double-sided loo roll exactly right.

When Mr Spud finally launched 'Bumfresh', it was an instant phenomenon. Mr Spud sold a billion rolls around the world every day. And every time a roll was sold, he made 10p. It all added up to an awful lot of money, as this simple maths equation shows.

10p x 1,000,000,000 rolls x 365 days a year = a lot of wonga.

Joe Spud was only eight at the time 'Bumfresh' was launched, and his life was turned upside down in a heartbeat. First, Joe's mum and dad split up. It turned out that for many years Joe's mum Carol had been having a torrid affair with Joe's Cub Scout leader, Alan. She took a ten billion pound divorce settlement; Alan swapped his canoe for a gigantic yacht. Last anyone had heard, Carol and Alan were sailing off the coast of Dubai, pouring vintage champagne on their Crunchy Nut Cornflakes every morning. Joe's dad seemed to get over the split quickly and began going on dates with all sorts of wildly unsuitable ladies.

Soon father and son moved out of their poky council flat and into an enormous stately home. Mr Spud named it 'Bumfresh Towers'.

The house was so large it was visible from outer space. It took five minutes just to motor up the drive. Hundreds of newly-planted, hopeful little trees lined the mile-long gravel track. The house had seven kitchens, twelve sitting rooms, forty-seven bedrooms and eighty-nine bathrooms.

Even the bathrooms had en-suite bathrooms. And some of those en-suite bathrooms had en-en-suite bathrooms.

Despite living there for a few years, Joe had probably only ever explored around a quarter of the main house. In the endless grounds were tennis courts, a boating lake, a helipad and even a 100m ski-slope complete with mountains of fake snow. All the taps, door handles and even toilet seats were solid gold. The carpets were made from mink fur, he and his dad drank orange squash from priceless antique medieval goblets, and for a while they had a butler called Otis who was also an orang-utan. But he had to be given the sack.

"Can I have a *proper* present as well, Dad?" said Joe, as he put the cheque in his trouser pocket. "I mean, I've got loads of money already."

"Tell me what you want, son, and I'll get one of my assistants to buy it," said Mr Spud. "Some solid gold sunglasses? I've got a pair. You can't see out of 'em but they are very expensive."

Joe yawned.

"Your own speedboat?" ventured Mr Spud.

Joe rolled his eyes. "I've got two of those. Remember?"

"Sorry, son. How about a quarter of a million pounds worth of WHSmith vouchers?"

"Boring! Boring! Boring!" Joe stamped his feet in frustration. Here was a boy with high-class problems.

Mr Spud looked forlorn. He wasn't sure there was anything left in the world that he could buy his only child. "Then what, son?"

Joe suddenly had a thought. He pictured himself going round the racetrack all on his own, racing against himself. "Well, there is something I really want…" he said, tentatively.

"Name it, son," said Mr Spud.

"A friend."

2

Bum Boy

"Bum boy," said Joe.

"*Bum Boy*?" spluttered Mr Spud. "What else do they call you at school, son?"

"The Bog Roll Kid..."

Mr Spud shook his head in disbelief. He had sent his son to the most expensive school in England. St Cuthbert's School for Boys. The fees were £200,000 a term and all the boys had to wear Elizabethan ruffs and tights. Here is a picture of Joe in his school uniform. He looks a bit silly, doesn't he?

So the last thing that Mr Spud expected was

that his son would get bullied. Bullying was
something that happened to poor people. But the
truth was that Joe had been picked on ever since
he started at the school. The posh kids hated him,

because his dad had made his money out of loo rolls. They said that was 'awfully vulgar'.

"Bottom Billionaire, The Bum-Wipe Heir, Master Plop-Paper," continued Joe. "And that's just the teachers."

Most of the boys at Joe's school were Princes, or at least Dukes or Earls. Their families had made their fortunes from owning lots of land. That made them 'old money'. Joe had quickly come to learn that money was only worth having if it was old. New money from selling loo rolls didn't count.

The posh boys at St Cuthbert's had names like Nathaniel Septimus Ernest Bertram Lysander Tybalt Zacharias Edmund Alexander Humphrey Percy Quentin Tristan Augustus Bartholomew Tarquin Imogen Sebastian Theodore Clarence Smythe.

That was just one boy.

The subjects were all ridiculously posh too. This was Joe's school timetable:

Monday

Latin

Straw Hat wearing

Royal studies

The study of etiquette

Show-jumping

Ballroom dancing

Debating Society ('This house believes that it is vulgar to do up the bottom button on your waistcoat')

Scone eating

Bow-tie tying

Punting

Polo (the sport with horses and sticks, not the mint)

Tuesday

Ancient Greek

Croquet

Pheasant shooting

Being beastly to servants class

Mandolin level 3

History of Tweed

Nose in the air hour

Learning to step over the homeless person as
you leave the opera

Finding your way out of a maze

Wednesday

Fox-hunting

Flower arranging

Conversing about the weather

History of cricket

History of the brogue

Playing Stately Home Top Trumps

Reading *Harper's Bazaar*

Ballet appreciation class

Top-hat polishing

Fencing (the one with swords, not selling stolen goods)

Thursday

Antique furniture appreciation hour

Range Rover tyre changing class

Discussion of whose daddy is the richest

Competition to see who is best friends with
Prince Harry

Learning to talk posh

Rowing club

Debating Society ('This house believes that
muffins are best toasted')

Chess

The study of coats of arms

A lecture on how to talk loudly in restaurants

Friday

Poetry reading (Medieval English)

History of wearing corduroy

Topiary class

Classical sculpture appreciation class

Spotting yourself in the party pages of *Tatler* hour

Duck hunting

Billiards

Classical music appreciation afternoon

Dinner party discussion topic class (e.g. how the working classes smell)

However, the main reason why Joe hated going to St Cuthbert's wasn't the silly subjects. It was the fact that everyone at the school looked down on him. They thought that someone whose papa made their money from bog rolls was just too, too frightfully common.

"I want to go to a different school, Dad," said Joe.

"No problem. I can afford to send you to the poshest schools in the world. I heard about this place in Switzerland. You ski in the morning and then—"

"No," said Joe. "How about I go to the local comp?"

"*What*?" said Mr Spud.

"I might make a friend there," said Joe. He'd seen the kids milling around the school gates when he was being chauffeured to St Cuthbert's. They all looked like they were having such a great time – chatting, playing games, swapping cards. To Joe, it all looked so fabulously *normal*.

"Yes, but the local comp..." said Mr Spud, incredulously. "Are you *sure*?"

"Yes," replied Joe, defiantly.

"I could build you a school in the back garden if you like?" offered Mr Spud.

"No. I want to go to a normal school. With normal kids. I want to make a *friend*, Dad. I don't have a single friend at St Cuthbert's."

"But you can't go to a normal school. You are a billionaire, boy. All the kids will either bully you or want to be friends with you just because you are rich. It'll be a nightmare for you."

"Well, then I won't tell anyone who I am. I'll just be Joe. And maybe, just maybe, I'll make a friend, or even two..."

Mr Spud thought for a moment, and then relented. "If that's what you really want, Joe, then OK, you can go to a normal school."

Joe was so excited he bumjumped* along the sofa nearer to his dad to give him a cuddle.

"Don't crease the suit, boy," said Mr Spud.

[*Bumjumping (verb) *bum-jump-ing*. To move places while sitting using only your bottom to power you, thus meaning you do not have to get up. Much favoured by the overweight.]

"Sorry Dad," said Joe, bumjumping back a little. He cleared his throat. "Um... I love you, Dad."

"Yes, son, ditto, ditto," said Mr Spud, as he rose to his feet. "Well, have a good birthday, mate."

"Aren't we going to do something together tonight?" said Joe, trying to hide his disappointment. When he was younger, Joe's dad would always take him to the local burger restaurant as a birthday treat. They couldn't afford the burgers, so they would just order the chips, and eat them with some ham and pickle sandwiches that Mr Spud would smuggle in under his hat.

"I can't son, sorry. I've got a date with this stunning model tonight," said Mr Spud, indicating an advert in the magazine.

Joe looked at the page. There was a photograph of a woman's hand squirting toilet cleaner around a U-bend. "Well I say model, she is a hand model really. I can't wait to see her face." Underneath the image it read, 'Sapphire, 19, from Bradford. Likes shopping, hates thinking.'

"Don't you think Sapphire's a little young for you, Dad?" asked Joe.

"It's only a twenty-seven-year age gap," replied Mr Spud in an instant.

Joe wasn't convinced. "Well, where are you taking this Sapphire?"

"A nightclub."

"A *nightclub*?" asked Joe.

"Yes," said Mr Spud, in an offended tone. "I am not too old to go to a nightclub!" As he spoke he opened a box and pulled out what looked like a hamster that had been flattened by a mallet and put it on his head.

"What on earth is that, Dad?"

"What's what, Joe?" replied Mr Spud with mock innocence, as he adjusted the contraption to cover his bald dome.

"That thing on your head."

"Ooh, this. It's a toupee, boy! Only ten grand each. I bought a blonde one, a brown one, a ginger one, and an afro for special occasions. It makes me look twenty years younger, don't you think?"

Joe didn't like to lie. The toupee didn't make his dad look younger – instead, it made him look like a man who was trying to balance a dead rodent on his head. Therefore, Joe chose a non-committal, "Mmm."

"Right. Well, have a good night," Joe added, picking up the remote. It looked like it would be just him and the 100-inch TV again.

"There's some caviar in the fridge for your tea, son," said Mr Spud as he headed for the door.

"What's caviar?"

"It's fish eggs, son."

"Eurgh…" Joe didn't even like normal eggs much. Eggs laid by a fish sounded really revolting.

"Yeah, I had some on toast for me breakfast. It's absolutely disgusting, but it is very expensive so we should start eating it."

"Can't we just have bangers and mash or fish

and chips or Shepherd's Pie or something, Dad?"

"Mmm, I used to love Shepherd's Pie, son…" Mr Spud drooled a little, as if imagining the taste of Shepherd's Pie.

"Well then…?"

Mr Spud shook his head impatiently. "No no no, we are rich son! We have to eat all this posh stuff now like proper rich people do. See you later!" The door slammed behind him and moments later Joe heard the deafening roar of his father's lime-green Lamborghini speeding off into the night.

Joe was disappointed to be on his own again, but he still couldn't suppress a small smile as he turned on the TV. He was going to go to an ordinary school again and be an ordinary boy. And maybe, *just maybe*, make a friend.

The question was, how long could Joe keep the fact that he was a billionaire a secret…?

3

Who's the Fattiest?

Finally, the big day came. Joe took off his diamond-encrusted watch and put his gold pen in the drawer. He looked at the designer black snakeskin bag his dad had bought him for his first day at his new school and put it back in his cupboard. Even the bag that bag had *come in* was too posh, but he found an old plastic one in the kitchen and put his school books in that. Joe was determined not to stand out.

From the back seat of his chauffeur-driven Rolls Royce he had passed the local comprehensive many times on his way to St Cuthbert's, and seen the kids pouring out of the school. A rushing river of swinging bags and swear words and hair gel. Today, he was going to enter the gates for the first time. But he didn't want to arrive by Rolls Royce – that would be a pretty good hint to the other kids that he was rich. He instructed the chauffeur to drop him off at a nearby bus stop. It had been quite a few years since he had travelled by public transport, and as he waited at the bus stop Joe tingled with excitement.

"I can't change that!" said the bus driver.

Joe hadn't realised that a £50 note was not going to be welcome to pay for a two-pound fare, and had to get off the bus. Sighing, he began to walk the two miles to school, his flabby thighs rubbing together as he took each step.

Finally, Joe reached the school gates. For a moment he loitered nervously outside. He had spent so long living a life of wealth and privilege – how on earth was he going to fit in with these kids? Joe took a deep breath and marched across the playground.

At registration, there was only one other kid sitting on his own. Joe looked over at him. He was fat, just like Joe, with a mop of curly hair. When he saw Joe looking at him, he smiled. And when registration was finished, he came over.

"I'm Bob," said the fat boy.

"Hi Bob," replied Joe. The bell had just rung and they waddled along the corridor to the first lesson of the day. "I'm Joe," he added. It was weird to be in a school where no one knew who he was. Where he wasn't Bum Boy, or Billionaire Bum, or the Bumfresh Kid.

"I am so glad you're here, Joe. In the class I mean."

"Why's that?" asked Joe. He was excited. It

looked like he might have found his first friend already!

"Because I'm not the fattest boy in the school anymore," Bob said confidently, as if stating an independently verified fact.

Joe scowled, then stopped for a second and studied Bob. It looked to him like he and the other boy were about the same level of fattiness.

"How much do you weigh then?" demanded Joe grumpily.

"Well, how much do you weigh?" said Bob.

"Well, I asked you first."

Bob paused for a second. "About eight stone."

"I'm seven stone," said Joe, lying.

"No way are you seven stone!" said Bob angrily. "I'm twelve stone and you are much fatter than me!"

"You just said you were eight stone!" said Joe accusingly.

"I *was* eight stone…" replied Bob, "when I was a baby."

That afternoon it was cross-country running. What a dreadful ordeal for any day at school, not least your first day. It was a yearly torture that seemed designed solely to humiliate those kids who weren't sporty. A category Bob and Joe could definitely be squeezed into.

"Where is your running kit, Bob?" shouted Mr Bruise, the sadistic PE teacher, as Bob made his way onto the playing field. Bob was wearing his Y-fronts and vest, and his appearance was greeted by a huge wave of laughter from the other kids.

"S-s-s-someone m-m-must have hidden it S-s-s-sir," answered a shivering Bob.

"Likely story!" scoffed Mr Bruise. Like most PE teachers, it was difficult to imagine him

wearing anything other than a tracksuit.

"D-d-do I still have to do the r-r-r-run S-s-s-s-s-s-s-sir....?" asked a hopeful Bob.

"Oh yes, boy! You don't get off that easily. Right everyone, on your marks, get set... wait for it! GO!"

At first, Joe and Bob sprinted away like all the other kids, but after about three seconds they were both out of breath and were forced to walk. Soon everyone else had disappeared into the distance and the two fat boys were left alone.

"I come last every year," said Bob, unwrapping a Snickers and taking a large bite. "All the other kids always laugh at me. They get showered and dressed and wait at the finish line. They could all go home, but instead they wait just to jeer at me."

Joe frowned. That didn't sound like fun. He decided he didn't want to be last, and quickened his pace a little, making sure he was at least half a step ahead of Bob.

Bob glared at him, and piled on the speed, going up to at least half a mile an hour. From the determined expression on his face, Joe knew that

Bob was hoping that this year was his golden chance not to finish last.

Joe sped up a little more. They were now almost jogging. The race was on. For the ultimate prize: who was going to finish… second to last! Joe really didn't want to be beaten at cross-country running by a fat boy in his vest and pants on his first day at school.

After what seemed like an eternity the finish line hazed into sight. Both boys were out of breath with all this power-waddling.

Suddenly, disaster struck Joe. A painful stitch burst in his side.

"Ooww!" cried Joe.

"What's the matter?" asked Bob, now quite a few centimetres in the lead.

"I've got a stitch… I've got to stop. Owww…"

"You're bluffing. A fifteen-stone girl pulled

that on me last year and ended up beating me by a fraction of a second."

"Oww. It's true," said Joe, holding his side tightly.

"I ain't falling for it, Joe. You are going to be last, and this year all the kids in the year are gonna be laughing at you!" said Bob triumphantly, as he edged ahead still further.

Being laughed at on his first day at school was the last thing Joe wanted. He'd had enough of being laughed at when he was at St Cuthbert's. However, the stitch was becoming more and more painful with every step. It was as if it was burning a hole in his side. "How about I give you a fiver to come last?" he said.

"No way," replied Bob, through heaving breaths.

"A tenner?"

"No."

"Twenty quid?"

"Try harder."

"Fifty quid."

Bob stopped, and looked around at Joe.

"Fifty quid…" he said. "That's a lot of chocolate."

"Yeah," said Joe. "Tons."

"You've got yourself a deal. But I want the wonga now."

Joe searched through his shorts and pulled out a fifty-pound note.

"What's that?" asked Bob.

"It's a fifty pound note."

"I've never seen one before. Where did you get it?"

"Oh, erm, it was my birthday last week you see…" said Joe, stumbling over his words a little. "And my dad gave me that as a present."

The marginally fatter boy studied it for a moment, holding it up to the light as if it was a priceless artefact. "Wow. Your dad must be *loaded*," he said.

The truth would have blown Bob's fat mind. That Mr Spud had given his son two million pounds as a birthday present. So Joe kept schtum.

"Nah, not really," he said.

"Go on then," said Bob. "I'll come last again. For fifty quid I would finish tomorrow if you like."

"Just a few paces behind me will be fine," said Joe. "Then it will look real."

Joe edged ahead, still gripping his side in pain. Hundreds of little cruelly smiling faces were coming into focus now. The new boy crossed the finish line with only a hum of mocking laughter. Trailing behind was Bob, clutching his fifty-pound note, since there were no pockets in his Y-fronts. As he neared the finish line the kids started chanting.

"BLOB! BLOB! BLOB! BLOB!
BLOB! BLOB! BLOB! BLOB!
BLOB! BLOB! BLOB! BLOB!
BLOB! BLOB! BLOB! BLOB!
BLOB! BLOB! BLOB!"

The chants grew louder and louder.

"BLOB! BLOB! BLOB!
BLOB! BLOB! BLOB!
BLOB! BLOB! BLOB!
BLOB! BLOB! BLOB!
BLOB! BLOB! BLOB!
BLOB! BLOB! BLOB!
BLOB! BLOB! BLOB!
BLOB! BLOB! BLOB!
BLOB! BLOB! BLOB!
BLOB! BLOB! BLOB!
BLOB! BLOB! BLOB!
BLOB! BLOB! BLOB!"

They started clapping in time now.

BLOB! BLOB! BLOB! BLOB!
BLOB! BLOB! BLOB! BLOB!
BLOB! BLOB! BLOB! BLOB!
BLOB! BLOB! BLOB! BLOB!
BLOB! BLOB! BLOB! BLOB!
BLOB! BLOB! BLOB! BLOB!
BLOB! BLOB! BLOB! BLOB!
BLOB! BLOB! BLOB! BLOB!
BLOB! BLOB! BLOB! BLOB!
BLOB! BLOB! BLOB! BLOB!
BLOB! BLOB! BLOB! BLOB!
BLOB! BLOB! BLOB! BLOB!
BLOB! BLOB! BLOB! BLOB!
BLOB! BLOB! BLOB! BLOB!
BLOB! BLOB! BLOB! BLOB!
BLOB! BLOB!"

Undeterred, Bob hurled his body across the finish line.

"HA! HA! HA! HA!
HA! HA! HA! HA! HA!
HA! HA! HA! HA! HA!
HA! HA! HA! HA! HA! HA! HA!
HA! HA! HA! HA! HA! HA! HA!
HA! HA! HA! HA! HA! HA!
HA! HA! HA! HA! HA!
HA! HA! HA! HA! HA!
HA! HA! HA! HA! HA!

HA! HA! HA! HA! HA!
HA! HA! HA! HA! HA!
HA! HA! HA! HA! HA! HA!
HA! HA! HA! HA! HA! HA! HA!
HA! HA! HA! HA! HA! HA! HA!
HA! HA! HA! HA! HA! HA! HA!
HA!"

The other kids fell around laughing, pointing at Bob, as he bent over and panted for breath.

Turning around, Joe felt a sudden twinge of guilt. As the school kids dispersed, he went over to Bob and helped him stand up straight.

"Thanks," said Joe.

"You're welcome," said Bob. "To be honest I should have done that anyway. If you came last on your very first day, you'd never hear the end of it. But next year you're on your own. I don't care if you give me a million pounds – I ain't coming last again!"

Joe thought about his two million pound birthday cheque. "What about two million pounds?" he joked.

"Deal!" said Bob, laughing. "Imagine if you really did have that much money. It would be crazy! I guess you could have everything you ever wanted!"

Joe forced a smile. "Yeah," he said. "Maybe..."

4

"Loo Rolls?"

"So, did you forget your kit on purpose?" asked Joe.

Mr Bruise had locked up the changing rooms by the time Joe and Bob had finished their cross-country run... well, cross-country walk. They stood outside the grey concrete building, Bob shivering in his pants. They'd already been to find the school secretary, but there was absolutely no one left in the whole place. Well, apart from the caretaker. Who didn't seem to speak English. Or any other language for that matter.

"No," replied Bob, a little hurt at the suggestion. "I may not be the fastest runner, but I'm not that much of a coward."

They trudged through the school grounds, Joe in his singlet and shorts, and Bob in his vest and pants. They looked like two rejects from a boy band audition.

"So who took it?" said Joe.

"I dunno. It might be the Grubbs. They're the school bullies."

"The Grubbs?"

"Yeah. They're twins."

"Oh," said Joe. "I haven't met them yet."

"You will," replied Bob, dolefully. "You know, I feel really bad about taking your birthday money off you…"

"You don't have to," said Joe. "It's fine."

"But fifty pounds is a lot of money," Bob protested.

Fifty pounds was not a lot of money to the Spuds. Here are a few things Joe and his dad would do with fifty-pound notes:

- Light them instead of bits of old newspaper to get the barbecue going
- Keep a pad of them by the telephone and use them as post-it notes
- Line the hamster cage with handfuls of them and then throw them out after a week when they began to smell of hamster wee

- Let the same hamster use one as a towel after it's had a shower
- Filter coffee through them
- Make paper hats out of them to wear on Christmas day
- Blow their noses on them

- Spit chewed-up chewing gum into them before crumpling them and placing them in the hand of a butler who would then put them in the hand of a footman who would then put them in the hand of a maid who would then put them in the bin
- Make paper aeroplanes out of them and throw them at each other
- Wallpaper the downstairs loo with them

"I never asked," said Bob. "What does your dad do?"

Joe panicked for a moment. "Erm, he, er, he makes loo rolls," he said, only lying a tiny bit.

"*Loo rolls?*" said Bob. He couldn't suppress his smile.

"Yes," replied Joe defiantly. "He makes loo rolls."

Bob stopped smiling. "That doesn't sound like it pays all that well."

Joe winced. "Er... no, it doesn't."

"Then I guess your dad had to save for weeks to give you £50. Here you go." Bob carefully handed the now-slightly-crumpled fifty-pound note back to Joe.

"No, you keep it," protested Joe.

Bob pressed the note into Joe's hand. "It's your birthday money. You keep it."

Joe smiled uncertainly and closed his hand

over the money. "Thank you, Bob. So, what does *your* dad do?"

"My dad died last year."

They continued walking in silence for a moment. All Joe could hear was the sound of his heart beating. He couldn't think of anything to say. All he knew was that he felt awful for his new friend. Then he remembered that when someone died people sometimes said, 'I'm sorry'.

"I'm sorry," he said.

"It's not your fault," said Bob.

"I mean, well, I'm sorry he died."

"I'm sorry too."

"How did he… you know?"

"Cancer. It was really scary. He just got more and more ill and then one day they took me out of school and I went to the hospital. We sat by his bed for ages and you could hear his breath rattling and then suddenly the sound just stopped. I ran outside to get the nurse and she came in and said he was 'gone'. It's just me and my mum now."

"What does your mum do?"

"She works at Tesco. On the checkout. That's where she met my dad. He would shop on Saturday mornings. He used to joke that he 'only came in for a pint of milk but left with a wife!'"

"It sounds like he was funny," said Joe.

"He was," said Bob, smiling. "Mum's got another job too. She's a cleaner at an old people's home in the evenings. Just to make ends meet."

"Wow," said Joe. "Doesn't she get tired?"

"Yeah," said Bob. "So I do a lot of the cleaning and stuff."

Joe felt really sorry for Bob. Since he was eight, Joe had never had to do anything at home – there was always the butler or the maid or gardener or the chauffeur or whoever to do everything. He took the note out of his pocket. If there was one person who needed the money more than him it was Bob. "Please, Bob, keep the £50."

"No. I don't want to. I'd feel bad."

"Well, let me at least buy you some chocolate."

"You've got a deal," said Bob. "Let's go to Raj's."

5

Out of Date Easter Eggs

D<small>ING</small>!

No, reader, that's not your doorbell. No need
to get up. It's the sound of the bell tinkling in
Raj's shop as Bob and Joe opened the door.

"Ah, Bob! My favourite customer!" said Raj.
"Welcome, welcome!"

Raj ran the local newsagent's shop. All the
local kids adored him. He was like the funny
uncle you always wished you had. And even
better than that, he sold sweets.

"Hi, Raj!" said Bob. 'This is Joe."

"Hello Joe," exclaimed Raj. "Two fat boys in

my shop at one time! The Lord must be smiling on me today! Why have you both got so little on?"

"We came straight from cross-country running Raj," explained Bob.

"Fantastic! How did you do?"

"First and second…" replied Bob.

"That's wonderful!" exclaimed Raj.

"…to last," finished Bob.

"That's not so good. But I imagine you boys must be hungry after all that exercise. How can I help you today?"

"We'd like to buy some chocolate," said Joe.

"Well, you have come to the right place. I have the finest selection of chocolate bars in this parade!" Raj announced triumphantly. Considering the only other shops in the parade were a launderette and a long since closed florist that wasn't saying much, but the boys let it pass.

Now, one thing Joe knew for certain was that chocolate didn't have to be expensive to taste nice. In fact, after a few years of gorging themselves on the finest chocolates from Belgium or Switzerland, he and his dad had realised that they weren't half as delicious as a Yorkie. Or a bag of Minstrels.

Or, for the true connoisseur, a Double Decker.

"Well, let me know if I can help you gentlemen," said the newsagent. The stock in Raj's shop was haphazardly laid out. Why was a car magazine next to the Tipp-ex? If you couldn't find the Jelly Tots, it was entirely possible that they might be hiding under a copy of the *Sun* from 1982. And did the post-it notes really have to be in the freezer?

However, local people kept coming to the shop because they loved Raj, and he loved his customers too, particularly Bob. Bob was one of his absolute best customers.

"We are happy just to browse thanks," replied Bob. He was studying the rows and rows of confectionery, looking for something special. And today money wasn't a problem. Joe had a fifty-pound note in his pocket. They could even afford one of Raj's out of date Easter eggs.

"The Wispas are very good today, young Sirs. Fresh in this morning," ventured Raj.

"We are just looking thank you," replied Bob politely.

"The Cadbury's Creme Eggs are in season," suggested the newsagent.

"Thank you," said Joe politely, smiling.

"Just to say, gentlemen, I am here to help," said Raj. "If you have any questions please don't hesitate to ask."

"We will," said Joe.

There was a brief moment of silence.

"Just to let you know the Flake is off today, Sirs," continued Raj. "I should have said. A problem with the supplier, but I should have them back on sale tomorrow."

"Thanks for letting us know," said Bob. He and Joe shared a look. They were beginning to wish the newsagent would let them shop in peace.

"I can recommend a Ripple. I had one earlier and they are exquisite at the moment."

Joe nodded politely.

"I'll leave you alone to make up your own mind. As I say, I am here to help."

"Can I have one of these?" said Bob, lifting up a giant bar of Cadbury's Dairy Milk to show Joe.

Joe laughed. "Of course you can!"

"An excellent choice, gentlemen. I have those on special offer today. Buy ten get one free," said Raj.

"I think we just need the one right now, Raj," said Bob.

"Buy five get half a one free?"

"No thanks," said Joe. "How much is it?"

"£3.20 please."

Joe took out the fifty-pound note.

Raj looked at it in wonder. "Oh my! I have never seen one of those before. You must be a very rich young man!"

"Not at all," said Joe.

"His dad gave it to him for his birthday," chimed in Bob.

"Lucky boy," said Raj. He peered at Joe. "You know, you look familiar, young man."

"Do I?" replied Joe nervously.

"Yes I am sure I have seen you somewhere before." Raj tapped his chin as he thought. Bob stared at him, baffled. "Yes," said Raj eventually. "Only the other day I saw a picture of you in a magazine."

"I doubt it, Raj," scoffed Bob. "His dad

makes loo rolls!"

"That's it!" exclaimed Raj. He riffled through a pile of old newspapers and pulled out the *Sunday Times Rich List*.

Joe started to panic. "I've got to go…"

The newsagent flicked through the pages. "There you are!" Raj indicated a photograph of Joe sitting awkwardly on the front of his Formula One racing car, and then read aloud from the magazine. "Britain's Richest Children. Number one: Joe Spud, age twelve. Bumfresh heir. Estimated worth, ten billion."

A large lump of chocolate dropped from Bob's mouth onto the floor. "Ten *billion*?"

"No way have I got ten billion," protested Joe. "The press always exaggerate. I've got eight billion at the most. And I won't even get most of it till I'm older."

"That's still a lot of money!" exclaimed Bob.

"Yes, I suppose it is."

"Why didn't you tell me? I thought we were mates."

"I'm sorry," stammered Joe. "I just wanted to be normal. And it's so embarrassing being the son of a bog-roll billionaire."

"No no no you should be proud of your dad!" exclaimed Raj. "His story is an inspiration to all of us. A humble man who became a billionaire with one simple idea!"

Joe had never really thought of his dad like that.

"Leonard Spud revolutionised the way we wipe our bottoms forever!" Raj chuckled.

"Thanks, Raj."

"Now, please tell your father I have just started using Bumfresh and I love it! My bottom has never been so sparkling! See you next time!"

The two boys walked along the street in

silence. All you could hear was Bob sucking the chocolate from between his teeth.

"You lied to me," said Bob.

"Well I did tell you he worked in bog rolls," said Joe, uncomfortably.

"Yeah but…"

"I know. I'm sorry." It was Joe's first day at school, and his secret was already out. "Here, have the change," said Joe, reaching in his pocket for the two twenty-pound notes.

Bob looked crushed. "I don't want your money."

"But I'm a billionaire," said Joe. "And my dad's got squillions. I don't even know what that means, but I know it's loads. Just take it. Here, have this lot too." He pulled out a roll of £50 notes.

"I don't want it," said Bob.

Joe's face crinkled with incredulity. "Why not?"

"Because I don't care about your money. I just liked hanging out with you today."

Joe smiled. "And I liked hanging out with you." He coughed. "Look, I really am sorry. It's just... the kids at my old school used to bully me because I was the Bumfresh boy. I wanted to just be a normal kid."

"I can understand that," said Bob. "I mean, it would be nice to start again."

"Yeah," said Joe.

Bob stopped, and held out his hand. "I'm Bob," he said.

Joe shook his hand. "Joe Spud."

"No other secrets?"

"No," said Joe, smiling. "That's it."

"Good," said Bob, smiling too.

"You won't tell anyone at school, will you?" said Joe. "About me being a billionaire. It's so embarrassing. Especially when they find out how my dad became rich. Please?"

"Not if you don't want me to."

"I don't. I really don't."

"Well, I won't then."

"Thanks."

The two continued down the street. After a few paces Joe couldn't wait any longer. He turned to Bob, who had already polished off half the massive bar of Dairy Milk. "Can I have some chocolate then?" he asked.

"Yes of course. This is for us to share," said Bob, as he broke off his friend a tiny square of chocolate.

6

The Grubbs

"OI! BLOB!" came a shout from behind them.

"Just keep walking," said Bob.

Joe turned to look around and glimpsed a pair of twins. They looked terrifying – like gorillas in human suits. These must be the dreaded Grubbs Bob had talked about.

"Don't look round," said Bob. "I'm serious. Just keep walking."

Joe was beginning to wish he was luxuriating in the safety of the back seat of his chauffeur-driven Rolls Royce, rather than walking to the bus stop.

"FATSO!"

As Joe and Bob walked faster, they could hear footsteps behind them. Although it was still early, the winter sky was blackening. The street lamps flickered on and blotches of yellow light spilled onto the wet ground.

"Quick, let's run down here," said Bob. The boys dashed down an alley, and hid behind a giant green wheely bin that was parked at the back of a Bella Pasta.

"I think we've lost them," whispered Bob.

"Are those the Grubbs?" asked Joe.

"Shh. Keep your voice down!"

"Sorry," whispered Joe.

"Yeah, it's the Grubbs."

"The ones who bully you?"

"That's them. They're identical twins. Dave and Sue Grubb."

"*Sue*? One of them's a girl?" Joe could swear that when he'd turned around and seen the twins following them, both of them had thick facial hair.

"Sue's a girl, yes," said Bob, as if Joe was some kind of idiot.

"Then they can't be identical," whispered Joe. "I mean, if one's a boy and one's a girl."

"Well, yes, but no one can tell them apart."

Suddenly Joe and Bob heard footsteps coming closer and closer.

"I can smell fat boys!" came a voice from the other side of the bin. The Grubbs wheeled the bin away to reveal the two boys crouching behind it. Joe took his first good look at the pair. Bob was right. The Grubbs were identical. They both had matching crew-cuts, hairy knuckles and moustaches. All of which seemed unfortunate for both of them.

Let's play spot the difference with the Grubbs.

Can you spot the ten differences between these two?

No you can't. They are exactly the same.

A gust of cold wind hummed through the alley. An empty can trundled past on the ground. Something twitched in the bushes.

"How was the cross-country run without your kit today Blob?" chuckled one Grubb.

"I knew that was you two!" Bob replied angrily. "So what did you do with it?"

"It's in the canal!" chuckled the other.

"Now give us your chocolate." Even hearing their voices didn't give any clues as to who was Dave and who was Sue. Both their voices wavered high and low in one sentence.

"I'm taking some home for my mum," protested Bob.

"I don't care," said the other Grubb.

"Give us it you little ****," said the other one.

I have to confess, reader, that the **** bit was a swear word. Other swear words include ****,

******** and of course the incredibly rude
*************************. If you don't know
any swear words it's best to ask a parent or
teacher or other responsible adult to make a list
for you.

For example, here are some of the rude words
I know:

Puttock

Krunter

Noog

Smagger

Mingming

Klazbo

Furp

Fedger

Nadgers

Blimblam

Coobdrizz

Trunt

Joofer

Klootzak

Bullmunter

Gunder

Whizzplop

Huppeltrut

Bwatter

Lopcrock

Moozer

Frink

Dangle Spangles

Boola Boola

Burmnop

Oodplops

Lingpoop

Twutter

Ploomfizz

Lumweed

Moomers

Blamfan

Pognots

Voogan Bits

Zucky zuck

Sming

Kumbo Drops

Poot Puddle

Kungo

Bimbim

Paffer

Goollyging

Nonkey

Humbum

Ponk

Hool

Blunkers

Pumpum

Minki

Gruntbunt

Poob

Drazz

Nockynooters

Luzzer

Plimplam

Vart

All of those words are so rude I wouldn't dream of putting them in this book.

"Don't pick on him!" said Joe. Then he instantly regretted drawing attention to himself again as the Grubbs took a step towards him.

"Or what?" said either Dave or Sue, their breath toxic from a bag of Skips they had recently snatched from a little girl in year five.

"Or…" Joe searched his mind for something to say that would crush these bullies forever. "Or I'll be very disappointed with you both."

That wasn't it.

The Grubbs laughed. They snatched what was left of the Cadbury's Dairy Milk bar from Bob's hand and then grabbed his arms. They lifted him up and, as Bob yelled for help, they deposited him into the wheely bin. Before Joe could say anything else the Grubbs were stomping off down the road laughing, with their mouths full of stolen chocolate.

Joe dragged a wooden crate over, then stood on it to give himself more height. He leaned down into the bin and caught hold of Bob under the armpits. With a great heave, he started to pull his heavy friend out of the bin.

"Are you OK?" he asked, as he strained to take Bob's weight.

"Oh, yeah. They do this to me most days," said Bob. He pulled some spaghetti and parmesan cheese out of his curly hair – some of it might have been there since the last time the Grubb twins deposited him in a bin.

"Well, why don't you tell your mum?"

"I don't want to make her worry about me. She's got enough to worry about already," replied Bob.

"Maybe you should tell a teacher then."

"The Grubbs said if I ever told anyone that they would really beat me up. They know where I live and even if they got expelled they could still find me," said Bob. He looked like he was about to cry. Joe didn't like to see his new friend upset. "One day, I'll get them back. I will. My dad always used to say the best way to beat bullies is to stand up to them. One day I will."

Joe looked at his new friend. Standing there in his underwear, covered in scraps of Italian food. He thought of Bob standing up to the Grubbs. The fat boy would get massacred.

But maybe there's another way, he thought. *Maybe I can get the Grubbs off his back forever.*

He smiled. He still felt bad about paying Bob to come last in the race. Now he could make up for it. If his plan worked, he and Bob were going to be more than just friends. They'd be *best* friends.

7

Gerbils on Toast

"I bought you something," said Joe. He and Bob were sitting on the bench in the playground, watching the more agile kids play football.

"Just because you are a billionaire, doesn't mean you have to buy me anything," said Bob.

"I know, but…" Joe brought a large bar of Dairy Milk out of his bag. Bob's eyes couldn't help but light up a little.

"We can share it," said Joe, before snapping off a tiny square of chocolate. Then breaking that tiny square in half.

Bob's face fell.

"I'm only joking!" said Joe. "Here." He handed Bob the bar to help himself.

"Oh, no," said Bob.

"What?" said Joe.

Bob pointed. The Grubbs were walking slowly across the playground towards them, right through the games of football. Not that anyone dared to complain.

"Quick, let's make a run for it," said Bob.

"Where?"

"The dining room. They wouldn't dare go in there. No one does."

"Why?"

"You'll see."

When they burst into the dining room it was completely empty, aside from a lone dinner lady.

The Grubbs burst in a few paces behind them,

their genders still uncertain.

"If you aren't eating, get out!' shouted Mrs Trafe.

"But Mrs Trafe…?" said either Dave or Sue.

"I SAID 'OUT'!"

The twins reluctantly retreated, as Joe and Bob tentatively made their way to the serving counter.

Mrs Trafe was a large, smiley soul, of dinner-lady age. Bob had explained on the way to the canteen that she was nice enough, but her food was truly revolting. The kids in the school would rather die than eat anything she cooked. In fact they probably *would* die if they ate anything she cooked.

"Who's that, then?" said Mrs Trafe, peering at Joe.

"This is my friend, Joe," said Bob.

Despite the vile smell in the canteen, Joe felt

warmth spread through him. No one had ever called him their friend before!

"Now what would you like today, boys?" Mrs Trafe said with a warm smile. "I have a very nice badger and onion pie. Some deep-fried rust. Or for the vegetarians I have jacket potatoes with sock cheese."

"Mmm, it all looks so nice," said Bob, lying, as the Grubbs stared in at them through the grimy windows.

Mrs Trafe's cooking was truly unspeakable. A typical week's menu for the school canteen looked like this:

Monday

Soup of the day – wasp

Gerbils on toast

Or

Hair lasagne (vegetarian option)

Or

Brick cutlet

All served with deep-fried cardboard

Dessert – A slice of sweat cake

Tuesday

Soup of the day – Caterpillar consommé

Macaroni snot (vegetarian option)

Or

Road-kill bake

Or

Slipper frittata

All served with spider's web salad

Dessert – Toenail ice cream

Wednesday

Soup of the day – Cream of hedgehog

Parrot kedgeree (may contain nuts)

Or

Dandruff risotto

Or

Bread sandwich (slice of bread between two slices of bread)

Or

Char-grilled kitten (healthy option)

Or

Soil bolognese

All served with either boiled wood or deep fried iron filings

Dessert – Squirrel dropping tart with cream or ice cream

Thursday: Indian Day

Soup of the Day – Turban

To start – Paper poppadoms (A4 or A3 sizes) with chutney

Main course – Wet-wipe tandoori (vegan)

Or

Moth korma (spicy)

Or

Newt vindaloo (very spicy)

All served with bogey bhajis

Dessert – a refreshing sand sorbet

Friday

Soup of the day – Terrapin

Pan-fried otter steaks

Or

Owl quiche (kosher)

Or

Boiled poodle (not suitable for

vegetarians)

All served with a slice of gravy

Dessert – Mouse mousse

"It's so hard to choose…" said Bob, desperately scouring the trays of food for something edible. "Mmm, I think we will just have two jacket potatoes please."

"Is there any chance I could have it without the sock cheese?" pleaded Joe.

Bob looked hopefully at Mrs Trafe.

"I could sprinkle on some ear-wax shavings if you prefer? Or a showering of dandruff?" offered Mrs Trafe with a smile.

"Mmm, I think I will just have it totally plain please," said Joe.

"Some boiled mould on the side perhaps? You are growing boys…" offered Mrs Trafe, wielding a serving spoon of something green and unspeakable.

"I'm on a diet, Mrs Trafe," said Joe.

"Me too," said Bob.

"That's a shame, boys," said the dinner lady

dolefully. "I have a smashing dessert on today. Jellyfish and custard."

"My absolute favourite too!" said Joe. "Never mind."

He took his tray to one of the empty tables and sat down. As he put his knife and fork into the potato he realised that Mrs Trafe had forgotten to cook it.

"How are your spuds?" called Mrs Trafe across the hall.

"Delicious, thank you, Mrs Trafe," Joe called back, as he pushed his raw potato round the plate. It was still covered in soil and he noticed a maggot burrowing out of it. "I hate it when they are too well done. This is perfect!"

"Good good!" she said.

Bob was trying to chew his but it was so utterly inedible he started crying.

"Something the matter, boy?" called Mrs Trafe.

"Oh no, it's so delicious that these are tears of joy!" said Bob.

DDDDDDDDDRRRRRRRRRRIIII IIIIIIIIINNNNNNNNNNGGGG GGGGGGG!

Once again, that wasn't your doorbell, reader. That was the bell to signal the end of lunch.

Joe let out a sigh of relief. Dinner hour was over.

"Oh, what a shame, Mrs Trafe," said Joe. "We have to go to our Maths lesson now."

Mrs Trafe limped over and inspected their plates.

"You've hardly touched them!" she said.

"Sorry. It was just so filling. And really really tasty though," said Joe.

"Mmm," seconded Bob, still crying.

"Well it doesn't matter. I can put them in the

fridge for you and you can finish them off tomorrow."

Joe and Bob shared a horrified look.

"Really, I don't want you to go to any trouble," said Joe.

"No trouble at all. See you then. And I've got some specials tomorrow. It's the anniversary of the bombing of Pearl Harbour, so it's Japanese day. I'm doing my armpit hair sushi, followed by tadpole tempura... Boys...? Boys...?"

"I think the Grubbs have gone," said Bob as they sneaked out of the canteen. "I've just got to use the bog."

"I'll wait for you," said Joe. He leaned against the wall, as Bob disappeared through a door. Usually Joe would have said that the lavatories were smelly – and he'd have been horrified to have to use them, after the privacy of his own en-en-suite bathroom, with emperor-size bath.

But the truth was that the toilets didn't smell as bad as the canteen.

Suddenly Joe sensed two figures looming behind him. He didn't need to turn round. He knew it was the Grubbs.

"Where is he?" said one.

"He's in the boys' loo, but you can't go in there," said Joe. "Well, not both of you, anyway."

"Where's the chocolate bar?" asked the other.

"Bob's got it," said Joe.

"Well, we'll wait for him then," said the Grubb.

The other Grubb turned to Joe, a deadly look in its eye. "Now give us a pound. Unless you want a dead arm, that is."

Joe gulped. "Actually... I'm glad I bumped into you two guys, well, guy and a girl, obviously."

"Obviously," said Dave or Sue. "Give us a pound."

"Wait," said Joe. "It's just… I wondered if—"

"Give him a dead arm, Sue," said a Grubb, revealing for perhaps the first time which of the twins was male and which was female. But then the Grubbs grabbed Joe and spun him around, and he lost track again.

"No! Wait," said Joe. "The thing is, I want to make you two an offer…"

8

The Witch

DDDDDDDRrrrrrrrriiiiiiiiiiNNN NNNNGGGGGGGGG!

"The bell is a signal for me, not you!" said Miss Spite sharply. Teachers love saying that. It's one of their catchphrases, as I'm sure you know. The all-time top ten of teachers' catchphrases goes like this:

 At ten… "Walk, don't run!"

 A non-mover at nine… "Are you chewing?"

Up three places to eight... "I can still hear talking."

A former number one at seven... "It doesn't need discussion."

A new entry at six... "How many times do you need to be told?"

Down one place at five... "Spelling!"

Another non-mover at four... "I will not tolerate litter!"

New at three... "Do you want to pass your GCSEs?"

Just missing the top spot at two... "Would you do that at home?"

And still at number one... "It's not just yourself you've let down, but the whole school."

Taking the History lesson was Miss Spite. Miss Spite smelt of rotten cabbage. That was the nicest thing about her. She was one of the school's most feared teachers. When she smiled she looked like a crocodile that was about to eat you. Miss Spite loved nothing more than giving out punishments, once suspending a girl for dropping a pea on the floor of the school canteen. "That pea could have had someone's eye out!" she had yelled.

Kids at the school had fun thinking up

nicknames for their teachers. Some were fond, others cruel. Mr Paxton the French teacher was 'Tomato', as he had a big round red face like a tomato. The headmaster, Mr Dust, was called 'The Tortoise' as he looked like one. He was very old, extremely wrinkly, and walked impossibly slowly. The deputy head, Mr Underhill, was 'Mr Underarms', as he ponged a bit, especially in the summer. And Mrs MacDonald, the biology teacher, was called either 'The Bearded Lady' or even 'Hairy Maclary from Donaldson's Dairy' as she... well, I imagine you can guess why.

But the kids just called Miss Spite 'The Witch'. It was the only name that really ever fitted and was passed down through generations of pupils at the school.

All the kids she taught passed their exams though. They were too scared not to.

"We still have the small matter of last night's

homework," Miss Spite announced with an evil relish that suggested she was desperate for someone to have failed to do it.

Joe reached his hand into his bag. Disaster. His exercise book wasn't there. He had spent all night writing this intensely boring 500-word essay about some old dead Queen, but in the rush to get to school on time he must have left it on his bed.

Oh, no, he thought. *Oh no no no no no...*

Joe looked over at Bob, but all his friend could do was grimace sympathetically.

Miss Spite stalked the classroom like a Tyrannosaurus Rex deciding which little creature it was going to eat first. To her evident disappointment, a field of grubby little hands held aloft essay after essay. She gathered them up, before stopping at Spud.

"Miss...?" he stammered.

"Yeeeessss Sssppppuuudddd?" said Miss Spite, drawing out her words as long as possible so she could relish this delicious moment.

"I did do it, but…"

"Oh yes, of course you did it!" The Witch cackled. All the other pupils except Bob sniggered too. There was nothing more pleasurable than seeing someone else get into trouble.

"I left it at home."

"Litter duty!" the teacher snapped.

"I am not lying, Miss. And my dad will be at home today, I could—"

"I should have known. Your father is clearly penniless and on the dole, sitting at home watching daytime TV – much as you will no doubt be doing in ten years' time. Yes…?"

Joe and Bob couldn't help but share a smirk at this.

"Er…" said Joe. "If I called him and asked

him to run the essay over here would you believe me?"

Miss Spite smiled broadly. She was going to enjoy this.

"Spud, I will give you fifteen minutes exactly to place said essay in my hand. I hope your father is quick."

"But—" started Joe.

"No 'buts' boy. Fifteen minutes."

"Well thank you Miss," said Joe sarcastically.

"You're quite welcome," said the Witch. "I like to think that everyone gets a fair chance to rectify their errors in my class."

She turned to the rest of the class. "The rest of you are dismissed," she said.

Kids started to spill out into the corridor. Miss Spite leaned after them and screamed, "Walk, don't run!"

Miss Spite couldn't resist another catchphrase.

She was the queen of the catchphrase. And now she couldn't stop.

"It doesn't need discussion!" she called after her pupils, randomly. Miss Spite was on a roll now. "Are you chewing?" she howled down the corridor to a passing school inspector.

"Fifteen minutes, Miss?" said Joe.

Miss Spite studied her little antique watch. "Fourteen minutes, fifty one seconds, in point of fact."

Joe gulped. Was Dad going to be able to get there that fast?

9

"Finger?"

"Finger?" asked Bob, as he offered half of his Twix to his friend.

"Thank you, mate," said Joe. They stood in a quiet corner of the playground and contemplated Joe's bleak fate.

"What are you going to do?"

"I dunno. I texted my dad. But there's no way he can get here in fifteen minutes. What can I do?"

A few ideas raced through Joe's mind.

He could invent a time machine and travel

back in time and remember not to forget his homework. It might be a bit hard to do though, as if time machines *had* ever been invented then maybe someone would have come back from the future and prevented Piers Morgan's birth.

Joe could go back to the classroom and tell Miss Spite that 'the tiger had eaten it'. This would only be half a lie, as they did have a private zoo and a tiger. Called Geoff. And an alligator called Jenny.

Become a nun. He would have to live in a nunnery and spend his days saying prayers and singing hymns and doing general religious stuff. On the one hand the nunnery would give him sanctuary from Miss Spite and he did look good in black, but on the other hand it might get a bit boring.

Go and live on another planet. Venus is nearest, but it might be safer to go to Neptune.

Live the rest of his life underground. Perhaps even start a tribe of below-the-surface-of-the-earth dwellers and create a whole secret society of people who all owed Miss Spite some homework.

Have plastic surgery and change his identity. Then live the rest of his life as an old lady called Winnie.

Become invisible. Joe wasn't sure how this might be achieved.

Run to the local bookshop and buy a copy of *How to Learn Mind Control in Ten Minutes* by Professor Stephen Haste and very quickly hypnotise Miss Spite into thinking he had already given her his homework.

Disguise himself as a plate of spaghetti Bolognese.

Bribe the school nurse into telling Miss Spite he had died.

Hide in a bush for the rest of his life. He could survive on a diet of worms and grubs.

Paint himself blue and claim to be a Smurf.

Joe had barely had time to consider these options when two familiar shadows loomed behind them.

"Bob," said one of them, in a voice neither high nor low enough to determine its gender.

The boys turned around. Bob, tired of

fighting, simply handed them his slightly nibbled finger of Twix.

"Don't worry," he whispered to Joe. "I've concealed a large number of Smarties down my sock."

"We don't want your Twix," said Grubb number one.

"No?" said Bob. His mind started racing. Could the Grubbs possibly know about the Smarties?

"No, we wanted to say we are very sorry for bullying you," said Grubb number two.

"And as a peace gesture we would like to invite you round for tea," prompted Grubb number one.

'Tea?" asked Bob, incredulous.

"Yes, and maybe we can all play Hungry Hippos together," continued Grubb number two.

Bob looked at his friend, but Joe just shrugged.

"Thank you, guys, I mean guy and girl, obviously..."

"Obviously," said an unidentified Grubb.

"...but I am a bit busy tonight," continued Bob.

"Maybe another time," said a Grubb, as the twins lolloped off.

"That was weird," said Bob, retrieving some Smarties that now had a faint taste of sock. "I couldn't imagine a night when I would want to go and play Hungry Hippos with those two. Even if I lived until I was a hundred."

"Yeah, how strange..." said Joe. He glanced away quickly.

At that moment, a deafening roar silenced the playground. Joe looked up. A helicopter was hovering overhead. Very quickly all the football games broke up, and the kids raced out of the way of the descending aircraft. Items from hundreds of packed lunches were whisked up in the air by the force of the blades. Packets of Quavers, a mint-chocolate Aero, even a Müller Fruit Corner danced about in the whirling air, before smashing to the ground as the engine shut down and the blades slowed to a stop.

Mr Spud leaped out of the passenger seat and raced across the playground holding the essay.

Oh no! thought Joe.

Mr Spud was wearing a brown toupee that he held on to his head with both hands, and an all-in-one gold jumpsuit with 'BUM AIR'

emblazoned on the back in sparkly letters. Joe felt like he was going to die of embarrassment. He tried to hide himself behind one of the older kids. However, he was too fat and his dad spotted him.

"Joe! Joe! There you are!" shouted Mr Spud.

All the other kids stared at Joe Spud. They hadn't paid much attention to this short fat new boy before. Now it turned out his dad had a helicopter. A real-life helicopter! Wow!

"Here's your essay, son. I hope that's OK. And I realised I forgot to give you your dinner money. Here's £500."

Mr Spud pulled out a wad of crisp new £50 notes from his zebra-skin wallet. Joe pushed the money away, as all the other kids looked on in envy.

"Shall I pick you up at 4pm son?" asked Mr Spud.

"It's OK, thanks, Dad, I'll just get the bus," muttered Joe, looking down at the ground.

"You can pick *me* up in your helicopter, mate!" said one of the older boys.

"And me!" shouted another.

"And me!"

"Me!"

"ME!!"

"PICK ME!!!"

Soon all the kids in the playground were shouting and waving to get this short, fat, gold-jumpsuited man's attention.

Mr Spud laughed. "Maybe you can invite some of your friends over at the weekend and they can all have a helicopter ride!" he pronounced with a smile.

A huge cheer echoed around the playground.

"But Dad..." That was the last thing Joe wanted. For everyone to see how monstrously expensive their house was and how much crazy stuff they owned. He checked his plastic digital watch. He had less than 30 seconds to go.

"Dad, I gotta run," blurted out Joe. He snatched the essay out of his father's hands and raced into the main school building as fast as his short fat legs would take him.

Running up the staircase, he raced past the unfeasibly old headmaster, who was making his way down on a Stannah Stairlift. Mr Dust looked at least 100 years old, but was probably older. He was more suited to being an exhibit in the Natural History Museum than administrating a school, but he was harmless enough.

"Walk, don't run!" he mumbled. Even very old teachers are fond of catchphrases.

Hurling himself along the corridor to the classroom where Miss Spite was waiting, Joe realised half the school was following him. He even heard someone shout, "Hey, Bumfresh Boy!"

Unnerved, he pushed on, bursting into the classroom. The witch was holding her watch in her hand.

"I've got it, Miss Spite!" proclaimed Joe.

"You are five seconds late!" she proclaimed.

"You have got to be kidding Miss!" Joe couldn't believe anyone could be so mean. He glanced back behind him and saw hundreds of pupils were staring at him through the glass. Such was the eagerness to catch a glimpse of the richest boy in the school, or perhaps even the world, noses were pushed up against the glass so they looked like a tribe of pig-children.

"Litter duty!" said Miss Spite.

"But Miss—"

"A week's litter duty!"

"Miss—"

"One month's litter duty!"

Joe decided to say nothing this time and sloped across the classroom. He closed the door behind him. In the corridor hundreds of little pairs of eyes were still staring at him.

"Oi! Billionaire Boy!" came a deep voice from the back. It was one of the older boys, but Joe couldn't tell which one. In the sixth form *all* the boys had moustaches and Ford Fiestas. All the little mouths laughed.

"Lend us a million quid!" someone shouted. The laughter was now deafening. The noise clouded the air.

My life is officially over, thought Joe.

10

Dog Spit

As Joe scurried across the playground to the dining room, all the other kids swarmed around him. Joe kept his head down. He didn't like this instant superstardom at all. Voices whirled around him.

"Hey, Bum Boy! I'll be your best friend!"

"My bike got nicked. Buy us a new one mate."

"Lend us a fiver…"

"Let me be your bodyguard!"

"Do you know Justin Timberlake?"

"Me granny needs a new bungalow, give us a hundred grand will ya?"

"How many helicopters have you got?"

"Why do you bother going to school anyway, you are rich!"

"Can I have your autograph?"

"Why don't you have a massive party at yours on Saturday night?"

"Can I have a lifetime's supply of bog rolls?"

"Why don't you buy the school and sack all the teachers?"

"Can't you just buy me a bag of Maltesers? All right then, one Malteser? You are sooo mean!"

Joe started running. The crowd started running too. Joe slowed down. The crowd slowed down too. Joe turned and walked in the other direction. The crowd turned and walked in the other direction.

A little ginger-haired girl tried to grab his bag, and he thumped her hand away with his fist.

"Ow! My hand is probably broken," she cried. "I am going to sue you for ten million pounds!"

"Hit me!" said another voice.

"No me! Hit me!" said another.

A tall boy with glasses had a better idea. "Kick me in the leg and we can settle out of court for two million! Please?"

Joe sprinted into the school dining room. That was one place that was guaranteed to be empty at lunchtime. Joe struggled to force the double doors back on the tsunami of schoolchildren, but it was no use. They burst through, flooding the room.

"FORM AN ORDERLY QUEUE!" shouted the dinner lady, Mrs Trafe. Joe walked up to the serving counter.

"Now what would you like today, young Joe?" she said with a warm smile. "I have a very stinging nettle soup to start today."

"I am not that hungry today, maybe I'll go straight to a main course Mrs Trafe."

"It's chicken breast."

"Ooh, that sounds nice."

"Yes it comes in a dog spit sauce. Or for vegetarians I have deep fried Blu-tack."

Joe gulped. "Mmm, it's so hard to decide. See, I had some dog spit only last night."

"That's a shame. I'll give you a plate of the fried Blu-Tack then," said the dinner lady, as she dumped a lump of something blue and greasy and vomit-inducing on to Joe's plate.

"If you ain't having lunch then get out!" cried Mrs Trafe at the crowd still cowering at the doors.

"Spud's dad has got a helicopter Mrs Trafe," came a voice from the back.

"He's super-rich!" came another.

"He's changed!" came a third.

"Just give me a dead arm, Spud, and I will take a quarter of a million," came a tiny voice from the back.

"I SAID OUT!" shouted Mrs Trafe. The crowd reluctantly retreated, and contented themselves with staring at Joe through the grimy windows.

With his knife he removed the batter from the blue lump underneath. Now that raw potato seemed like food of the gods. After a few moments Mrs Trafe limped over to his table.

"Why are they all staring at you like that?" she asked kindly, as she slowly slumped her heavy frame down next to him.

"Well, it's a long story Mrs Trafe."

"You can tell me, pet," said Mrs Trafe. "I'm a school dinner lady. I reckon I've heard it all."

"Right, well…" Joe finished chewing the large lump of Blu-Tack he had in his mouth, and told the old dinner lady everything. About how his father had invented 'Bumfresh', how they now lived in a massive mansion, how they once had an orang-utan as a butler (she was very jealous of that bit), and how no one would have guessed a thing had his stupid dad not landed his stupid helicopter in the playground.

All the time he talked, the other kids continued to stare through the windows at him like he was an animal in the zoo.

"I am so sorry, Joe," said Mrs Trafe. "It must

be awful for you. You poor thing. Well not *poor* exactly, but you know what I mean."

"Thank you Mrs Trafe." Joe was surprised anyone would ever feel sorry for someone who had everything. "It's not easy. I don't know who to trust any more. All the kids in the school seem to want something from me now."

"Yeah, I bet," said Mrs Trafe, bringing out an M&S sandwich from her bag.

"You bring a packed lunch?" asked Joe, surprised.

"Oh yes, I wouldn't eat this filth. It's disgusting," she said. Her hand crept across the table and rested on his.

"Well, thanks for listening Mrs Trafe."

"That's OK, Joe. I am here for you anytime. You know that – anytime." She smiled. Joe smiled too. "Now…" said Mrs Trafe. "I just need ten thousand quid for a hip replacement…"

11

Camping Holiday

"You missed a bit," said Bob.

Joe bent down and picked up another piece of litter from the playground and put it in the bin liner Miss Spite had so generously provided. It was five o'clock now and the playground was empty of children. Only their litter remained.

"I thought you said you were going to help me," accused Joe.

"I am helping you! There's another bit." Bob pointed to another sweet wrapper that was lying on the asphalt, as he munched a bag of crisps. Joe bent down to pick it up. It was a Twix wrapper.

Probably the one he himself had dropped on the ground earlier that day.

"Well I guess everyone knows how rich you are now, Joe," said Bob. "Sorry about that."

"Yeah, I guess so."

"I suppose now all the kids at the school are going to want to be your friend..." said Bob, quietly. When Joe looked at him, Bob turned away.

"Maybe," Joe smiled. "But it means more that we were friends before everyone knew."

Bob grinned. "Cool," he said. Then he pointed to the ground at his feet. "You missed another bit there, Joe."

"Thanks, Bob," sighed Joe, as he bent down again, this time to pick up the crisp packet his friend had just dropped.

"Oh, no," said Bob.

"What's the matter?"

"Grubbs!"

"Where?"

"Over by the bike shed. What do they want?"

Lurking behind the shed were the twins. When they spotted Joe and Bob, they waved.

"I don't know what was worse," continued Bob. "Being bullied by them or being invited around for tea."

"HELLO, BOB!" shouted one Grubb, as they started lolloping towards them.

"Hello, Grubbs," Bob called back wearily.

Inexorably, the two bullies reached where the two boys were standing.

"We have been thinking," continued the other. "We are going on a camping trip at the weekend. Would you like to come?"

Bob looked at Joe for help. A camping holiday with these two was not an inviting invitation.

"Oh, what a terrible shame," said Bob. "I am busy this weekend."

"Next weekend?" asked Grubb one.

"That one too, I'm afraid."

"The one after that?" asked the other.

"Completely..." stammered Bob, "...chock full of things I've got to do. So sorry. It sounds so much fun. Anyway, see you two tomorrow, sorry, I would love to chat but I have to help Joe with his litter duty. Bye!"

"Any weekend next year?" asked the first Grubb.

Bob stopped. "Um... er... um... next year is, really busy for me. So I'd really really love to but I am so so sorry..."

"How about the year after?" asked Grubb Two. "Any free weekends? We have a lovely tent."

Bob couldn't keep it in any longer. "Look.

One day you're bullying me, the next you are inviting me to spend the weekend with you in a tent! What on earth is going on?"

The Grubbs looked to Joe for help. "Joe?" said one of them.

"We thought it would be easy being nice to Blob," said the other. "But he just says no to everything. What do you want us to do, Joe?"

Joe coughed, not very subtly. But the Grubbs didn't seem to get the hint.

"You paid them not to bully me, didn't you?" demanded Bob.

"No," replied Joe unconvincingly.

Bob turned to the Grubbs. "*Did* he?" he demanded.

"Noyes..." said the Grubbs. "We mean yesno."

"How much did he pay you?"

The Grubbs looked at Joe for help. But it was too late. They were all busted.

"Ten pounds each," said a Grubb. "And we *saw* the helicopter, Spud. We're not stupid. We want more cash."

"Yeah!" continued the other. "And you're

going in the bin, Joe, unless you give us eleven pounds each. First thing tomorrow."

The Grubbs stomped off.

Bob's eyes filled with angry tears. "You think money is the answer to everything don't you?"

Joe was baffled. He had paid off the Grubbs to *help* Bob. He was utterly perplexed as to why his friend was so upset. "Bob, I was just trying to help you, I didn't—"

"I am not some charity case, you know."

"I know that, I was just..."

"Yes?"

"I just didn't want to see you put in the bin again."

"Right," said Bob. "So you thought it would be better if the Grubbs were really weird and friendly and going on about camping trips."

"Well, they sort of came up with the camping trip on their own. But yes."

Bob shook his head. "I can't believe you. You're such a... such a... spoiled brat!"

"What?" said Joe. "I was just helping you out! Would you really rather be put in the bin and have your chocolate stolen?"

"Yes!" shouted Bob. "Yes, I would! I'll fight my own battles, thank you!"

"Suit yourself," said Joe. "Have fun being dumped in the bin."

"I will," replied Bob before storming off.

"Loser!" shouted Joe, but Bob didn't turn back.

Joe stood alone. A sea of litter surrounded him. He stabbed at a Mars wrapper with his litter stick. He couldn't believe Bob. He thought he'd found a friend, but all he'd really found was a selfish, bad tempered, ungrateful... *Ploomfizz*.

12

Hand Model

"... and the Witch still made me do litter duty!" said Joe. He was sitting with his dad at one end of the highly polished thousand-seater dining-room table waiting for his dinner. Impossibly large diamond candelabras hung overhead, and paintings that weren't very nice but cost millions of pounds adorned the walls.

"Even after I dropped your homework off in the chopper?" said Mr Spud, angrily.

"Yeah, it was so unfair!" replied Joe.

"I did not invent a double sided moist/dry toilet tissue for my son to be put on litter duty!"

"I know," said Joe. "That Miss Spite is such a cow!"

"I am going to fly to the school tomorrow and give that teacher of yours a piece of my mind!"

"Please don't, Dad! It was embarrassing enough when you turned up today!"

"Sorry, son," said Mr Spud. He looked a little hurt, which made Joe feel guilty. "I was just trying to help."

Joe sighed. "Just don't do it again, Dad. It's so awful everyone knowing I am the son of the Bumfresh man."

"Well, I can't help that, boy! That's how I made all this money. That's why we are living in this big house."

"Yeah… I guess," said Joe. "Just don't come turning up in your Bum Air helicopter or anything, yeah?"

"OK," said Mr Spud. "So, how's that friend

of yours working out?"

"Bob? He's not really my friend any more," replied Joe. He hung his head a little.

"Why's that?" asked Mr Spud. "I thought you and him were getting on really well?"

"I paid off these bullies to help him," said Joe. "They were making his life a misery, so I gave them some cash to leave him alone."

"Yeah, so?"

"Well, he found out. And then, get this, he got all upset. He called me a spoiled brat!"

"Why?"

"How do I know? He said he'd rather get bullied than have me help him."

Mr Spud shook his head in disbelief. "Bob sounds a bit of a fool to me. The thing is, when you've got money like we do, you meet a lot of ungrateful people. I reckon you're better off without this Bob character. It sounds like he doesn't understand the importance of money. If he wants to be miserable, let him."

"Yeah," agreed Joe.

"You'll make another friend at school, son," said Mr Spud. "You're rich. People like that. The sensible ones, anyway. Not like this idiot Bob."

"I'm not so sure," said Joe. "Not now everyone knows who I am."

"You will Joe. Trust me," said Mr Spud with a smile.

The immaculately attired butler entered the dining room through the vast oak panelled double doors. He did a little theatrical cough to get his master's attention. "Miss Sapphire Stone, gentlemen."

Mr Spud swiftly put on his ginger toupee as renowned hand model Sapphire clip-clopped into the room in her impossibly high heels.

"Sorry I'm late, I was just at the tanning

salon," she announced.

This was evident. Sapphire had fake tan smeared over every inch of her skin. She was now orange. As orange as an orange, if not orangier. Think of the orangiest person you've ever met, then times their orangeness by ten. As if she didn't look frightful enough already, she was wearing a lime green mini-dress and clutching a shocking pink handbag.

"What's *she* doing here?" demanded Joe.

"Be nice!" mouthed Dad.

"Nice pad," said Sapphire, looking round admiringly at the paintings and chandeliers.

"Thank you. It's just one of my seventeen homes. Butler, please tell Chef that we want our dinner now. What are we having tonight?"

"Foie gras, Sir," replied the butler.

"What's that?" asked Mr Spud.

"Specially fattened goose liver, Sir."

Sapphire grimaced. "I'll just have a bag of crisps."

"Me too!" said Joe.

"And me!" said Mr Spud.

"Three packets of potato crisps coming right up, Sir," sneered the butler.

"You look beautiful tonight, my angel!" said Mr Spud, before approaching Sapphire for a kiss.

"Don't smudge me lip liner!" said Sapphire, as she repelled him forcefully with her hand.

Mr Spud was clearly a little hurt, but tried to hide it. "Please take a seat. I see you brought the new Dior handbag I sent you."

"Yeah, but this bag comes in eight colours," she complained. "One for each day of the week. I thought you were gonna buy me all eight."

"I will, my sweet princess…" spluttered Mr Spud.

Joe stared at his dad. He couldn't believe he

had fallen for such a wrong'un.

"Dinner is served," announced the butler.

"Here, my beautiful angel of love, take a seat," said Mr Spud, as the butler pulled out a chair for her.

Three waiters entered the room carrying silver trays. They carefully placed the plates down on the table. The butler nodded and the waiters lifted the silver covers to reveal three packets of Salt n' Vinegar crisps. The trio started eating. Mr Spud initially attempted to eat his crisps with his knife and fork to appear posh, but soon gave up.

"Now me birfday's only eleven months away," said Sapphire. "So I've made a little wish-list of presents you are going to buy me…"

Her fingernails were so long and fake she could barely fish the piece of paper from her pink handbag. It was like watching one of those grabber machines at the fair where you never win anything. Eventually she grasped it and passed it over to Mr Spud. Joe looked over his dad's shoulder and read what she had scribbled.

Sapphire's Birfday Wish-list

A solid gold Rolls Royce convertible

A million pounds in cash

500 pairs of Versace sunglasses

A holiday home in Marbella (large)

A bucket of diamonds

A unicorn

A box of Ferrero Rocher chocolates (large)

A great big massive like really big yacht

A large tank of topical fish*

'Beverly Hills Chihuahua' on DVD

I think she must mean tropical fish, rather than fish that are up on the news and current affairs.

5000 bottles of Chanel perfume

Another million pounds in cash

Some gold

Lifetime subscription to *OK* magazine

A private jet (new please, not second-hand)

A talking dog

General expensive stuff

100 designer dresses (I don't mind which ones as long as they are expensive. Any ones I don't like me mum can flog down the market)

A pint of semi-skimmed milk

Belgium

"Of course I will get all these things for you, my angel sent from heaven," slobbered Mr Spud.

"Thanks, Ken," said Sapphire, her mouth full of crisps.

"It's Len," corrected Dad.

"Oh, sorry, yeah! LOL! Len! Silly me!" she said.

"You can't be serious!" said Joe. "You're not really going to buy her all that stuff are you?"

Mr Spud gave Joe an angry look. "Why not, son?" he said, trying to control his temper.

"Yeah, why not, you little git?" said Sapphire. Definitely not controlling *her* temper.

Joe hesitated for a moment. "It's plain to see you're only with my dad for the money."

"Don't talk to your mother like that!" shouted Mr Spud.

Joe's eyes nearly popped out of his head. "She's not my *mother*, she's your stupid girlfriend and she's only seven years older than me!"

"How dare you!" fumed Mr Spud. "Say sorry."

Joe defiantly remained silent.

"I said, 'say sorry'!" shouted Mr Spud.

"No!" shouted Joe.

"Go to your rooms!"

Joe pushed back his chair, making as much of a clatter as possible, and stomped upstairs, as the staff pretended not to see.

He sat on the edge of his bed and cradled himself in his arms. It was a long, long time since anyone had hugged him, so he hugged himself. He squeezed his own sobbing plumpness. He was beginning to wish that Dad had never invented 'Bumfresh' and they were all still living in the council flat with Mum. After a few moments, there was a knock on the door. Joe sat in defiant silence.

"It's your dad."

"Go away!" shouted Joe.

Mr Spud opened the door and sat down next to his son on the bed. He nearly slid off the bedspread onto the floor. Silk sheets may look nice, but they aren't very practical.

Mr Spud bumjumped a little nearer to his son.

"I don't like to see my little Spud like this. I know you don't like Sapphire, but she makes me happy. Can you understand that?"

"Not really," said Joe.

"And I know you had a tough day at school too. With that teacher, the Witch, and with that ungrateful boy, Bob. I'm sorry. I know how much you wanted a friend, and I know I didn't make it any easier. I will have a quiet word with the headmaster. Try and sort things out for you if I can."

"Thanks, Dad." Joe sniffed. "I'm sorry I was crying." He hesitated for a moment. "I do love you, Dad."

"Ditto, son, ditto," replied Mr Spud.

13

New Girl

The half-term holidays came and went, and when Joe returned to school on the Monday morning he found he wasn't the centre of attention any more. There was a new girl at school, and because she was soooooooo pretty everyone was talking about her. When Joe walked into his classroom there she was, like a giant unexpected present.

"So what's the first lesson today?" she asked as they walked across the playground.

"Sorry?" spluttered Joe.

"I said, 'what's the first lesson today?'"

the new girl repeated.

"I know, it's just... you're really talking to me?" Joe couldn't believe it.

"Yes, I am talking to you," she laughed. "I'm Lauren."

"I know." Joe wasn't sure if the fact that he had remembered her name made him sound suave or like a stalker.

"What's your name?" she asked.

Joe smiled. At last there was someone at the school who knew nothing about him.

"My name is Joe," he said to Lauren.

"Joe what?" asked Lauren.

Joe didn't want her to know that he was the Bumfresh billionaire. "Erm, Joe Potato."

"Joe Potato?" she asked, more than a little surprised.

"Yes..." stammered Joe. In the moment he had been too overwhelmed by her beauty to be able to come up with a better alternative to 'Spud'.

"Unusual name, Potato," said Lauren.

"Yes, I suppose it is. It is actually spelt with an 'e' at the end. Joe *Potatoe*. So it's not quite the vegetable 'potato'. That would be ridiculous! Ha ha!"

Lauren tried to laugh too, but she was looking at Joe a little oddly. *Oh no*, thought Joe. *I only met this girl one minute ago and she already thinks I'm nuts.* He quickly tried to change the subject. "We've got Maths next with Mr Crunch," he said.

"OK."

"And then we've got History with Miss Spite."

"I hate History, it's so boring."

"You'll hate it even more with Miss Spite. She's a good teacher, I suppose, but all us kids

hate her. We call her 'The Witch'!"

"That's so funny!" said Lauren, giggling.

Joe felt ten feet tall.

Bob bobbed into view. "Er… Hi Joe."

"Oh, hi Bob," Joe replied. The two former
friends hadn't seen each other over the half term.
Joe had spent his days alone racing around and
around his racetrack in a new Formula One car
his dad had bought him. And Bob had spent
most of the week in a bin. Wherever Bob was the

Grubbs seemed to find him, lift him up by his ankles and deposit him in the nearest skip. Well, that *was* what Bob had said he wanted.

Joe had missed Bob, but this wasn't good timing. Right now he was talking to the prettiest girl in the school, maybe even the prettiest girl in the whole of the local area!

"I know we haven't seen each other in a while. But… well… I've been thinking about what we said when you were doing litter duty…" stammered Bob.

"Yeah?"

Bob seemed a little taken aback by Joe's impatient tone, but pressed on. "Well, I am sorry we fell out, and I would like us to be friends again. You could move your desk back so that—"

"Do you mind if I talk to you later, Bob?" said Joe. "I am quite busy right now."

"But—" began Bob, a wounded expression on his face.

Joe ignored it. "I'll see you around," he said.

Bob marched off ahead.

"Who was that? A friend of yours?" enquired Lauren.

"No no no, he's not my friend," replied Joe. "Bob's his name, but he's so fat everyone calls him 'Blob'!"

Lauren laughed again. Joe felt a tiny bit sick, but he was so pleased to be making the pretty new girl laugh that he pushed the feeling all the way down inside him.

For the duration of the maths class Lauren kept on looking over at Joe. It put him right off his algebra. In History she was definitely gazing in his direction too. As Miss Spite droned on and on about the French revolution, Joe started to daydream about kissing Lauren. She was so very pretty that Joe wanted to kiss her more than anything. However, being only twelve Joe had never kissed a girl before, and had no idea how to make it happen.

"And the name of the king of France in 1789 was…? Spud?"

"Yes, Miss?" Joe stared at Miss Spite, horrified. He hadn't been listening at all.

"I asked you a question, boy. You haven't been paying attention, have you? Do you want to pass your exam?"

"Yes, Miss. I was listening…" stammered Joe.

"What is the answer then, boy?" demanded Miss Spite. "Who was the king of France in 1789?"

Joe had no idea. He was pretty sure it wasn't King Kevin II, or King Craig IV, or King Trevor the Great, because kings didn't tend to have names like that.

"I am waiting," pronounced Miss Spite. The bell rang. *I'm saved!* thought Joe.

"The bell is a signal for me, not you!" pronounced Miss Spite. Of course she was going to say that. She lived to say that. It would probably be written on her tombstone. Lauren was sitting behind where Miss Spite was standing, and she suddenly waved at Joe to get his attention. He was confused for a moment, then realised she was trying to help him by miming the answer. First she acted out someone going to the bathroom.

"King Toilet the…?" offered Joe.

The class all burst out laughing. Lauren shook her head. Joe had another try. "King Lavatory?"

They laughed again.

"King Bog?"

They laughed even harder this time.

"King Loo…? Ah, King Louis the…"

"Yes, boy?" Miss Spite continued her interrogation. Behind her Lauren mimed numbers with her fingers.

"King Louis the fifth, the tenth, the fifteenth, sixteen! King Louis the sixteenth!" declared Joe.

Lauren mimed a little clap.

"That's right, Spud," said a suspicious Miss Spite, before turning to the board and writing on it. "King Louis the sixteenth."

Stepping out into the spring sunshine, Joe turned to Lauren. "You totally saved my butt in there."

"That's OK. I like you." She smiled.

"Really...?" asked Joe.

"Yes!"

"Well, then, I wonder if..." Joe stumbled over his words. "If, well..."

"Well, what...?"

"If you, well, I mean you probably wouldn't,

in fact you definitely wouldn't, I mean, why would you? You are so pretty and I am just a big lump, but…" The words were spiralling out of his mouth in all directions now, and Joe was beginning to blush fiercely with embarrassment. "Well, if you wanted to…"

Lauren took over the speaking for a bit. "If I wanted to go for a walk in the park after school and maybe grab an ice lolly? Yes, I would love to."

"*Really*?" Joe was incredulous.

"Yes, really."

"With me?"

"Yes, with you, Joe Potatoe."

Joe was a hundred times happier than he could ever remember. It didn't even matter that Lauren thought his last name was Potatoe.

14

The Shape of a Kiss

"Oi!"

It had all been going perfectly. Joe and Lauren had been sitting on a park bench eating their lollies from Raj's shop. Raj could see Joe was trying to impress this girl, and so made a ridiculous fuss of him, giving him a one-penny discount on their lollies, and offering Lauren a free browse of *Now* magazine.

At last, though, they had escaped the newsagent's shop and found a quiet corner of the park, where they had been talking and talking as the melted red goo of their lollies dribbled down their fingers. They spoke about everything except Joe's family life. Joe didn't want to lie to Lauren. He already liked her too much for that. So when she asked him what his parents did he just told her his dad worked in 'human waste management' and unsurprisingly Lauren didn't enquire any further. Joe desperately didn't want Lauren to know how ridiculously rich he was. Having observed how Sapphire shamelessly used his dad, he knew only too well how money could ruin things.

Everything was perfect... until the sound of that "Oi!" spoiled everything.

The Grubb twins had been hanging around by the swings aching for someone to tell them off. Unfortunately for them, the police, the park-keeper and the local vicar were all otherwise engaged. So when one of them spotted Joe they bounced over grinning, no doubt hoping to relieve their boredom by making someone else's life a misery for a bit.

"Oi! Give us some more money or we'll put you in a bin!"

"Who are they talking to?" whispered Lauren.

"Me," said Joe reluctantly.

"Money!" said a Grubb. "Now!"

Joe reached into his pocket. Maybe if he gave them each a £20 note they would leave him alone, for today at least.

"What are you doing, Joe?" asked Lauren.

"I just thought…" he stammered.

"What's it to you, you moo?" said Grubb One.

Joe looked down at the grass, but Lauren handed Joe what was left of her lolly and rose from the bench. The Grubbs shifted around uneasily. They weren't expecting a thirteen-year-old girl to literally stand up to them.

"Sit down!" said Grubb Two, as he or she put his or her hand on Lauren's shoulder to force her down onto the bench. Lauren, however, grabbed his or her hand and twisted it behind his or her back, and then pushed him or her to the ground. The other Grubb charged her, so Lauren leaped into the air and kung-fu kicked him or her to the ground. Then the other

one leaped up and tried to grab her, but she karate-chopped him or her on his or her shoulder and he or she raced off screaming in pain.

It really is quite hard writing this when you don't know someone's gender.

Joe felt it was about time he did something so he stood up and, his legs shaking in fear, approached the Grubb. It was only then that Joe realised he was still holding two melting ice lollies. The remaining twin stood its ground for a moment, and then when Lauren stood behind Joe he or she ran off, whimpering like a dog.

"Where did you learn to fight like that?" said Joe, astounded.

"Oh, I've just done a few martial arts classes, here and there," replied Lauren, a little unconvincingly.

Joe reckoned he might have found his dream

girl. Not only could Lauren be his girlfriend, she could be his bodyguard too!

They walked through the park. Joe had walked through it many times before, but today it seemed more beautiful than ever. As the sunlight danced through the leaves on the trees on this Autumn afternoon, for a moment everything in Joe's life seemed perfect.

"I'd better head home," Lauren said, as they neared the gate.

Joe tried to hide his disappointment. He could have strolled round the park with Lauren forever.

"Can I buy you lunch tomorrow?" he asked.

Lauren smiled. "You don't have to buy me anything. I'd love to have lunch with you, though, but I'm paying, you understand?"

"Well, if you really want to," said Joe. Wow. This girl was too good to be true.

"What's the school canteen like?" said Lauren.

How could Joe find the words? "Um, well, it's… it's great if you are on a very strict diet."

"I love healthy food!" said Lauren. That wasn't quite what Joe meant, but it was the best place at school for a date as it was guaranteed to be quiet.

"See you tomorrow then," said Joe. He closed his eyes and made his lips the shape of a kiss. And waited.

"See you tomorrow Joe," said Lauren, before skipping off down the path. Joe opened his eyes and smiled. He couldn't believe it! He had nearly kissed a girl!

15

Nip and Tuck

There was something very peculiar about Mrs Trafe today. She looked the same but different. As Joe and Lauren approached the serving counter, Joe realised what had changed.

The loose skin on her face had been lifted.

Her nose was smaller.

Her teeth were capped.

The lines on her forehead had been erased.

Her eye bags had disappeared.

Her wrinkles had gone.

Her breasts were much, much bigger.

But she was still limping.

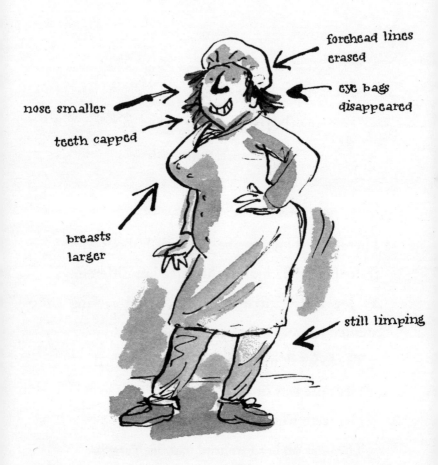

forehead lines
erased

eye bags
disappeared

nose smaller

teeth capped

breasts
larger

still limping

"Mrs Trafe, you look really… different…" Joe
said, staring at her.

"Do I?" replied the old dinner lady with mock
innocence. "Now, what do you two fancy today?

174

Roast bat with all the trimmings? Soap soufflé? Cheese and polystyrene pizza?"

"It's hard to choose…" faltered Lauren.

"You are new, are you, girl?" asked Mrs Trafe.

"Yes, I just joined the school yesterday," replied Lauren, surveying the dishes, and trying to work out which one was the least horrible.

"Yesterday? That's strange. I'm sure I've seen you somewhere before," said the dinner lady, studying Lauren's perfect face. "You look very familiar."

Joe butted in. "Did you have the hip replacement operation yet, Mrs Trafe?" He was becoming increasingly suspicious. "The one I gave you the money for a couple of weeks ago," he whispered, so Lauren wouldn't hear.

Mrs Trafe began to jabber nervously. "Um, well, no, not yet dear, why don't you have a large slice of my very tasty underpant flan…?"

"You spent the money I gave you on plastic surgery, didn't you?" hissed Joe.

A bead of sweat trickled down her face and plopped into her badger snot soup.

"I am sorry, Joe, I just, well, I just always wanted to have a few things done…" pleaded the dinner lady.

Joe was so furious he felt he had to leave instantly. "Lauren, we're going," he announced, and she followed as he stormed out of the dining room. Mrs Trafe limped after them.

"If you could just lend me another £5000, Joe, I promise I'll have it done this time!" she called after him.

When Lauren finally caught up with Joe, he was sitting alone in the far corner of the playground. She gently put her hand on his head to comfort him.

"What was all that about lending her £5000?" she asked.

Joe looked at Lauren. There was no way of avoiding telling her now. "My dad is Len Spud," he said sorrowfully. "'The Bumfresh billionaire'. My name's not Potatoe. I just said that so you wouldn't know who I was. The truth is, we're stupidly rich. But when people find out... it tends to ruin everything."

"You know what, some of the other kids told me this morning," said Lauren.

Joe's sadness lifted for a moment. He reminded himself that Lauren had still gone for an ice lolly with him yesterday when she thought he was just Joe. Maybe it wouldn't ruin things this time. "Why didn't you say anything?" he asked.

"Because it doesn't matter. I don't care about all that. I just like you," she said.

Joe was so happy he wanted to cry. It's strange how sometimes you can be so happy it goes all the way around to sadness. "I really like you too."

Joe moved closer to Lauren. This was the moment to kiss! He closed his eyes and pushed his lips together.

"Not here in the playground, Joe!" Lauren pushed him away laughing.

Joe felt embarrassed he had even tried. "I'm sorry." He quickly changed the subject. "I was just trying to do something kind for that old bag, and she goes and gets her knockers done!"

"I know, it's unbelievable."

"It's not the money, I don't care about the money…"

"No, it's that she took your generosity for granted," offered Lauren.

Joe looked up to meet her gaze. "Exactly!"

"Come on," said Lauren. "I think what you need is some chips. I'll buy you some."

The local chippy was bursting with kids from the comprehensive. It was against the rules to leave the school premises at lunchtime, but the food in the canteen was so abhorrent there wasn't much choice. The Grubbs were at the front of the queue, but fled as soon as they saw Lauren, leaving their battered sausages sizzling on the counter.

The pair stood outside on the pavement and ate their chips. Joe couldn't remember the last time he had enjoyed such a simple pleasure. It must have been when he was really, really little. Before the Bumfresh billions came and changed everything. Joe wolfed his chips down, and noticed Lauren had barely touched hers. He was still hungry, but wasn't sure whether their relationship had advanced to the point where he could start helping himself to her food. That was normally after a few years of marriage, and they weren't even engaged yet.

"Have you finished with yours?" he ventured.

"Yes," she replied. "I don't want to eat too much. I am working next week."

"Working? Doing what?" said Joe.

Lauren suddenly looked very flustered. "What did I say?"

"I thought you said you were working."

"Yeah yeah yeah, I *am* working." She paused, and then took a breath. "Just in a shop…"

Joe wasn't convinced. "So why would you

need to be thin to work in a shop?"

Lauren looked uncomfortable. "It's a very narrow shop," she said. She checked her watch. "We've got double Maths in ten minutes. We'd better go."

Joe frowned. There was something strange going on here…

16

Peter Bread

"The Witch is dead!" sang a spotty little boy. "Ding-dong, the wicked witch is dead!" It wasn't even registration time yet, but already the news was spreading across the school like flu.

"What do you mean?" asked Joe as he took his seat in his classroom. On the other side of the class, he could see Bob, looking over at him with a pained expression. *Probably jealous about Lauren*, thought Joe.

"Haven't you heard?" said another even spottier little boy behind him. "Spite's been sacked!"

"Why?" asked Joe.

"Who cares?!" said a slightly less spotty boy. "No more boring History lessons!"

Joe smiled, then frowned. He hated Miss Spite and her tedious lessons like everybody else, but wasn't sure she had done anything to deserve losing her job. Even though she was horrible, she was actually a good teacher.

"Spite's been sacked," blurted Joe to Lauren as she walked in.

"Yes, I heard," she replied. "It's brilliant news, isn't it?"

"Erm, well, I suppose so," said Joe.

"I thought that's what you wanted? You said you couldn't stand her."

"Yes, but…" Joe hesitated for a moment. "I just feel a bit, you know, sorry for her."

Lauren pulled a dismissive face.

Meanwhile, a gang of fierce-looking girls were

sat on desks at the back of the class. The smallest of the group was pushed over in Lauren's direction as the others looked on smirking.

"Got any Pot Noodles then?" she asked, much to the amusement of the gang.

Lauren shot a look at Joe. "I don't know what you mean," she protested.

"Don't lie," said the girl. "You look different in it, but I well reckon it's you."

"I have no idea what you're talking about," said Lauren, a little flustered.

Before Joe could speak a young man in old man's clothes entered the classroom and took his position uncertainly by the blackboard. "Simmer down please," he said quietly. No one in the classroom took any notice, except Joe.

"I said, 'simmer down please'…"

The new teacher's second sentence was barely more audible than the first. Still none of the other kids took any notice. In fact, if anything they started making even more noise than before.

"That's better," said the little man, trying to make the best of it. "Now, as you may know Miss Spite isn't here today—"

"Yeah, she's been given the boot!" shouted a loud fat girl.

"Well, that's not… well, yes, it is true…" the teacher continued in his faint monotone. "Now I am going to be taking over from Miss Spite as your form teacher, and also to teach you History and English. My name is Mr Bread." He began writing his name neatly on the board. "But you can call me Peter."

Suddenly there was quiet, as thirty little brains whirred.

"Pita Bread!" proclaimed a ginger-haired boy from the back. A huge wave of laughter crashed over the classroom. Joe had tried to give this poor man a chance, but he couldn't help but laugh.

"Please, please, can I have some quiet?" pleaded the unfortunately named teacher. But there was no use. The whole class was in uproar. The new form teacher had committed the biggest blunder any teacher can make – having a silly name. This is a serious point. If you have a name like any of those in the list below it is very, very important you don't become a teacher:

Sue Doku

Tom Atoe

Justin Case

Neil Down

Will Ing

Bob Head

Terry Daktul

Clare Voyant

Mel Formed

Rachel Prejudice

Mona Lott

Herbie Hind

Ima Hogg

Carol Singer

Dick Tate

Don Keigh

Rhoda Camel

Robin Banks

Felix Cited

Gerry Atrick

Bea O'Problem

Mya Bumreeks

Anita Bath

Sue Age

Marcus Absent

Al Gebra

Barbara Blacksheep

Kitty Litter

Mary Christmas

Jim Class

Doris Closed

Doris Locked

Wayne Dear

Dan Druff

Humphrey Dumpty

Stan Dupp

Cliff Hanger

Hugh Idiot

Lee King

Manuel Labour

Ruth Less

Willie Mammoth

Marsha Mellow

Walter Melon

Hazel Nut

Luke Out

Stu Pidd

Lolly Popp

Chuck Up

Seriously. Don't even consider it. The kids in your class will make your life a living hell.

Now, back to the story…

"Right," said the unfortunately named teacher. "I am going to take the register. Adams?"

"Don't forget Tara Mosalata!" shouted a skinny blonde-haired boy. The laughter swept up again.

"I did ask for quiet," said Mr Bread, pathetically.

"Or Ted Ziki!" hollered another kid. The laughter was deafening now.

Peter Bread put his head in his hands. Joe could almost feel sorry for him. This grey little man's life was going to be an utter misery from this day forward.

Oh, no, thought Joe. *We're all going to fail our exams.*

17

A Knock on the Toilet Door

There are a number of things you don't want to hear when you sit on the toilet.

A fire alarm.

An earthquake.

The roar of a hungry lion in the cubicle next door.

A large group of people shouting 'Surprise!' to you.

The sound of the entire toilet block being demolished by a giant wrecking ball.

The clicking sound of someone taking a photograph.

The sound of an electric eel swimming up the U-bend.

Someone drilling a hole in the wall.

JLS singing. (Admittedly that wouldn't be welcome at any time.)

A knock on the door.

That last one was exactly what Joe heard at break time when he took a seat in the boys' toilet.

RAT TAT TAT.

To be clear, that isn't a knock at *your* door, readers. It's a knock on Joe's toilet door.

"Who is it?" asked Joe, irritated.

"It's Bob," replied... yes, you've guessed correctly: Bob.

"Go away, I'm busy," said Joe.

"I need to talk to you."

Joe pulled the chain, and opened the door. "What do you want?" he said angrily as he made his way to the sink. Bob trailed after him munching on a bag of crisps. It was only an hour since he'd been eating chips like everyone else, but obviously Bob got hungry very easily.

"You shouldn't eat crisps in a toilet, Bob."

"Why not?"

"Because… because… I don't know, because the crisps wouldn't like it." Joe whacked the tap on to wash his hands. "Anyway, what do you want?"

Bob put the bag in his trouser pocket and stood behind his former friend. He looked into Joe's eyes in the mirror. "It's Lauren."

"What about her?" Joe had *known* it. Bob was just jealous.

Bob looked away for a second and took a deep breath. "I don't think you should trust her," he said.

Joe turned around, shaking with fury. "*What*

did you say?" he shouted.

Bob stepped away, taken aback. "I just think she's…"

"SHE'S WHAT?"

"She's fake."

"Fake?" Joe felt white-hot with fury.

"Lots of the other kids reckon she's an actress. They said she's in some advert, or something. And I saw her out with this other boy at the weekend."

"What?"

"Joe, I think she's just pretending to like you."

Joe put his face next to Bob's. He hated being this angry. It was scary being so out of control. "SAY THAT AGAIN…"

Bob backed away. "Look, I'm sorry, I don't want a fight, I am just telling you what I saw."

"You're lying."

"I'm not!"

"You're just jealous because Lauren likes me, and you're a fatty with no friends at all."

"I'm not jealous, I'm just worried for you, Joe. I don't want you to get hurt."

"Yeah?" said Joe. "You sounded really *worried about me* when you called me a spoiled brat."

"Honestly, I—"

"Just leave me alone, Bob. We're not friends any more. I felt sorry for you and talked to you and that was that."

"What did you just say? You felt 'sorry for me'?" Bob's eyes were wet with tears.

"I didn't mean..."

"What, because I'm fat? Because the other kids bully me? Because my dad's dead?" Bob was shouting now.

"No... I just... I didn't mean..." Joe didn't know what he meant. He reached into his pocket and pulled out a wad of £50 notes, and offered

Billionaire Boy

them to Bob. "Look, I'm sorry, here you go. Buy
your mum something nice."

Bob knocked the money out of Joe's hand
and the notes fell onto the damp floor. "How
dare you?"

"What have I done now?" protested Joe. "What's the matter with you, Bob? I'm just trying to help you."

"I don't want your help. I don't want to ever speak to you again!"

"Fine!"

"And you are the one people should feel sorry for. You're pathetic." Bob stormed out.

Joe sighed, then got down on his knees and started picking up the wet bank notes.

"That's ridiculous!" said Lauren later, with a laugh. "I'm not an actress. I don't think I'd even get a part in the school play!"

Joe tried to laugh too, but he couldn't quite. They sat together on the bench in the playground, shivering slightly at the cold. Joe found it hard to say the next sentence. He did and didn't want to know the answer. He took a deep breath. "Bob said he saw you with some other boy. Is that true?"

"What?" said Lauren.

"At the weekend. He said he saw you out with someone else." Joe looked straight at her, trying to read her face. For a moment she seemed to retreat to the back of her eyes.

"He's a liar," she said after a moment.

"I thought so," said Joe, relieved.

"A big fat liar," she continued. "I can't believe you were ever friends with him."

"Well, it was only for a bit," squirmed Joe. "I don't like him anymore."

"I hate him. Lying pig. Promise me you won't ever speak to him again," said Lauren urgently.

"Well..."

"Promise, Joe."

"I promise," he replied.

A wicked wind whipped through the playground.

18

The Vortex 3000

Lauren didn't think the petition to get Miss Spite reinstated was going to be popular.

And she was right.

By the end of the day Joe had only got three signatures – his, Lauren's and Mrs Trafe's. The dinner lady had only signed it because Joe had agreed to try one of her Hamster Dropping Tartlets. It tasted worse than it sounded. Despite having what was essentially not much more than a blank sheet of paper, Joe still felt it was worth presenting his petition to the headmaster. He didn't like Miss Spite one bit, but he didn't understand why she had been sacked. Despite everything, she was a good teacher, certainly a lot better than Naan Bread, or whatever his stupid name was.

"Hello, children!" said the headmaster's secretary brightly. Mrs Chubb was a very fat jolly lady who always wore glasses with brightly coloured frames. She was always sitting in the headmaster's office behind her desk. In fact, no one had ever seen her stand up. It was not inconceivable that she was so big she was permanently wedged into her chair.

"We are here to see the headmaster, please," declared Joe.

"We have a petition for him," added a supportive Lauren, holding the piece of paper in her hand demonstratively.

"A petition! What fun!" beamed Mrs Chubb.

"Yes, it's to get Miss Spite her job back," said

Joe in a manly way that he hoped might impress Lauren. For a moment he toyed with the idea of thumping his fist on the desk to add emphasis, but he didn't want to topple over any of Mrs Chubb's abundant collection of lucky gonks.

"Oh, yes. Miss Spite, wonderful teacher. Don't understand that at all, but children I am sorry to say you have just missed Mr Dust."

"Oh, no," said Joe.

"Yes, he just left. Oh, look, there he goes." She pointed one of her bejewelled sausage fingers to the car park. Joe and Lauren peered through the glass. The headmaster was edging his way along at a snail's pace with his Zimmer frame.

"Slow down, Mr Dust, you'll do yourself a mischief!" she called after him. Then she turned back to Joe and Lauren. "He can't hear me. Well in truth he can't hear a thing! Do you want to leave that little petition thing with me?" She angled her head and studied it for a moment. "Oh dear, it looks like all the signatures have fallen off."

"We were hoping for more," said Joe, weakly.

"Well if you run you might just catch him!" said Mrs Chubb.

Joe and Lauren shared a smile, and walked slowly out to the car park. To their surprise Mr Dust had abandoned his Zimmer frame and was clambering astride a shiny new Harley Davidson motorbike. It was the brand new jet-powered Vortex 3000. Joe recognised it, because his dad had a small collection of 300 motorbikes and was always showing his son brochures of new ones he was going to buy. The superbike, at £250,000, was the most expensive motorbike ever produced. It was wider than a car, taller than a lorry, and blacker than a black hole. It shone with a very different chrome to that of the headmaster's Zimmer frame.

"Headmaster!" called Joe, but he was too late. Mr Dust had already put on his helmet and revved the engine. He put the beast into gear and

it roared past the other teachers' humble cars at a hundred miles an hour. It went so fast that the Headmaster was clinging on by his hands, his little old legs dangling up in the air behind him.

"YYYIIIıIPPPPPPPPPPEEEEEEEEE…..!" cried the Headmaster as he and his preposterous machine disappeared off into the distance, becoming a dot on the horizon in a matter of seconds.

"There is something very strange going on," said Joe to Lauren. "The Witch gets the sack, the headmaster gets a £250,000 motorbike…"

"Joe, you're being silly! It's just coincidence!" laughed Lauren. "Now, am I still invited for dinner tonight?" she added, rapidly changing the subject.

"Yes yes yes," said Joe eagerly. "How about I meet you outside Raj's in an hour?"

"Cool. See you in a bit."

Joe smiled too, and watched her walk away.

But that bright golden glow that surrounded Lauren in Joe's mind was beginning to darken. Suddenly something felt very wrong…

19

A Baboon's Bottom

"Maybe your headmaster is simply having a mid-life crisis," pronounced Raj.

Stopping off at the newsagent's shop on the way home from school, Joe had told Raj about the curious events of the day.

"Mr Dust is about a hundred. He's got to be more than mid-way through his life!" said Joe.

"What I mean, Clever Clogs," continued Raj, "is that perhaps he was just trying to feel young again."

"But it's the most expensive motorbike in the world. It costs a quarter of a million pounds.

He's a teacher not a footballer, how could he afford it?!" proclaimed Joe.

"I don't know... I am no detective like Miss Marbles, or the great Shylock Holmes," said Raj, before looking around his shop and lowering his voice to a whisper. "Joe, I need to ask you about something in the strictest confidence."

Joe lowered his voice too. "Go ahead."

"This is very embarrassing, Joe," whispered Raj. "But do you use your dad's special toilet paper?"

"Yes, of course, Raj. Everybody does!"

"Well, I have been using his new one for a few weeks now."

"The mint-flavoured bum wipes?" asked Joe. There was now a huge range of Bumfresh products including:

HOTBUMFRESH – warms your bottom as you wipe.

LADYBUMFRESH – specially soft wipes for ladies' bottoms.

MINTYBUMFRESH – leaves your bottom with a cool, minty aroma.

"Yes, and…" Raj took a deep breath. "My bottom has come up all… well… purple."

"Purple!" said Joe with a shocked laugh.

"This is a very serious matter," chided Raj. He looked up suddenly. "One copy of the *Daily Mail* and a packet of Rolos, that will be 85p, be careful with those Rolos on your dentures, Mr Little."

He waited for the pensioner to leave the shop. *Ding* went the bell on the door.

"I didn't see him there. He must have been lurking behind the Quavers," said Raj, a little shaken at what the pensioner might have heard.

"You are joking aren't you, Raj?" said Joe with a quizzical smile.

"I am deadly serious, Joe," said Raj gravely.

"Show me, then!" said Joe.

"I can't show you my bottom Joe! We've only just met!" exclaimed Raj. "But let me draw you a simple graph."

"A graph?" asked Joe.

"Be patient, Joe."

As the boy looked on Raj grabbed some paper and pens and drew this simple graph.

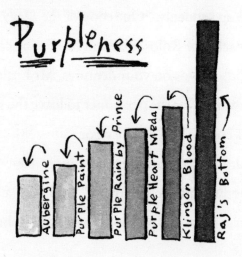

"Wow, that is purple!" said Joe, studying the graph. "Is it painful?"

"It is a little sore."

"Have you seen a doctor?" asked Joe.

"Yes, and he said he had seen hundreds of people in the local area with brightly coloured bottoms."

"Oh no," said Joe.

"Maybe I will have to have a bum transplant!"

Joe couldn't help but laugh. "A bum transplant?!"

"Yes! This isn't a laughing matter, Joe," chided Raj. There was hurt in his eyes that his bottom had become the subject of mockery.

"No, sorry," said Joe, still giggling.

"I think I will stop using your dad's new Bumfresh wipes and go back to the shiny white my wife used to buy."

"I'm sure it isn't the bum wipes," said Joe.

"What else could it be?"

"Look, Raj, I'd better go," Joe said. "I have invited my girlfriend over later."

"Oooh, girlfriend is it now? The pretty girl you came in with when I sold you the ice lollies?" said the newsagent brightly.

"Yes, that's her," said Joe shyly. "Well, I don't know if she really is my girlfriend, but we've been spending lots of time together..."

"Well, have a lovely evening!"

"Thanks." Arriving at the door Joe turned back to the newsagent. He couldn't help himself. "Oh, by the way, Raj, good luck with the bum transplant..."

"Thank you, my friend."

"I hope they can find one big enough!" Joe laughed.

"Out of my shop! Out! Out!" said Raj.

Ding.

"Cheeky boy," muttered the newsagent with a smile, as he rearranged his Curly Wurlys.

20

A Beach Ball Rolled in Hair

Bumfresh Towers pulsated with music. Coloured lights spun in every room. Hundreds of people swarmed around the house. This was a party that was going to get complaints about the noise.

From people in Sweden.

Joe had no idea that there was a party at the house tonight. Dad hadn't mentioned anything at breakfast and Joe had invited Lauren over for dinner. As it was a Friday night they could stay up late too. It was going to be perfect. Maybe tonight they might even kiss.

"Sorry, I had no idea about all this," said Joe,

as they approached the giant stone steps at the front of the house.

"It's cool, I love a party!" replied Lauren.

As darkness fell and strangers tumbled out of the house clutching bottles of champagne, Joe took Lauren's hand, and led her through the huge oak front door.

"Wow, this is some house," shouted Lauren over the music.

"What?" said Joe.

Lauren put her mouth to Joe's ear so she could be heard. "I said, 'wow, this is some house'." But Joe still couldn't really hear. Feeling the heat of her breath so close to him was so exhilarating he stopped listening for a moment.

"THANK YOU!" shouted Joe back into Lauren's ear. Her skin smelt sweet, like honey.

Joe searched all over the house for his dad. It was impossible to find him. Every room was oozing with people. Joe didn't recognise a single one of them. Who on earth were they all? Guzzling cocktails and gobbling finger food like there was no tomorrow. Being short, Joe really found it hard to see over them. His dad wasn't in the snooker room. He wasn't in the dining room. He wasn't in the massage room. He wasn't in the library. He wasn't in the other dining room. He wasn't in his bedroom. He wasn't in the reptile house.

"Let's try the pool room!" shouted Joe in Lauren's ear.

"You've got a pool! Cool!" she shouted back.

They passed a woman bent over vomiting by the sauna as a man (presumably her boyfriend) patted the small of her back supportively. Some party guests had either dived or fallen into the pool, and were bobbing around in the water. Joe enjoyed swimming, and the thought that none of these people looked like they would get out of the pool if they needed a pee, clouded his mind.

Just then he spotted his dad – wearing just a pair of swimming trunks and his curly afro toupee, and dancing to a completely different song than the one that was playing. Covering the wall behind him was a vast mural of a strangely muscle-bound version of himself reclining in a thong. The real Mr Spud boogied badly in front of it, looking more like a beach ball that had been rolled in hair.

"What's going on, Dad?" Joe shouted, half because the music was so loud and half because he was angry his dad hadn't told him anything about the party. "Who are all these people? Your friends?"

"Oh no, I hired them in. £500 each. Partyguests.com."

"What's the party for, Dad?"

"Well, I know you will be so pleased to know that Sapphire and I have got engaged!" shouted Mr Spud.

"What the—?" said Joe, not able to disguise his shock.

"It's great news isn't it?" Dad yelled. Still the music boom boom boomed.

Joe didn't want to believe it. Did the hand model really have to be his new mum?

"I asked her yesterday and she said 'no', but then I asked her again today and gave her a great big diamond ring and she said 'yes'."

"Congratulations, Mr Spud," said Lauren.

"So you must be a friend of my son's from school?" said Mr Spud, his words tumbling out clumsily.

"That's right, Mr Spud," replied Lauren.

"Call me Len, please," said Mr Spud with a smile. "And you must meet Sapphire. SAPPHIRE!" he shouted.

Sapphire tottered over in her shocking yellow high heels and even more shocking yellow mini-dress.

"Would you show Joe's friend the engagement ring, my gorgeous lady love of all time? Twenty million quid, just for the diamond."

Joe spied the diamond on his soon to be stepmother's finger. It was the size of a small bungalow. Her left arm was dangling lower than the right with the weight of it.

"Er… er… oh… It's so heavy, I can't lift my hand but if you bend down you can see it…" said Sapphire. Lauren stepped closer to get a better look. "Haven't I seen ya somewhere before?" Sapphire asked.

Mr Spud leaped in. "No, you haven't, my one true love."

"Yes I have!" said Sapphire.

"No, my angel cake!"

"OMG! I know where I seen ya!"

"I said shut it, my chocolate sprinkled princess!" said Mr Spud.

"You done that ad for Pot Noodle!" Sapphire exclaimed.

Joe turned to Lauren, who looked at the floor.

"It's well good, you know the one, Joe," continued Sapphire. "For the new sweet and sour flavour. The one where she has to do karate to stop people from nicking it!"

"You *are* an actress!" spluttered Joe. The advert was coming back into focus in his mind. Her hair was a different colour, and she wasn't wearing an all in one yellow catsuit, but it was Lauren all right.

"I better go," said Lauren.

"And did you lie about having a boyfriend too?" demanded Joe.

"Goodbye Joe," said Lauren, before weaving past the guests in the poolroom as she ran off.

"LAUREN!" shouted Joe after her.

"Let her go, son," said Mr Spud sadly.

But Joe raced after her, and caught up with her just as she reached the stone steps. He grabbed her arm, harder than he had anticipated and she turned around in pain.

"Oww!"

"Why did you lie to me?" Joe stammered.

"Just forget it, Joe," said Lauren. She suddenly seemed a different person. Her voice was more posh now and her face less kind. The twinkle in her eye had definitely gone, and the glow around her had turned into a shadow. "You don't want to know."

"Don't want to know what?"

"Look, if you must know your dad saw me on that Pot Noodle advert and called my agent. Said you were unhappy at school, and paid me to be your friend. It was all fine until you tried to kiss me."

She skipped down the steps and ran off down the long drive. Joe watched her go for a few moments, before the pain in his heart was so great he had to bend over to stop it. He fell to his knees. A party guest stepped over him. Joe didn't even look up. He felt he was so sad that he was never going to be able to get up again.

21

A GCSE in Make-Up

"DAD!" screamed Joe. He had never been this angry before, and hoped he never would be again. He ran into the pool room to confront his father.

Mr Spud nervously straightened his toupee as his son approached.

Joe stood in front of his dad hyperventilating. He was too angry to speak.

"I am sorry, son. I thought that's what you wanted. A friend. I just wanted to make things better for you at school. I got that teacher you hated sacked too. All I had to do was buy the headmaster a motorbike."

"So.... You got an old lady sacked from her job... And then, and then... you... paid a girl to like me..."

"I thought that's what you wanted."

"*What*?"

"Listen, I can buy you another friend," said Mr Spud.

"YOU DON'T GET IT DO YOU?" screamed Joe. "Some things can't be bought."

"Like what?"

"Like friendship. Like feelings. Like love!"

"Actually, that last one can," offered Sapphire, still unable to lift her hand.

"I hate you Dad, I really do," shouted Joe.

"Joe, please," pleaded Mr Spud. "Look, please calm down. How about a nice little cheque for five million quid?"

"Ooh, yes please," said Sapphire.

"I don't want any more of your stupid money," sneered Joe.

"But son…" spluttered Mr Spud.

"The last thing I want to do is end up like you… A middle-aged man with some brain-dead teenage fiancée!"

"Excuse me, I've got a GCSE in make-up," said Sapphire angrily.

"I never want to see either of you again!" said Joe. He ran out of the room, pushing the vomiting lady out of his way and into the pool as he did so. Then he slammed the huge door behind him. One of the mural tiles from Mr Spud's thong fell off the wall and smashed onto the floor.

"JOE! JOE! WAIT!" shouted Mr Spud.

Joe dodged past the hordes of guests and ran up to his room, shutting the door firmly behind him. There wasn't a lock, so he grabbed a chair and wedged it under the door handle so it wouldn't open. As the beat of the music thumped through the carpet, Joe grabbed a bag and started filling it with clothes. He didn't know where he was going, so wasn't sure what he needed. All he knew was that he didn't want to be in this ridiculous house for another minute. He grabbed a couple of his favourite books (*The*

Boy in the Dress and *Mr Stink*, both of which he found hilarious and yet heart-warming).

Then he looked on his shelf at all his expensive toys and gadgets. His eyes were drawn to the little loo-roll rocket that his dad had given him when he still worked at the factory. He remembered it was a present for his eighth birthday. His mum and dad were still together then and Joe thought it might have been the last time he was truly happy.

As his hand reached out to take it there was a loud thump on the door.

"Son, son, let me in…"

Joe didn't say a word. He had nothing more he wanted to say to the man. Whoever his dad had been was lost years ago.

"Joe, please," said Mr Spud. Then there was a pause.

TTTTHHHHHUUUUUMMMM
MPPPPP.

Joe's dad was trying to force the door open.

"Open this door!"

TTTTTTTTTTTTHHHH
HHHHHHHHHHHHHH
HUUUUUUUUUUUM
MMMMMMMPPPPPPP
PPPP.

"I've given you everything!" He was putting all his weight behind it now, and the chair legs heroically dug themselves deeper into the carpet. He made one last try.

TTTTTTTTTTTTT
TTHHHHHHHHH
HHHHHHHHHHH
HHHUUUUUUUU

UUUUUUUUMM MMMMMMMMMM MMMMMMMPPPP PPPPPPPPPPPPPPP PPPPPPPPPPP.

Joe then heard a much smaller thump as his dad gave in and leaned his body against the door. This was followed by a squeak as his bulk slid down the door, and a few whimpering cries. Then the light in the gap under the door was blocked. His dad must have been slumped on the floor.

Spud Junior felt unbearably guilty. He knew all he needed to do to stop his dad's pain was open that door. He put his hand on the chair for a moment. *If I open that door now*, he thought, *nothing is going to change*.

Joe took a deep breath, lifted his hand, grabbed his bag and walked to the window. He opened it slowly so his dad wouldn't hear, and then climbed onto the windowsill. Joe took one last look at his bedroom before jumping out into the darkness, and a new chapter.

22

A New Chapter

Joe ran as fast as he could – which wasn't that fast, in all honesty. But it felt fast to him. He ran down the long, long drive. Dodged past the guards. Jumped over the wall. Was that wall to keep people out or keep him in? He'd never thought about it before. But there wasn't time to think about it now. Joe had to run. And keep running.

Joe didn't know where he was running to. All he knew was where he was running from. He couldn't live in that stupid house with his stupid dad for one moment longer. Joe ran down the road. All he could hear was his own breath, getting faster and faster. There was a faint taste of blood in his mouth. Now he wished he had tried harder in the school cross-country run.

It was late now. After midnight. The lamp posts pointlessly illuminated the empty little town. Reaching the town centre, Joe slowed to a stop. A lone car crouched in the road. Realising he was alone, Joe suddenly felt a shiver of fear. The reality of his great escape dawned on him. He looked at his reflection in the window of the darkened KFC. A chubby twelve-year-old boy with nowhere to go looked back at him. A police car rolled past slowly and silently. Was it looking for him? Joe hid behind the big plastic bin. The smell of fat and ketchup and hot cardboard was so stomach-churning it almost made him choke. Joe covered his mouth to stifle the sound. He didn't want the policemen to discover him.

The police car turned a corner and Joe ventured out into the street. Like a hamster that had escaped from its cage, he kept close to the edges and corners. Could he go to Bob's? *No*, thought Joe. In the exhilaration of meeting Lauren or whatever her stupid name really was, he had badly let down his only friend. Mrs Trafe had been a sympathetic ear, but it turned out she was after his money all along.

How about Raj? *Yes*, thought Joe. He could go and live with the purple-bottomed newsagent. Joe could set up camp behind the fridge. Hidden safely there, Joe could read *Nuts* magazine all day, and feast on slightly out of date confectionery. He couldn't imagine a more charmed life.

Joe's mind was racing, and soon his legs were too. He crossed the road and turned left. Raj's shop was only a few streets away now.

Somewhere above him in the black air he heard a distant whirr. The whirr became louder. More of a buzz. Then a drone.

It was a helicopter. A searchlight danced across the streets. Mr Spud's voice came out of a loudspeaker.

"JOE SPUD, THIS IS YOUR DAD SPEAKING. GIVE YOURSELF UP. I REPEAT, GIVE YOURSELF UP."

Joe dashed into the entrance of The Body Shop. The searchlight had just missed him. The smell of pineapple and pomegranate body wash and dragonfruit foot scrub pleasingly tickled its way up his nostrils. Hearing the helicopter passing overhead, Joe dashed to the other side of the street, and crept past Pizza Hut, and then Pizza Express, before seeking sanctuary in the doorway of a Domino's Pizza. Just as he stepped out to make a dash past Bella Pasta, the helicopter whooshed back overhead. Suddenly Joe Spud was caught in the dead centre of the searchlight.

"**DON'T MOVE. I REPEAT, DON'T MOVE,**" the voice thundered.

Joe looked up into the light as his body trembled from the force of the rotor blades. "Shove off!" he shouted. "I repeat, shove off!"

"COME HOME NOW, JOE."

"No."

"JOE, I SAID..."

"I heard what you said and I'm not coming home. I'm not ever coming home," shouted Joe. Standing there in the bright light he felt like he was on stage in a particularly dramatic school play. The helicopter whirred overhead for a moment as the loudspeaker crackled in silence.

Then Joe made a run for it, dashing down an alley behind Argos, through the NCP car park, and round the back of Superdrug. Soon the helicopter was nothing more than a distant buzz, no louder than the sleepless birds.

Arriving at Raj's, Joe knocked gently on the metal shutters. There was no answer, so he banged this time until the shutters shook with the force of his fists. Still no answer. Joe looked at his watch. It was two o'clock in the morning. No wonder Raj wasn't in his shop.

It looked like Joe would have to be the very first billionaire to ever sleep rough.

23

Canal Boat Weekly

"What are you doing in there?"

Joe wasn't sure if he was awake, or simply dreaming that he was awake. He certainly couldn't move. His body felt stiff with cold, and every part of him ached. Joe couldn't open his eyes yet, but knew without doubt that he hadn't woken up between the silk sheets of his four-poster bed.

"I said, what are you doing in there?" came the voice again. Joe frowned, puzzled. His butler didn't have an Indian accent. Joe struggled to unglue eyes that had been stuck together with sleep. He saw a big smiley face hovering over his.

It was Raj's.

"Why are you here at this ungodly hour, Master Spud?" asked the kindly newsagent.

As dawn was beginning to glow through the gloom, Joe took in his surroundings. He had climbed into a skip outside Raj's shop and fallen asleep. Some bricks had been his pillow, a piece of tarpaulin his duvet, and a dusty old wooden door his mattress. No wonder every part of his body ached.

"Oh, er, hello Raj," croaked Joe.

"Hello Joe. I was just opening up my shop and heard some snoring. There you were. I was quite surprised, I must tell you."

"I don't snore!" protested Joe.

"I regret to inform you that you do. Now would you be so kind as to climb out of the skip and step inside my shop, I think we need to talk," said Raj, in a deadly serious tone.

Oh no, thought Joe, *now I'm in trouble with Raj.*

Although Raj was adult in age and size, he was nothing like a parent or a teacher, and it was really difficult to get into trouble with him. Once one of the girls from Joe's school had been caught trying to steal a bag of Wotsits from the newsagent and Raj had banned her from his shop for all of five minutes.

The dusty billionaire clambered out of the skip. Raj fashioned him a stool from a stack of *Heat* magazines, and wrapped a copy of the *Financial Times* over his shoulders like it was a big pink boring blanket.

"You must have been outside in the cold all night, Joe. Now, you must eat some breakfast. A nice hot mug of Lilt perhaps?"

"No thanks," said Joe.

"Two Rolo eggs, poached?"

Joe shook his head.

"You need to eat, boy. A toasted Galaxy bar?"

"No thanks."

"A hearty bowl of Pickled Onion Monster Munch perhaps? With warm milk?"

"I am really not hungry, Raj," said Joe.

"Well, my wife has put me on a strict diet so I am only allowed fruit for breakfast now," announced Raj as he unwrapped a Terry's Chocolate Orange. "Now, are you going to tell me why you slept in a skip last night?"

"I ran away from home," announced Joe.

"I guessed that much," slurred Raj, chewing away on multiple segments of Terry's Chocolate Orange. "Oooh, pips," he said before spitting something into the palm of his hand. "The question is, why?"

Joe looked ill at ease. He felt the truth shamed him as much as his dad. "Well you know that girl I brought in here the day we got some ice lollies?"

"Yes, yes! You know I said I had seen her

somewhere before? Well, she was on TV last night! On an advert for Pot Noodle Snacks! So did you finally kiss her?" exclaimed an excited Raj.

"No. She was only pretending to like me. My dad paid her to be my friend."

"Oh dear," said Raj. His smile fell from his face. "That's not right. That's not right at all."

"I *hate* him," said Joe hotly.

"Please don't say that, Joe," said Raj, shocked.

"But I do," said Joe, turning to Raj with fire in his eyes. "I hate his guts."

"Joe! You must stop talking like this right now. He is your father."

"I hate him. I never want to see him again for as long as I live."

Tentatively, Raj reached out and put his hand on Joe's shoulder. Joe's anger immediately turned to sadness, and with his head bowed he began to weep into his own lap. His body shook involuntarily as the waves of tears ebbed and flowed through him.

"I can understand your pain, Joe, I really can," ventured Raj. "I know from what you said that you really liked that girl, but I guess your dad was, well… just trying to make you happy."

"It's all that money," said Joe, barely audible through the tears. "It's ruined everything, I even lost my only friend over it."

"Yes, I haven't seen you and Bob together for a while. What happened?"

"I've behaved like an idiot too. I said some really mean things to him."

"Oh dear."

"We fell out when I paid some bullies to leave him alone. I thought I was helping him, but he got all angry about it."

Raj nodded slowly. "You know, Joe…" he

said slowly. "It doesn't sound as though what you did to Bob is so very different to what your father did to you."

"Maybe I am a spoiled brat," Joe told Raj. "Just like Bob said."

"Nonsense," said Raj. "You did a stupid thing, and you must apologise. But if Bob has any sense, he will forgive you. I can see that your heart was in the right place. You meant well."

"I just wanted them to stop bullying him!" Joe said. "I just thought, if I gave them money…"

"Well, that's no way to beat bullies, young man."

"I know that now," admitted Joe.

"If you give them money they'll just come back and back for more."

"Yes, yes, but I was only trying to help him."

"You have to realise money can't solve

everything, Joe. Maybe Bob would have stood up to the bullies himself, eventually. Money is not the answer! You know I was once a very rich man?"

"Really?!" said Joe, instantly embarrassed that he sounded a little too surprised. He sniffed and wiped his wet face on his sleeve.

"Oh, yes," replied Raj. "I once owned a large chain of newsagent shops."

"Wow! How many shops did you have, Raj?"

"Two. I was taking home literally hundreds of pounds a week. If I wanted anything I would simply have it. Six Chicken McNuggets? I would have nine! I splashed out on a flash brand new second-hand Ford Fiesta. And I would think nothing of returning a DVD to Blockbuster a day late and thus incurring a £2.50 fine!"

"So, um, yeah, that sounds like quite a rollercoaster ride," said Joe, not sure what else to say. "What went wrong?"

"Two shops meant I was working very long hours, young Joe, and I forgot to spend time with the one person I really loved. My wife. I would buy her lavish gifts. Boxes of After Eight mints, a gold-plated necklace from the Argos catalogue, designer dresses from George at Asda. I thought that was the way to make her happy, but all she really wanted was to spend time with me," concluded Raj with a sad smile.

"That's all I want!" exclaimed Joe. "To just spend time with my dad. I don't care about all the stupid money," said Joe.

"Come on, I am sure your father loves you very much, he'll be worried sick. Let me take you home," said Raj.

Joe looked at Raj and managed a little smile.

"OK. But can we stop off at Bob's on the way? I really need to talk to him."

"Yes, I think you are right. Now, I believe I have his address somewhere as his mum gets the *Mirror* delivered," said Raj as he began to flick through his address book. "Or is it the *Telegraph*? Or is it *Canal Boat Weekly*? I never can remember. Ah, here we are. Flat 112. The Winton Estate."

"That's miles away," said Joe.

"Don't worry, Joe. We will take the Rajmobile!"

24

The Rajmobile

"*This* is the Rajmobile?" asked Joe.

He and Raj were looking at a tiny girl's tricycle. It was pink and had a little white basket on the front and would have been too small for a girl of six.

"Yes!" said Raj proudly.

When Raj had mentioned the Rajmobile, Joe's mind had conjured up images of Batman's Batmobile or James Bond's Aston Martin, or at least Scooby Doo's van.

"It's a little small for you, don't you think?" he asked.

"I bought it on eBay for £3.50, Joe. It looked

a lot bigger in the photograph. I think they had a very small man stand next to it in the picture! Still, at that price, quite a bargain."

Reluctantly, Joe sat in the basket at the front, as Raj took his place on the saddle.

"Hold on tight, Joe! The Rajmobile is quite a beast!" said Raj, before he started pedalling, and the trike trundled off slowly, squeaking with every turn of the wheels.

dr**ING**.

That wasn't… Oh, I think I've done that joke too many times now.

"Hello?" said a kindly but sad-looking lady at the door of Flat 112.

"Are you Bob's mum?" asked Joe.

"Yes," said the woman. She squinted at him. "You must be Joe," she said, in a not-very-friendly tone. "Bob has told me all about *you*."

"Oh," squirmed Joe. "I'd like to see him, if that's OK."

"I'm not sure he'll want to see you."

"It's really important," said Joe. "I know I've treated him badly. But I want to make up for it. Please."

Bob's mum sighed, then opened the door. "Come in then," she said.

Joe followed her into the little flat. The whole thing could have fitted into his en-suite bathroom. The building had definitely seen better days. Wallpaper was peeling off the walls, and the carpet was worn in places. Bob's mum led Joe along the corridor to Bob's room and knocked on his door.

"What?" came Bob's voice.

"Joe is here to see you," replied Bob's mum.

"Tell him to get lost."

Bob's mum looked at Joe, embarrassed.

"Don't be rude, Bob. Open the door."

"I don't want to talk to him."

"Maybe I should go?" whispered Joe, half turning towards the front door. Bob's mum shook her head.

"Open this door at once, Bob. You hear me? At once!"

Slowly the door opened. Bob was still in his pyjamas, and stood staring at Joe.

"What do you want?" he demanded.

"To talk to you," replied Joe.

"Go on then, talk."

"Shall I make you two some breakfast?" asked Bob's mum.

"No, he's not staying," replied Bob.

Bob's mum's tutted and disappeared into the kitchen.

"I just came to say I'm sorry," spluttered Joe.

"It's a bit late for that, isn't it?" said Bob.

"Look, I am so, so sorry for all the things I said."

Bob was defiant in his anger. "You were really nasty."

"I know, I'm sorry. I just couldn't work out why you were so upset with me. I only gave the Grubbs money because I wanted to make things easier for you—"

"Yes, but—"

"I know, I know," said Joe hurriedly. "I realise

now it was the wrong thing to do. I'm just explaining how I felt at the time."

"A true friend would have stuck up for me. Supported me. Instead of just flashing their money around to make the problem go away."

"I am an idiot, Bob. I know that now. A great big fat stinking idiot."

Bob smiled a little, though he was clearly trying hard not to.

"And you were right about Lauren, of course," continued Joe.

"About her being a fake?"

"Yes, I found out my dad was paying her to be my friend," said Joe.

"I didn't know that. That must have really hurt."

Joe's heart ached, as he remembered how much pain he had felt at the party last night. "It did. I really liked her."

"I know. You forgot who your *real* friends were."

Joe felt so guilty. "I know... I'm so sorry. I do really like you, Bob. I really do. You're the only kid at school who ever liked me for me, not just my money."

"Let's not fall out again. Eh Joe?" Bob smiled.

Joe smiled too. "All I ever really wanted was a friend."

"You're still my friend, Joe. You always will be."

"Listen," Joe said. "I've got something for you. A present. To say sorry."

"Joe!" said Bob, frustrated. "Look, if it's a new Rolex or a load of money I don't want it, all right?"

Joe smiled. "No, it's just a Twix. I thought we could share it."

Joe pulled out the chocolate bar and Bob

chuckled. Joe chuckled too. He opened the packet and handed Bob one of the fingers. But just as Joe was about to scoff the chocolate and caramel topped biscuit...

"Joe?" called Bob's mum from the kitchen. "You better come quickly. Your dad is on the TV..."

25

Broken

Broken. That's the only word that could describe how Joe's dad looked. He was standing outside Bumfresh Towers, in his dressing gown. Mr Spud addressed the camera, his eyes red from crying.

"I've lost everything," he said slowly, his whole face shattered with emotion. "Everything. But all I want is my son back. My beautiful boy."

Then the tears welled up in Mr Spud and he had to catch his breath.

Joe looked over at Bob and his mum. They stood in the kitchen staring at the screen. "What does he mean? He's lost everything?"

"It was just on the news," she replied. "Everyone is suing your dad. Bumfresh has made everyone's bottom go purple."

"*What*?" replied Joe. He turned back to the TV.

"If you are watching out there, son... Come home. Please. I beg you. I need you. I miss you so much..."

Joe reached out and touched the screen. He could feel tears welling in the corners of his eyes. A little hiss of static danced on his fingertips.

"You'd better go to him," said Bob.

"Yeah," said Joe, too shocked to move.

"If you and your dad need anywhere to stay, you are both welcome here," said Bob's mum.

"Yeah, of course," chimed in Bob.

"Thanks so much. I'll tell him," said Joe. "Look, I've gotta go."

"Yeah," said Bob. He opened his arms and gave Joe a hug. Joe couldn't remember the last time anyone had hugged him. It was one thing money couldn't buy. Bob was a brilliant hugger too. He was all squidgy.

"I'll see you later, I suppose," said Joe.

"I'll make a Shepherd's Pie," said Bob's mum with a smile.

"My dad loves Shepherd's Pie," replied Joe.

"I remember," said Bob's mum. "Me and your dad were at school together."

"Really?" asked Joe.

"Yes, he had a bit more hair and a bit less money back then!" she joked.

Joe allowed himself a little laugh. "Thank you so much."

The lift was out of order so Joe raced down the stairs, bouncing off the walls as he did so. He ran out into the car park where Raj was waiting.

"Bumfresh Towers, Raj. And step on it!"

Raj pedalled hard and the trike trundled off down the street. They passed a rival newsagent's shop and Joe clocked the headlines on the papers in racks outside. Dad was on every front page.

BUMFRESH SCANDAL said *The Times*.

BILLIONAIRE SPUD FACING RUIN ran the *Telegraph*.

BUMFRESH IS HARMFUL TO BOTTOMS exclaimed the *Express*.

IS YOUR BOTTOM PURPLE? enquired the *Guardian*.

BUMFRESH PURPLE BOTTOM NIGHT-MARE! screamed the *Mirror*.

QUEEN HAS BABOON'S BUM claimed the *Mail*.

BUM HORROR yelled the *Daily Star*.

POSH SPICE CHANGES HAIRSTYLE announced the *Sun*.

Well, nearly every front page.

"You were right, Raj!" said Joe, as they sped up the high street.

"About what in particular?" replied the

newsagent, as he mopped the sweat from his brow.

"About Bumfresh. It has made everyone's bottom go purple!"

"I told you so! Did you inspect yours?"

So much had happened since Joe had left Raj's shop yesterday afternoon he had completely forgotten. "No."

"Well?" prompted the newsagent.

"Pull over!"

"What?"

"I said, 'pull over'!"

Raj swerved the Rajmobile on to the verge. Joe leaped off, looked over his shoulder and pulled down the back of his trousers a little.

"Well?" asked Raj.

Joe looked down. Two great purple swollen cheeks stared back at him. "It's purple!"

Let's have another look at Raj's graph. If Joe's

bottom was added to it, it would look like this:

In short Joe's bum was **very very very very very very very very very very very very very very very very very very very very very very very very very very very very very very very very very very very very very very very very very very very very very very very very very very very very very very very**

very very very very very very very very very very very very very very very very very very very very very very very very very very...

...*purple*.

Joe pulled up his trousers and jumped back on the Rajmobile. "Let's go!"

As they approached Bumfresh Towers, Joe saw that there were hundreds of journalists and camera crews waiting outside the gates of his house. As they approached, all the cameras turned to them, and hundreds of flashes went off. They were blocking their entrance and Raj had no choice but to stop the trike.

"You are live on Sky News! How do you feel now your father faces financial ruin?"

Joe was too shocked to reply, but still men in raincoats continued to shout questions at him.

"BBC News. Is there going to be a compensation

package for the millions of people around the world whose bums have gone purple?"

"CNN. Do you think your father will face criminal charges?"

Raj cleared his throat. "If I may make a short statement gentlemen."

All the cameras turned to the newsagent and there was hushed silence for a moment.

"At Raj's shop in Bolsover Street I am doing a very special offer on Frazzles. Buy ten packets get one free! For a limited time only."

The journalists all sighed loudly and muttered their annoyance.

Ding ding!

Raj rang the bell on his trike and the sea of reporters parted, to let him and Joe through.

"Thank you so much!" chirped Raj with a smile. "And I have some out of date Lion Bars at half price! Only slightly mouldy!"

26

A Blizzard of Banknotes

As Raj pedalled hard up the long driveway, Joe was shocked to see that there was already a fleet of lorries parked up by the front door. An army of bulky men in leather jackets were carrying out all of his dad's paintings and chandeliers and diamond-encrusted golf clubs. Raj stopped the bike and Joe leaped out of the basket and ran up the huge stone steps. Sapphire was hurrying out in a pair of impossibly high heels, laden with a huge suitcase and numerous handbags.

"Out of my way!" she hissed.

"Where's my dad?" demanded Joe.

"I dunno and I don't care! The idiot has lost all of his money!"

As she ran down the steps the heel of her shoe broke off and she took a tumble. The case crashed on the stone floor and broke open. A blizzard of banknotes swirled into the air. Sapphire began screaming and crying, and as mascara ran down her cheeks she leaped up, trying desperately to catch them. Joe looked back at her with a mixture of anger and pity.

He then raced into the house. It was now completely bare of any belongings. Joe fought past the bailiffs and sprinted up the grand spiral staircase. He passed a couple of burly men making off with hundreds of miles of his Scalextric track. For a millisecond Joe felt a pang of regret, but he carried on running and burst through the door to his dad's bedroom. The room was white and bare, almost serene in its emptiness. Hunched on a bare mattress with his back to the door was his dad, wearing only a vest and a pair of boxer shorts, his fat hairy arms and legs contrasting with his bald head. They had even taken his toupee.

"Dad!" shouted Joe.

"Joe!" Dad turned around. His face was red and raw from crying. "My boy, my boy! You came home."

"I'm sorry I ran away, Dad."

"I am so upset I hurt you with all that business with Lauren. I just wanted to make you happy."

"I know, I know, I forgive you, Dad." Joe sat down next to his father.

"I've lost everything. Everything. Even Sapphire's gone."

"I am not sure she was the one, Dad."

"No?"

"No," replied Joe as he tried not to shake his head too hard.

"No, maybe not," said Dad. "Now we've got no house, no money, no private jet. What are we gonna do, son?"

Joe reached into his trouser pocket and pulled out a cheque. "Dad?"

"Yes, my boy?"

"The other day I was going through my pockets and I found this."

Dad studied it. It was the one he had written his son for his birthday. For two million pounds.

"I never paid it in," said Joe excitedly. "You can have it back. Then you can buy us somewhere to live, and still have loads of money left over."

Dad looked up at his son. Joe wasn't sure if his father was happy or sad.

"Thank you so much, boy. You are a great lad, you really are. But I am sorry to say this cheque is worthless."

"Worthless?" Joe was shocked. "Why?"

"Because I have no money left in my bank

account," explained Dad. "There are so many law suits against me the banks have frozen all my accounts. I'm bankrupt now. If you had paid it in when I gave it to you, we would still have two million pounds."

Joe felt a little bit frightened that somehow he had done the wrong thing. "Are you angry with me, Dad?"

Dad looked at Joe and smiled. "No, I'm pleased you didn't cash it in. All that money never really made us happy, did it?"

"No," said Joe. "In fact it made us sad. And I am sorry too. You brought my homework to school and I shouted at you for embarrassing me. Bob was right, I *have* behaved like a spoiled brat at times."

Dad chuckled. "Well, just a little!"

Joe bumjumped along closer to his dad. He needed a hug.

At that moment two burly bailiffs entered the room. "We've got to take the mattress," announced one.

The Spuds offered no resistance, and stood up to let the men carry the last item out of the room.

Dad leaned over and whispered into his son's ear. "If there's anything you want to grab from your room, boy, I'd do it now."

"I don't need anything, Dad," replied Joe.

"There must be something. Designer shades, a gold watch, your iPod…"

They watched as the two men carried the mattress out of Mr Spud's bedroom. It was now completely bare.

Joe thought for a moment. "There is something," he said. He disappeared out of the room.

Mr Spud moved over to the window. He watched helpless as the leather-jacketed men carried out everything he owned, silver cutlery, crystal vases, antique furniture, everything... and loaded it into the trucks.

In a few moments Joe reappeared.

"Did you manage to grab anything?" asked Dad eagerly.

"Just one thing."

Joe opened his hand and showed his dad the sad little loo-roll rocket.

"But why?" said Dad. He couldn't believe his son had kept the old thing, let alone chosen it as the one thing he wanted to save from the house.

"It's the best thing you ever gave me," said Joe.

Dad's eyes clouded over with tears. "But it's just a loo roll with a bit of another loo roll stuck to it," he spluttered.

"I know," said Joe. "But it was made with

love. And it means more to me than all that expensive stuff you bought me."

Dad shook with uncontrollable emotion, and wrapped his short fat hairy arms around his son. Joe put *his* short, fat, less-hairy arms around his dad. He rested his head on his dad's chest. He felt that it was wet with tears.

"I love you, Dad."

"Ditto… I mean, I love you too, son."

"Dad…?" said Joe tentatively.

"Yes?"

"Do you fancy Shepherd's Pie for tea?"

"More than anything in the world," said Dad with a smile.

Father and son held each other tight.

Finally, Joe had everything he could ever need.

Postscript

So what happened to all the characters in the story?

 Mr Spud liked Bob's mum's Shepherd's Pie so much that he married her. And now they have it every night for their tea.

 Joe and Bob not only stayed best friends – when their parents got married they became stepbrothers too.

 Sapphire got engaged to a Premier League football team.

Raj and Mr Spud began working on a number of ideas together that they hoped would make them zillionaires. The five-fingered Kit Kat. The queen-size Mars Bar (in between king and normal size). Vindaloo-flavoured Polo mints. At time of writing none of these ideas have made them a penny.

No one ever worked out which Grubb was a he and which Grubb was a she. Not even their mum or dad. They were sent to a boot camp in America for juvenile delinquents.

The headmaster, Mr Dust, retired from the school on his hundredth birthday. He now races motorbikes full time.

Miss Spite the history teacher got her job back and gave Joe litter duty every day for the rest of his life.

The unfortunately named teacher Peter Bread changed his name. To Susan Jenkins. Which didn't really help.

Lauren continued her acting career, the only highlight of which was a part in the TV hospital drama *Casualty*. As a dead body.

The headmaster's secretary, Mrs Chubb, never did get out of her chair.

The Queen's bum remained purple.

She showed it to everyone in the country when she gave her yearly speech to the nation on Christmas Day, calling it her 'anus horribilis'.

And finally, Mrs Trafe released a best-selling cook book, *101 Recipes with Bat Sick*. Available from HarperCollins.

Have you got them all?

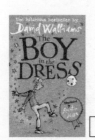

Illustrated in glorious colour!

Frank's dad was a champion banger racer, King of
the Track. Gilbert the Great! But, when a terrible
accident sees him go from hero to zero, Frank and
Gilbert are left with nothing – and in the grips of a
wicked crime boss and his henchmen.

Then, when Gilbert is thrown in prison,
only Frank can come to his rescue . . .

Jack's grandpa wears his slippers to the supermarket, serves up Spam à la Custard for dinner and often doesn't remember Jack's name, but he can still take to the skies in a speeding Spitfire and save the day…

When Tom gets hit on the head by a cricket ball, he finds himself at Lord Funt Hospital, and is greeted by a terrifying-looking porter. Things go from bad to worse when he meets the wicked matron in charge of the children's ward… But Tom is about to embark on the journey of a lifetime!

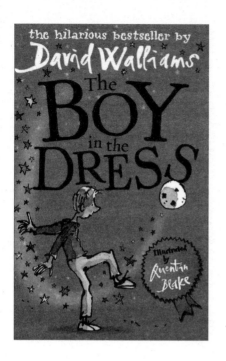

Dennis lives in a boring house in a boring street in a boring town. But he's about to find out that when you open your mind, life becomes anything but boring!

When Chloe makes friends with Mr Stink, the local tramp, she soon learns that some secrets have a way of leading to disaster. And that there just might be more to Mr Stink than meets the eye... or the nose.

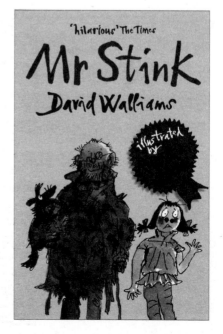

Meet Joe Spud, the richest twelve-year-old in the world. Joe has absolutely everything he could possibly want. But there's one thing he still really needs: a friend...

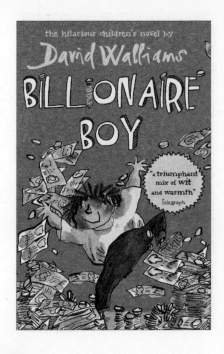

Ben's grandma is the boringest grandma ever: all she wants to do is to play Scrabble, and eat cabbage soup. But then he discovers she has a dark secret... She was once an international jewel thief!

Join Ben on the adventure of a lifetime – you'll never think of grannies in the same way again...

Zoe's got a lot of things to be unhappy about... Her stepmother's so lazy she gets Zoe to pick her nose for her. And the school bully loves flobbing on her head. Worst of all, the dastardly Burt has terrible plans for her pet rat. And guess what he's going to do with it? The clue is in the title.

Stella Saxby is the sole heir to Saxby Hall. But awful Aunt Alberta and her giant owl will stop at nothing to get it from her. Luckily Stella has a secret – and slightly spooky – weapon up her sleeve...

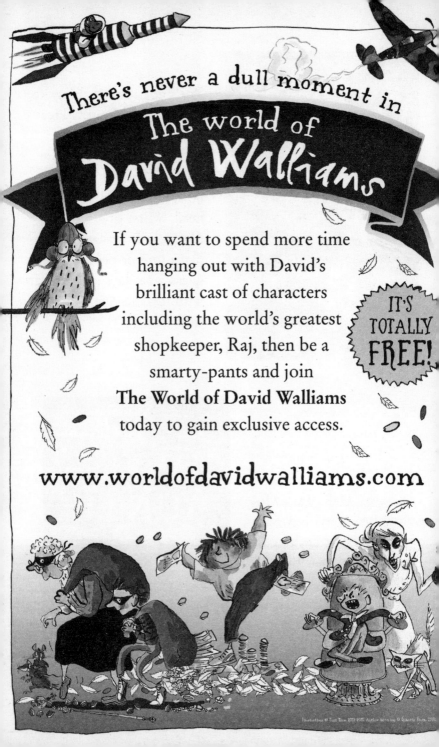

Praise for *The Boy in the Dress*

"Well written, funny, touching" *Observer*

"Charming, funny, with lovely illustrations from Quentin Blake" *The Times*

"A great and comic tale – Walliams is a natural wit and good with words" *Evening Standard*

"Walliams's storytelling has a lovely Dahlian fluency to it" *Time Out*

"The *Little Britain* star's debut novel is a passionate celebration of individuality" *Telegraph*

"I was surprised by how tender and kind Walliams's first book for children is... a touching story" *Independent on Sunday*

"Believable characters and a story that's original and intriguing: *****" *Heat Magazine*

"Has an old-fashioned, spiky morality that those of us who grew up on Roald Dahl know and love" *Observer Woman*

"Charming, surprising and hilarious – everything you would expect from David Walliams: ****" *Look Magazine*

"Hilariously funny – just as you'd expect!" *Mizz*

David Walliams

The BOY in the DRESS

Illustrated by Quentin Blake

HarperCollins *Children's Books*

First published in hardback in Great Britain by HarperCollins
Children's Books 2008
First published in paperback in Great Britain by HarperCollins
Children's Books 2009
HarperCollins *Children's Books* is a division of
HarperCollinsPublishers Ltd
1 London Bridge Street, London SE1 9GF

The HarperCollins website address is:
www.harpercollins.co.uk

HarperCollins*Publishers*
1st Floor, Watermarque Building, Ringsend Road
Dublin 4, Ireland

99

ISBN 978-0-00-727904-3

Printed and bound by
CPI Group (UK) Ltd, Croydon, CR0 4YY

For Eddie,

What joy you have given us all.

1

No Hugging

Dennis was different.

When he looked in the mirror he saw an ordinary twelve-year-old boy. But he *felt* different – his thoughts were full of colour and poetry, though his life could be very boring.

The story I am going to tell you begins here, in Dennis's ordinary house on an ordinary street in an ordinary town. His house was nearly exactly the same as all the others in the street. One house had double glazing, another did not. One had a gravel drive, another had crazy paving. One had a Vauxhall Cavalier in the drive, another a Vauxhall Astra. Tiny differences that only really pointed out the sameness of everything.

It was all so ordinary, something extraordinary just had to happen.

Dennis lived with his dad – who did have a name, but Dennis just called him Dad, so I will too – and his older brother John, who was fourteen. Dennis found it frustrating that his brother would always be two years older than him, and bigger, and stronger.

Dennis's mum had left home a couple of years ago. Before that, Dennis used to creep out of his room and sit at the top of the stairs and listen to his mum and dad shout at each other until one day the shouting stopped.

She was gone.

Dad banned John and Dennis from ever mentioning Mum again. And soon after she left, he went around the house and took down all the photographs of her and burnt them in a big bonfire.

But Dennis managed to save one.

One solitary photograph escaped the flames, dancing up into the air from the heat of the fire, before floating through the smoke and on to the hedge.

As dusk fell, Dennis snuck out and retrieved the photo. It was charred and blackened around the edges and at first his heart sank, but when he turned it to the light he saw that the image was as bright and clear as ever.

It showed a joyful scene: a younger John and Dennis with Mum at the beach, Mum wearing a lovely yellow dress with flowers on it. Dennis loved that dress; it was full of colour and life, and soft to the touch. When Mum put it on, it meant that summer had arrived.

It had been warm outside after she had left, but it hadn't really been summer in their house again.

In the picture Dennis and his brother were in swimming trunks holding ice-cream cones, vanilla ice cream smeared around their smiling mouths. Dennis kept the photo in his pocket and looked at it secretly every day. His mum looked so achingly beautiful in it, even though her smile was uncertain. Dennis stared at it for hours on end, trying to imagine what she had been thinking when it was taken.

After Mum left, Dad didn't say much, but when he did he would often shout. So Dennis ended up watching a lot of television, and especially his favourite show, *Trisha*. Dennis had seen a *Trisha* episode about people with depression, and thought maybe his dad had that. Dennis loved *Trisha*. It was a daytime talk show where ordinary people were given the opportunity to talk about their problems, or yell abuse at their relatives, and it was all presided over by a kindly-looking but judgemental woman conveniently called... Trisha.

For a while Dennis thought life without his mum would be some kind of adventure. He'd stay up late, eat takeaways and watch rude comedy shows. However, as the days turned into weeks, and the weeks turned into months, and the months turned into years, he realised that it wasn't an adventure at all.

It was just sad.

Dennis and John sort of loved each other in that way that they had to because they were brothers. But John tested this love quite often by doing things he thought were funny, like sitting on Dennis's face and farting. If farting had been an Olympic sport (at time of writing I am told it isn't, which I feel is a shame), he would have won a number of gold medals and probably received a knighthood from the Queen.

Now, reader, you might be thinking that, as their mum had left, the two brothers would be brought closer together.

Sadly, it only drove them apart.

Unlike Dennis, John was full of silent rage with his mum for leaving, and agreed with Dad that it was better never to mention her again. It was one of the rules of the house:

No talking about Mum.

No crying.

And worst of all – no hugging.

Dennis, on the other hand, was just full of sadness. Sometimes he missed his mum so much that he cried in bed at night. He tried to cry as quietly as possible, because he and his brother shared a room and he didn't want John to hear.

But one night Dennis's sobs woke John up.

"Dennis? Dennis? What are you crying for now?" demanded John from his bed.

"I don't know. It's just… well… I just wish that Mum was here, and everything," came the reply from Dennis.

"Well, don't cry. She's gone and she's not coming back."

"You don't know that…"

"She's never coming back, Dennis. Now stop crying. Only girls cry."

But Dennis *couldn't* stop crying. The pain ebbed and flowed inside him like the sea, crashing down on him, almost drowning him in tears. He didn't want to upset his brother, though, so he cried as quietly as he possibly could.

So why was Dennis so different, I hear you ask? After all, this boy lived in an ordinary house, in an ordinary street, in an ordinary town.

Well, I'm not going to tell you why yet, but the clue might be in the title of this book...

2

Fat Dad

Dennis's dad jumped up and down and shouted with joy. Then he pulled Dennis into a tight hug.

"Two nil!" he said. "We showed 'em, eh, son?"

Yes, I know I said there was no hugging in Dennis's house. But this was different.

It was football.

In Dennis's house, talking about football was easier than talking about feelings. He, John and Dad all loved football, and together shared the highs and (more often) lows of supporting their local third-division team.

But as soon as the match finished and the referee blew his whistle it was as if that sound also signalled a return to their strict no-hugging policy.

Dennis did miss being hugged. His mum had hugged him all the time. She was so warm and soft; he loved being held by her. Most children can't wait to grow up and get bigger, but Dennis missed being small and being picked up by his mother. It was in her arms that he had felt most safe.

It was a shame Dennis's dad hardly ever hugged him. Fat people are good at hugs; they're nice and soft, like a big comfy sofa.

Oh, yes, didn't I mention? Dad was fat.

Really fat.

Dad worked as a long-distance lorry driver. And all that sitting down and driving had taken its toll, only stretching his legs to go to the

service station café and eat various combinations
of eggs, sausage, bacon, beans and chips.

Sometimes, after breakfast, Dad would eat
two packets of crisps. He just got fatter and
fatter after Mum left. Dennis had seen a *Trisha*
episode about a man called Barry who was so
fat he couldn't wipe his own bum. The studio
audience were told about his daily food intake

and "oohed" and "aahed" with a strange mixture of delight and horror. Then Trisha asked him, "Barry, does the fact that you have to get your mum or dad to wipe your... underneath... not make you want to lose weight?"

"Trisha, I just love me food," was Barry's smirking reply.

Trisha put it to Barry that he was "comfort

eating". Trisha was good with phrases like that. She had after all been through a lot of difficult times herself. Barry cried a bit at the end, and as the credits rolled Trisha smiled sadly and gave him a hug, though it was hard for her to really get her arms round Barry as he was the size of a small bungalow.

Dennis wondered whether his dad was comfort eating too, having one more sausage or slice of fried bread at breakfast to – in Trisha's words – "fill the emptiness inside". But he didn't dare share that thought with his dad. Dad wasn't keen on Dennis watching the show anyway. He said, "It's just for girls, that."

Dennis dreamed of one day having his own *Trisha* episode, with the title "My brother's farts smell well bad" or "My dad has a chocolate Hobnob problem". (Dad ate a whole packet of the admittedly more-ish biscuits every day when he got home from work.)

So when Dennis, his dad and John played football, Dad would always go in goal, because he was so fat. He liked it because it meant he didn't have to run around that much. The goal was an upturned bucket and an empty beer keg, a remnant from a long-forgotten barbecue they'd once had when Mum was still around.

They didn't have barbecues any more. These days they had battered sausages from the local chippy, or bowls of cereal, even when it wasn't breakfast.

What Dennis loved most about playing football with his family was that he was the best. Even though his brother was two years older, Dennis could run rings round him in the garden, tackling, dribbling and scoring with great skill. And it wasn't like it was *easy* to get

the ball past his dad. Not because Dad was good
in goal – it was just that he was so *big*…

On Sunday mornings Dennis used to play
football for his local club. He dreamed of being
a professional footballer, but after his mum and
dad split up he stopped going. He had always

relied on his mum to give him a lift – Dad
couldn't take him as he was forever driving up
and down the country in his lorry trying to
make ends meet.

So Dennis's dream floated quietly away.

Dennis did play football for his school,

though, and was his team's number one...
shooter?

Sorry, reader, I must look this up.

Ah, *striker*.

Yes, Dennis was his team's number one striker,
scoring over a million goals in a year.

Excuse me again, reader, I don't know much
about football, maybe a million is too much. A
thousand? A hundred? Two?

Whatever, he scored the most goals.

As a result, Dennis was incredibly popular
with his team-mates – except the captain,
Gareth, who picked Dennis up on every little
mistake on the pitch. Dennis suspected that
Gareth was jealous of him because he was a
better footballer. Gareth was one of those boys
who are unusually large for their age. In fact,
you wouldn't be surprised to find he was really
five years older than everyone else in his year,

but had just been held back on account of being a bit thick.

Once, Dennis was off school with a really bad cold on a match day. He had just finished watching that day's *Trisha*, a gripping episode about a woman who discovered she was having an affair with her own husband. Then he was looking forward to some Heinz tomato soup and his second favourite show, *Loose Women*, where a panel of angry-looking ladies debated important issues of the day – like diets and leggings.

But just as the signature tune was starting there was a knock at the door. Dennis got up grumpily. It was Darvesh, Dennis's best friend at school.

"Dennis, we desperately need you to play today," pleaded Darvesh.

"I'm sorry, Darvesh, I'm just not feeling well.

I can't stop sneezing or coughing. Aaachoooo! See?" replied Dennis.

"But it's the quarter finals today. We've always got knocked out at the quarter finals before. Please?"

Dennis sneezed again.

"Aaaaaaaaaaaaaaaaaaaaaccccccccccchhhhh hhhhhooooooooooooooooooooOOO!"
It was such a strong sneeze he thought he was going to turn inside out.

"Pleeeaaassseee," said Darvesh hopefully as he discreetly wiped some of Dennis's stray snot from his tie.

"OK, I'll try," coughed Dennis.

"Yeeeessss!" exclaimed Darvesh, as if victory was already theirs.

Dennis gulped down a couple of mouthfuls of soup, grabbed his kit and ran out of the house.

Darvesh's mum was sitting in her little red

Ford Fiesta outside, with the engine running. She worked on the tills at Sainsbury's, but lived to see her son play football. She was the proudest mum in the world, which always made her son squirm a little.

"Thank goodness you have come, Dennis!" she said as Dennis clambered on to the back seat. "The team needs you today, it's a very important match. Without doubt the most important match of the season!"

"Just drive please, Mum!" said Darvesh.

"All right! All right! We're going! Don't talk to your mother like that, Darvesh!" she shouted, pretending to be angrier than she really was. She put her foot on the accelerator and the car lurched uncertainly off towards the school playing fields.

"Oh, you've decided to come, have you?" growled Gareth as they pulled up. Not only was he bigger than everyone else, he had a deeper voice, and was disturbingly hairy for a boy his age.

When he showered, he looked like a big monkey.

"Sorry, Gareth, I just wasn't feeling well. I have a pretty bad..."

Before Dennis could say "cold", he sneezed again even more violently than before.

"Aaaaaaaaaaaaaaaaaaaaaaaaaaaaaaaaaaaaaaaa
aaaaaaaaaaaaaaaaaaaaaaaaaccccccccc
cccccccccccccccccccccccchcccc
cchhhhhhhhhhhhhhhhhhhhhhhh
hhhhhhhoooooooooooooooo
ooooooooooooooOOOOOO!"

"Oh sorry, Gareth," said Dennis, wiping a small gloop of snot from Gareth's ear with a tissue.

"Let's just do this," said Gareth.

Feeling weak with illness, Dennis ran on to the school pitch with his team, coughing and spluttering all the way.

"Good luck, boys! Especially my son Darvesh, and of course his friend Dennis! Let's win this for the school!" shouted Darvesh's mum from the side of the pitch.

"My mum is like so embarrassing," rumbled Darvesh.

"I think it's cool she comes," said Dennis. "My dad's never seen me playing in a match."

"Let's see a nice goal from you today please, Darvesh my son!"

"Mmm, maybe she *is* a bit embarrassing," agreed Dennis.

That afternoon they were playing St Kenneth's School for Boys, one of those schools where the pupils felt a little superior just because their parents had to pay for them to go there. They were a very good team, though, and within the first ten minutes had scored. The pressure was immediately on, and Darvesh stole the ball off a boy who looked twice his size and passed it to Dennis.

"Lovely tackle, Darvesh my son!" shouted Darvesh's mum.

The thrill of possessing the ball made Dennis forget his cold for a moment, and he weaved his way through the defence and approached the goalkeeper, a luxuriant-haired boy sporting brand-new kit, who was probably called Oscar or Tobias or something. All of a sudden they were face to face, and Dennis sneezed again uncontrollably.

"Aaaaaaaaaaaaacccccccccccchhhhhhhh hhhooooooooooooooOOO!!!!"

The snot exploded on to the goalie's face, blinding him for a moment, and all Dennis needed to do was tap the ball past the line.

"Foul!" shouted the goalkeeper, but the referee allowed it. It was foul, but not technically *a* foul.

"I'm sorry about that," said Dennis. He really hadn't meant to do it.

"Don't worry, I have a tissue!" exclaimed Darvesh's mum. "I always carry a packet with me." She hurtled on to the pitch, hitching up her sari to avoid the mud and ran up to the goalie. "There you go, posh boy," she said, handing him the tissue. Darvesh rolled his eyes at his mother's one-woman pitch invasion. The goalie tearfully wiped Dennis's mucus from his floppy hair. "Personally I think St Kenneth's doesn't stand a chance," she added.

"Mummmm!" shouted Darvesh.

"Sorry! Sorry! Play on!"

Four goals later – one from Dennis, one from Gareth, one from Darvesh and one "accidental" deflection from Darvesh's mum – and the game was won.

"You are through to the semi-finals, boys! I can't wait!" exclaimed Darvesh's mum as she drove the boys home, beeping out tunes on the Ford Fiesta's horn in celebration. For her it was as if England had won the World Cup.

"Oh, please don't come, Mum, I beg you. Not if you're gonna do that again!"

"How dare you, Darvesh! You know I wouldn't miss the next game for the world. Oh, you make me so proud!"

Darvesh and Dennis looked at each other and smiled. For a moment their victory on the pitch made them feel like they owned the universe.

Even Dad raised a smile when Dennis told him that his team were through to the semi-finals.

But Dad wasn't going to stay happy for long...

3

Under the Mattress

"What the hell *is* this?" said Dad. His eyes were popping out he was so angry.

"It's a magazine," replied Dennis.

"I can see it's a magazine."

Dennis wondered why his dad was asking, if he already knew what it was, but he kept that thought to himself.

"It's *Vogue* magazine, Dad."

"I can see it's *Vogue* magazine."

Dennis fell silent. He had bought the magazine from the newsagent's a few days before. Dennis liked the picture on the cover. It was of a very pretty girl in an even prettier yellow dress with what looked like roses sewn on the front, and it really reminded him of the dress his mum was wearing in the photograph he'd kept. He just had to buy it, even though the magazine was £3.80, and he only got £5 a week pocket money.

ONLY 17 SCHOOLCHILDREN ALLOWED IN AT ONE TIME read the sign in the newsagent's shop window. The shop was run by a very jolly man called Raj, who laughed even when nothing funny was happening. He laughed when he said your name as you walked through the door – and that was just what he did when Dennis went into the shop.

"Dennis! Ha ha!"

Seeing Raj laugh it was impossible not to laugh too. Dennis visited Raj's shop most days on his way to or from school, sometimes just to chat to Raj, and after he picked up the copy of *Vogue* he felt a twinge of embarrassment. He knew it was usually women who bought it, so he also picked up a copy of *Shoot* on the way to the counter, hoping to hide the *Vogue* underneath it. But after ringing up the *Shoot* magazine on the till, Raj paused.

He looked at the *Vogue* magazine, then at Dennis.

Dennis gulped.

"Are you sure you want this, Dennis?" asked Raj. "*Vogue* is mainly read by ladies, and your drama teacher Mr Howerd."

"Umm…" Dennis hesitated. "It's a present for a friend, Raj. It's her birthday."

"Oh, I see! Maybe you'd like some wrapping paper to go with it?"

"Um, OK." Dennis smiled. Raj was a wonderful businessman and very skilled at getting you to buy things you didn't really want.

"All the wrapping paper is over there by the greetings cards."

Dennis reluctantly wandered over.

"Oh!" said Raj, excited. "Maybe you need a card to go with it too! Let me help."

Raj bounded out from behind the counter and began to proudly show Dennis his range of cards. "These are very popular with the ladies. Flowers. Ladies love flowers." He pointed out another. "Kittens! Look at these lovely kittens. And PUPPIES!" Raj was really excited now. "Look at those lovely puppies! They're so beautiful, Dennis, that they make me want to cry."

"Er…" said Dennis, looking at the card with puppies on it, trying to understand why it might make someone shed actual tears.

"Does this lady friend of yours prefer kittens or puppies?" Raj asked.

"I'm not sure," said Dennis, unable to think what this "lady friend" of his might like, if she existed. "Puppies, I think, Raj."

"Puppies it is! These puppies are so beautiful I want to kiss them all over!"

Dennis tried to nod his head in agreement, but his head wouldn't move.

"Is this wrapping paper OK?" asked Raj as he pulled out a roll of what looked suspiciously like unsold Christmas wrapping paper.

"It's got Father Christmas on it, Raj."

"Yes, Dennis, and he's wishing you a very happy birthday!" said Raj confidently.

"I think I'll just leave it, thanks."

"Buy one extra roll, I'll give you a third free," said Raj.

"No, thanks."

"Three rolls for the price of two! That's a very good offer!"

"No, thanks," said Dennis again.

"Seven rolls for the price of five?"

Dennis only got Ds in maths, so wasn't sure if

that was a better offer or not. But he didn't want seven rolls of Father Christmas wrapping paper, especially in March, so again he said, "No, thanks."

"Eleven rolls for the price of eight?"

"No, thanks."

"You're a madman, Dennis! That's three rolls free!"

"But I really don't need eleven rolls of wrapping paper," said Dennis.

"OK, OK," said Raj. "Let me just put these through the till for you."

Dennis followed Raj to the till. He glanced briefly at the sweets on the counter.

"*Vogue* magazine, *Shoot* magazine, card, and now you're eyeing up my Yorkie bars, aren't you?" said Raj, laughing.

"Well, I was just..."

"Take one."

"No, thanks."

"Take one," insisted Raj.

"It's OK."

"Please, Dennis, I want you to have a Yorkie bar."

"I don't really like Yorkie bars…"

"Everyone likes Yorkie bars! Please take one."

Dennis smiled and picked up a Yorkie.

"One Yorkie bar, sixty pence," said Raj.

Dennis's face dropped.

"So that's five pounds in total please," continued the shopkeeper.

Dennis rummaged in his pocket and pulled out some coins.

"As my favourite customer," said Raj, "I give you a discount."

"Oh, thank you," said Dennis.

"Four pounds and ninety-nine pence, please."

Dennis had walked halfway up the street before he heard a voice shout, "Sellotape!"

He looked round. Raj was holding a large box of Sellotape. "You need Sellotape to wrap the present!"

"No, thanks," said Dennis politely. "We've got some at home."

"Fifteen rolls for the price of thirteen!" Raj shouted.

Dennis smiled and carried on walking. He felt a sudden surge of excitement. He couldn't wait to get home and open the magazine, and gaze at its hundreds of glossy, colourful pages. He walked faster, then started jogging, and when he really couldn't contain his excitement any more he started running.

When he got home, Dennis bounded upstairs. He closed the bedroom door, lay down on his bed and turned the first page.

Like a treasure box from an old film, the magazine seemed to shine a golden light on his face. The first hundred pages were all adverts, but in a way they were the best bit – pages and pages of glorious photographs of beautiful women in beautiful clothes and make-up and jewellery and shoes and bags and sunglasses. Names like Yves Saint-Laurent, Christian Dior, Tom Ford, Alexander McQueen, Louis Vuitton, Marc Jacobs and Stella McCartney ran underneath the images. Dennis didn't know who any of them were, but he loved the way their names looked on the page.

The adverts were followed by a few pages of writing – they looked boring so he didn't read them – then pages and pages of fashion shoots. These were not very different from the adverts, featuring more beautiful women in photographs that were moody and fabulous. The magazine even smelled exotic, as it had special pages where you pulled open a flap to have a sniff of the newest perfume. Dennis pored over every page, mesmerised by the dresses – their colour, their length, their cut. He could lose himself in the pages forever.

The glamour.

The beauty.

The perfection.

Suddenly he heard a key in the door. "Dennis? Oi, bro? Where are you?"

It was John.

Dennis quickly hid the magazine under his mattress. He knew somehow that he didn't want his brother to see it.

He opened the bedroom door and called down as innocently as he could from the top of the stairs, "I'm just up here."

"What are you doing?" asked John as he

leaped up the stairs, a Jaffa Cake in his mouth.

"Nothing. Just got home."

"Do you wanna have a kick about in the garden?"

"Yeah, OK."

But all the time they played, Dennis couldn't help thinking about the magazine. It was as if it was glowing like gold from under the mattress. That night, when his brother was in the bath, he quietly lifted the copy of *Vogue* from under the mattress and silently turned the pages, studying every hem, every stitch, every fabric.

Every moment he could, Dennis returned to this glorious world. It was his Narnia, only without the talking lion that's supposed to be Jesus.

But Dennis's escape to that magical world of glamour ended the day his dad discovered the magazine.

"I can see it's *Vogue.* What I want to know is why a son of mine wants to *look* at a fashion magazine?"

It sounded like a question, but there was such anger and force in Dad's voice Dennis wasn't sure if he really wanted an answer. Not that Dennis could think of one anyway.

"I just like it. It's only pictures and things about dresses and that."

"I can see that," said Dad, looking at the magazine.

And that was when he paused and a funny look crossed his face. He studied the cover for a moment – the girl in the flowery frock. "That dress. It's like the one your m—"

"Yes, Dad?"

"Nothing, Dennis. Nothing."

Dad looked for a moment like he was going to cry.

"It's OK, Dad," said Dennis softly, and he slowly moved his hand and placed it over his dad's. He remembered doing the same with his mum once when Dad had made her cry. He remembered how strange it felt too, a little boy comforting a grown-up.

Dad let Dennis hold his hand for a moment,

before moving it away, embarrassed. He raised his voice again. "No, son, it's just not right. Dresses. It's weird."

"Well, Dad, what are you doing looking under my mattress in the first place?"

In truth Dennis knew *exactly* why his dad was looking under his mattress. Dad owned a copy of a rude magazine like the ones on the top shelf at Raj's shop. Sometimes John would sneak into their dad's room and smuggle it out and look at it. Dennis looked at it too, sometimes, but didn't find it all that exciting. He was disappointed when the ladies took their clothes off – he preferred looking at what they were wearing.

Anyway, when John "borrowed" his father's magazine, it wasn't really like when you borrow a book from the library. There wasn't an inlay card that would have to be stamped by a bespectacled librarian, and you didn't incur fines if you returned it late.

So John usually just kept it.

Dennis guessed his dad's magazine had gone missing again, and he had been looking for it when he found the copy of *Vogue*.

"Well, I was just looking under your mattress because..." Dad looked uncomfortable, and then angry. "It doesn't matter why I was looking under your mattress. I'm your dad. I can look under your mattress any time I like!" He finished his speech with the tone of triumph grown-ups sometimes use when they are talking nonsense and they know it.

Dennis's dad brandished the magazine. "This is going in the dustbin, son."

"But, Dad..." Dennis protested.

"I'm sorry. It's just not right. A boy your age reading *Vogue* magazine." He said "*Vogue* magazine" as if he was talking a foreign language he didn't understand. "It's just not right," he muttered over and over as he left the room.

Dennis sat on the edge of his bed. He listened as his dad clumped his way down the stairs, and then lifted the dustbin lid. Finally he heard a clanging *thud* as the magazine hit the bottom of the bin.

4

Wanting to Disappear

"Morning, Dennis, or should I say Denise!" said John, laughing cruelly.

"I told you not to mention it," said Dad sternly as he coated his white toast with an inch-thick layer of butter. When Mum was around, she'd have made him have margarine.

And brown bread.

Dennis slumped down at the kitchen table in silence, not even looking at his brother. He poured himself some Rice Krispies.

"Seen any nice dresses recently?" taunted John. He laughed again.

"I told you to leave it alone!" said Dad, even louder than before.

"Magazines like that are for girls! And woofters!"

"SHUT UP!" said Dad.

Dennis suddenly didn't feel hungry any more, and picked up his bag and walked out of the door. He slammed it behind him. He could still hear Dad, saying, "What did I say, John? It's over, OK? It's in the bin."

Dennis walked unwillingly to school. He didn't want to be at home *or* at school. He was afraid his brother would tell somebody and he'd be laughed at. He just wanted to disappear. When he was much younger, he used to believe that if he closed his eyes no one else could see him.

Right now he wished it was true.

The first lesson of the day was history. Dennis

liked history – they were studying the Tudor dynasty, and he loved looking at the pictures of the kings and queens in all their finery. Especially Elizabeth I, who really knew how to "power dress", an expression he had read in *Vogue* next to a shoot of a model in a beautifully cut business suit. But Dennis always found chemistry – the next lesson – mind-numbingly boring. He spent most of the lesson staring at the periodic table, trying to fathom what it was.

When break-time came, Dennis played football as usual in the playground with his friends. He was having fun until he saw John with a group of his mates, the bad boys with short hair who the careers' advisors would probably advise to become nightclub bouncers or criminals. They ambled through the middle of the makeshift pitch.

Dennis held his breath.

John nodded at his brother, but said nothing.

Dennis let out a sigh of relief.

He was pretty sure his brother couldn't have told anyone that he'd bought a women's fashion magazine. After all, Darvesh was playing football with him as he always did. They played with an old tennis ball that Darvesh's dog Odd-Bod had chewed. It was a school rule that footballs weren't allowed in the playground in case a window got broken. Darvesh set Dennis up to score with a daring cross.

Then Dennis headed the ball and it flew too high up past what was meant to be the goal...

... and through the window of the headmaster's office.

John and his friends stared, mouths open. The playground fell silent.

You could have heard a pin drop, in the

unlikely event that someone had dropped a pin at that exact moment.

"Oops," said Darvesh.

"Yes, oops," said Dennis.

"Oops" was really an understatement. The headmaster, Mr Hawtrey, hated children. Actually, he hated everybody, probably even himself. He wore an immaculate three-piece grey suit, with a charcoal-coloured tie and dark-framed glasses. His hair was meticulously combed and parted, and he had a thin, black moustache. It was as if he actively wanted to look sinister. And he had a face that someone who has spent their whole life grimacing ends up with.

A permanently grimacing one.

"He might not be in his office," ventured Darvesh hopefully.

"Maybe," said Dennis, gulping.

At that moment the headmaster's face peered

out of the window. "SCHOOL!" he bellowed. The playground fell silent. "Who kicked this ball?" He held the tennis ball between his fingers with the same sense of disgust that dog owners do when they are forced to pick up their dog's doo-doo.

Dennis was too scared to say anything.

"I asked a question. WHO KICKED IT?"

Dennis gulped. "I didn't kick it, sir," he offered tentatively. "But I *did* header it."

"Detention today, boy. Four o'clock."

"Thank you, sir," said Dennis, not sure what else to say.

"Because of your behaviour all ball games in the playground are banned for today," added Mr Hawtrey before disappearing back into his study. A sigh of angry disappointment echoed around the playground. Dennis hated it when teachers did that, when they made everyone suffer to make you unpopular with your classmates. It was a cheap trick.

"Don't worry, Dennis," said Darvesh. "Everyone knows Mr Hawtrey's a total—"

"Yeah, I know."

They sat on their bags by the wall of the science block and opened their lunch boxes, devouring the sandwiches that were meant for lunch.

Dennis hadn't told Darvesh about buying *Vogue* – but he wanted to find out what his friend thought about it – in a roundabout way.

Darvesh was Sikh. As he was in the same year as Dennis and only twelve he didn't wear a turban yet. He wore a *patka*, a bobble-hat-type thing that kept his hair out of his face. That's because Sikh men aren't supposed to cut their hair. There were lots of different types of kids at the school, but Darvesh was the only one who wore a *patka*.

"Do *you* feel different, Darvesh?" asked Dennis.

"In what way?"

"Well, just, you know, you're the only boy in school who has to wear one of those things on your head."

"Oh, that, yeah. Well, with my family of course I don't. And when Mum took me to India at Christmas to visit Grandma I didn't at all. All the Sikh boys were wearing them."

"But at school?"

"At first I did, yes. I felt a bit embarrassed cos I knew I looked different to everyone."

"Yeah."

"And then I suppose as people got to know me they realised I wasn't really that different. I just wear this funny thing on my head!" He laughed.

Dennis laughed too.

"Yeah, you're just my mate Darvesh. I don't really think about the thing on your head at all. In fact, I'd quite like one."

"No, you wouldn't. It itches like hell! But, you know, it would be boring if we were all the same, wouldn't it?"

"It certainly would." Dennis smiled.

5

Just Doodling

Dennis had never had a detention before, so in a way he was quite looking forward to it. When he turned up at classroom 4C to report to the French teacher, Miss Windsor, he noticed there was only one other person who had been sentenced to an hour's incarceration. It was Lisa.

Lisa James.

Only the most beautiful girl in the school.

She was super cool too, and somehow she always made her school uniform look like it was a costume in a pop video. Even though they had never spoken, Dennis had a really big crush on Lisa.

Not that anything would ever happen, though – her being two years older and six inches taller made her literally out of reach.

"Hi," Lisa said. She had a gorgeous voice, rough round the edges but soft inside.

"Oh, hi, um…" Dennis pretended not to remember her name.

"Lisa. What's your name?"

Dennis thought for a moment about changing his name to something cooler like "Brad" or "Dirk" to try and impress her, but realised that would be insane.

"Dennis."

"Hi, Dennis," said Lisa. "What are you in for?"

"I headed a ball into Hawtrey's office."

"Cool!" said Lisa, laughing.

Dennis laughed a little too. She obviously assumed that he had headed the ball into the headmaster's office on purpose and he wasn't about to correct her.

"What about you?" asked Dennis.

"I wasn't 'wearing the correct school uniform'. This time Hawtrey said my skirt was too short."

Dennis looked down at Lisa's skirt. It *was* quite short.

"I don't care really," she continued. "I'd rather wear what I want and get the odd detention now and again."

"Sorry," interrupted Miss Windsor. "There's not really meant to be any talking in detention."

Miss Windsor was one of the nice teachers who didn't really enjoy telling pupils off. She would usually say "excuse me" or "sorry" before she did. She was probably in her late forties. Miss Windsor didn't wear a wedding ring or seem to have any kids. She liked to exude a little French sophistication, throwing colourful silk scarves over her shoulder with mock nonchalance, and devouring four-packs of croissants from the Tesco Metro at break-time.

"Sorry, Miss Windsor," said Lisa.

Dennis and Lisa smiled at each other. Dennis got back to his lines.

I must not header balls into the headmaster's window.

I must not header balls into the headmaster's window.

I must not header balls into the headmaster's window.

He looked over at what Lisa was doing. Instead of her lines, she was idly sketching some dress designs. A ball gown with a plunging back looked like it wouldn't be out of place in *Vogue*. She turned over the page and started sketching a strapless top and pencil skirt. Next to that she drew a long flowing white suit that went in and out in all the right places. Lisa clearly had a real flair for fashion.

"Excuse me," said Miss Windsor. "But you should really concentrate on your own work, Dennis."

"Sorry, miss," said Dennis. He started his lines again.

I must not header balls into the headmaster's window.

I must not header Vogue into the headmaster's window.

I must not read Vogue into the headmaster's

Dennis sighed and rubbed out the last few lines. He was getting distracted.

After about forty-five minutes, Miss Windsor looked at her watch anxiously and addressed the class of two.

"I'm sorry," she said, "but would either of you mind if we finished this detention fifteen minutes early? Only I would quite like to get home in time for *Neighbours*. Lassiter's coffee shop is re-opening today after the dramatic fire."

"No problem, miss," said Lisa, smiling. "Don't worry, we won't tell anyone!"

"Thank you," said Miss Windsor, confused for a moment that somehow the roles had been reversed, and it was Dennis and Lisa who were letting her off.

"Do you wanna walk me home, Dennis?" asked Lisa.

"What?" said Dennis, in a panic.

"I said, 'do you want to walk me home?'"

"Um, yeah, OK," said Dennis, trying to sound cool.

Dennis felt like a celebrity as he walked down the road with Lisa. He walked slowly so he could be with her for as long as possible.

"I couldn't help noticing your drawings. Those dress designs. They're brilliant," said Dennis.

"Oh thanks. They were nothing really. I was just doodling."

"And I love the way you look."

"Thank you," replied Lisa, trying not to laugh.

"I mean *dress*," Dennis corrected himself. "Dress, I love the way you dress."

"Thanks," said Lisa, smiling again. She looked so unutterably gorgeous when she smiled that Dennis could barely look at her. Instead he looked down at her shoes, noticing they were round-toed.

"Beautiful shoes," he offered.

"Well, thank you for noticing."

"Apparently round-toed shoes are in this year. Pointy-toed are out."

"Where did you read that?"

"*Vogue*. I mean…"

"You read *Vogue*?"

Dennis caught his breath. What had he said? In all the excitement of being with Lisa his tongue was running away with itself.

"Um… no… erm… well, yeah, once."

"I think that's cool."

"You *do*?" asked Dennis, incredulous.

"Yeah. Not nearly enough boys are into fashion."

"I suppose not…" Dennis said. He wasn't sure if he *was* into fashion, or just liked looking at pictures of pretty dresses, but he chose not to mention it.

"Do you have a favourite designer?" Lisa asked.

Dennis wasn't sure if he did, but he remembered really liking one of the dresses in the magazine, a cream floor-length ball gown, designed by John Gally something.

"John Gally something," he said.

"John Galliano? Yeah, he's amazing. A legend. He designs all the pieces for Dior too."

Dennis loved that she said "pieces". That was the word they'd used in *Vogue* for items of clothes.

"Well, this is my house. Thanks, Dennis. Bye," said Lisa. Dennis's heart sank a little that their walk was already over. She went to go towards the front door, then stopped for a moment. "You could come over at the weekend if you like," she said. "I've got loads of great fashion magazines I could show you. I really want to be a designer or a stylist or something when I'm older."

"Well, you *are* very stylish," said Dennis. He meant it sincerely, but somehow it sounded cheesy.

"Thank you," said Lisa.

She knew she was.

Everyone knew she was.

"It's Saturday tomorrow. Is eleven o'clock any good for you?"

"Er... I think so," said Dennis. As if any event in his past or future could prevent him from being at her house at eleven.

"See you then," she said as she gave him a smile and passed out of view.

And, just like that, Dennis's world went back to normal again, like when the lights go on in the cinema at the end of a film.

6

Forever and a Moment

At 10:59am Dennis was waiting outside Lisa's house. She had said eleven o'clock, but he didn't want to seem too keen. So he waited for his watch to count the seconds until eleven.

54.

55.

56.

57.

58.

59.

00.

He pressed the bell. The faint sound of Lisa's

voice floated down the stairs, and the blurry vision of her through the glass of the door was enough to make his heart beat faster.

"Hey," she said, smiling.

"Hey," he said back. Not that he'd ever said "hey" to anyone before, but he wanted to be like Lisa.

"Come in," she said, and he followed her into the house. It was very similar to the one Dennis lived in, but where his was gloomy, Lisa's was full of light and colour. There were paintings and family pictures haphazardly arranged on the walls. A sweet smell of freshly baked cake lingered in the hall. "Do you want a drink?"

"A glass of white wine, perhaps?" said Dennis, trying to act three times his age.

Lisa looked bemused for a moment. "I don't have any wine. What else do you like?"

"Um Bongo."

Lisa raised her eyebrows. "I think we've got some Um Bongo."

She found a carton and poured a couple of glasses, then they went upstairs to her room.

Dennis instantly adored it. In truth it was how he would like his room to be. She had pictures from fashion magazines all over the walls, stylish shots of beautiful women in glamorous locations. On the shelves were books about fashion or famous film stars like Audrey Hepburn or Marilyn Monroe. A sewing machine sat in the corner of the room and she had a big pile of *Vogues* by the bed.

"I'm collecting them," she said. "I've got an Italian one too. It's hard to get here, but it's amazing. The best *Vogue* is Italian. Heavy, though! Would you like to see it?"

"I'd love to," said Dennis. He'd had no idea there were different *Vogues* around the world.

They sat on her bed together, slowly turning the pages. The first shoot was in colour, but featured dresses that were only black or white, or a combination of the two.

"Wow, that dress is gorgeous," said Dennis.

"Chanel. It's probably madly expensive, but it is beautiful."

"I love the sequins."

"And that slit up the side," said Lisa. She traced her fingers longingly along the page.

What seemed like forever and a moment went by, as they studied every page, discussing each detail of every dress. When they reached the end, they felt like they'd been friends forever.

Lisa pulled out another magazine to show him one of her favourite shoots, or "stories" as she called them. It was from an old British *Vogue*, and featured lots of models in wigs and metallic dresses. It looked like a scene from an old science-fiction film. Dennis loved the extravagance of these fantasies, so different from the grey cold reality of his own life.

"You'd look stunning in that gold dress," said Dennis, pointing to a girl with similar hair colouring to Lisa.

"Anyone would. It's an amazing dress. I could never afford any of these, but I like to look at these pictures and get ideas for my own designs. Do you want to see?"

"Oh yeah!" replied Dennis excitedly.

Lisa pulled a large scrapbook from her shelf. It was full of brilliant illustrations she had drawn of skirts and blouses and dresses and hats. Next to these Lisa had stuck lots of things on to the page: strips of glittering fabric, cut-out photographs of film costumes, even buttons.

Dennis stopped Lisa turning the page at an especially gorgeous drawing she had done of an orange sequined dress.

"That one is *beautiful*," he said.

"Thanks, Dennis! I'm really pleased with it. I'm making it right now."

"Really? Can I see?"

"Of course."

She reached into her cupboard and pulled out the half-finished dress.

"I got this material really cheap. It was just from down the market," she said. "But I think it's going to look really good. It's a little bit 1970s, I think. Very glamorous."

She held up the dress by its hanger. Although it was still cut a little roughly around the edges, and had a few loose threads, it was covered in hundreds of little round sequins and twinkled effortlessly in the morning sunlight.

"It's amazing," said Dennis.

"It would look good on you!" said Lisa. She laughed and held the dress next to Dennis. He laughed too, and then looked down at it, allowing himself to imagine for a moment what he would look like wearing it, but then told himself to stop being silly.

"It's really beautiful," he said. "It's not fair, though, is it? I mean boy's clothes are so boring."

"Well, I think all those rules are boring. About what people can and can't wear. Surely everyone should be able to wear whatever they like?"

"Yes, I suppose they should," said Dennis. He had never really been encouraged to think like this before. She was right. What was wrong with wearing the things you liked?

"Why don't you put it on?" Lisa asked with a cheeky smile.

There was silence for a moment.

"Maybe that's a crazy idea," Lisa said, backtracking as she sensed Dennis's awkwardness. "But dresses can be beautiful, and dressing up is fun. I love putting on pretty dresses. I bet some boys would like it too. It's no big deal."

Dennis's heart was beating really fast – he wanted to say "yes", but he couldn't. He just couldn't. This was all a bit much...

"I've got to go," he snapped.

"Really?" asked Lisa, disappointed.

"Yes, I'm sorry, Lisa."

"Well, will you come and visit me again? Today has been really fun. The next issue of *Vogue* is out next week. Why don't you come over next Saturday?"

"I don't know…" said Dennis as he rushed out of the house. "But thanks again for the Um Bongo."

7

Watching the Curtain Edges
Grow Light

"Happy birthday, Dad!" exclaimed Dennis and John excitedly.

"I don't like birthdays," said Dad.

Dennis's face fell. Sunday was always a miserable day for him. He knew that loads of families were sitting down together for a roast dinner, and that only made him think about Mum. When Dad did try to cook a Sunday roast for his sons, it only made their loss more painful. It was as if there was a place laid in all their minds for someone they loved who wasn't there.

And, anyway, Dad was *not* a good cook.

But this Sunday was even worse than usual – it was Dad's birthday and he was determined not to celebrate it.

Dennis and John had waited all afternoon to wish him a happy birthday. He had left for work very early that day – now it was seven o'clock at night and Dad had just got in. The boys had crept downstairs to the kitchen to surprise him, where he was sitting alone wearing the same red-checked jacket he always did. He had a can of cheap lager and a bag of chips.

"Why don't you go and play, boys? I just want to be on my own."

The card and cake Dennis and John were holding seemed to fade away in their hands at Dad's words.

"I'm sorry, boys," he said, catching their hurt. "It's just there's not much to celebrate, is there?"

"We got you a card, Dad, and a cake," offered John.

"Thanks." He opened the card. It was from Raj's shop and featured a big smiling cartoon bear inexplicably wearing sunglasses and Bermuda shorts. Dennis had chosen it from Raj's shop because it had "Happy Birthday to the Best Dad in the World" written on it.

"Thanks, boys," said Dad as he looked at it. "I don't deserve it, though. I'm not the best dad in the world."

"Yes you are, Dad," said Dennis.

"*We* think you are," added John tentatively.

Dad stared at the card again. Dennis and John had thought it would make him happy, but it seemed to be having the opposite effect.

"I'm sorry, boys, it's just I find birthdays hard, you know, since your mum left."

"I know, Dad," said Dennis. John nodded and tried to smile.

"Dennis scored a goal today. For the school," said John, trying to change the subject to something happy.

"Did you, son?"

"Yes, Dad," said Dennis. "It was the semi-final today, and we won 2–1. I got one goal and Darvesh scored the other. We're through to the final."

"Well that's good," said Dad, staring into the distance. He took another gulp from his can. "Sorry. I just need to be alone for a bit."

"OK, Dad," said John, nodding to Dennis that they should leave. Dennis touched his dad's shoulder for a moment, before they retreated from the room. They had tried. But birthdays, Christmas, going on holiday and even day trips to the sea – slowly all those things had disappeared. Mum had always organised them, and now they seemed a lifetime away. Home was becoming a very cold, grey place.

"I need a hug," said Dennis.

"I ain't hugging you."

"Why not?"

"I'm your brother. I ain't hugging you. It's weird. I've gotta go anyway. I told the boys I was gonna hang around on the wall outside the offy with them for a bit."

Dennis needed to get out of the house too. "I'm going to Darvesh's, then. See you later."

As he walked across the park, he felt bad for leaving his dad on his own in the kitchen. He wished he could make Dad happy.

"What's up?" asked Darvesh, as they were looking at videos on YouTube in his bedroom.

"Nothing," said Dennis unconvincingly. He wasn't a good liar, but then lying is not a thing that it's good to be good at.

I, myself, have never ever lied.

Apart from just then.

"You seem, like, really distracted."

Dennis *was* distracted. Not only was he thinking about his dad, he couldn't stop thinking about that orange sequined dress.

"I'm sorry. Darvesh, you'd be my friend whatever, wouldn't you?"

"Of course."

"Darvesh! Dennis! Would you boys like some refreshing Lucozade drink?" shouted Darvesh's mum from the next room.

"No thanks, Mum!" Darvesh shouted back, before sighing loudly. Dennis just smiled.

"It's a high-energy beverage! It'll get your strength up for the final!" came the insistent reply.

"All right, Mum, maybe later!"

"Good boys! You'll make me very proud if you win. But you know I'll still be proud if you don't."

"Yes, yes..." said Darvesh. "She's so embarrassing."

"It's only because she loves you," said Dennis.

Darvesh went silent for a moment so Dennis changed the subject.

"Can I try on your hat thing?" he asked.

"My *patka*?"

"Yes your *patka*."

"Sure, if you really want. I've got a spare one here I think," said Darvesh as he rummaged in his drawer before pulling out another hat. He passed it to Dennis, and Dennis carefully put it on.

"How do I look?" asked Dennis.

"Like a bit of a prat!"

They both laughed loudly. Then Darvesh thought for a moment. "I mean, it doesn't make you Sikh, does it? On you it's just a hat. It's just dressing up, innit?"

Dennis walked home feeling a bit brighter. He'd even laughed at some of the stupid videos they'd found, particularly one of a cat clambering over a baby and putting its bum in the baby's face.

But when he walked in he saw that Dad was

still sitting at the kitchen table where they had left him, with another can of lager but the same cold and soggy chips.

"Hi, Dad," said Dennis, trying to sound happy to see him.

His dad looked up for a moment, and then sighed heavily.

John had already gone to bed. When Dennis went up, John didn't even bother saying anything. As they lay there, the silence was deafening. There was nothing that could be said. Dennis couldn't sleep at all, and spent all night watching the curtain edges grow light.

Only one thing stopped him suffocating: thinking about Lisa, the world she had opened up for him, and that sequined orange dress, sparkling and sparkling and sparkling in the sunlight...

8

Lying on the Carpet with Lisa

Lisa held out the orange sequined dress. "I finished it!" she said.

It was the next Saturday and back in Lisa's bedroom she and Dennis had been poring over every page of the new issue of *Vogue*, before she surprised him.

The dress was perfect.

"That is the most beautiful thing," said Dennis, "that I've ever seen."

"Why, thank you, Dennis!" Lisa laughed a little, slightly embarrassed by the weight of the compliment. "Actually, I want you to have it. It's a present."

"For *me*?" asked Dennis.

"Yes, Dennis, you love it so much. You should have it."

"I couldn't…"

"Yes, you could."

She handed him the dress.

"Er, thanks Lisa," said Dennis, taking it from her. It was heavier than he imagined, and the sequins felt unlike anything he had felt before. It was a work of art. Quite simply the best present he had ever been given. But where would he keep it? He couldn't exactly hang it next to his anorak in the wardrobe he shared with his brother.

And what was he going to *do* with it?

"Why don't you try it on?" said Lisa.

Dennis's stomach did a flip. He felt how a new companion on *Dr Who* must feel when they're about to enter the Tardis for the first time. Now this really *was* going to be different.

"It'll be fun," said Lisa.

Dennis looked at the dress. It *would* be fun to try it on. "Well... if you're sure."

"I'm sure."

Dennis took a deep breath.

"Just for a moment, though," he said.

"Yay!"

Dennis started to take off his clothes, then suddenly felt really embarrassed.

"Don't worry, I won't look," said Lisa, closing her eyes.

Dennis undressed down to his socks and pants, and then stepped into the dress and pulled it up over his shoulders. It felt different to wearing his normal boy's clothes. The fabric felt so unfamiliar next to his skin – all silky and smooth. He reached around for the zip at the back.

"I'm not sure I can…"

"Let me," said the expert, opening her eyes. "Turn around." She guided the zip up his back. "It looks great. How does it feel?"

"Nice. It feels nice." In fact, it felt more than nice; it felt wonderful. "Can I see in the mirror?"

"Not yet. We haven't found the shoes!" Lisa pulled out some stunning high-heeled gold shoes with red soles on the bottom. "I got these in Oxfam. They're Christian Louboutins, but the old dear in the shop only charged me two quid for them!"

Dennis wondered if Christian Louboutin might ever need them back.

He bent down to put the shoes on. "You'd better take your socks off first," Lisa said, looking down at his bedraggled grey socks. His big toe poked out of one particularly large hole.

They *were* rather spoiling the look.

"Oh, yes, of course," said Dennis, before tugging them off, and placing his feet in the narrow shoes. The heels were quite high and he felt for a second that he might topple over. Lisa held his hand to steady him.

"*Now* can I look in the mirror?" he asked.

"You haven't got any make-up on yet."

"No, Lisa, no!"

"You've got to do this properly, Dennis." Lisa reached for her make-up bag. "This is so much fun! I always wanted a little sister. Now, do this with your lips." She stretched her mouth open and he copied her. She rolled the lipstick gently across his lips. It felt weird. Nice, but weird. He never knew lipstick tasted like that – oily and waxy.

"Eye shadow?"

"No I really don't—" protested Dennis.

"Just a little!"

He closed his eyes as she lightly applied some silver eye shadow with a little brush. "Looking good, Dennis," she said. "Or should I say Denise!"

"That's what my brother called me when he found out about the magazine."

"Well, that's your girl's name I suppose. Your *name* is Dennis, but if you were a girl you'd be called Denise."

"Can I look in the mirror yet?" he asked.

Lisa adjusted the dress expertly before silently leading him to the mirror on the

bedroom wall. Dennis gazed at himself. For a moment he was shocked by what he saw. Then the shock turned to wonder, and he laughed. He felt so happy he wanted to dance. Sometimes you feel things so deeply that words aren't enough. He started to move around in front of the mirror. Lisa joined in, humming some made-up music.

For a moment they were in their own crazy little musical, before they fell to the floor laughing.

"I guess you like it, then?" asked Lisa, still giggling.

"Yes… it's just a bit…"

"Strange?"

"Yes. A bit strange."

"You look good, though," offered Lisa.

"Really?" said Dennis. He was enjoying lying on the carpet with Lisa a little too much and felt embarrassed, so he got up and looked at himself in the mirror again. Lisa followed him.

"Yeah, in fact, you look great," she said. "You know what?"

"What?" asked Dennis eagerly.

"I think you could fool anybody dressed like that. You look just like a girl."

"Really? Are you sure?" Dennis looked at himself again in the mirror, squinting. He tried to imagine that he was looking at a stranger.

He *did* look a bit like a girl…

"Yeah," said Lisa. "I'm sure. You look amazing. Do you want to try on something else?"

"I don't know if I should," said Dennis, suddenly self-conscious. "Someone might come in."

"My mum and dad are at the garden centre. It's so boring but they love it there! Trust me, they won't be back for hours."

"Well, maybe this one, then?" said Dennis, displaying a long purple dress that Lisa had copied from one she'd seen Kylie wear at an awards do.

"Nice choice!"

Then he tried on a short red dress that Lisa's mum had bought for her to wear to a family wedding, then a little yellow puff-ball skirt from the 1980s that her Auntie Sue had passed on to her, then a lovely nautical-themed blue and white striped dress that Lisa had found in Cancer Research.

That afternoon, Dennis ended up trying on everything in Lisa's wardrobe. Gold shoes, silver shoes, red shoes, green shoes, boots, big handbags, little handbags, clutch bags, blouses, long flowing skirts, miniskirts, earrings, bangles, hair scrunchies, fairy wings, even a tiara!

"It's not fair," said Dennis. "Girls have got all the best stuff!"

"Rules don't apply here," laughed Lisa. "Dennis, you can be whoever you want to be!"

9

Bonjour, Denise

The next morning Dennis was in bed lying perfectly still, but he felt like he was on a rollercoaster. His mind was racing. Dressing up had made him feel like he didn't have to be boring Dennis living his boring life any more. *I can be whoever I want to be!* he thought.

He took a shower. The bathroom was dark green like an avocado. Dennis had never understood why his parents had chosen such a revolting colour for a bathroom. If he had been consulted, he would have installed a white antique bath, which he would have complemented with black and white tiles. But, being a child, he'd never been asked for his opinion.

To use the shower you needed the precision of a safe cracker. Turn the dial one millimetre to the left or right and the water would go either ice cold or boiling hot. Dennis positioned the dial exactly where it should be so as not to be frozen or scalded to death, and squeezed some Imperial Leather shower gel on his hand. It was what he did every morning. It was part of the grinding routine of his life. Yet somehow the world was burning with possibilities.

Downstairs in the kitchen, John was eating his toast and chocolate spread and watching the *Hollyoaks* omnibus.

"Dad gone already?" asked Dennis.

"Yeah, I heard him leave at four. Didn't the lorry wake you up?"

"No. Don't think so."

"He said something about having to be up early to take some cat food to Doncaster."

Dennis thought how his dad's life as a lorry driver wasn't as glamorous as it sounded.

And it didn't sound that glamorous to begin with.

Dennis poured himself some Rice Krispies, and just as he was about to eat a spoonful the doorbell rang. It was a confident ring, long and loud.

DRRRRIIIIIIiiiiiiiiiiiiIIIIING!

Dennis and John were so curious about who it could be at the door on a Sunday morning that they both rushed to open it. The postman didn't come on a Sunday, nor indeed in the morning any more, preferring to do his round at some hour of his choosing in the afternoon.

It wasn't the postman.

It was Lisa.

"Hi," she said.

"Er..." said John, now suddenly unable to form words.

Dennis knew John fancied Lisa – he stared at her all the time at school. But then *everybody* fancied Lisa. She was so utterly gorgeous that probably even the hearts of squirrels missed a beat when she walked by.

"Um, what do you want?" asked John awkwardly, unable to function properly in this close proximity to beauty.

"I've come to see Dennis," she said.

"Oh," said John. He turned to Dennis with a look of hurt and injustice in his eyes, like a dog about to be put down.

"Come in," said Dennis, loving how much all this was winding John up. "I'm just having breakfast."

Dennis led Lisa into the kitchen. They sat down.

"Oh, I love *Hollyoaks*," said Lisa.

"Yeah, I do too," said Dennis.

John shot him a look that clearly stated, *You filthy liar, you have never previously expressed any interest in the long-running, Chester-based teen soap opera.*

Dennis ignored him. "Do you want anything to eat?" he asked Lisa.

"No, I'm fine. I'd love a cup of tea, though."

"Cool," said Dennis, and put some water in the kettle. John gave him another look. This one clearly said, *You never say "cool". I'm so angry I'm going to have to tear off your head and use it as a football.*

"I had fun yesterday," said Lisa.

"Y-yes," said Dennis tentatively, not wanting to give too much away in front of his brother. "I had a great time…" He knew he was driving his brother insane with jealousy so added, "…with you."

"WE ARE MEANT TO BE GOING UP THE PARK TO PLAY FOOTBALL NOW," said John, trying to put emphasis on every word to sound authoritative, but actually only sounding a bit mad.

"You go ahead. I'm gonna chill with Lisa for a while." Dennis looked at John and smiled. Lisa smiled too.

They smiled John out of the room.

Lisa and Dennis listened to the door shutting behind him. Lisa laughed excitedly at all the intrigue.

"Well, how do you feel today?" she asked.

"Well… I just feel… great!" said Dennis.

"I've had an idea," said Lisa. "Crazy, but…"

"Go on."

"Well, you know what I said about how you could fool everyone into thinking you were a girl?"

"Yes…" said Dennis, nervously.

"Well, some of the kids at school just had French exchange students staying with them…"

"So?" said Dennis.

"So, I thought… this is crazy but… I thought

I could dress you up as a girl and take you to Raj's and say you were my French pen pal or something. You wouldn't have to say much, because, you know, you'd be French!"

"No!" said Dennis. He felt the exhilaration and fear of somebody who has just been chosen to assassinate a president.

"It could be fun."

"Absolutely not."

"How amazing would it be, though? To pass you off as a girl."

"It's insane! I go into Raj's shop every day. He'd know for certain it was me."

"I bet he wouldn't," said Lisa. "I've got a wig my mum bought for a fancy-dress party. I could put some make-up on you like yesterday. It'd be so much fun – let's do it today!"

"*Today?*"

"Yeah, it's Sunday so there should be less

people about. I brought a dress with me, cos I was hoping you'd say yes."

"I don't know, Lisa. I've got a lot of homework to do."

"I've got you a handbag too…"

Ten minutes later Dennis looked at himself in the hall mirror. He was wearing a short, electric-blue dress and holding a silver clutch bag. It was a party dress, really, not what anyone would wear on a Sunday morning to a newsagent's shop.

Least of all a twelve-year-old boy.

But having Lisa fuss over him, applying make-up to his face, squeezing his feet into matching silver high-heeled shoes, and styling the wig, had been so much fun he didn't complain.

"Is Raj really going to believe I'm your French pen pal?" he asked.

"You look amazing. And it's all about confidence. If you believe it, everyone else will too."

"Maybe…"

"Come on, let's see you walk."

Dennis trotted up and down the hall, doing his best impression of a catwalk model.

"Mmm, it's like Bambi taking his first steps," said Lisa with a laugh.

"Thanks a lot."

"Sorry, just joking. Look, you've got to stand upright in heels like these."

Dennis copied Lisa's posture and immediately felt a little more confident in the silver shoes. "I quite like this actually," he said.

"Yes, it's a good feeling, being that little bit taller. And it makes your legs look great."

"Is Denise a French name too?" he asked.

"If you say anything in a French accent, it sounds French," said Lisa.

"De-neeze," said Dennis, laughing. "*Bonjour, je m'appelle De-neeze.*"

"*Bonjour, Denise. Vous êtes très belle,*" said Lisa.

"*Merci beaucoup, Mademoiselle Lisa.*"

They both laughed.

"Are you ready?" Lisa asked.

"Ready to…?"

"To go outside."

"No, of course I'm not."

"But?"

"But I will!"

They both laughed again. Lisa opened the door and Dennis stepped out into the sunshine.

10

Pickled Onion Monster Munch

At first Lisa held Dennis's hand to steady him. After a few paces the tottering calmed down a little, and Dennis began to walk more easily.

High heels do take a bit of getting used to. Not that I would know, reader. Someone told me.

Soon they arrived at Raj's shop. Lisa squeezed Dennis's hand reassuringly. He took a deep breath and they went inside.

"A good morning to you, Miss Lisa," said Raj, smiling broadly. "I have the new copy of Italian *Vogue* for you. Oh my word, it's heavy, though!

Like a brick! I ordered it in specially for you."

"Wow, thanks so much, Raj," said Lisa.

"And who is your new friend?"

"Oh, this is my French exchange person...
student, Denise," said Lisa.

Raj studied Dennis for a moment. Had they
fooled him? Dennis mouth was dry with nerves.

"Ah, hello, Denise, welcome to my shop,"
said Raj. Lisa and Dennis smiled at each other.
Dennis looked so good as Denise that Raj
clearly didn't suspect a thing. "It is possibly the
finest shop of this kind in the whole of England!
Now you can get all your postcards to send
back home!" Raj picked up a packet of plain
white postcards.

"They're blank, Raj," said Lisa.

"Yes, you will have to draw some sights of
London on these. I stock an unrivalled selection
of felt-tipped pens. So you are from France?"

"Yes," replied Lisa.

"*Oui*," added Dennis, tentatively.

"I've always wanted to go to France," said Raj. "It's in France, isn't it?"

Lisa and Dennis shared a confused look.

"Well, if there is anything I can do whilst you are in England, Miss... forgive me, what is your name again?" asked Raj.

"De-neeze," replied Dennis.

"It's a lovely accent you have, Miss Denise."

"*Merci*."

"What did she say?" asked Raj.

"Thank you," said Lisa.

"Oh! *Merci, merci*," said Raj, delighted at this discovery. "I can speak French now! If there is anything I can do, please let me know. Now, Lisa, before you go, I have some special offers today I would like to tell you about."

Lisa and Dennis both rolled their eyes. "Nine Kinder Eggs for the price of eight."

"No, thanks," said Lisa.

"*Non, merci*," added Dennis, growing in confidence.

"I have some excellent bags of pickled onion Monster Munch, only slightly out of date. Fifteen bags for the price of thirteen. They are a British delicacy. Your French friend may wish to try them, and take a box home for her loved ones."

"I'll just take the Italian *Vogue* thanks, Raj," said Lisa as she put her money down on the counter. "Goodbye."

"*Au revoir*," added Dennis.

"Goodbye, ladies. Do come back soon."

They left the shop giddy with excitement, running away as they carried the exceptionally heavy magazine between them. Raj came out of the shop holding a box of crisps and shouted, "You drive a hard bargain, Lisa. I'll throw in another box of roast beef Monster Munch absolutely free!"

Raj's voice echoed down the street as Dennis and Lisa ran, breathless with excitement.

11

"These high heels are killing me"

"You did it!" said Lisa as they sat on a wall to recover their breath.

"He really thought I was a girl!" exclaimed Dennis. "That's the best fun I've had... well, ever!"

"Well, let's go into town, then! There should be loads of people there!"

"I'd love to Lisa, but these high heels are killing me!" said Dennis.

"Not easy being a girl, is it?" she said.

"No, I had no idea your shoes were so painful. How do you wear them every day?"

He took his shoes off and rubbed his feet. They felt like they'd been put in a vice from the metalwork room. "Aah, let's just go back, Lisa. I need to get changed and go and meet John up the park anyway. He'll be wondering where I am."

"Oh!" Lisa couldn't hide her disappointment. "Spoilsport."

"Morning, Lisa!"

It was Mac, a boy from Lisa's year. He huffed and puffed his way up the street to join them. Mac was one of the fattest boys in the school, and endured the unwelcome celebrity that went with it. He had been to Raj's shop as he did every day, and was carrying a bag of goodies.

"Oh, hi," said Lisa brightly, before whispering to Dennis, "Don't worry, just keep quiet." She raised her voice and said, "So, Mac, have you got anything nice there?"

Unlike most of the pupils, Lisa called Mac by his name, rather than his nickname, "Big Mac and Fries". Sometimes children pass on cruelty unthinkingly like they would a cold, but Lisa was different.

"Oh, it's just my breakfast, Lisa. A couple of bags of Maltesers, a Toblerone, a Bounty, Jelly Tots, some Skips, seven bags of Monster Munch – Raj was doing a special offer on those – a box of Creme Eggs and a can of Diet Coke."

"*Diet* Coke?" asked Lisa.

"Yeah, I'm trying to lose some weight," said Mac without irony.

"Well, good luck with that," said Lisa, *almost* without irony. "You know it wouldn't do if we were all thin you know."

"Maybe not. Who's your lovely friend then?" he asked with a smile, as he popped a whole Creme Egg in his mouth.

"Oh, this is my French pen-pal, Denise. She's staying with me for a bit."

Dennis smiled at Mac uncertainly. Mac stared at him and kept chewing. It was quite a long time before he had demolished enough of the Creme Egg in his mouth to resume speaking. "*Bonjour*, Denise," he mumbled through the chocolate.

"*Bonjour*, Mac," replied Dennis, praying the conversation wouldn't continue past the few French words he knew.

"*Parlez-vous Anglais?*" Mac asked.

"*Oui*, I mean, yes, a little," said Dennis awkwardly.

"I had a French pen pal come to stay once. Hervé was his name. Nice guy. Smelled a bit though. He wouldn't take a shower so in the end we had to hose him down at the end of the garden." He was still chewing. "Hervé came into school with me – are you coming in with Lisa tomorrow? I do hope so. I think French girls are gorgeous." As he said this a little spittle of chocolate egg ran down his chin. Dennis looked at Lisa with panic in his eyes.

"Erm yes, of course Denise is coming in with me tomorrow," said Lisa.

"I am?" said Dennis, so shocked he nearly lost his lady voice and his French accent all at once.

"Yes, of course you are. We'll see you tomorrow, Mac."

"OK, girls, *au revoir!*" said Mac, before he made his way down the street, joyfully swinging his bag of confectionary as he went.

"Oh no!" said Dennis.

"Oh yes!" said Lisa.

"Are you out of your mind?"

"Come on, at least think about it. What if you could fool everyone at school? It would be such a laugh, and it would be our little secret."

"Well, I suppose it *would* be the most amazing thing," said Dennis, a smile broadening across his face. "If the teachers, my friends, my brother, if everyone believed I was a girl…"

"Well…?"

"OK, but I'm gonna need some different shoes!"

But little did Dennis know, as he tottered home in his uncomfortable shoes, that he was about to take a tumble…

12

Another World

"I'm still worried about these shoes," said Dennis.

"They're fine. You can't even tell they're extra wides."

It was Monday morning, and Lisa and Dennis stood outside the school gates. Dennis was dressed as Denise again, in the orange dress he loved so much. Maybe it was the sequins, or maybe it was his nerves, but he was sweating.

"I can't do it..." said Dennis.

"It'll be *fine*," assured Lisa in hushed tones as pupils and teachers made their way in to school.

"You won't have to say much. No one here can speak French. They can barely speak English."

Dennis was too tense to laugh at Lisa's joke. "Fooling Raj and Mac was one thing, but the whole school? I mean, someone's bound to recognise me..."

"They won't. You look so different. No one in a million years is going to think you're Dennis."

"Not so loud!"

"Sorry. Look, trust me, no one's going to have a clue as to who you are. But, you know, we could just go home instead..."

Dennis thought for a moment. "No. That would be the boring thing to do."

Lisa simply smiled. Dennis smiled back and sashayed into the playground. Lisa had to quicken her pace.

"Calm down," said Lisa. "You're a French

exchange student, not a supermodel."

"Sorry – I mean, *desolée.*"

Some of the kids stopped and stared. The boys always stared at Lisa anyway because she was so wildly attractive. And the girls liked to check out what she was wearing, even the jealous ones who invented reasons not to like her. But now she was with this new girl not wearing school uniform there was even more reason to look. Dennis could sense all those eyes on him, and loved it. He spotted Darvesh waiting for him outside the classroom as he always did. Sometimes they would have a quick kick-about before the bell rang. Darvesh scrutinised Dennis for a moment, then looked away. *Wow,* thought Dennis. *Even my best friend doesn't recognise me.*

Lisa's classroom was on the top floor of the main school building. Although John was in the same year as Lisa, he wasn't in the same class. And kids two years older than Dennis didn't know him, just as he didn't know them, so Dennis had never met most of the people in Lisa's class. In a school of nearly a thousand pupils, it was very easy to feel anonymous.

Unless, of course, you were unutterably gorgeous like Lisa, or had once put your willy in a test-tube in the middle of a chemistry lesson, like Rory Malone.

By the time they reached the classroom, the bell had already rung. They entered just as Lisa's form teacher Miss Bresslaw was calling the register. Miss Bresslaw was a well-liked PE teacher, even though she had quite bad breath. It was school legend that her breath had once broken a window in the staff room, but only the new kids tended to believe it.

"Steve Connor."

"Here."

"Mac Cribbins."

"Here."

"Louise Dale."

"Yep."

"Lorna Douglas."

"Here."

"And Lisa James… you are late."

"Sorry, miss."

"Who is this with you?" asked the teacher.

"It's my French exchange student, Miss. Denise."

"I wasn't told anything about this," said Miss Bresslaw.

"Oh, were you not? Sorry. I did clear it with Hawtrey."

"*Mr* Hawtrey, Lisa," chided Miss Bresslaw.

"Sorry, Mr Hawtrey, the headmaster bloke. I cleared it with him."

Miss Bresslaw rose from her chair, and approached the new arrival. As she scrutinised Dennis, she breathed over him slightly. *Mmm, that does smell bad,* thought Dennis. A sort of mixture of cigarettes, coffee and poo. He held his breath. He could feel himself sweating profusely now. He feared his make-up was going to melt and start collecting in a puddle on the floor. There was silence for a moment. Lisa smiled. Miss Bresslaw smiled back, finally.

"Well, that's fine, then," she said. "Denise, please take a seat. Welcome to the school."

"*Merci beaucoup*," said Dennis. He and Lisa sat down together. Miss Bresslaw continued to read out the register.

Lisa reached for Dennis's hand under the desk. She squeezed it softly to say, *Don't worry*. Dennis held on to her hand and squeezed it back, just because it felt nice.

As they made their way down the corridor to Lisa's history class, Mac huffed and puffed his way to catch up with them. "Hi, girls."

"Oh hi, Mac," said Lisa. "How's the diet coming along?"

"Slowly," said Mac as he unwrapped a Twix.

"*Bonjour*, Denise," Mac offered nervously.

"*Bonjour* again, Mac," replied Dennis.

"Ummm... I was just, you'll probably say no, but if you weren't doing anything after school with Lisa I was wondering if you might like to come and get an ice cream or two with me."

Dennis looked at Lisa with panic. Lisa took over. "You know what, Mac, Denise and I have already made plans for after school. But I know she'd really love to. Maybe next time she's over, OK?"

Mac looked disappointed, but not heartbroken. Dennis was impressed by how tactfully Lisa had turned him down on his behalf.

"Maybe I'll see you again later, then," said Mac. He smiled shyly and overtook them, munching on his Twix and unwrapping a Walnut Whip as he went.

Lisa waited until he was out of earshot before saying, "He really fancies you."

"Oh no!" said Dennis.

"Don't worry – it's cool," said Lisa. "It's great, in fact. It must mean you're very convincing as a girl," she laughed.

"That's not funny."

"Yes, it is," she replied, and laughed again.

The first lesson of the day, geography, passed without incident. Though Dennis didn't think his new-found knowledge of oxbow lakes would ever be of use in the adult world.

Unless of course he wanted to be a geography teacher.

He got away with it in the second lesson too, physics. Magnets and iron filings. Fascinating! Dennis hadn't understood this subject as a boy, and understood it even less as a girl. He was quickly learning that:

It was best to remain silent in class,

Remember to cross your legs when you are wearing a dress, and, most importantly,

Don't catch the boys' eyes as you might be more attractive than you thought!

The bell rang again not a moment too soon. It was break-time.

"I need to go to the loo," said Dennis, with a sense of urgency.

"I do too," said Lisa. "Let's go together." Lisa took Dennis's hand and they went through the doors of the girls' toilet.

And into another world...

Boys treated the "boys' room" as a purely functional place. You did what you needed to do, maybe wrote something rude about Mr Hawtrey on the toilet door and then you left. Inside the girls' room, it was like a party.

It was rammed.

Dozens of girls competed for space around the mirrors, while others chatted to their neighbours in the next cubicles.

Lisa and Dennis joined a queue for one of the toilets. Dennis wasn't used to queuing but found that he loved it. Listening to all the girls chatter to each other and then bustle around each other seemed so new. Without the presence of boys, girls seemed to behave so differently. They talked and laughed and shared everything.

The giggles, the glitter, the glamorous make-up... what a perfect world it was!

Lisa touched up her lipstick. She was about to put her make-up bag away when she paused.

"Do you want me to do yours too?" she asked.

"Oh, yes, please," said Dennis in his best French accent.

"Let me see," said Lisa, reaching into her

bag. "Maybe we should try a different lipstick colour?"

"I've got a lovely pink one here, Lisa," chirped one of the girls.

"I just bought this new eye shadow," said another. Before Dennis could say anything, all these girls were fussing around him, helping to apply lip liner, foundation, blusher, eye liner, mascara, lipstick... everything.

Dennis hadn't been so happy in years. All these girls chatting to him, making him feel special. He was in heaven.

13

Double French

"This is hell," whispered Dennis.

"Shush," said Lisa.

"You didn't tell me you had *French* today."

"I forgot."

"You *forgot*?" said Dennis.

"Shush. And, actually, it's double French."

"*Double* French?"

"*Bonjour, la classe*," said Miss Windsor loudly as she entered. Dennis prayed she wouldn't recognise him from the detention.

"*Bonjour, Mademoiselle Windsor*," said the class in unison. Miss Windsor always started the

classes in French. It gave the false impression that the pupils were all fluent French speakers. Suddenly, she spotted the girl in the orange dress and all the make-up. Miss Windsor couldn't fail to notice her, really. She stood out like a disco-ball in the gloom of the classroom.

"*Et qui êtes-vous?*" she enquired. Dennis sat frozen with fear, with a terrible feeling he was about to throw up or pee, or both

simultaneously, if that was at all possible.

Frustrated by the lack of response, Miss Windsor abandoned the French speaking, as she usually had to within a few seconds of entering the classroom, and continued in English.

"Who are you?" she repeated.

Still Dennis sat in silence.

Everyone looked at Lisa. She gulped. "She's my German pen pal, miss," she said.

"I thought you said she was French," said Mac innocently, his voice slightly muffled by the Rolo he was chewing.

"Oh, yes, sorry. French pen pal. *Thanks*, Mac," said Lisa pointedly. She shot him an angry look and he frowned, looking hurt and baffled.

Miss Windsor's face instantly glowed with joy. She hadn't smiled so much since winning her campaign for the school canteen to serve baguettes at lunchtime.

"*Ah, mais soyez la bienvenue! Quel grand plaisir de vous accueillir dans notre humble salle de classe! C'est tout simplement merveilleux! J'ai tant de questions à vous poser. De quelle région de la France venez-vous? Comment sont les écoles là-bas? Quel est votre passe-temps favori? Que font vos parents dans la vie? S'il-vous-plaît, venez au tableau et décrivez votre vie en France pour que nous puissions tous en bénéficier. Ces élèves pourraient tirer grand profit d'un entretien avec une vraie Française telle que vous! Mais rendez-moi un service, ne me corrigez pas devant eux!"*

Like everyone in the class, and indeed like most people reading this book except for the exceptionally clever or French ones, Dennis had absolutely no idea what Miss Windsor was going on about. I don't know either – I had to get a friend who had passed their French GCSE to translate it for me. Basically, though, Miss Windsor is delighted to have a real French person in her class and is asking lots of questions about life in France. I hope so anyway, unless my friend is playing a horrible joke on me and Miss Windsor is talking about her favourite episodes of *Spongebob Squarepants* or something.

"Er... *oui*," said Dennis, hoping that by simply saying yes he couldn't get himself into too much trouble. Unfortunately, Miss Windsor became even more animated, and led Dennis up to the front of the class, still declaiming excitedly in French.

"*Oui, c'est vraiment merveilleux. On devrait faire cela tous les jours! Faire venir des élèves dont le français est la langue maternelle! Ce sont les jours comme celui-ci que je me souviens pourquoi j'ai voulu devenir prof. S'il-vous-plaît, racontez-nous vos premières impressions de l'Angleterre.*"

Dennis stood still in front of everyone. Lisa looked like she wanted to shout out and help, but couldn't make a sound.

Dennis felt as if he was underwater or in a dream. He looked out into the eerie stillness of the room. Everyone stared at him. Nothing moved except Mac's jaw.

Rolos are extremely chewy.

"May I speak in English one moment?" asked Dennis in a tentative French accent.

Miss Windsor looked a little surprised and a lot disappointed. "Yes, of course."

"Errrm, 'ow can I put this, 'ow you say… politely?"

"*Poliment, oui.*"

"Madame Windsor," continued Dennis, "your French accent is very poor and I am very sorry but I cannot understand anything you are saying."

Some of the pupils laughed cruelly. A single tear appeared in Miss Windsor's eye and rolled down her cheek.

"Are you all right, miss? Do you need a tissue?" asked Lisa, before shooting Dennis a furious look.

"No, no, I'm perfectly fine, thank you, Lisa.

I've just got something in my eye, that's all."

Miss Windsor stood there swaying like she had been shot, but hadn't quite fallen to the floor yet. "Um, why don't you all get on with some private reading. I just need to step outside to get some air for a moment." She tottered uncertainly out of the classroom, as if the bullet was slowly making its way to her heart. She closed the door behind her. For a moment there was silence. Then from outside the classroom they heard a huge wail.

"Aaaaaaaaaaaaaaaaaaaaaaaaaaaaaaah."

Then silence again.

Another wail. "Aaaaaaaaaaaaaaaaaaah."

A little more silence and then an even longer one. "Aaaaaaaaaaaaaaaaaaaaaaaaaaaaaaaa aaaaaaaaaaaaaaaaaaaaaaaaaaaaaaaaaaa aaaaaaaaaaaaaaaaaaaaaaaaaaaaaaaaaa aaaaaaaaaaaaaaaaaaaaaaaaaaaaaaaaaaaaaa

aaaaaaaaaaaaaaaaaaaaaaaaaaaaaaaaaaaaaa
aaaaaaaaaaaaaaaaaaaaaaaaaaaaaaaaaaaaaaaaaaaa
aaaaaaaaaaaaaaaaaaaaaaaaaaaaaaaaaaaaaaaaa
aaaaaaaaaaaaaaaaaaaaaaaaaaaaaaaaaaaaaaaaa
aaaaaaaaaaaaaaaaaaaaaaaaaaaaaaaaaaaaaaaaaa
aaaaaaaaaaaaaaaaaaaaaaaaaaaaaaaaaaaaaaaaaaaa
aaaaaaaaaaaaaaaaaaaaaaaaaaaaaaaaaaaaaaa
aaaaaaaaaaaaaaaaaaaaaaaaaaaaaaaaaaaaaaa
aaaaaaaaaaaaaaaaaaaaaaaaaaaaaaaaaaaaaaaaaaaa
aaaaaaaaaaaaaaaaaaaaaaaaaaaaaaaaaaaaaaa

aaaaaaaaaaaaaaaaaaaaaaaaa
aaaaaaaaaaaaaaaaaaaaaaaaaaaaa
aaaaaaaaaaaaaaaaaaaaaaaaaaaaaaaaaaaaaaaaaaaaaaa
aaaaaaaaaaaaaaaaaaaaaaaaaaaaaaaaaaaaaaaaaaaaaaa
aaaaaaaaaaaaaaaaaaaaaaaaaaaaaaaaaaaaaaaaaaaaaaa
aaaaaaaaaaaaaaaaaaaaaaaaaaaaaaaaaaaaaaaaaaa
aaaaaaaaaaaaaaaaaaaaaaaaaaaaaaaaaaaaaaaaaaa
aaaaaaaaaaaaaaaaaaaaaaaaaaaaaaaaaaaaaaaaaaaaaaa
aaaaaaaaaaaaaaaaaaaaaaaaaaaaaa
aaaaaaaaaaaaaaaaaaaaaaaaaaaaaaaaaaaaaaaaaaaa
aaaaaaaaaaaaaaaaaaaaaaaaaaaaaaaaaaaaa
aaaaaaaaaaaaaaaaaaaaaaaaaaaaaaaaaaaaaaaaaaaaaaaaa
aaaaaaaaaaaaaaaaaaaaaaaaaaaaaaaa
aaaaaaaaaaaaaaaaaaaaaaaaaaaaaaaaaaaaaaaaaaaaaaa
aaaaaaaaaaaaaaaaaaaaaaaaaaaaaaa
aaaaaaaaaaaaaaaaaaaaaaaaaaaaaaaaaaaaaaaa
aaaaaaaaaaaaaaaaaaaaaaaaaaaaaaaaaaaaaaaaaaaaa
aaaaaaaaaaaaaaaaaaaaaaaaaaaaaaaaaaaaaah."

The mouths of those pupils who had laughed

now closed tight with regret. Lisa looked at Dennis, who bowed his head. He returned to his seat, scraping his high heels along the floor sorrowfully.

A few more seconds passed like hours, before Miss Windsor returned to the classroom. Her face was red and puffy from crying.

"Right, so, um... right, good... turn to page fifty-eight in your textbooks and answer questions (a), (b) and (c)."

The pupils all began their work, more silent and compliant than they had ever been before.

"Would you like a Rolo, miss?" ventured Mac. No one was more aware of the momentary comfort chocolate could give in moments of despair.

"No, thank you, Mac. I don't want to spoil my lunch. It's bœuf bourguignon..."

She started crying uncontrollably again.

14

Silence like Snow

"You complete &**%$£%!"

Oops, sorry. I know even though real children do swear, you mustn't have swearing in a children's book. Please forgive me, I really am %$£@$*& sorry.

"You shouldn't swear, Lisa," said Dennis.

"Why not?" Lisa asked angrily.

"Because a teacher might hear you."

"I don't care who hears me," said Lisa. "How could you do that to poor Miss Windsor?"

"I know... I feel so bad..."

"She's probably weeping into her bœuf

bourguignon now," said Lisa as they stepped out into the busy playground. It was lunchtime, and people stood in groups, chatting and laughing, enjoying their hour of partial freedom. Football games were breaking out everywhere – games that Dennis would normally have joined in with, had he not been wearing a wig, make-up and an orange sequined dress.

And high heels.

"Maybe I should go and apologise," said Dennis.

"*Maybe?*" said Lisa. "You have to. Let's go and find her in the dining hall. She should be there, unless she's jumped in the River Seine."

"Oh, don't make me feel any worse."

As they made their way across the playground, a football rolled past them. "Kick it back, love," shouted Darvesh.

Dennis couldn't help it – the urge to kick the ball was too strong.

"Don't be too flash," said Lisa as he ran after the ball. But Dennis couldn't help himself, and chased it aggressively. He stopped it neatly, then took a run up to kick it back to his friend.

But as he kicked the ball his high-heeled shoe flew off, and he toppled backwards.

At that moment his wig slipped back off his head and on to the ground.

Denise became Dennis again.

Time seemed to slow down. There Dennis was, standing in the middle of the playground, in a girl's dress and make-up with one shoe on. Silence spread across the playground like snow. Everyone stopped what they were doing and turned to look at him.

"Dennis…?" asked Darvesh incredulously.

"No, it's Denise," replied Dennis. But the game was up.

Dennis felt like he'd looked at Medusa, that Greek mythological monster who turned people to stone. He couldn't move. He looked at Lisa. Her face was dark with worry. Dennis tried to smile.

Then out of the silence came a laugh.

Then another.

Then another.

Not the kind of laughter that greets something funny, but that cruel, mocking laugh, meant to hurt and humiliate. The laughter became louder and louder and louder, and Dennis felt as if the whole world was laughing at him.

For all eternity.

"Hahahahahahahahahahahaha Hahahahaha**hahahahahaha**hahahahaha

Hahahahahahahahahahahahahahahah
Hahahahahahahahahahahahahahahaha
hahahaHhahahahahahahahahahahahahaha
ahahahahHahahahahahahahahahahahaha
hahahahHahahahahahahahahaha
ahahahahahahahahHahahahahahahahahah
ahahahhahahahahahaHahahahahahahahaha
hahahahahahahahaHahahahahahahah
hahahahahahahahahahahahHahahaha
h a h a h ahahahahahahahahahahahahaha
hahhahahahahahahahahahahahahahah

Hahahahahahahahahahahahahahah
Hahahahahahahahahahahahahahahaha
hahahaHahahahahahahahahahahahahaha
hahahahHahahahahahahahahahahahahah
hahahahHahahahahahahahahhha
hahahahahahahahahahahHahahahahahaha
ahahahahahhahahahahahahahahhahahaha
hahahahahahahahaHahahahahahahahaha
hahahahahahahahahahahahahaHahahaha
ahahahahahahahahahahahahahahahahaha
hahahahahahahahahahahahahahahaha

haHahahahahahahahahahahahah
ahHahahahahahahahahahahahahahahaha
hahahahahahahahahHahahahahaha
hahahahahahahahahahahahahahahaha
hahahahahahahahahahahahahahaha
hahahahahahaHahahahahahahahahahahaha
hahahahahahahahahaHahahahahahahahaha
Hahahahahahahahahahahahaha
hahahahahahahahahahahahHahahaha
hahahahahahahahahahahahahahahahahaha
hahhahahahahahahahahahahaha
ahahaHahahahahahahahahahahah
ahahHahahahahahahahahahahahahahaha
hahahahahaHhahahahahahahahahahahaha
hahahahahHahahahahahahahahahahaha
hahhahahahHahahahahahaha
hahahahhahahahahahahahahahahahahHah
ahahahahahahhhahahahahahahahaH
ahahahahahahahahahahahaHahahahahahaha!"

"You, boy," boomed a voice from the school building. The laughter stopped in an instant as the school looked up. It was Mr Hawtrey, the headmaster with the heart of darkness.

"Me, sir?" asked Dennis, with a misguided tone of innocence.

"Yes, you. The boy in the dress."

Dennis looked around the playground. But he was the only boy wearing a dress. "Yes, sir?"

"Come to my office. NOW."

Dennis started to walk slowly towards the school building. Everyone watched him take each uncertain, wobbling step.

Lisa picked up the other shoe. "Dennis..." she called after him.

He turned round.

"I've got your other shoe."

Dennis turned back.

"There's no time for that, boy," bellowed

Mr Hawtrey, his little moustache twitching with rage.

Dennis sighed and click-clacked his way to the headmaster's office.

Everything in the office was black, or very dark brown. Leather volumes of school records lined the shelves, along with some old black-and-white photographs of previous headmasters, whose stern expressions made Mr Hawtrey look almost human. Dennis had never been in this room before. But then it wasn't a room you ever wanted to visit. Seeing inside meant only one thing.

YOU WERE IN DEEP POO.

"Are you deranged, boy?"

"No, sir."

"Then why are you wearing an orange sequined dress?"

"I don't know, sir."

"You don't know?"

"No, sir."

Mr Hawtrey leaned forward. "Is that *lipstick*?"

Dennis wanted to cry. But even though Mr Hawtrey could see a tear welling up in Dennis's eye he continued his assault.

"Dressing up like that in make-up and high heels. It's disgusting."

"Sorry, sir."

A tear rolled down Dennis's cheek. He caught it with his tongue. That bitter taste again. He hated that taste.

"I hope you are utterly ashamed of yourself," continued Mr Hawtrey. "Are you ashamed of yourself?"

Dennis hadn't felt ashamed of himself before. But he did now.

"Yes, sir."

"I can't hear you, boy."

"YES, SIR." Dennis looked down for a moment. Mr Hawtrey had black fire in his eyes and it was hard to keep looking at him. "I am really sorry."

"It's too late for that, boy. You've been skiving off your lessons, upsetting teachers. You're a disgrace. I am not having a degenerate like you in my school."

"But, sir…"

"You are expelled."

"But what about the cup final on Saturday, sir? I have to play!"

"There will be no more football for you, boy."

"Please, sir! I'm begging you…"

"I said, 'YOU ARE EXPELLED!' You must leave the school premises immediately."

15

There Was Nothing More to Say

"Expelled?"

"Yes, Dad."

"EXPELLED?"

"Yes."

"What on earth for?"

Dennis and his dad were sitting in the lounge. It was 5pm and Dennis had washed the make-up from his face and changed back into his own clothes. He'd hoped this might at least soften the blow.

He'd been wrong.

"Well..." Dennis wasn't sure he could find

the words. He wasn't sure if he could ever find the words.

"HE WENT TO SCHOOL DRESSED UP AS A GIRL!" shouted John, pointing at Dennis as if he was an alien who had momentarily fooled everyone by taking human form. He had clearly been listening at the door.

"You got dressed up as a girl?" asked Dad.

"Yes," replied Dennis.

"Have you done this before?"

"A couple of times."

"A couple of times! Do you *like* dressing up as a girl?" Dad had a look of distress in his eyes that Dennis hadn't seen since his mum left.

"A bit."

"Well either you do or you don't."

Deep breath.

"Well, yes, Dad. I do. It's just... fun."

"What have I done to deserve this? My son likes wearing dresses!"

"*I* don't, Dad," said John, eager to score a point. "I've never put on a dress, not even as a joke, and I never will."

"Thanks, John," said Dad.

"That's OK, Dad. Can I go to the freezer and have a Magnum?"

"Yes," said Dad, distracted. "You can have a Magnum."

"Thanks, Dad," said John, glowing with pride as if he had just been given a badge that said "Number One Son" on it.

"That's it. No more watching that show *Small England* or whatever it's called where those two idiots dress up as 'laydees'. It's a bad influence."

"Yes, Dad."

"Now go to your room and do your homework," barked Dad.

"I haven't got any homework. I've been expelled."

"Oh, yes." Dennis's dad thought for a moment. "Well, just go to your room, then."

Dennis passed John, who was sitting on the stairs gleefully enjoying his Magnum. He lay on his bed in silence, thinking how everything had been ruined, simply by putting on a dress. Dennis took out the photograph he had saved from the bonfire of him, John and Mum at the beach. It was all he had left now. He gazed at the picture. He would give anything to be on that beach again with ice cream round his mouth, holding on to his mum's hand. Maybe if he stared long enough into it he would disappear back into that happy scene.

But suddenly the picture was torn out of his hands.

Dad held it up. "What's this?"

"It's just a picture, Dad."

"But I burnt them all. I don't want any reminders of that woman in the house."

"I'm sorry, Dad. It just floated out of the bonfire on to a hedge."

"Well, now it's going in the bin, like your magazine."

"Please, Dad, don't! Let me keep it." Dennis snatched the photograph back.

"How dare you! Give it to me! NOW!" shouted Dad.

Dennis had never seen him so angry. He tentatively handed the picture back.

"Have you got any others?"

"No, Dad. That was the only one, I promise."

"I don't know what to believe any more. I blame your mother for all this dressing up business anyway. She was always too soft on you."

Dennis was silent. There was nothing more to say. He carried on looking forward. He heard the door slam. An hour went by, or was it a day, or a month, or a year? Dennis wasn't sure any more. The present was somewhere he didn't want to be, and he couldn't see a future.

His life was over – and he was only twelve.

The doorbell rang, and a few moments later Dennis heard Darvesh's voice downstairs. Then his dad's.

"He's not allowed out of his room I'm afraid, Darvesh."

"But I really need to see him, Mr Sims."

"It's not possible I'm afraid. Not today. And if you see that stupid girl Lisa, who John says put him up to this dressing-up thing, tell her to never show her face again."

"Can you tell him I'm still his friend? Whatever's happened. He's still my friend. Can you tell him that?"

"I'm not talking to him at the moment, Darvesh. It's best you go."

Dennis heard the door shut, and then went to the window. He could see Darvesh walking slowly down the drive, his *patka* getting wet in the rain. Darvesh turned back, and caught sight of Dennis up at his bedroom window. He smiled sadly, giving a little wave. Dennis put his hand up to wave back. Then Darvesh disappeared out of sight.

Dennis spent the whole day holed up in his room hiding from his dad.

Just as night fell Dennis heard a quiet tapping on the window. It was Lisa. She was standing on a ladder and trying to talk in as hushed a tone as possible.

"What do *you* want?" asked Dennis.

"I need to speak to you."

"I'm not allowed to speak to you any more."

"Just let me in for a minute. Please?"

Dennis opened the window and Lisa climbed in. He sat back down on the bed.

"I'm sorry, Dennis. I'm really sorry. I thought it would be fun. I didn't think it would end up like this." She put a hand on his shoulder, stroking his hair. No one had stroked Dennis's hair for years. His mum used to do it every night when she tucked him into bed. Somehow it made him want to cry.

"It's ridiculous, isn't it?" Lisa whispered. "I mean, why are girls allowed to wear dresses and boys aren't? It doesn't make any sense!"

"It's OK, Lisa."

"I mean, *expelled*? It's just not fair. Karl Bates didn't even get expelled for mooning the school inspectors!"

"And I'm going to miss the football final."

"I know, I'm sorry. Look, I never meant all this to happen. It's just crazy. I'm going to get Hawtrey to have you back at the school."

"Lisa…"

"I am. I don't know how yet, but I promise."

Lisa hugged him and kissed him for a moment just shy of his lips. It was a glorious kiss. How could it be anything but glorious? After all, her mouth was shaped like a kiss.

"Dennis, I promise."

16

With or Without the Dress

It wasn't until the weekend that Dennis was allowed out of the house. Dad had locked the computer away in a cupboard, and Dennis was forbidden to watch the television so he had missed a number of episodes of *Trisha*.

Finally, on Saturday morning, Dad relented and Dennis was let out for the day. He wanted to go round to Darvesh's flat to wish him luck for the final. On the way he stopped off at Raj's to get something to eat. He only had 13p to spend, as his pocket money had been frozen indefinitely. Raj greeted him as warmly as he always did.

"Ah, my favourite customer!" exclaimed Raj.

"Hi, Raj," said Dennis mutedly. "Have you got anything for 13p?"

"Erm, let me think. Half a Chomp bar?"

Dennis smiled. It was the first time he had smiled in a week.

"It's nice to see you smile, Dennis. Lisa told me what happened at school. I am very sorry."

"Thanks, Raj."

"I must say you had me fooled, though! Very good you looked, Denise! Ha ha! But I mean, being expelled for putting on a dress. It's absurd! You haven't done anything wrong, Dennis. You mustn't be made to feel like you have."

"Thanks, Raj."

"Please help yourself to some free confectionery…"

"Wow, thanks…" Dennis's eyes lit up.

"…to the value of 22p."

Watching Darvesh pack his football kit for the final was harder than Dennis had imagined. Not being able to play was the worst part of being expelled.

"I'm gutted you're not in the team today, Dennis," said Darvesh as he sniffed his socks to check they were clean. "You're our star striker."

"You guys will be OK," said Dennis supportively.

"We don't stand a chance without you and you know it. That Hawtrey is so evil, expelling you."

"Well, it's done now, isn't it? There's nothing I can do."

"There must be something. It's so unfair. It's only dressing up. It doesn't bother me, you know. You're still Dennis, my mate, with or without the dress."

Dennis was really touched, and wanted to hug Darvesh, but, being twelve-year-old boys, hugging wasn't really something they did.

"Those high heels must have been uncomfortable, though!" said Darvesh.

"They're murder!" said Dennis, laughing.

"Here's your pre-match snack!" said Darvesh's mum as she entered the room, carrying a tray piled high with food.

"What's all this, Mum?" moaned Darvesh.

"I made you a little masala, some rice, dahl, a chapatti, samosas, followed by a Wall's Vienetta…"

"I can't eat all this now, Mum! I'll throw up! The game is in an hour!"

"You need your strength, boy! Doesn't he, Dennis?"

"Well, yes…" Dennis hesitated. "I suppose…"

"You tell him, Dennis. He won't listen to me! You know I'm so sad you're not playing today."

"Thanks, it's been a horrible week," replied Dennis.

"You poor boy, expelled just for not wearing the correct school uniform. Darvesh never told me – what exactly *were* you wearing?"

"Erm, it really doesn't matter, Mum…" said Darvesh. He attempted to hurry her out of his room.

"No, it's OK," said Dennis. "I don't mind her knowing."

"Knowing what?" asked Darvesh's mum.

"Well," Dennis paused, before continuing in a serious tone. "I went to school wearing an orange sequined dress."

There was silence for a moment.

"Oh, Dennis," she said. "What a terrible thing to do!"

Dennis paled.

"I mean, orange is *really* not your colour, Dennis," she continued. "With your light hair you would probably look better in a pastel colour like pink or baby blue."

"Um… thank you," said Dennis.

"My pleasure. You can come to me any time for style advice. Now come on, Darvesh, eat up. I'll just go and start the car," she said as she left the room.

"Your mum's cool," said Dennis. "I love her!"

"I love her too, but she's nuts!" said Darvesh with a laugh. "So are you going to come and watch the game, then? Everyone will be there."

"I don't know…"

"I know it will be a bit weird for you, but come with us. It won't be the same without you. We need you there, Dennis, if only to cheer us on. Please?"

"I don't know if I should…" said Dennis.

"Please?"

17

Maudlin Street

Dennis felt sick as the referee's whistle blew for the start of the game. Pupils, parents and teachers were all grouped excitedly around the pitch. Darvesh's mum looked like she was going to explode with excitement. She had elbowed her way to the front of the crowd.

"Come on, football!" she kept shouting with joyful anticipation.

Mr Hawtrey was next to Darvesh's mum. He was sitting on a strange contraption that was half walking stick and half seat. The fact that the headmaster was the only person sitting made him look very important, even if what he was sitting on looked bum-numbingly uncomfortable. Dennis pulled up the hood on his anorak so that Mr Hawtrey wouldn't spot him.

He didn't even go to the school any more, and the headmaster *still* terrified him.

Dennis was surprised to see Lisa standing in the crowd with Mac. "What are you doing here?" he asked. "I didn't know you liked football."

"Well it *is* the final," said Lisa casually. "I just wanted to come and support like everyone else."

"I feel a bit embarrassed now, Dennis," said Mac tentatively. "Asking you out on a date and everything."

"Oh, don't worry, Mac," said Dennis. "I was flattered in a way."

"Well, you did look very pretty as a girl," said Mac.

Lisa burst out laughing.

"Prettier than Lisa?" joked Dennis.

"Oi, watch it, you!" said Lisa, smiling.

Out of the corner of his eye Dennis saw Miss Windsor making her way across the pitch to take her place in the crowd.

"Have you apologised to Miss Windsor yet, Dennis?" asked Lisa, with a tone that suggested she knew the answer already.

"Erm not yet, Lisa, but I will," squirmed Dennis.

"Dennis!" said Lisa sharply.

"I will."

"You did really upset her," added Mac as he somehow managed to put a whole Caramac into his mouth. "I saw her in Raj's shop yesterday, and she cried when she saw a bottle of Orangina."

"Yeah, all right, I will. I just can't do it right now, can I? Not with Hawtrey sitting right there," said Dennis, concealing himself behind Mac's bulk and turning his attention to the match.

The opposition was Maudlin Street. They had lifted the trophy every year for the last three years. It was a notoriously rough school, and their team played dirty, going in really hard for tackles, elbowing opponents, even once poking a referee in the eye. Dennis's school, or rather ex-school, had never won, and all most people were expecting of them was a heroic defeat. Especially now that their best player had been expelled...

True to form, Maudlin Street got off to a strong start, scoring in the first few minutes. One of their team was given the yellow card for administering a Chinese burn to one of the defenders before they scored another goal.

Then another.

Darvesh ran up to Gareth. "We don't stand a chance. We need Dennis!"

"He's expelled, Darvesh. Come on, we can win this without him."

"No we can't. And you know it!"

Gareth ran off after the ball. Another goal from Maudlin Street.

4–0.

This was turning into a massacre.

There was a lull for a moment as Darvesh's mum and Miss Windsor stretchered off one of the school's team. One of the Maudlin Street centre forwards had "accidentally" stamped on his leg. Darvesh shouted at Gareth, "Please, Gareth. Do something!"

Gareth sighed and ran over to Mr Hawtrey.

"What do you want, boy? This is a disaster!

You're bringing shame on the school!" snarled the headmaster.

"I'm sorry, sir. But you expelled our best player. We don't have a chance without Dennis."

"That boy is not playing."

Gareth's face fell. "But, sir, we *need* him."

"I'm not having that dress-wearing disgrace of a boy representing the school."

"Please, sir...?"

"Play on, boy," said Mr Hawtrey with a dismissive wave of his hand.

Gareth ran back on to the pitch. Within moments he was lying in agony on the wet grass, after one of Maudlin Street's forwards booted the ball straight at his groin. The striker then regained possession of the ball and hammered it into the goal.

5–0.

"You know you should really let the boy play, Mr Headmaster," said Darvesh's mum urgently.

"I'd be grateful if you minded your own business, madam," snapped Mr Hawtrey in reply.

"Come on, Mac," said Lisa bossily. "I need a hand."

"Where are you guys going?" asked Dennis.

"You'll see," replied Lisa with a wink. She marched off across the playing fields with Mac trailing behind.

The Maudlin Street supporters once again howled with delight. Another goal.

6–0.

Dennis closed his eyes. He couldn't watch any more.

18

A Thousand Smiles

"Where the hell are they?" yelled Mr Hawtrey at no one in particular.

The second half was about to begin, and Maudlin Street were all waiting on the pitch, eager to finish off their demolition job. The school's team was nowhere to be seen. Had they run away?

Then, suddenly, Lisa stepped out of the changing room and held the door open.

First Gareth ran out wearing a gold lamé ball gown...

Then Darvesh followed in a yellow polka-dot frock...

Then the defenders were right behind in matching red cocktail dresses...

The rest of the team followed in a variety of outfits from Lisa's wardrobe... And finally Dennis came out of the dressing room – in a pink bridesmaid's dress.

There was a huge cheer from the crowd. Dennis looked at Lisa and smiled.

"Go get 'em, kid!" she said.

As they ran on to the pitch, Mr Hawtrey bellowed at Gareth.

"WHAT ON EARTH DO YOU THINK YOU ARE DOING, BOY?"

"You expelled Dennis for wearing a dress. But you can't expel us all, sir!" he shouted back triumphantly.

All the boys in the team lined up defiantly behind their captain, striking poses like they were dancers in a Madonna video. The crowd went wild.

"THIS IS A DISGRACE!" bellowed Mr Hawtrey. He stormed off, angrily brandishing his walking stick/seat thing.

Gareth smiled at Dennis.

"Come on, boys. Let's do it!" said Gareth.

The bemused referee blew his whistle before it fell out of his mouth. Within seconds Dennis had scored a goal. The Maudlin Street team were in shock.

They were still 6–1 down, but Dennis and his team-mates were back in the game.

"Woo!" shouted Darvesh as he hitched up his skirt and weaved round a defender.

Laughing, Dennis scored again. He was on his way to a hat-trick and he was a hundred times happier than he had ever been. He was doing the two things he loved most at once: playing football and wearing a dress. Then Darvesh scored, sliding across the pitch and adding a large grass stain to his frock as he sneaked the ball past the Maudlin Street goalie.

6–3.

"My boy! My boy in the yellow polka-dot dress has scored!" shouted Darvesh's mum.

They were on fire. Dennis set up a fantastic cross for Gareth, who just had to tap it into the net.

6–4.

Gareth being Gareth celebrated like this goal would be replayed forever on *Match of the Day*, doing three victory laps of the pitch, and hitching up his gold lamé ball gown as he ran. The crowd laughed and cheered. Then another goal followed. And another.

6–6.

Now there were only a few more minutes of the game to play.

One more to go. And they'd have done it.

"Come on, Dennis," shouted Lisa. "You can do it!"

Dennis looked over at her and smiled. *It would be really cool if I scored now,* he thought, *especially in front of Lisa... my future wife.*

But, at that moment, Dennis fell to the ground in pain.

The crowd gasped.

One of the Maudlin Street strikers had nobbled him. Kicked him right in the shin when he didn't even have the ball. Dennis lay there in the mud, holding his leg in agony. The referee had seen nothing.

"He's putting it on, ref!" protested the Maudlin Street boy. The crowd booed.

Dennis was trying really hard not to cry. He opened his eyes, and his vision swam.

Lying there, grass pressing into his cheek, he peered up at the crowd. Through the tears he glimpsed a red-checked jacket that looked very familiar…

And then the red-checked jacket turned into a man…

And then the man shouted, in a deep voice

that was even more familiar.

"OI! WHAT'S GOING ON HERE?"

Dad.

Dennis couldn't believe it. Dad had never come to see him play for the school before, and now here Dennis was, lying on the ground with tears in his eyes wearing a dress. He was going to be in so much trouble…

But Dad looked at Dennis and smiled.

"OI! REF!" he shouted. "That kid kicked my son!"

Dennis rose to his feet, his leg still glowing with pain but a warm feeling spreading through him. He steadied himself. Then smiled back over at Dad.

"You OK?" asked Darvesh.

"Yeah," said Dennis.

"COME ON, SON!" shouted Dennis's dad, really getting into it now. "YOU CAN DO IT!"

"I called him at half-time," said Darvesh. "After what you said about your dad never seeing you play in a match, I thought you wouldn't want him to miss this."

"Thanks, mate," said Dennis. Whenever he thought Darvesh couldn't surprise him any more, couldn't be a better friend, he went ahead and did it.

Gareth tackled the ball off one of the Maudlin Street boys. Darvesh ran up the outside, and

Gareth passed to him. Maudlin Street charged towards Darvesh and he passed back to Gareth. Gareth panicked for a moment, then passed to Dennis, who weaved straight past the defence before booting it right over the goalie's head and into the back of the net.

The keeper didn't stand a chance.

6–7!

The final whistle blew. It was all over.

"Yyyyyyyyyyyyyyyyeeeeeeeeeeeeeeeeeee
eeeeesssssssssssssssssssss!" shouted the crowd.
"GGGGGGOOOOOOOOONNNNNNN
MYYYYYSSSSOOOOONNNNNN!!!"
shouted Dennis's dad.

Dennis looked over and smiled. For a moment
he thought he saw John's face in the crowd, but
he couldn't be sure as everything seemed to
blur in all the excitement. Gareth was first to go
up and hug Dennis. Darvesh was next. Within
moments they were all hugging excitedly,
celebrating their victory. The school had never
even got to the semis before – and now they'd
won the cup!

Dad couldn't contain his excitement and ran
on to the pitch. He scooped Dennis up into his
arms and sat him on his shoulders.

"This is my son! This is my boy!" shouted
Dad, helpless with pride.

The crowd erupted with cheers again. Dennis smiled a thousand smiles. He looked down at Gareth, Darvesh and the rest of the team all wearing their dresses.

There's just one problem, Dennis thought. *I don't feel that different any more.*

But he kept that thought to himself.

19

Dragged in the Mud

The Maudlin Street team and their supporters stomped off muttering things like "fix", "re-match" and "bunch of woofters!"

Gareth passed the gleaming silver cup to Darvesh to hold.

The crowd cheered.

"My son! My son the footballer! And yellow is *so* your colour!" exclaimed Darvesh's mum. Darvesh looked over at his mum, and held the cup up to her.

"This is for you, Mum," he said.

She pulled out one of her tissues and wiped

a tear from her eye. Darvesh then passed the cup to Dennis. At that moment Mr Hawtrey reappeared.

"NOT YOU, BOY!"

"But, sir?" implored Dennis.

"You are still expelled from this school."

The crowd started booing. Mac took a toffee bon-bon out of his mouth momentarily and joined in. Even Miss Windsor allowed herself a little French revolutionary boo.

"SILENCE!"

And there was silence. Even the adults were scared.

"But I thought…" said Dennis.

"Whatever you thought, boy, was wrong," snarled Mr Hawtrey. "Now get off the school premises before I call the police."

"But, sir…"

"NOW!"

Dad waded in.

"You're a right idiot, you," he said. Mr Hawtrey was taken aback. No one had spoken to him like that before. "My boy just won the cup for your school."

"My son Darvesh helped too!" added Darvesh's mum.

"Dennis was expelled, though," said Mr Hawtrey with a sickeningly smug smile.

"You know what? I've got a good mind to shove that cup up your whatsit!" said Dad.

"Oh dear, he's more embarrassing than me," muttered Darvesh's mum.

"Look, Mr…"

"Sims. And he's Dennis Sims. My son, Dennis Sims. Remember that name. He'll be a famous footballer one day. You mark my words. And I'm his dad, and I couldn't be prouder. Come on, son, let's go home," said Dad, as he took Dennis's hand, and led him home across the pitch.

Dennis's dress dragged in the mud, but he held Dad's hand tightly as he sloshed through the puddles.

20

Blouse and Skirt

"I'm sorry there's mud all over this," said Dennis as he handed back the bridesmaid dress to Lisa. It was later that afternoon and they were sat on the floor in her bedroom.

"Dennis, I'm sorry. I tried," said Lisa.

"Lisa. You were amazing. Thanks to you I got to play in the final. That's what really mattered. I guess I just need to find another school that might take me – the boy in the dress."

"Maudlin Street maybe?" said Lisa with a smile.

Dennis laughed. They sat in silence for a

moment. "I am going to miss you," he said.

"I'm gonna miss you too, Dennis. It's gonna be sad not seeing you at school, but we can still get together at the weekends, can't we?"

"I want to. Thank you for everything, Lisa."

"What have you got to thank me for? I got you expelled!"

Dennis paused.

"Lisa, I want to thank you for opening my eyes."

Lisa looked down, shyly. Dennis had never seen her look like that before.

"Well, thank you, Dennis. That's the loveliest thing anyone has ever said to me."

Dennis smiled, and his confidence grew for a moment.

"And I have to tell you something, Lisa. Something I've wanted to tell you for ages."

"Yes?"

"I am completely, madly…"

"Completely, madly what?"

But he just couldn't say it. Sometimes it's hard to say the things you feel.

"I'll tell you when I'm older."

"Promise, Dennis?"

"I promise."

I hope he does. We all have someone who, when we are near them, our heart feels like it is in the sky. But, even when you're a grown-up, sometimes it's hard to say the things you feel.

Lisa ran her hands through Dennis's hair. He shut his eyes so he could feel it more.

On the way home, Dennis walked past Raj's shop. He wasn't going to stop, but Raj spotted him and came out of the shop to see him.

"Dennis, you look so sad! Come in, come in! What on earth is the matter, young man?"

Dennis told him what had happened at the

football match, and Raj shook his head in disbelief.

"You know the irony, Dennis?" proclaimed Raj. "Those people who are so quick to judge, be they teachers or politicians or religious leaders or whatever, are normally up to far worse themselves!"

"Maybe," murmured Dennis, half listening.

"Not maybe, Dennis. It's true. You know that headmaster of yours, what's his name?'

"Mr Hawtrey."

"That's it. Mr Hawtrey. I could swear there's something strange going on with him."

"Strange?" asked Dennis, intrigued.

"I don't know for sure," continued Raj, "but you see he used to come in here every Sunday morning at seven o'clock in the morning for his *Telegraph*. Same time every week, on the dot. And then after a while he stopped coming and his sister came instead. At least, he *said* it was his sister."

"What do you mean?"

"Well, I can't put my finger on it, but there's something very peculiar about that woman."

"Really? What?"

"Come tomorrow at seven o'clock and see for yourself." Raj tapped his nose. "Now, do you want the other half of that Chomp bar? I can't seem to shift it."

"It's very early for a Sunday," complained Lisa. "It's six forty-five. I should be in bed."

"I'm sorry," said Dennis.

"So Hawtrey's got a sister. So what?"

"Well, Raj said there was something funny about her. Look, we'd better hurry up if we want to be there for seven."

They quickened their pace along the cold,

misty streets. The ground was damp from an overnight storm. No one else was up yet, and the absence of people gave the town an eerie feel. Lisa was of course wearing heels, though Dennis wasn't on this particular occasion. All that could be heard was the click-clacking of her heels down the street.

Then, out of the grey mist stepped a very tall woman dressed in black. She entered the shop. Dennis checked his watch.

Seven o'clock precisely.

"That must be her," whispered Dennis. They tiptoed over to the shop window and peered through the glass. This woman was indeed buying a copy of the *Sunday Telegraph*.

"So she's buying a newspaper? So what?" whispered Lisa.

"Shush," shushed Dennis. "We haven't had a proper look at her yet."

Raj spotted Dennis and Lisa through the glass and gave them a big wink as the woman turned around. They retreated behind a bin as she made her way out of the shop. Neither Dennis nor Lisa could believe what they saw. If it was Mr Hawtrey's sister it must have been his twin. She even had a moustache!

The figure looked about to see no one was around and then hurried down the street. Dennis and Lisa looked at each other and smiled.

Gotcha!

"MR HAWTREY!" shouted Dennis.

The figure turned and said in a low, manly voice, "Yes?" before immediately raising its voice for a lady-like tone, "Um, I mean no!"

Dennis and Lisa approached.

"I'm not Mr Hawtrey. No... no... definitely not. I'm his sister Doris."

"Come off it, Mr Hawtrey," said Lisa, "we may be kids but we're not stupid."

"And why have you got a moustache?" accused Dennis.

"I have a very slight facial-hair problem!" was the high-pitched reply. Dennis and Lisa just laughed. "Oh, it's you. The boy in the dress," snarled Mr Hawtrey in a low voice. He knew the game was up now.

"Yes," replied Dennis, "the boy you *expelled* for wearing a dress. And here you are wearing one yourself."

"It's not a dress, boy. It's a blouse and skirt," snapped Mr Hawtrey.

"Nice heels, sir," said Lisa.

Mr Hawtrey's eyes bulged. "What do you want from me?" he demanded.

"I want Dennis reinstated at the school," demanded Lisa.

"Impossible, I'm afraid. Not wearing the correct school uniform is a very serious offence," said Mr Hawtrey with headmasterly confidence.

"Well, what if it got out that you liked dressing like this?" asked Lisa. "You'd be a laughing stock."

"Are you trying to blackmail me?" Mr Hawtrey asked severely.

"Yes," said Lisa and Dennis simultaneously.

"Oh," said Mr Hawtrey, suddenly deflated. "Well, it seems like I have no choice, then. Come back to school on Monday morning. In correct school uniform, boy. But you need to swear that you will never mention this to anyone," added Mr Hawtrey sternly.

"I swear," said Dennis.

Mr Hawtrey looked at Lisa. She was silent for a moment, enjoying the power she still had over him. She smiled wider than a grand piano.

"Oh, OK, I swear too," she said eventually.

"Thank you."

"Oh, and another thing I almost forgot," said Dennis.

"Boy?"

"Yeah, let's have proper footballs allowed in the playground at break-time from now on," continued Dennis confidently. "It's no good playing with tennis balls."

"Anything else?" roared Mr Hawtrey.

"No, I think that's everything," said Dennis. "If we think of anything else, we'll let you know," added Lisa.

"Thank you so much," said Mr Hawtrey sarcastically. "You know, it's not always easy being a headmaster. Shouting at people all the time, telling them off, expelling them. I need to dress up like this to unwind."

"Well, that's cool, but why don't you try being a bit nicer to everyone?" asked Lisa.

"Utterly absurd idea," replied Mr Hawtrey.

"See you on Monday then, miss!" said Dennis laughing. "Sorry, I mean, sir!"

Mr Hawtrey turned and began to run home as fast as his heels would let him. Just as he was about to disappear round the corner, he kicked his shoes off, picked them up and started sprinting.

Dennis and Lisa laughed so loudly they woke up the whole street.

21

Big Hairy Hands

"What are you wearing that for?" asked Dad.

It was Monday morning and he was staring at Dennis, who was sitting at the kitchen table eating his Rice Krispies, and for the first time in a week wearing his school uniform.

"I'm going back to school today, Dad," replied Dennis. "The headmaster has changed his mind about me being expelled."

"He has? Why? He's a nasty piece of work that man."

"It's a long story. I suppose he thought that the dressing up wasn't so bad after all."

"Well, he's right. It isn't. You know, I was very proud of you out there on that pitch. You were very brave."

"That boy really did kick me pretty hard," said Dennis.

"I don't just mean that. I mean going out there in a dress. *That* was brave. I wouldn't be able to do it. You're a great lad really, you are. It hasn't been easy for you since your mum left. I've been very unhappy and I know sometimes I've taken it out on you and your brother, and I am sorry for that."

"It's OK, Dad. I still love you."

Dad reached into his jacket pocket and pulled out the photograph he had taken of his family at the beach.

"I didn't have the heart to burn it, son. It's just too painful for me to look at photos like that. I loved your mum very much, you see?

I still love her now, after everything. Being a grown-up is complicated like that. But it's your photo, Dennis. You keep it safe." Dad's hand trembled as he passed the charred photograph back to his son. Dennis looked at it again, then slid it carefully into his breast pocket.

"Thanks, Dad," he said.

"All right?" said John as he entered the room. "You coming back to school, then?"

"Yeah," replied Dennis.

"That stupid headmaster changed his mind," added Dad.

"Well, I think you're very brave going back," said John as he put some stale slices of bread in the toaster. "Some of the older kids might pick on you."

Dennis looked down at the lino.

"Well, you need to look after your brother, then, don't you, John?" said Dad.

"Yeah, I will. If anyone has a go, I'll have a go back. You're my brother and I'll protect you."

"Good boy, John," said Dad, trying not to cry. "I've gotta go, boys. I've gotta drive a load of bog rolls to Bradford." He walked over to the door, and then turned back for a moment. "I am very proud of you both, you know. Whatever you do, you'll always be my boys.

You're all I've got." He couldn't quite look at them as he spoke, and then he quickly left, shutting the door behind him.

Dennis and John looked at each other. It was as if an ice age had thawed, and the sun was shining for the first time in a million years.

"It's a shame you missed the final," said Dennis as they walked to school together.

"Yeah…" said John. "I just had to, you know, hang around outside the leisure centre with my mates."

"That's funny. I thought for a moment I saw your face in the crowd, but I suppose it must have been someone else."

John coughed. "Well… actually, I sort of *was* there…"

"I knew it!" said Dennis, smiling. "Why didn't you let on?"

"I was going to," spluttered John. "But I just

couldn't run on to the pitch at the end and do all that hugging stuff. I wanted to, honest, but... I dunno. I'm sorry."

"Well, I'm glad you were there, even if you didn't tell me. You don't need to be sorry."

"Thanks. Sorry."

They walked in silence for a moment.

"What I still don't get, though," ventured John, "is why you did it?"

"Did what?"

"Put on that dress in the first place."

"I don't know really," said Dennis, a puzzled look crossing his face. "I suppose because it was fun."

"Fun?" said John.

"Well, you know when we were younger and we used to run around the garden pretending to be Daleks or Spider-Man or whatever?"

"Yeah."

"It felt like that. Like playing," said Dennis confidently.

"I used to like playing," said John, almost to himself, as they continued down the street.

"What the...?" said John, as he and Dennis entered Raj's shop to find Raj resplendent in a bright green sari.

And wig.

And full make-up.

"Morning, boys!" said Raj in a ridiculously high-pitched voice.

"Morning, Raj," said Dennis.

"Oh no, I'm not Raj," said Raj. "Raj is not here today, but he has left me in charge of the shop. I'm his Aunt Indira!"

"Raj, we know it's you," said John.

"Oh dear," said Raj, dejected. "I've been up since dawn putting this look together.

What gave it away so quickly?"

"The stubble," said Dennis.

"The Adam's apple," added John.

"Those big hairy hands," continued Dennis.

"All right, all right, I get the point," said Raj hurriedly. "I was hoping I'd get my own back by fooling you, Dennis, after you played that trick on me!"

"Well, you very nearly did fool me, Raj," said Dennis kindly. "You were incredibly convincing as a woman." He smiled, looking admiringly at Raj's outfit. "So where did you get the sari?"

"It's my wife's. Luckily she's a very big lady so it's a good fit." Raj lowered his voice for a moment and looked around so no one else could hear. "She doesn't know I've got it on so if you see her it's best not to mention it."

"It's OK, Raj, we won't," said Dennis.

"Thank you so much. Good tip about your headmaster Mr Hawtrey, yes?" said Raj with a wink of his eye-liner-caked eye.

"Oh yes, thank you, Raj," said Dennis, winking back.

"What's that about Hawtrey?" asked John.

"Oh nothing. He just likes to read the *Sunday Telegraph*, that's all," said Dennis.

"Well, we'd better go. We're gonna be late,"

said John, tugging his brother's arm. "Erm, just this bag of Quavers, please, Raj."

"Buy two bags of Quavers, I give you one extra one free," said Raj with great delight at his new special offer.

"All right, then," said John. "That sounds good." He picked up another bag of Quavers and gave it to Dennis.

Raj then produced a single Quaver from a bag. "And there is your free Quaver. So that's two bags of Quavers… 58p. Thank you so much!"

John looked confused.

"Good luck today, Dennis," exclaimed Raj as the two boys left his shop. "I'll be thinking of you."

22

One Thing Left to Do

Entering the school gates, Dennis spotted Darvesh waiting for him, holding a brand-new football.

"Do you fancy a kick-about?" asked Darvesh. "My mum bought me this yesterday. We're allowed to play with proper footballs in the playground now," he added, bouncing the ball triumphantly.

"Really?" said Dennis. "I wonder why Hawtrey changed his mind…"

"Do you wanna play, then?" asked Darvesh eagerly.

At that moment Dennis saw Miss Windsor parking her yellow Citroen 2CV. It wasn't so much a car, more a dustbin on wheels, but it was French, and she loved it.

"I'll catch up with you at break, OK?" said Dennis.

"OK, Dennis, we'll have a proper game then," replied Darvesh, doing keepie-uppies as he made his way to the classroom.

"John, wait here a moment, will you?" said Dennis. "There's one thing I still need to do."

Dennis took a deep breath. "Miss?" he called out. John hung back a little.

"Oh, it's you," said Miss Windsor frostily. "What do you want?"

"I just wanted to say I'm really sorry. I am. I'm sorry. I really shouldn't have said that you didn't have a good French accent."

Miss Windsor remained silent and Dennis

squirmed, trying to think of something else to say.

"Because you do. You actually have a really good French accent, miss. *Mademoiselle*. It sounds like you are actually a proper French person."

"Well, thank you, Dennis, or '*merci beaucoup, Dennis*' as I would say in *Français*," said Miss Windsor, warming a little. "Well done on Saturday. Wonderful match. You actually looked very convincing in a dress, you know."

"Thank you, miss."

"Actually, I'm glad you're here," said Miss Windsor. "You see, I've written a play…"

"Oh yes…" said Dennis with trepidation.

"It's a play about the life of Joan of Arc, the fifteenth-century French religious martyr…"

"Wow, that sounds… erm."

"None of the girls want to play her. Anyway,

I thought it would be fascinating to have a boy play her, as she of course was a girl who wore boy's clothing. Dennis, I think you would make a very memorable Joan."

Dennis looked to his brother for help, but John just smirked.

"Well it certainly sounds... interesting..."

"Wonderful. Let's meet up at break-time and discuss it over a *pain au chocolat*."

"OK, miss," said Dennis, trying to hide his dread. He walked away slowly and quietly, as you might retreat from a bomb that may be about to go off.

"Oh, I should have said – the play is entirely in French. *Au revoir!*" she called after him.

"*Au revoir*," he called back in the most un-French accent he could manage.

"Now *that* I can't wait to see!" said John, laughing.

As they walked off together towards the main school building, John put his arm around him. Dennis smiled.

The world felt different.

Thank-yous:

I would like to thank my literary agent at Independent Talent, Paul Stevens; Moira Bellas and everyone at MBC PR; all at HarperCollins, especially my publisher Ann-Janine Murtagh and my editor Nick Lake for their belief in the project and tremendous support of me; James Annal, the cover designer; Elorine Grant, interior designer; Michelle Misra, eagle-eyed copy-editor; the other side of my brain that is Matt Lucas; my greatest fan and mum, Kathleen; and my sister Julie for dressing me up in the first place.

Most of all, though, I would like to thank the great Quentin Blake, who has brought more to this book than I could have ever dared to dream.

Have you got them all?

Illustrated in glorious colour!

GANGSTA GRANNY

Books by David Walliams:

THE BOY IN THE DRESS
MR STINK
BILLIONAIRE BOY
GANGSTA GRANNY
RATBURGER
DEMON DENTIST
AWFUL AUNTIE
GRANDPA'S GREAT ESCAPE
THE MIDNIGHT GANG
BAD DAD
THE ICE MONSTER

Illustrated in glorious colour:
THE WORLD'S WORST CHILDREN
THE WORLD'S WORST CHILDREN 2
THE WORLD'S WORST CHILDREN 3

Also available in picture book:
THE SLIGHTLY ANNOYING ELEPHANT
THE FIRST HIPPO ON THE MOON
THE QUEEN'S ORANG-UTAN
THE BEAR WHO WENT BOO!
THERE'S A SNAKE IN MY SCHOOL!
BOOGIE BEAR
GERONIMO

David Walliams
GANGSTA GRANNY

Illustrated by Tony Ross

HarperCollins *Children's Books*

First published in hardback in Great Britain
by HarperCollins *Children's Books* in 2011
First published in paperback in Great Britain by
HarperCollins *Children's Books* in 2012
HarperCollins *Children's Books* is a division of HarperCollins*Publishers* Ltd
1 London Bridge Street, London, SE1 9GF

HarperCollins*Publishers*
1st Floor, Watermarque Building, Ringsend Road
Dublin 4, Ireland

The HarperCollins website address is
www.harpercollins.co.uk

109

ISBN 978-0-00-737146-4

Printed and bound by
CPI Group (UK) Ltd, Croydon, CR0 4YY

MIX
Paper from
responsible sources
FSC™ C007454

For Philip Onyango...

...the bravest little boy I have ever met.

Thank-yous:

I would like to thank a few people who helped me with this book.

First, the hugely talented Tony Ross for his magical illustrations. Next, Ann-Janine Murtagh, the brilliant head of children's books at HarperCollins. Nick Lake, my hard-working editor and friend. The fantastic designers James Stevens and Elorine Grant, who worked on the cover and text respectively. The meticulous copy editor Lizzie Ryley. Samantha White, for her brilliant work publicising my books. The lovely Tanya Brennand-Roper who produces the audio versions. And of course my very supportive literary agent Paul Stevens at Independent.

Most of all I would like to thank you kids for reading my books. I am genuinely humbled that you come and meet me at signings, write me letters or send me drawings. I really love telling you stories. I do hope I can dream up some more. Keep reading, it's good for you!

1

Cabbagy Water

"But Granny is soooo boring," said Ben. It was a cold Friday evening in November, and as usual he was slumped in the back of his mum and dad's car. Once again he was on his way to stay the night at his dreaded granny's house. "*All* old people are."

"Don't talk about your granny like that," said Dad weakly, his fat stomach pushed up against the steering wheel of the family's little brown car.

"I hate spending time with her," protested Ben. "Her TV doesn't work, all she wants to do is play Scrabble and she stinks of cabbage!"

"In fairness to the boy she does stink of cabbage," agreed Mum, as she applied some last minute lip-liner.

"You're not helping, wife," muttered Dad. "At worst my mother has a very slight odour of boiled vegetables."

"Can't I come with you?" pleaded Ben. "I love ball-whatsit dancing," he lied.

"It's called ballroom dancing," corrected Dad. "And you don't love it. You said, and I quote, 'I would rather eat my own bogeys than watch that rubbish'."

Now, Ben's mum and dad *loved* ballroom dancing. Sometimes Ben thought they loved it more than they loved him. There was a TV show on Saturday evenings that Mum and Dad never missed called *Strictly Stars Dancing*, where celebrities would be paired with professional ballroom dancers.

In fact, if there was a fire in their house, and Mum could only save either a sparkly gold tap-shoe once worn by Flavio Flavioli (the shiny, tanned dancer and heartbreaker from Italy who appeared on every series of the hit TV show) or her only child, Ben thought she would probably go for the shoe. Tonight, his mum and dad were going to an arena to see *Strictly Stars Dancing* live on stage.

"I don't know why you don't give up on this pipe dream of becoming a plumber, Ben, and think about dancing professionally," said Mum, her lip-liner scrawling across her cheek as the car bounced over a particularly bumpy speed bump. Mum had a habit of applying make-up in the car, which meant she often arrived somewhere looking like a clown. "Maybe, just maybe, you could end up on *Strictly*!" added Mum excitedly.

"Because prancing around like that is stupid," said Ben.

Mum whimpered a little, and reached for a tissue.

"You're upsetting your mother. Now just be quiet please, Ben, there's a good boy," replied Dad firmly, as he turned up the volume on the stereo. Inevitably, a *Strictly* CD was playing. *50 Golden Greats from the Hit TV Show* was emblazoned on the cover. Ben hated the CD, not least because he had heard it a million times. In fact, he had heard it so many times it was like torture.

Ben's mum worked at the local nail salon, 'Gail's Nails'. Because there weren't many customers, Mum and the other lady who worked there (unsurprisingly called Gail) spent most days doing each other's nails. Buffing, cleaning, trimming, moisturising, coating, sealing, polishing, filing, lacquering, extending and painting. They were doing things to each other's nails all day long (unless Flavio Flavioli was on daytime TV). That meant Mum would always come home with extremely long multi-coloured plastic extensions on the end of her fingers.

Ben's dad, meanwhile, worked as a security guard at the local supermarket. The highlight of his twenty-year career thus far was stopping an old man who had concealed two tubs of margarine down his trousers. Although Dad was now too fat to run after any robbers, he could certainly block their escape. Dad met Mum when he wrongly accused her of shoplifting a bag of crisps, and within a year they were married.

The car swung around the corner into Grey Close, where Granny's bungalow squatted. It was one of a whole row of sad little homes, mainly inhabited by old people.

The car came to a halt, and Ben slowly turned his head towards the bungalow. Looking expectantly out of the living-room window was Granny. Waiting. Waiting. She was always waiting by the window for him to arrive. *How long has she been there?* thought Ben. *Since last week?*

Ben was her only grandchild and, as far as he knew, no one else ever came to visit.

Granny waved and gave Ben a little smile, which his grumpy face just about permitted him to reluctantly return.

"Right, one of us will pick you up tomorrow morning at around eleven," said Dad, keeping the engine running.

"Can't you make it ten?"

"Ben!" growled Dad. He released the child lock and Ben grudgingly pushed the door open and stepped out. Ben didn't need the child lock, of course: he was eleven years old and hardly likely to open the door while the car was driving. He suspected his dad only used it to stop him from diving out of the car when they were on their way to Granny's house. *Clunk* went the door behind him, as the engine revved up again.

Before he could ring the bell, Granny opened the door. A huge gust of cabbage blasted in Ben's face. It was like a great big slap of smell.

She was very much your textbook granny:

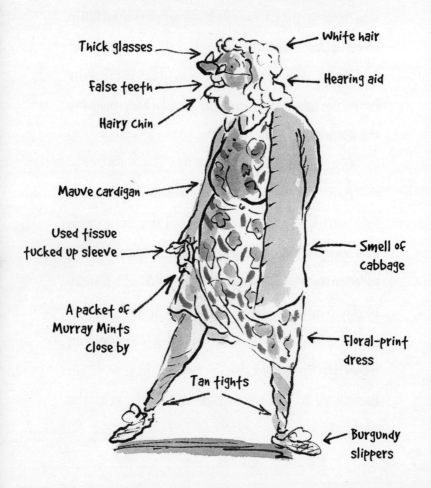

Thick glasses

White hair

False teeth

Hearing aid

Hairy chin

Mauve cardigan

Used tissue tucked up sleeve

Smell of cabbage

A packet of Murray Mints close by

Floral-print dress

Tan tights

Burgundy slippers

"Are Mummy and Daddy not coming in?" she asked, a little crestfallen. This was one of the things Ben couldn't stand about her: she was always talking to him like he was a baby.

Broom-broom-brrooooooooooommm.

Together Granny and Ben watched the little brown car race off, leaping over the speed bumps. Mum and Dad didn't like spending time with her any more than Ben did. It was just a convenient place to dump him on a Friday night.

"No, erm... Sorry, Granny..." spluttered Ben.

"Oh, well, come in then," she muttered. "Now, I've set up the Scrabble board and for your tea, I've got your favourite... cabbage soup!"

Ben's face dropped even further. *Noooooooo oooooooooo!* he thought.

2

A Duck Quacking

Before long, granny and grandson were sitting opposite each other in deadly silence at the dining-room table. Just like every single Friday night.

When his parents weren't watching *Strictly* on TV, they were eating curry or going to the movies. Friday night was their 'date night', and ever since Ben could remember, they had been dropping him off with his granny when they went out. If they weren't going to see *Strictly Stars Dancing Live On Stage Live!*, they would normally go to the Taj Mahal (the curry house on the high street, not the ancient white marble monument in India) and eat their own bodyweight in poppadums.

All that could be heard in the bungalow was the ticking of the carriage clock on the mantelpiece, the clinking of metal spoons against porcelain bowls, and the occasional high-pitched whistle of Granny's faulty hearing aid. It was a device whose purpose seemed to be not so much to aid Granny's deafness, but to cause deafness in others.

It was one of the main things that Ben hated about his granny. The others were:

1) Granny would always spit in the used tissue she kept up the sleeve of her cardigan and wipe her grandson's face with it.

2) Her TV had been broken since 1992. And

now it was covered in dust so thick it was like fur.

3) Her house was stuffed full of books and she was always trying to get Ben to read them even though he loathed reading.

4) Granny insisted you wore a heavy winter coat all year round even on a boiling hot day, otherwise you wouldn't "feel the benefit".

5) She reeked of cabbage. (Anyone with a cabbage allergy would not be able to come within ten miles of her.)

6) Granny's idea of an exciting day out was feeding mouldy crusts of bread to some ducks in a pond.

7) She constantly blew off without even acknowledging it.

8) Those blow-offs didn't just smell of cabbage. They smelled of rotten cabbage.

9) Granny made you go to bed so early it seemed hardly worthwhile getting up in the first place.

10) She knitted her only grandson jumpers for Christmas with puppies or kittens on them, which he was forced to wear during the whole festive period by his parents.

"How's your soup?" enquired the old lady.

Ben had been stirring the pale green liquid around the chipped bowl for the last ten minutes hoping it would somehow disappear.

It wouldn't.

And now it was getting cold.

Cold bits of cabbage, floating around in some cold cabbagy water.

"Erm, it's delicious, thank you," replied Ben.

"Good."

Tick tock tick tock.

"Good," said the old lady again.

Clink. Clink.

"Good." Granny seemed to find it as hard to speak to Ben as he did to her.

Clink clank. Whistle.

"How's school?" she asked.

"Boring," muttered Ben. Adults always ask kids how they are doing at school. The one subject kids absolutely hate talking about. You don't even want to talk about school when you are *at* school.

"Oh," said Granny.

Tick tock clink clank whistle tick tock.

"Well, I must check on the oven," said Granny after the long pause stretched out into an even *longer* pause. "I've got your favourite cabbage pie on the go."

She rose slowly from her seat and made her

way to the kitchen. As she took each step a little bubble of wind puffed out of her saggy bottom. It sounded like a duck quacking. Either she didn't realise or was extremely good at pretending she didn't realise.

Ben watched her go, and then crept silently across the room. This was difficult because of the piles of books everywhere. Ben's granny LOVED books, and always seemed to have her nose in one. They were stacked on shelves, lined up on windowsills, piled up in corners.

Crime novels were her favourite. Books about gangstas, bank robbers, the mafia and the like. Ben wasn't sure what the difference between a gangsta and a gangster was, but a gangsta seemed much worse.

Although Ben hated reading, he loved looking at all the covers of Granny's books. They had fast cars and guns and glamorous ladies luridly painted on them, and Ben found it hard to believe this boring old Granny of his liked reading stories that looked so thrilling.

Why is she obsessed with gangstas? thought Ben. *Gangstas don't live in bungalows. Gangstas don't play Scrabble. Gangstas probably don't smell of cabbage.*

Ben was a very slow reader, and the teachers at school made him feel stupid because he couldn't keep up. The headmistress had even put him down a year in the hope that he would catch up on his reading. As a result, all his friends were in a different class, and he felt nearly as lonely at school as he did at home, with his parents who only cared about ballroom dancing.

Eventually, after a hairy moment where he nearly knocked over a stack of real-life crime books, Ben made it to the pot plant in the corner.

He quickly tipped the remainder of his soup

into it. The plant looked as if it was already dying, and if it wasn't dead yet, Granny's cold cabbage soup was sure to kill it off.

Suddenly, Ben heard Granny's bum squeaking again as she made her way into the dining room, so he sped back to the table. He sat there trying to look as innocent as possible, with his empty bowl in front of him and his spoon in hand. "I've finished my soup, thank you, Granny. It was yummy!"

"That's good," said the old lady as she trundled back to the table carrying a saucepan on a tray. "I've got plenty more here for you, boy!" Smiling, she served him up another bowl.

Ben gulped in terror.

3

Plumbing Weekly

"I can't find *Plumbing Weekly*, Raj," said Ben.

It was the next Friday, and the boy had been scouring the magazine shelves of the local newsagent's shop. He couldn't find his favourite publication anywhere. The magazine was aimed at professional plumbers, and Ben was beguiled by pages and pages of pipes, taps, cisterns, ballcocks, boilers, tanks and drains. *Plumbing Weekly* was the only thing he enjoyed reading – mainly because it was crammed full of pictures and diagrams.

Ever since he had been old enough to hold

things, Ben had *loved* plumbing. When other children were playing with ducks in the bath, Ben had asked his parents for bits of pipe, and made complicated water channelling systems. If a tap broke in the house, he fixed it. If a toilet was blocked, Ben wasn't disgusted, he was ecstatic!

Ben's parents didn't approve of him wanting to be a plumber, though. They wanted him to be rich and famous, and to their knowledge there had never been a rich and famous plumber. Ben was as good with his hands as he was rubbish at reading, and was absolutely fascinated when a plumber came round to fix a leak. He would watch in awe, as a junior doctor might watch a great surgeon at work in an operating theatre.

But he always felt like a disappointment to his mum and dad. They desperately wanted him to fulfil the ambition they had never managed: to become a professional ballroom dancer.

Ben's mum and dad had discovered their love of ballroom dancing too late to become champions themselves. And, to be honest, they seemed to prefer sitting on their bums watching it on TV to actually taking part.

As such, Ben tried to keep his passion private. To avoid hurting his mum and dad's feelings, he stashed his copies of *Plumbing Weekly* under his bed. And he had made an arrangement with Raj, so that every week the newsagent would keep the plumbing magazine aside for him. Now, though, he couldn't find it anywhere.

Ben had searched for the magazine behind *Kerrang* and *Heat* and even looked underneath *The Lady* (not an actual lady, I mean the magazine called *The Lady*), all to no avail. Raj's store was madly messy, but people came from miles away to shop there as he always brought a smile to their faces.

Raj was halfway up a stepladder, putting up Christmas decorations. Well, I say 'Christmas decorations' – he was actually putting up a banner that read 'Happy Birthday', though he had Tippexed out the word 'Birthday' and replaced it in scratchy biro with 'Christmas'.

Raj carefully stepped down off the ladder to help Ben with his search.

"Your *Plumbing Weekly*... mmm... Let me think, have you looked beside the toffee bonbons?" said Raj.

"Yes," replied Ben.

"And it's not underneath the colouring books?"

"No."

"And you have checked behind the penny chews?"

"Yes."

"Well, this is very mysterious. I know I

ordered one in for you, young Ben. Mmm, very mysterious…" Raj was speaking extremely slowly, in that way people do when they are thinking. "I am so sorry, Ben, I know you love it, but I don't have a clue where it is. I do have a special offer on Cornettos."

"It's November, Raj, it's freezing outside!" said Ben. "Who would want to eat a Cornetto now?"

"Everyone when they hear my special offer! Wait until you hear this: buy twenty-three Cornettos, get one free!"

"Why on earth would I want twenty-four Cornettos?!" said Ben with a laugh.

"Erm, well, I don't know, you could maybe eat twelve, and put the other twelve in your pocket to enjoy later."

"That's a lot of Cornettos, Raj. Why are you so keen to get rid of them?"

"They go out of date tomorrow," said Raj, as he lumbered over to the freezer cabinet, slid open the glass top and pulled out a cardboard box of Cornettos. A freezing cold mist immediately

shrouded the shop. "Look! Best Before 15th of November."

Ben studied the box. "It says Best Before 15th of November 1996."

"Well," said Raj. "Even more reason to put them on special offer. OK, Ben, this is my final offer. Buy one box of Cornettos, I will give you ten boxes absolutely free!"

"Really Raj, no thanks," said Ben. He peered into the freezer cabinet to see what else might be lurking in there. It had never been defrosted and Ben wouldn't have been surprised to find a perfectly preserved woolly mammoth from the Ice Age inside.

"Hang on," he said, as he moved a few frost-encrusted ice lollies out of the way. "It's in here! *Plumbing Weekly*!"

"Ah yes, I remember now," said Raj. "I put it in there to keep it fresh for you."

"Fresh?" said Ben.

"Well, young man, the magazine comes out on a Tuesday, but it's Friday today. So I put it in the freezer to keep it fresh for you, Ben. I didn't want it to go off."

Ben wasn't sure how any magazine could ever go off, but he thanked the newsagent anyway. "That's very kind of you, Raj. And I'll have a packet of Rolos, please."

"I can offer you seventy-three packets of Rolos for the price of seventy-two!" exclaimed the newsagent with a smile that was meant to entice.

"No thanks, Raj."

"One thousand packets of Rolos for the price of nine hundred and ninety-eight?"

"No thanks," said Ben.

"Are you mad, Ben? That's a wonderful offer. All right, all right, you drive a hard bargain, Ben.

One million and seven packets of Rolos, for the price of a million and four. That's three packets of Rolos absolutely free!"

"I'll just take one packet and the magazine, thank you."

"Of course, young sir!"

"I can't wait to get stuck into *Plumbing Weekly* later. I have to go and spend the whole night with my boring old granny again."

It had been a week since Ben's last visit, and the dreaded Friday had rolled around once more. His parents were going to see a 'chick flick', according to his mum. Romance and kissing and all that goo. Yuckety yuck yuck.

"Tut tut tut," said Raj, shaking his head as he counted out Ben's change.

Ben instantly felt ashamed. He had never seen the newsagent do this before. Like all the other local kids, Ben regarded Raj as 'one of us' not 'one of them'. He was so full of life and laughter, Raj seemed a world away from parents and teachers and all the grown-ups who felt they could tell you off because they were bigger than you.

"Just because your granny is old, young Ben," said Raj, "doesn't mean that she is boring. I am getting on a bit myself. And whenever I have met your granny I have found her to be a very interesting lady."

"But—"

"Don't be too hard on her, Ben," pleaded Raj. "We will all be old one day. Even you. And I'm sure your granny will have a secret or two. Old people always do…"

4

Mystery and Wonder

Ben wasn't at all sure that Raj was right about Granny. That night it was the same old story. Granny served up cabbage soup, followed by cabbage pie and for dessert it was cabbage mousse. She even found some cabbage-flavoured after-dinner chocolates* somewhere. After dinner, Granny and Ben sat down together on the musty sofa as they always did.

"Scrabble time!" exclaimed Granny.

*Cabbage-flavoured chocolates are not as nice as they sound, and they don't sound that nice.

Great, thought Ben. *Tonight's going to be a million times more boring than last week!*

Ben detested Scrabble. If he had his way, Ben would build a rocket, and blast all the Scrabble boards in the world into outer space. Granny pulled out the dusty old Scrabble box from the sideboard and set up the game on the pouf.

Ben sighed.

What seemed like decades later, but was probably just hours, Ben stared at his letters, before scanning the board. He had already put down:

BORING

ANCIENT

QUACK (double word score)

POINTLESS

PONGY (this had to be checked in the dictionary)

WRINKLES

CABBAGESICK (triple word score)

ESCAPE

HELP

IHATETHISSTUPIDGAME (Granny had disallowed this on account of it not being one word).

He had an 'E', an 'M', an 'I', a 'U' and a 'D'. Granny had just put down 'Murraymint' (double word score) so Ben used the 'T' at the end to form the word 'tedium'.

"Well, it's nearly eight o'clock, young man," announced Granny, looking at her little gold watch. "Time for your beddy-byes, I think…"

Ben groaned inwardly. Beddy-byes! He wasn't a toddler!

"But I don't have to go to bed until nine o'clock at home!" he protested. "And not until ten o'clock when I haven't got school in the morning."

"No, Ben, off you go to bed, please." The old lady could be quite firm when she wanted to be. "And don't forget to brush your teeth. I'll be up soon to give you a bedtime story, if you like. You always used to love a bedtime story."

Later, Ben stood at the sink in the bathroom. It was a cold damp room with no window. Some of the tiles had fallen off the wall. There was just one sad little frayed towel and a very worn bar of soap that looked like it was half soap, half mould.

Ben hated brushing his teeth. So he pretended to brush his teeth. Pretending to brush your teeth is simple. Don't tell your parents I told you, but if you want to try it for yourself, all you have to do is follow this handy step-by-step guide:

1) Turn on the cold tap

2) Wet the toothbrush

3) Squeeze a tiny amount of toothpaste on to your finger and place finger in mouth

4) Move the trace of toothpaste around your mouth with your tongue

5) Spit

6) Turn off the tap

See? It's so easy. Nearly as easy as brushing your teeth.

Ben looked at himself in the bathroom mirror. He was eleven years old, but shorter than he wanted to be, so he stood on his tiptoes for a moment. Ben was aching to be older.

Only a few more years, he thought, and he would be taller and hairier and spottier, and his Friday nights would be very different.

He wouldn't have to stay at boring old Granny's any more. Instead Ben would be able to do all the thrilling things the older kids in the town did on Friday nights:

Hang around with a gang of friends outside the off-licence waiting for someone to tell you off.

Or alternatively, sit at the bus stop with some girls in tracksuits and chew gum and never actually get on a bus.

Yes, a world of mystery and wonder awaited him.

However, for now, even though it was still light outside and he could hear boys in the nearby park playing football, it was time for Ben to go to sleep. In a hard little bed in a damp little room in his granny's rundown little bungalow. That smelled of cabbage.

Not just a little bit.

A lot.

Sighing, Ben got under the covers.

Just then, Granny gently opened the door to his bedroom. He quickly shut his eyes and pretended to be asleep. She lumbered over to the bed, and Ben could feel her standing over him for a moment.

"I was going to tell you that bedtime story," she whispered. The old lady had often told him stories when he was younger, about pirates and smugglers and master criminals, but he was far too old for all that nonsense now.

"What a shame you're asleep already," she said. "Well, I just wanted to say that I love you. Goodnight, my little Benny."

He hated being called 'Benny' too.

And 'little'.

The nightmare continued, as Ben sensed his granny bending over to give him a kiss. The prickly old hairs on her chin bristled uncomfortably against his cheek. Then he heard the familiar rhythmic quacking sound as her bum squeaked with every step. She squeaked her way back to the door and closed it behind her, sealing the smell in.

That's it, thought Ben. *I have to escape!*

5

A Little Broken

"*Aaaahhhhkkkk… pffftttt… aaaaaahhhhhhk kkkkk … ppppppppffffffffffftttttttt…*"

No, reader, you haven't bought the Swahili edition of this book by mistake. That was the sound Ben was waiting for.

Granny snoring.

She was asleep.

"*Aaaaaahhhhkkkkkkk… pppppffffffffftttttttt… aaaaaaaaaaaaahhhhhhkkkkkkk…*"

Ben crept out of his room and made his way over to the telephone in the hall. It was one of those old style telephones that purred like a cat when you dialled a number.

"Mum...?" he whispered.

"I CAN HARDLY HEAR YOU!" she shouted back. There was loud jazz music playing in the background. Mum and Dad were at the arena again watching *Strictly Stars Dancing Live On Stage Live!* She was probably drooling as Flavio Flavioli swivelled his hips and broke the hearts of thousands of women of a certain age. "What's the matter? Is everything all right? The old bat hasn't died, has she?"

"No, she's fine, but I hate it here. Can't you come and pick me up? Please," whispered Ben.

"Flavio hasn't even done his second dance yet."

"Please," he pleaded. "I want to come home. Granny is such a bore. It's torture spending time with her."

"Speak to your dad." Ben heard a muffled

sound as she passed the phone over.

"HELLO?" shouted Dad.

"Please keep your voice down!"

"WHAT?" he shouted again.

"Shhhh. Keep your voice down. You are going to wake up Granny. Can you come and pick me up, Dad? Please? I hate it here."

"No, we cannot. Seeing this show is a once in a lifetime experience."

"You saw it last Friday!" protested Ben.

"Twice in a lifetime then."

"And you said you were going again next Friday too!"

"Look, if I have any more of your cheek, young lad, you can stay with her until Christmas. Goodbye!"

With that, his dad hung up. Ben carefully placed the receiver back in its cradle, and the phone made the quietest *ting*.

Suddenly, he noticed that Granny's snoring had stopped.

Had she heard what he'd said? He looked behind him and thought he saw her shadow, but then it was gone.

It was true that Ben found her dreadfully dull, but he didn't want her to know that. After all she was a lonely old widow, and her husband had died long before Ben was even born. Guiltily, Ben crept back to the spare room and waited and waited and waited for the morning.

At breakfast Granny seemed different.

Quieter. Older maybe. A little broken.

Her eyes looked bloodshot as if she'd been crying.

Did she hear? thought Ben. *I really hope she didn't hear.*

She stood by the oven as Ben sat at the tiny

kitchen table. Granny was pretending to be interested in her calendar, which was pinned to the wall by the oven. Ben could tell she was pretending, because there was nothing interesting on her calendar.

This was a typical week in Granny's hectic life:

Monday: Make cabbage soup. Play Scrabble against yourself. Read a book.

Tuesday: Make cabbage pie. Read another book. Blow off.

Wednesday: Make the dish 'Chocolate Surprise'. The surprise is that it isn't made of chocolate at all. It is in fact 100% cabbage.

Thursday: Suck a Murray Mint all day. (She could make one mint last a lifetime.)

Friday: Still suck the same Murray Mint. My wonderful grandson visits.

Saturday: My wonderful grandson leaves. Have another nice sit down. Pooped!

Sunday: Eat roast cabbage, with braised cabbage and boiled cabbage on the side. Blow off all day.

Eventually, Granny turned away from the calendar. "Your mummy and daddy will be here soon," she finally said, breaking the silence.

"Yes," said Ben, looking at his watch. "Just a few more minutes."

The minutes felt like hours. Days even. Months!

A minute can be a long time. Don't believe me? Then sit in a room on your own and do nothing but count for sixty seconds.

Have you done it yet? I don't believe you. I'm not joking. I want you to really go and do it.

I am not carrying on with the story until you do.

It's not my time I'm wasting.

I've got all day.

Right, have you done it now? Good. Now back to the story...

At just after eleven o'clock, the little brown car pulled up in front of Granny's house. Much like a getaway driver for a bank robbery, Mum kept the engine running. She leaned over and opened the passenger door so Ben could dive in quickly and they could zoom off.

As Ben trudged towards the car, Granny stood at the front door. "Would you like to come in for a cup of tea, Linda?" she shouted.

"No thanks," said Ben's mum. "Quick, Ben, for goodness sake get in!" She revved the engine. "I don't want to have to talk to the old dear."

"Shh!" said Ben. "She'll hear you!"

"I thought you didn't like Granny?" said Mum.

"I didn't say that, Mum. I said I found her boring. But I don't want *her* to know that, do I?"

Mum laughed as they sped off out of Grey Close. "I wouldn't worry, Ben, your granny isn't really with it. She probably doesn't understand what you're saying half the time."

Ben frowned. He wasn't sure about that. He wasn't sure at all. He remembered Granny's face at the breakfast table. Suddenly, he had a horrible feeling she understood a lot more than he had ever realised…

6

Cold Wet Egg

This Friday night would have been just as spectacularly dull as the last, if Ben hadn't remembered to bring his magazine with him this time. Once again, Mum and Dad dumped their only child at Granny's.

As soon as he arrived, Ben rushed past her into his cold damp little bedroom, shut the door and read his copy of the latest *Plumbing Weekly* from cover to cover. There was an amazing guide, with lots and lots of colour photographs, showing how to install the new generation of combi boilers. Ben folded over the corner of the page. Now he knew what he wanted for Christmas.

Once he'd finished the magazine, Ben sighed and headed to the living room. He knew he couldn't stay in his bedroom all evening.

Granny looked up and smiled when she saw him. "Scrabble time!" she exclaimed cheerily, holding up the board.

The next morning the air was thick with silence.

"Another boiled egg?" said Granny, as they sat in her rundown little kitchen.

Ben didn't like boiled eggs and hadn't finished his first one yet. Granny could even ruin food this simple. The egg would always come out all watery, and the soldiers were always burnt to a cinder. When the old lady wasn't looking, Ben would flick the egg gloop out of the window with his spoon, and hide the soldiers behind the radiator. There must be a whole platoon of them back there by now.

"No thanks, Granny. I'm completely full," replied Ben. "Delicious boiled egg, thank you," he added.

"Mmm..." murmured the old lady, unconvinced. "It's a bit nippy. I'm just going to put another cardigan on," she said, even though she was already wearing two. Granny trundled out of the room, quacking as she went.

Ben flicked the rest of his egg out of the window, and then tried to find something else to eat. He knew that Granny had a secret stash of chocolate biscuits that she kept on a top shelf in the kitchen. Granny would give Ben one on his birthday. Ben would also help himself to one from time to time, when his granny's cabbage-based delicacies left him as hungry as a wolf.

So he quickly slid his chair over to the

cupboard and stood on it to reach the biscuits. He lifted the biscuit tin. It was a big Silver Jubilee assortment tin from 1977 that featured a scratched and faded portrait of a much younger Queen Elizabeth II on the lid. It felt really heavy. Much heavier than usual.

Strange.

Ben shook the tin a little. It didn't feel or sound like it had biscuits inside. It was like it had stones or marbles in it.

Even stranger.

Ben unscrewed the lid.

He stared.

And then he stared some more.

He couldn't believe what was inside.

Diamonds! Rings, bracelets, necklaces, earrings, all with great big sparkling diamonds. Diamonds, diamonds and more diamonds!

Ben was no expert, but he thought there must

be thousands of pounds worth of jewellery in the biscuit tin, maybe even millions.

Suddenly, he heard Granny quacking her way into the room. Fumbling desperately, he put the lid back on and placed the tin on the shelf. He leaped down, yanked his chair over and sat at the table.

Glancing at the window, he realised that his flicked egg hadn't flown out into the garden, but was smeared across the glass. Granny would need a blowtorch to get that off if it dried. So he rushed over to the window and sucked the cold wet egg off the glass, then returned to his seat. It was too unpleasant to swallow so, in a panic, Ben kept it in his mouth.

Granny shuffled back into the kitchen wearing her third cardigan.

Still quacking.

"Better get your coat on, young man. Your mummy and daddy will be here in just a tick," she said with a smile.

Ben reluctantly swallowed the cold wet egg. It slipped down his throat. Yuck, yuck and double yuck. "Yes," he said, fearing he would vomit and deposit the egg back on the window.

Scrambled.

7

Bags of Manure

"Can I stay at Granny's again tonight?" announced Ben from the backseat of his mum and dad's little brown car. The diamonds in the biscuit tin were so puzzling; he was desperate to do some detective work. Maybe even search every nook and cranny of the old lady's bungalow. This was all awfully mysterious. Raj had said his granny might have a secret or two. And it seemed like the newsagent was right! And whatever Granny's secret was, it must be pretty amazing to explain all those diamonds. What if she used to be a zillionaire? Or worked in a diamond mine? Or been left them by a Princess? Ben couldn't wait to find out.

"What?" asked Dad, astonished.

"But you said she was boring," said Mum, equally astonished, irritated even. "You said all old people are."

"I was just joking," said Ben.

Dad studied his son in the rear-view mirror. He found understanding his plumbing-obsessed son hard enough at the best of times. Right now Ben wasn't making any sense at all. "Mmm, well... if you are sure, Ben..."

"I am sure, Dad."

"I'll call her when we get home. Just to check she's not going out."

"Going out!" scoffed Mum. "The old dear hasn't gone out for twenty years!" she added with a chuckle.

Ben wasn't sure why this was funny.

"I took her out to the garden centre that time," protested Dad.

"It was only because you needed someone to help you carry a load of bags of manure," said Mum.

"She had a super day out, though," said Dad, sounding miffed.

Later, Ben sat alone on his bed. His mind was racing.

Where on earth had Granny got the diamonds?

How much were they worth?

Why would she live in that sad little bungalow if she was so rich?

Ben searched and searched his mind, but couldn't find any answers.

Then Dad entered the room.

"Granny's busy. She says she'd love to see you, but she's going out tonight," he announced.

"What?!" spluttered Ben. Granny hardly ever went out – Ben had seen her calendar. The mystery was getting even more mysterious…

8

A Small Wig in a Jar

Ben hid in the bushes outside Granny's bungalow. Whilst Mum and Dad were downstairs in the living room watching *Strictly Stars Dancing* on the TV, Ben had scaled down the drainpipe outside his bedroom window, and cycled the five miles to Granny's.

This alone was a sign of how curious Ben had become about his granny. He didn't like cycling. His parents were always encouraging him to get more exercise. They told him that being fit was absolutely necessary if you wanted to be a professional dancer. But since it didn't make much difference when you were lying under a sink, screwing in a new length of copper piping, Ben had never willingly taken any exercise.

Until now.

If Granny was really going out for the first time in twenty years, Ben had to know where. It might just hold the key to how she came to have a ton of diamonds in her biscuit tin.

So he huffed and puffed along the canal towpath on his clunky old bike, until he came to Grey Close. The only good thing was that, being November, instead of being drenched in sweat, Ben was only mildly moist.

He had pedalled fast because he knew he didn't have that much time. *Strictly Stars Dancing* seemed to go on for hours, days even, but it had taken Ben half an hour to cycle over to Granny's, and as soon as the show was over Mum would be calling him downstairs for his tea. Ben's parents loved all the dancing TV shows – *Dancing on Ice Skates, So You Think You Might Be Able To Dance A Bit?* – but they were completely obsessed with *Strictly Stars Dancing*. They had recorded every single episode, and had an unrivalled collection of *Strictly* memorabilia in the house, including:

- A lime green thong once worn by Flavio Flavioli, framed with a photograph of him wearing it

- A *Strictly Stars Dancing* real fake leather bookmark

- Some athlete's foot powder signed by Flavio's professional dance partner, the Austrian beauty, Eva Bunz

- His and Hers official *Strictly Stars Dancing* leg warmers

- A CD of songs nearly used on the show

- A small wig in a jar that had been worn by the presenter, Sir Dirk Doddery

- A lifesize cardboard cut-out of Flavio Flavioli that had some of Mum's lipstick smudged around the mouth

- Some earwax in a jar that belonged to a celebrity contestant, the politician, Dame Rachel Prejudice MP

- A pair of tan tights that smelled of Eva Bunz

- A doodle on a napkin of a man's bottom drawn by the nasty judge,

Craig Malteser-Woodward

- A set of official *Strictly Stars Dancing* eggcups
- A half full tube of raxjex used by Flavio Flavioli
- A Craig Malteser-Woodward poseable action figure
- A Hawaiian Hot pizza crust that had been left by Flavio (complete with a signed letter of authenticity from Eva Bunz)

It was a Saturday, so after the show had finished the family were going to be having Cheesy Beans and Sausage. Neither Mum nor Dad could cook, but of all the readymade meals Ben's mum took out of the freezer, pricked with a fork and placed in the microwave for three minutes, this was his favourite. Ben was hungry and didn't want to miss it – which meant he needed to get back from Granny's house quickly. If it had been a Monday night, say, and they were having Chicken Tikka Lasagne, or a Wednesday and Doner Kebab Pizza, or a Sunday and Yorkshire Pudding Chow Mein* was on the menu, Ben wouldn't have been so bothered.

Night was falling. As it was late November it was rapidly growing colder and darker, and Ben was shivering in the bushes as he spied on his granny. *Where can she be going?* thought Ben. *She hardly ever goes out.*

*The supermarket chain where Ben's dad worked liked to bring the cuisine of two countries together in one easily microwaveable pack. By combining dishes from different countries, perhaps they would be able to bring peace to a deeply divided world. Or maybe not.

He saw a shadow move in her bungalow. Then her face appeared at the window, and Ben quickly shot out of view. The bushes rustled. *Shhh!* thought Ben. Had the old lady seen him?

After a few moments the front door opened slowly, and out stepped a figure dressed entirely in black. A black jumper, black leggings, black gloves, black socks, probably even a black bra and knickers. A black balaclava disguised the face, but from the stoop Ben knew it was Granny. She looked like someone from one of the covers of the books she loved reading. She straddled her mobility scooter and revved the engine.

Where on earth was she going?

And, more importantly, why was she dressed like a ninja?

Ben propped his bike against the bushes, and got ready to tail his own grandmother.

Which was one thing he had never in a million years dreamed of doing.

Like a spider scuttling around a bathroom trying not to be seen, Granny steered her scooter close to the walls. Ben followed on foot as quietly as possible. It wasn't too difficult to keep up, as the top speed of the mobility scooter was four miles per hour. Whirring across the road, she suddenly looked back as if she had heard something, and Ben dived behind a tree.

He waited, holding his breath.

Nothing.

After a few moments, he poked his head around the trunk, and saw that Granny had reached the end of the road. He continued his chase.

Soon they were near the town's high street. It was all but deserted. As it was early evening, all the shops had shut for the day and the pubs and restaurants had yet to open for the night. Granny stayed out of the glow of the streetlights, swerved into doorways, as she neared her destination.

Ben gasped when he saw where she had parked.

The jeweller's shop.

Necklaces and rings and watches sparkled in the window. Ben couldn't believe his eyes as Granny took out a tin of cabbage soup from the scooter's basket. She glanced around theatrically then pulled back her arm in readiness to smash the tin through the jeweller's shop window.

"Nooooo!" shouted Ben.

Granny dropped the tin. It crashed to the ground and cabbage soup oozed on to the pavement.

"Ben?" hissed Granny. "What are you doing here?"

9

The Black Cat

Ben stared at his granny as she stood by the jeweller's shop, dressed all in black.

"Ben?" she prompted. "What are you doing following me?"

"I just… I…" Ben was so shocked he couldn't form a sentence.

"Well," she said. "Whatever you're doing here, you'll have the cops on us in no time. We'd better get out of here. Quick, jump on."

"But I can't—"

"Ben! We've got about thirty seconds before that CCTV camera comes on." She pointed to a camera screwed to the wall of an apartment block next to the row of shops.

Ben jumped on the back of her mobility scooter. "You know when the CCTV cameras come on?" he asked.

"Oh," said Granny, "you'd be surprised by what I know."

Ben looked at her back as she drove. He'd just seen her preparing to rob a jeweller's shop, how could he be *more* surprised? Clearly there was a lot more to his granny than he had ever known.

"Hold on," said Granny. "I'm going full throttle."

She violently twisted the handle of the scooter, to absolutely no effect that Ben could feel. They hummed off in the dark, going about three miles per hour with the increased weight.

✳

"'The Black Cat'?" repeated Ben. They were finally back sitting in Granny's living room. She had made a pot of tea and laid out some chocolate biscuits.

"Yes, that's what they called me," replied Granny. "I was the most wanted jewel thief in the world."

Ben's head was exploding with a million questions. *Why? Where? Who? What? When?* It was impossible to know what to ask first.

"No one else knows except you, Ben," continued Granny. "Even your granddad went to his grave not knowing. Can you keep a secret? You have to swear not to tell a soul."

"But—"

Granny's face looked fierce for a moment. Her eyes narrowed and darkened like a snake about to bite.

"You have to swear," the old lady said with

an intensity Ben had never witnessed before. "Us criminals take our oaths very seriously. Very seriously *indeed*."

Ben gulped, a little scared. "I swear not to tell anyone."

"Not even your mother and father!" barked Granny, nearly spitting out her false teeth in the process.

"I said, I swear not to tell anyone," barked back Ben.

Ben had been learning about Venn diagrams in school recently. As he had sworn not to tell anyone, and let's say that 'anyone' is Set A, then Mum and Dad are obviously included in Set A and are of course a subset of it, so there was really no need for Granny to ask Ben to swear a second time.

Take a look at this handy diagram:

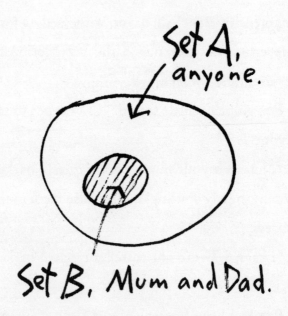

Set A, anyone.

Set B, Mum and Dad.

But Ben didn't think his granny would be interested in Venn diagrams right now. Since she was still staring at him with those scary eyes, he sighed, and said, "All right, I swear not to tell Mum and Dad."

"Good boy," said Granny as her hearing aid began to whistle.

"Erm, on one condition," ventured Ben.

"What's that?" said Granny, seeming a little startled by his nerve.

"You have to tell me everything…"

10

Everything

"I was about your age when I stole my first diamond ring," said Granny.

Ben was astonished; partly at the idea that Granny had ever been his age, which seemed impossible, and partly because of the obvious fact that eleven-year-old girls do not usually steal diamonds. Glitter pens, hairclips, toy ponies maybe, diamonds definitely not.

"I know you look at me with my Scrabble and my knitting and my fondness for cabbage, and think I am just some boring old dear…"

"No…" said Ben, not entirely convincingly.

"But you forget, child, that I was young once."

"What was the first ring you stole?" said Ben eagerly. "Did it have a really big diamond on it?"

The old lady chuckled. "Not so big! No, it was my first one. I've still got it somewhere. Go into the kitchen will you, Ben, and fetch the Silver Jubilee biscuit tin from the shelf."

Ben shrugged as if he knew nothing about the Silver Jubilee biscuit tin, and its incredible contents.

"Whereabouts is it, Granny?" asked Ben as he left the living room.

"Just on top of the larder, boy!" called Granny. "Chop-chop. Your mummy and daddy will be wondering where you are soon." Ben remembered that he had wanted to rush home for Cheesy Beans and Sausage. Suddenly that seemed colossally unimportant. He wasn't even feeling hungry any more.

Ben re-entered the room holding the tin. It was even heavier than he remembered. He passed it to his granny.

"Good boy," she said as she rummaged through the tin, and picked out a particularly beautiful little sparkler.

"Aah, yes, this is it!"

To Ben, all the diamond rings looked pretty much the same. However, Granny seemed to know each of them as if they were her oldest friends. "Such a little beauty," she said as she brought the ring up to her eye for closer inspection. "This is the first one I stole, back when I was a nipper."

Ben couldn't imagine what Granny would have been like young. He had only known her as an old lady. He even imagined she had been born an old lady. That years ago in the hospital when her mother had given birth and asked the midwife if it was a boy or a girl, the midwife might have replied, "It's an old lady!"

"I grew up in a small village, and my family were very poor," continued Granny. "And up at the top of the hill was this grand country house where a Lord and Lady lived. Lord and Lady Davenport. It was just after the war and we didn't have much food in those days. I was hungry, so one night at midnight, when everyone was asleep I crept out of my mother and father's little cottage. Under the cover of darkness, I made my way through the woods and up the hill to Davenport House."

"Weren't you scared?" asked Ben.

"Yes, of course I was. Being alone in the dark woods at night, it was terrifying. There were guard dogs at the house. Great big black Dobermans. So as quietly as I could, I climbed a drainpipe and found an unlocked window. I was a very little girl at eleven, small for my age. So I managed to squeeze myself through a tiny gap in the window, and landed behind a velvet curtain. When I pulled back the curtain I realised I was in Lord and Lady Davenport's bedroom."

"Oh no!" said Ben.

"Oh yes," continued the old lady. "I thought I might just take some food perhaps, but next to the bed I saw this little beauty." She indicated the diamond ring.

"So you just took it?"

"Being an international jewel thief is never that simple, young man," said Granny. "The Lord and Lady were snoring heavily, but if I woke them I'd be dead. The Lord always slept with a shotgun by the bed."

"A shotgun?" asked Ben.

"Yes, he was posh, and being posh he liked hunting pheasants, so he owned many guns."

Ben was sweating with nerves. "But he didn't wake up and try and shoot you, did he?"

"Be patient, young man. All in good time. I crept over to Lady Davenport's side of the bed and picked up the diamond ring. I couldn't believe how beautiful it was. I had never seen one up close before. My mother would never have dreamed of owning one. 'I don't need jewels,' she would say to us children. '*You* are my little diamonds.' I wondered at the diamond in my hand for a moment. It was the most gorgeous thing I had ever seen in my life. Then, suddenly, there was an almighty noise."

Ben frowned. "What was it?"

"Lord Davenport was a big fat greedy man. He must have had too much to eat earlier because he let out the most enormous burp!"

Ben laughed and Granny laughed too. He knew burps weren't supposed to be funny, but couldn't help laughing.

"It was so loud!" said Granny, still chuckling.

"BBBBBBBBBBB BUUUUUUUUUU UUUUUURRRRR RRRRRRRRPPPP PPPPPPPP!!!!!!!!"
she mimicked.

Ben was helpless with laughter now.

"It was so loud," continued Granny, "that I was startled and dropped the ring on the polished wooden floor. It made quite a bang as it hit the teak, and both Lord and Lady Davenport woke up."

"Oh no!"

"Oh yes! So I grabbed the ring and ran back to the open window. I didn't dare look behind me, as I could hear Lord Davenport cocking his shotgun. I leapt down on to the grass, and all of a sudden the lights in the house came on and the dogs were barking and I was running for my life. Then I heard a deafening sound…"

"Another burp?" asked Ben.

"No, a gunshot this time. Lord Davenport was shooting at me as I ran down the hill and back to the woods."

"Then what happened?"

Granny looked at her little gold watch. "My dear, you had better head home. Your mummy and daddy will be worried sick."

"I doubt it," said Ben. "All they care about is stupid ballroom dancing."

"That's not true," said Granny unexpectedly. "You know they love you."

"I want to hear the end of the story," said Ben, frustrated. He was desperate to know what happened next.

"You will. Another day."

"But Granny…"

"Ben, you have to go home."

"That's not fair!"

"Ben, you must leave now. I can tell you what happened when you come another day."

"BUT!"

"To be continued," she said.

11

Cheesy Beans and Sausage

Ben sped home on his bike, not even noticing his burning legs and aching chest. He was going so fast he thought the police might give him a speeding ticket. As the wheels raced round so did his mind.

Could his boring old granny really be a gangsta?!

A Gangsta Granny?!

That must be why she liked books about gangstas so much – she was one!

He slid through the back door just as the familiar *Strictly Stars Dancing* theme tune blasted out from the living room. He had made it home just in time.

But as Ben was about to disappear upstairs and pretend he had been in his bedroom doing his homework, Mum burst into the kitchen.

"What are you doing?" she asked suspiciously. "You look very sweaty."

"Oh, nothing," said Ben, feeling very sweaty.

"Look at you," she continued, as she approached him. "You are sweating like a pig."

Ben had seen a few pigs in his life and none of them had been sweating. In fact, pig fans everywhere will tell you that pigs don't even have sweat glands, so they can't sweat.

Wow, this book is actually really educational.

"I'm not sweating," Ben protested. Being accused of sweating made him sweat even more.

"You *are* sweating. Have you been out running?"

"No," replied a now very sweaty Ben.

"Ben, don't lie to me, I'm your mother," she said, pointing at herself, a false nail flying off into the air in the process.

Her false nails came off a lot. Once Ben had even found one in his microwaveable paella Bolognese.

"If you haven't been out running, Ben, then why are you sweating?"

Ben had to think fast. The *Strictly Stars Dancing* theme tune was coming to an end.

"I was dancing!" he blurted out.

"Dancing?" Mum didn't look convinced. Ben was no Flavio Flavioli. And of course he hated ballroom dancing.

"Yes, well, I have changed my mind about ballroom dancing. I love it!"

"But you said you hated it," shot back an increasingly suspicious Mum. "Many many

many times. Only the other week you said that you would rather 'eat your own bogeys than watch that rubbish'. Hearing you say that was like a dagger through my heart!"

Mum was becoming visibly upset at the memory.

"I'm sorry, Mum, I really am."

Ben reached out a hand to comfort her and another false nail fell on to the floor. "But now I love it, honestly. I was just watching *Strictly* through the crack in the door, and copying all the moves."

Mum beamed with pride. She looked as if her whole life suddenly had meaning. Her face turned strangely happy yet sad, as if this was destiny.

"Do you want to be a..." She took a deep breath, "...professional dancer?"

"Where's my Cheesy Beans and Sausage,

wife?!" called Dad from the living room.

"Shut your face, Pete!" Mum's eyes were wet with tears of joy.

She hadn't cried so much since Flavio was kicked out of the show in week two last year. Flavio had been forced to partner Dame Rachel Prejudice, who was so podgy all he could do was drag her around the floor.

"Well... erm... aah..." Ben desperately searched for a way to get out of this one. "... yeah."

That really wasn't it.

"Yes! I knew it!" cried Mum. "Pete, come in here a moment. Ben has got something he needs to tell you."

Dad trudged in wearily. "What is it, Ben? You're not joining the circus, are you? My word, you are sweaty."

"No, Pete," said Mum, slowly and deliberately

as if she was about to read out the name of a winner at an awards ceremony. "Ben doesn't want to be a silly old plumber any more—"

"Thank goodness for that," said Dad.

"He wants to be…" Mum looked at her son. "Tell him, Ben."

Ben opened his mouth, but before he could say anything Mum chimed in. "Ben wants to be a ballroom dancer!"

"Oh, there is a God!" exclaimed Dad. He looked up at the nicotine-stained ceiling as if he might catch a glimpse of the divine one.

"He was just practising in the kitchen," jabbered Mum excitedly. "Copying all the moves from the show…"

Dad looked into his son's eyes and shook his hand manfully. "That's wonderful news, my boy! Your mum and me haven't achieved much in our lives. What with Mum being a nail polisher—"

"I am a nail technician, Pete!" corrected Mum scornfully. "There is a world of difference, Pete, you do know that…"

"Nail technician. Sorry. And me being just a boring old security guard because I was too fat for the police. The most excitement I've had all year was when I stopped a man in a wheelchair speeding out of the store with a tin of custard concealed under his blanket. But you becoming a ballroom dancer, well… this… this is the greatest thing that's ever happened to us."

"The very greatest!" said Mum.

"The very very greatest," agreed Dad.

"Really it's the very very very greatest," said Mum.

"Let's just agree it's extremely great," said Dad, irritated. "Only, I warn you, boy, it's not going to be easy. If you train eight hours a day every day for the next twenty years, you might just get on the TV show."

"Maybe he can do the American version!" exclaimed Mum. "Oh Pete, just imagine, our boy a huge star in America!"

"Well, let's not jump the gun, wife. He's not won the British one yet. Right now we have to think about entering him for a junior competition."

"You're right, Pete. Gail told me there's one in the town hall just before Christmas."

"Crack open the sparkling wine, wife! Our son is going to be a cha-cha-cha champion!"

A naughty word exploded in Ben's head.

How on earth was he going to get out of this?!

12

The Love Bomb

Ben had spent the whole of Sunday morning being measured up by Mum for his dance outfit. She had stayed up through the night, sketching possible designs.

Under duress, he was forced to choose one, and pointed a limp finger at the one that he thought was the least hideous.

Mum's hand-drawn options ranged all the way from the embarrassing to the humiliating...

There was:

The Woodland

Fruit Cocktail

Thunder and Lightning

Accident and Emergency

Ice and a Slice

The Hedgerow and Badger

The Quality Street

Eggs 'n' Bacon

Confetti

The Underwater World

Burning Love

Cheese & Pickle

The Solar System

Piano Man

But the one that Ben thought was the *least* worst... was the Love Bomb:

"We will have to find you a nice young girl to partner with for the competition!" said Mum, excitedly, as she accidentally ran one of her fake nails under the sewing machine and it exploded.

Ben hadn't thought about dance partners. Not only was he going to have to dance, he was going to have to dance with a girl! And not just any girl, but a revoltingly precocious sparkly fake-tanned leotard-wearing over-made-up one.

Ben was still at the age when he thought girls were as appealing as frogspawn.

"Oh, I'm just going to dance on my own," he spluttered.

"A solo piece!" exclaimed Mum. "How original!"

"In fact, I can't stand here talking all day. I'd better go and practise," said Ben, as he disappeared upstairs to his room. He shut the door, turned on his radio, and then climbed out of the window and raced over to Granny's bungalow on his bike.

"So, you were running off into the woods, when Lord Davenport started shooting at you…" Ben was eagerly prompting his granny.

But for the moment her mind looked blank.

"Was I?" said Granny, looking increasingly befuddled.

"That's where the story ended last night. You said you had snatched the ring from the Davenports' bedroom, and were running across the lawn when you heard shots…"

"Oh yes, yes," muttered Granny, her face suddenly illuminated.

Ben smiled broadly. He suddenly remembered how he had used to love his granny telling stories when he was younger, transporting him to a magical world. A world where you paint pictures in your mind that are more thrilling than all the movies or TV shows or video games in the universe.

Only a couple of weeks ago he had pretended to be asleep to stop her telling him a bedtime story. Clearly he'd forgotten how thrilling stories could be.

"I was running and running," continued Granny breathlessly, as if she was actually running, "and I heard a shot ring out. Then another. I knew from the sound that it was definitely a shotgun rather than a rifle—"

"What's the difference?" asked Ben.

"Well, a rifle shoots one bullet and is more accurate. But a shotgun sprays hundreds of little deadly balls of lead. Any idiot can hit you if they fire a shotgun in your direction."

"And did he?" said Ben. His smile had faded now. He was genuinely worried.

"Yes, but luckily I was far away by then so I was only grazed. I could hear the dogs barking too. They were hunting me; and I was only a small girl. If they had caught me, the hounds would have ripped me to shreds..."

Ben gasped in horror. "So how did you get away?" he asked.

"I took a chance. I couldn't outrun the dogs through the forest. The fastest runner in the world couldn't. But I knew the woods really well. I used to play in them for hours with my brothers and sisters. I knew if I could just get across the stream, then the dogs would lose the scent."

"How come?"

"Dogs can't follow a scent across water. And there was a great oak tree just on the other side of the stream. If I climbed that tree, I might be safe."

Ben couldn't imagine his granny climbing stairs, let alone a tree. She had lived in her bungalow ever since he could remember.

"More shots rang out through the darkness as I ran towards the stream," continued the old lady. "And I stumbled in the gloom of the forest. I tripped on a tree root and fell face first in the mud. Scrambling to my feet, I turned round to see an army of men on horseback led by Lord

Davenport. They were carrying flaming torches and holding shotguns. The whole forest was lit up with the fire from the torches. I jumped into the stream. It was around this time of year; in the depth of winter and the water was icy. The cold shocked me and I could hardly breathe. I clapped my hand over my mouth to stifle a scream. I could hear the dogs getting nearer and nearer, barking and barking. There must have been dozens of them. I looked behind me and I could see their sharp teeth gleaming in the moonlight.

"So I waded across the stream and started climbing the tree. My hands were muddy, and my legs and feet were wet, and I kept slipping down the trunk. I frantically rubbed my hands on my nightshirt and began to climb again. I scrambled to the very top of the tree and stayed as still as I could. I heard the dogs and the army of Davenport's men follow the stream down to a different part of the forest. The dogs' ferocious barks became distant and after a while the torches were just specks in the distance. I was safe. I shivered up that tree for hours. I waited until dawn, slid down the tree, and made my way back to our cottage. I crept into bed and lay there for a few moments before the sun rose."

Ben could picture everything she described perfectly in his mind. Granny had him utterly spellbound.

"Did they come looking for you?" he asked.

"Well, no one got a good enough look at me, so Davenport had his men search everywhere in the village. Every cottage was turned upside down to look for the ring."

"Didn't you say anything?"

"I wanted to. I felt so guilty. But I knew if I owned up I would be in deep trouble. Lord Davenport would have had me publicly flogged in the village square."

"So what did you do?"

"I... swallowed it."

Ben couldn't believe his ears. "The ring, Granny? You swallowed the ring?"

"I thought it was the best way to hide it. In my stomach. A few days later it came out when I went to the toilet."

"That must have been painful!" said Ben, his bum wincing at the thought. Passing a big diamond ring out of his bottom didn't sound in any way enjoyable.

"It was painful. Excruciating, in fact." Granny grimaced. "The good thing was that our cottage had been searched already from top to bottom – not *my* bottom – the bottom of the cottage, I mean…" Ben chuckled. "…and Davenport's men had moved on to searching the next village. So one night I went off into the woods and hid the ring. I placed it where no one would ever look; under a rock in the stream."

"Clever!" said Ben.

"But that ring was only the first of many, Ben. Stealing it had been the biggest thrill of my life. And as I lay in bed each night, all I dreamed about was stealing more and more diamonds. That ring was just the beginning…" continued Granny in a low whisper, staring deep into Ben's innocent young eyes, "…of a lifetime of crime."

13

A Lifetime of Crime

Hours passed in what seemed like minutes, as Granny told her grandson how she had stolen every one of the dazzling items spread out on the living-room floor.

The huge tiara had belonged to the wife of the President of the United States of America, the First Lady. Granny told Ben how, over fifty years earlier, she had sailed all the way to America on a cruise liner to steal it from the White House in Washington. And that whilst sailing back home she had robbed every rich lady on the ship of her jewels! How she was caught red-handed by

the captain of the ship and escaped by diving
overboard and swimming the last few miles of
the Atlantic Ocean back to England with all of
the jewellery hidden in her knickers.

Granny told Ben that the sparkling emerald earrings that had been in her little bungalow for decades were worth over a million pounds each. They had once belonged to the wife of an enormously wealthy Indian maharajah; a maharani. The old lady recounted how she enlisted the help of a herd of elephants to steal them. She had coaxed the elephants to stand on top of each other to form a giant ladder so she could scale the wall of the fort in India where the earrings were kept in the royal bedchamber.

The most amazing tale of all was of how she stole the enormous deep blue diamond and sapphire brooch that sat sparkling on her worn living-room carpet. She told Ben that it had once belonged to the last Empress of Russia, who ruled with her husband the Tsar before the communist revolution of 1917. It had for many years been under bulletproof glass at the Hermitage museum in St Petersburg, guarded twenty-four hours a day, seven days a week, three hundred and sixty-five days a year by a platoon of fearsome Russian soldiers.

This theft had required the most elaborate plan of all. Granny had hidden in an ancient suit of armour in the museum, which dated back hundreds of years to the time of Catherine the Great. Each time the soldiers looked the other way, she would edge forward in the metal suit a few millimetres, until she got close enough to the brooch. It took her a week.

"What, like Granny's Footsteps?" asked Ben.

"Exactly, young man!" she replied. "Then I smashed the glass with the silver axe I was holding and grabbed the brooch."

"How did you escape, Granny?"

"That's a good question... now, how did I escape?" Granny looked flummoxed. "Sorry, it's my age, boy. I forget things."

Ben smiled supportively. "That's OK, Granny."

Soon the old lady's memory seemed to come

back into focus. "Oh yes, I remember," she continued. "I ran outside into the courtyard of the museum, leapt into the barrel of a huge cannon and then fired myself to safety!"

Ben pictured this for a moment: his granny, in deepest darkest Russia, flying through the air in an ancient suit of armour. It was hard to believe, but how else could this little old lady come to have such an astonishing collection of priceless gems?

Ben loved Granny's daring tales. At home, Ben had never had stories read or told to him. His parents always just switched on the television and slumped down on the sofa when they got home from work. Hearing the old lady talk was so exciting Ben wished he could move in with her. He could listen to Granny all day.

"There can't be a jewel in the world you haven't stolen!" said Ben.

"Oh yes there is, young man. Hang on, what's that?"

"What's what?" said Ben.

Granny was pointing behind Ben's head, an expression of horror on her face. "It's... It's..."

"*What*?" said Ben, not daring to turn around and see what she was pointing at. A shiver ran down his spine.

"Whatever you do," said Granny, "don't turn round..."

14

Nosy Neighbour

Ben couldn't help himself, and his eyes darted towards the window. For a brief moment he saw a dark figure wearing a strange hat peer through the dirty glass, and then quickly disappear out of view.

"There was a man peering in at the window," said Ben breathlessly.

"I know," said Granny. "I told you not to look."

"Shall I go out and see who it was?" said Ben, trying to hide the fact that he was more than a little frightened. Really, he wanted Granny to go out and see who it was.

"I bet it was my nosy neighbour, Mr Parker. He lives at number seven, he always wears a pork-pie hat, and he keeps spying on me."

"Why?" asked Ben.

Granny shrugged. "I don't know. I imagine he has a rather cold head, or something."

"What?" said Ben. "Oh. No, not his hat. I mean, why does he keep spying on you?"

"He's a retired Major, and now he runs the Neighbourhood Watch scheme in Grey Close."

"What's Neighbourhood Watch?" asked Ben.

"It's a group of local people who keep an eye out for burglars. But Mr Parker just uses it as an excuse to spy on everyone, the nosy old git. I often come back from the supermarket with my bag of cabbages and see he's hiding behind his net curtains spying on me with a pair of binoculars."

"Is he suspicious about you?" said Ben, more than a little panicked. He didn't want to be thrown in jail for aiding and abetting a criminal. He didn't really know what 'abetting' meant, actually, but he knew it was a crime, and he knew he was too young for prison.

"He is suspicious about everyone. We have to keep an eye out for him, young lad. The man is a menace."

Ben went over to the window and peered out. He couldn't see anyone.

BBBBBRRRRRRRRRIIIIIIIIIINNNNN NNNGGGGGGGGGGGGG!!!!!!!!!!!!!!!!!!!!!!

Ben's heart missed a beat. It was only the doorbell, but if they let Mr Parker inside he would see all the evidence the police would need to send Ben and his granny straight to prison.

"Don't answer it!" said Ben, as he ran to

the middle of the room and started stuffing all the jewels back in the tin, as quickly as he could.

"What do you mean, don't answer it?! He knows I am at home. He just saw us through the window. You answer the door and I will hide the jewels."

"Me?"

"Yes you! Hurry!"

BBBBBBBBBBBRRRRRRRRRRRRIIIIIIIII IIIIINNNNNNNNNNNNNNGGGGGGGG GGGG!!!

This ring was more insistent. Mr Parker had left his finger on the buzzer for even longer. Ben took a deep breath and walked calmly through the hall to the front door.

He opened it.

Outside stood a man in a very silly hat. Don't believe me? This is how silly his hat was:

"Yes?" said Ben in a squeaky high voice. "Can I help you?"

Mr Parker put his foot inside the bungalow so the front door couldn't be closed on him.

"Who are you?" he barked, nasally.

He had a very big nose, which made him

seem even nosier than he was, and he already seemed extremely nosy. Because he had a big nose he also had a very nasal voice, which made everything he said, however serious, seem a little bit absurd. But his eyes shone red like a demon.

"I am Granny's friend," spluttered Ben. *Why did I say that?* he thought. In truth, he was in a terrible panic, and his tongue was running away with him.

"Friend?" snarled Mr Parker, pushing open the front door. He was stronger than Ben, and soon forced his way inside.

"I mean grandson, Mr Parker, sir..." said Ben, retreating back towards the living room.

"Why are you lying to me?" he said, taking several paces forward as Ben took several paces back. It was if they were dancing the tango.

"I am not lying!" cried Ben.

They reached the living-room door.

"You can't go in there!" yelled Ben, thinking of the jewels still scattered all over the carpet.

"Why not?"

"Erm… umm… Because Granny is doing her naked yoga!"

Ben needed a dramatic excuse to stop Mr Parker barging through the door and seeing the jewels. He was pretty sure he had hit the jackpot as Mr Parker paused and furrowed his brow.

Sadly, the nosy neighbour was not convinced.

"Naked yoga?! A likely story! I need to talk to your grandmother right away. Now get out of my way, you nasty little worm of a boy!" he said as he shoved the boy aside and opened the living-room door.

Granny must have heard Ben through the door because when Mr Parker burst into the room she was standing in her bra and knickers in a tree pose.

"Mr Parker, do you mind?" said Granny, in mock horror that he had seen her in a state of undress.

Mr Parker's eyes spun around the room. He didn't know where to look, so he fixed his glare on the now bare carpet. "Excuse me, Madam, but I need to ask you, where are those jewels I saw a moment ago?"

Ben spied the Silver Jubilee biscuit tin poking out from behind the sofa. Surreptitiously he edged it out of view with his foot.

"What jewels, Mr Parker? Have you been spying on me again?" demanded Granny, still in her underwear.

"Well, I, err…" he spluttered. "I had good reason. I was suspicious when I saw a young gentleman enter your property. I thought he might be a burglar."

"I let him in through the front door."

"He might have been a very charming burglar. He might have weaselled his way into your confidence."

"He's my grandson. He stays every Friday night."

"Ah!" said Mr Parker, triumphantly. "But it's not Friday night! So you can see why my suspicions were raised. And as head of Grey Close's Neighbourhood Watch I must report anything suspicious I see to the police."

"I've got a good mind to report you to the police, Mr Parker!" said Ben.

Granny looked at him curiously.

"Whatever for?" said the man. His eyes narrowed. They were now so red it was like there was a fire in his brain.

"For spying on old ladies in their underwear!" said Ben triumphantly. Granny winked at Ben.

"She was fully clothed when I looked through the window…" protested Mr Parker.

"That's what they all say!" said Granny. "Now get out of my house before you are arrested for being a Peeping Tom!"

"You've not heard the last of me. Good day!" said Mr Parker. With that, he spun on his heels and left the room. Granny and Ben heard the front door slam behind him and they ran over to the window and watched him scuttle back to his bungalow.

"I think we frightened him off," said Ben.

"But he'll be back," said Granny. "We have to be very careful."

"Yes," said Ben, more than a little alarmed. "We'd better hide this tin somewhere else."

Granny thought for a moment. "Yes, I'll put it under the floorboards."

"OK," said Ben. "But first…"

"Yes, Ben?"

"You might want to get dressed."

15

Reckless and Thrilling

When Granny had put her clothes back on, she and Ben sat down on the sofa.

"Granny, before Mr Parker turned up you were telling me there was one jewel that you never stole," Ben whispered.

"There is something quite special that every great thief in the world would love to get their hands on. But it's impossible. It just can't be done."

"I bet you could do it, Granny. You're the greatest thief the world has ever known."

"Thank you, Ben, perhaps I am, or rather

was... and stealing these particular jewels might be every great thief's dream, but it would just be, well... impossible."

"Jewels? There's more than one?"

"Yes, my dear. The last time anyone tried to steal them was three hundred years ago. A Captain Blood I believe. And I am not sure the Queen would be pleased..." She chuckled.

"You don't mean...?"

"*The Crown Jewels*, yes, my boy."

Ben had learned about the Crown Jewels in a history lesson at school. History was one of the few subjects he liked, mainly because of all the gory punishments they used to have in the olden days. 'Hanged, drawn and quartered' was his absolute favourite, but he also liked the breaking wheel, being burned at the stake, and of course a red-hot poker up the bum.

Who doesn't?

At school, Ben had learned that the Crown Jewels were in fact a set of crowns, swords, sceptres, rings, bracelets and orbs, some of which were nearly a thousand years old. They were used when a new king or queen was crowned, and since 1303 (the year, not the time), they had been kept under lock and key in the Tower of London.

Ben had begged his parents to take him to see them, but they had moaned that London was too far away (even though it wasn't that far).

To be honest, they never really went anywhere as a family. When he was younger, Ben used to listen in silent wonder to his classmates, as they recounted their myriad adventures in 'show and tell'. Trips to the seaside, visits to museums, even holidays abroad. The knot in his stomach would tighten when his turn came. He was too embarrassed to admit that all he had done during the holidays was eat microwaveable meals and watch TV, so he would make up stories about flying kites and climbing trees and exploring castles.

But now he had the greatest 'show and tell' of all time. His granny was an international jewel thief. A gangsta! Except if he showed or told this, the old dear would be put in prison and they would throw away the key.

Ben realised that this was his big chance to do something crazy and reckless and thrilling.

"I can help you," said Ben in a cool and calm manner, though his heart was beating faster than ever.

"Help me do what?" replied the old lady, a little befuddled.

"Steal the Crown Jewels, of course!" said Ben.

16

'N' 'O' Spells 'NO'

"No!" shouted Granny as her hearing aid began whistling furiously.

"Yes!" shouted Ben.

"No!"

"Yes!"

"Nooo!"

"Yeeees!"

"NOOOOOOOOOOOOOOOOOOOO OOOOOOOOOOOOO!"

"YEEEEEEEEEEEEEEEEEEEEEEEEE EEEEEEEEEES!"

This went on for a few minutes, but to save

paper and therefore the trees and therefore the forests and therefore the environment and therefore the world I have tried to keep it short.

"There is absolutely no way I am letting a boy of your age come on a heist with me! Especially not to steal the Crown Jewels! And most important of all it's impossible! It can't be done!" exclaimed Granny.

"There must be a way…" pleaded Ben.

"Ben, I said 'no' and that's final!"

"But—"

"No buts, Ben. No. 'N' and 'O' spells 'no'."

Ben was bitterly disappointed, but the lady was not for turning. "I'd better go then," he said, despondently.

Granny looked a little downcast too. "Yes dear, you'd better, your mummy and daddy will be very worried about you."

"They won't be—"

"Ben! Home! Now!"

Ben was sad to see that Granny was becoming like one of the boring grown-ups again, just when she'd started to become interesting. Still, he did what she said. Apart from anything else, he didn't want to make his parents suspicious, so he raced home and climbed up the drainpipe to his bedroom window, before rushing downstairs to the living room.

Unsurprisingly, though, Mum and Dad hadn't been worried about where Ben was at all. They had been too busy planning their son's rise to dancing superstardom to notice he was gone.

Dad had been calling and calling the national under-twelve dance competition hotline until finally he got through and secured his son a place. Mum was right, the competition was at the town hall in just a couple of weeks' time. There was no time to lose, so Mum had been working every waking moment on her son's Love Bomb outfit.

"How's the rehearsals going, boy?" asked Dad. "You look like you've worked up quite a sweat."

"Fine, thank you, Dad," lied Ben. "I really am getting something really spectacular together for the big night."

Ben cursed his runaway mouth.

Something spectacular?

He'd be lucky if he didn't fall over and knock himself out.

"Well, we can't wait to see it! Not long to go!" said Mum, not even looking up from the sewing machine, as she stitched a row of hundreds of sparkling red hearts down the side of his Lycra trousers.

"I'd kind of like to practise on my own for now, Mum, you know..." Ben gulped nervously. "Until it's completely ready to show you."

"Yes, yes, we understand," said Mum.

Ben sighed with relief. He had bought himself a bit more time.

But only a little bit.

In a couple of weeks Ben was still going to have to perform a solo dance routine for the whole town.

He sat on his bed, and reached underneath it for his stash of *Plumbing Weeklys*. Flicking through an issue from the previous year, he saw that it contained a feature entitled 'A Short History of Plumbing', that focused on some of London's oldest sewage pipes. Ben frantically turned the pages to find it.

Eureka! There it was.

Hundreds of years ago the River Thames,

on the banks of which the Tower of London is situated, had been an open sewer. (Technically speaking, that means there was a lot of wee and poo in it.)

Buildings along the riverside simply had big pipes leading from their toilets straight into the river. In the magazine were detailed historical diagrams of various famous buildings in London, showing where their old sewage pipes connected to the river.

And...

Ben's finger ran down the article...

Yes! A chart of the sewer pipes at the Tower of London.

This could be the key to stealing the Crown Jewels. One pipe was nearly a metre wide, big enough for a child to swim up. And maybe big enough for a little old lady too!

The article also said that, when the plumbing

systems were modernised and proper sewers installed a lot of the old pipes were simply left where they were, because it was simpler than digging them up.

Ben's head spun as he thought about what this meant. It was possible – just possible – that there was still a huge pipe leading from the Thames into the Tower of London, and that most people, apart from very keen plumbing enthusiasts, had forgotten it was there. Ben wouldn't have known himself, if he hadn't been a long-term subscriber to *Plumbing Weekly*.

He and Granny could swim up that pipe, and get into the Tower…

Mum and Dad were wrong! he thought. *Plumbing can be exciting.*

Of course, it was a sewage pipe, which wasn't ideal, but any poo and wee still in it would be hundreds of years old.

Ben didn't know if that was a good or bad thing.

At that moment, he heard a creak in the floorboards and his bedroom door flew open. His mum burst in holding a big piece of Lycra that looked ominously like his 'Love Bomb' outfit.

Ben quickly concealed the magazine under his bed, which made him look incredibly guilty.

"I was just going to get you to try this on," said Mum.

"Oh yes," said Ben, as he sat on his bed awkwardly, his heels pushing the remaining *Plumbing Weeklys* out of sight of Mum's prying eyes.

"What's that?" she said. "What did you hide when I came in? Is that a rude magazine?"

"No," said Ben, swallowing his guilt. This looked way worse than it was. It looked like he was hiding a naughty magazine under the bed.

"It's nothing to be ashamed of, Ben. I think it's healthy you are expressing an interest in girls."

Oh no! thought Ben. *My mum's going to talk to me about girls!*

"There's nothing embarrassing about being interested in girls, Ben."

"Yes there is! Girls are gross!"

"No, Ben, it's the most natural thing in the world…"

She's just not stopping!

"THE DINNER IS NEARLY READY, LOVE!" came a shout from downstairs. "WHAT ARE YOU DOING UP THERE?"

"I AM TALKING TO BEN ABOUT GIRLS!" Mum shouted back.

Ben was so red that if he opened his mouth wide enough he might be mistaken for a postbox.

"WHAT?" cried Dad.

"GIRLS!" shouted Mum. "I AM TALKING TO OUR SON ABOUT GIRLS!"

"OH, RIGHT!" Dad shouted back. "I'LL TURN THE OVEN OFF."

"So, Ben, if you ever need to—"

BRING BRING. BRING BRING.

It was Mum's mobile phone going off in her pocket.

"Sorry dear," she said, placing the handset to her ear. "Gail, can I call you back? I am just talking to Ben about girls. OK, thanks, bub-bye."

She hung up the phone and turned to Ben.

"Sorry, where was I? Oh yes, if you ever need to have a little chat with me about girls, then please do. You can trust me to be very discreet..."

17

Planning the Heist

For the first time in his life, Ben skipped to school the following morning.

Through his love of plumbing, the previous night he had discovered that the Tower of London had a weakness. The most impregnable building in the world, where some of the country's most dangerous criminals had been imprisoned and executed, had a fatal flaw; a large sewage pipe that led directly into the River Thames.

That ancient tube would be his and Granny's way in and out of the Tower! It was a quite brilliant plan, and Ben's body couldn't hide its excitement at this amazing discovery.

That's why he was skipping.

Now he couldn't wait until Friday night when his mum and dad would once again pack him off to Granny's.

Then he would be able to convince the old lady that together they really could steal the Crown Jewels. Ben would bring along the diagram in *Plumbing Weekly* of the Tower of London's sewage system to show her. The two of them could stay up all night and work out every detail of the most daring robbery of all time.

The problem was that a whole fat week of lessons and teachers and homework stood between now and Friday night. However, Ben was determined to use the week at school wisely.

In his IT lesson, he looked up the Crown

Jewels and memorised every detail on the web page.

In History, he asked his teacher questions about the Tower of London and exactly where in the building the jewels were kept. (That would be the Jewel House, fact fans.)

In Geography, he found an atlas of the British Isles and pinpointed precisely where on the Thames the Tower is situated.

In PE, he didn't accidentally on purpose forget his kit like usual, instead he did extra press-ups so his arms would be strong enough to pull himself up the sewage pipe that led into the Tower.

In Maths, he asked the teacher how many packets of Rolos you could buy with five billion pounds (which is what the Crown Jewels were said to be worth). Rolos were Ben's absolute favourite sweets.

The answer is ten billion packets, or twenty-four billion actual Rolos. That's enough for a year at least.

And Raj was sure to throw in a few extra packets for free.

In his French class, Ben learned how to say, "I know nothing about the theft of, how you say, 'the Crown Jewels', I am but a poor French peasant boy", in case he needed to pretend he was a poor French peasant boy in order to escape from the scene of the crime.

In Spanish he learned to say, "I know nothing about, how you say, 'the Crown Jewels', I am but a poor Spanish peasant boy", in case he needed to pretend he was a poor Spanish peasant boy in order to escape from the scene of the crime.

In German he learned to say… well, I'm sure you get the idea.

In Science, Ben quizzed his teacher about how

you might be able to penetrate bulletproof glass. Even if you got into Jewel House, removing the jewels was not going to be easy, as they were kept behind glass that was inches thick.

In his Art class, he made a detailed scale model of the Tower of London out of matches so he could role play the daring robbery in miniature.

The week absolutely flew by, never had school been so much fun. Most importantly, for the first time in his life Ben couldn't wait to spend time with his granny.

By the end of school on Friday afternoon, Ben felt he had all the data he needed to put the daring plan into place.

The story of the theft of the Crown Jewels would be on the TV news for weeks, on every website, and emblazoned across every front page of every newspaper in every country in the world. However, no one, but no one, would suspect that the thieves were in fact a little old lady and an eleven-year-old boy. They were going to get away with the crime of the century!

18

Visiting Hours

"You can't stay with Granny tonight," said Dad. It was four o'clock on Friday afternoon, and Ben had just got home from school. It was strange that Dad was home so early. He usually didn't finish his shift at the supermarket until eight.

"Why not?" asked Ben, noticing his dad's face was dark with worry.

"I'm afraid I've got some bad news, son."

"What?" demanded Ben, his face darkening with worry too.

"Granny's in hospital."

*

A little while later, once they'd finally found a parking space, Ben and his parents went through the automatic doors of the hospital. Ben wondered if Mum and Dad were ever going to find Granny in here. The hospital was impossibly tall and wide, a great monument to illness.

There were lifts that took you to other lifts.

Mile-long corridors.

Signs everywhere that Ben couldn't comprehend:

CORONARY CARE UNIT
RADIOLOGY
OBSTETRICS
CLINICAL DECISION UNIT
MRI SCANNING ROOM

Confused-looking patients on trolleys or in wheelchairs were being wheeled up and down by porters, as doctors and nurses who looked like they hadn't been to bed for days, hurried past them.

When they finally found the wing Granny was in, right up on the nineteenth floor, Ben didn't recognise her at first.

Her hair was flat on her head, she didn't have her glasses on or her teeth in, and she was wearing not her own clothes, but a standard issue NHS nightgown. It was as if all of the things that made her Granny had been taken from her, and she was now just a shell.

Ben felt so sad to see her like this, but tried to hide it. He didn't want to upset her.

"Hello, dears," she said. Her voice was croaky, and her speech a little slurred. Ben had to take a deep breath to stop from bursting into tears.

"How are you feeling, Mum?" asked Ben's dad.

"Not too clever," she replied. "I had a fall."

"A fall?" said Ben.

"Yes. I don't remember much about it. One moment I was reaching in the larder for a tin of cabbage soup, the next thing I knew I was lying on the lino staring at the ceiling. My cousin Edna called me a number of times from her nursing home. When she couldn't get an answer, she called an ambulance."

"When did you fall over, Granny?" asked Ben.

"Let me think, I was lying on the kitchen floor for two days, so it must have been Wednesday morning. I couldn't get up to reach the telephone."

"I am so sorry, Mum," said Dad quietly. Ben had never seen his father look so upset.

"It's funny, because I meant to call you on Wednesday, you know just for a chat, to see how you are," said Mum, lying. She had never called the old lady in her life, and if Granny ever called the house Mum couldn't get off the phone quick enough.

"You weren't to know, my dear," said Granny. "They did all kinds of tests this morning to see what's wrong with me; X-rays and scans and the like. I'll get the results tomorrow. Hopefully I won't be in here too long."

"I hope so too," said Ben.

There was an uncomfortable silence.

No one quite knew what to say or do.

Mum hesitantly nudged Dad and mimed looking at her watch.

Ben knew hospitals made her uncomfortable. When he'd had his appendix out two years before she had only visited him a couple of times, and even then it had made her sweat and fidget.

"Well, we'd better be off," said Dad.

"Yes, yes, you go," said Granny, with lightness in her voice but sadness in her eyes. "Don't you worry about me, I'll be fine."

"Can't we stay a bit longer?" piped up Ben.

Mum shot him an anguished look, which Dad clocked.

"No, come along, Ben, your granny will need to go to sleep in a few hours," said Dad, as he stood up and readied himself to leave. "I'm quite busy, Mum, but I'll try and pop in over the weekend."

He patted his mother on the head, like one might a dog. It was an awkward gesture; Dad wasn't a hugger.

He turned to go, Mum smiled weakly, and

then pulled a reluctant Ben across the ward by his wrist.

Up in his bedroom, later that evening, Ben determinedly sorted all the information he'd gathered from school that week.

We'll show them, Granny, he thought fiercely. *I'm going to do it for you.* Now Granny was ill he was more determined to do it than ever.

He had until tea time to plan the greatest jewel theft in history.

19

A Small Explosive Device

The next morning, as Mum and Dad went through song after song to select some music for their son's upcoming dance competition, Ben sneaked out of the house and cycled to the hospital.

When he finally found Granny's ward, he saw that there was a bespectacled doctor perched on her bed. Nevertheless, he raced over excitedly to see the old lady, so he could share the plan with her.

The doctor was holding Granny's hand and talking to her slowly and quietly.

"Just give us a moment alone please, Ben," said Granny. "The doctor and I are just talking about, you know, lady things."

"Oh, er, OK," said Ben. He sloped back to the swing doors, and leafed through a sickly-looking copy of *Take a Break*.

The doctor passed him and said, "I'm sorry" before leaving the ward.

Sorry? thought Ben. *Why is he sorry?*

And he walked tentatively over to his granny's bed.

Granny was dabbing at her eyes with a tissue, and when she saw Ben approach she stopped and shoved it back up the sleeve of her nightdress.

"Are you OK, Granny?" he asked softly.

"Yes, I'm fine. I just have something in my eye."

"Then why did the doctor say 'I'm sorry' to me?"

Granny looked flustered for a moment.

"Erm, well, I imagine he was sorry that he wasted your time in coming here. There is absolutely nothing wrong with me, as it turns out."

"Really?"

"Yes, the doctor gave me the test results. I'm as fit as a butcher's dog."

Ben hadn't heard that expression before, but he imagined it must mean very, very fit.

"That's brilliant news, Granny," exclaimed Ben. "Now, I know you said 'no' before—"

"Is this what I think it is, Ben?" asked Granny.

Ben nodded.

"I said 'no' a hundred times."

"Yes, but—"

"But what, young man?"

"I've found a weakness in the Tower of London. And I have spent all week working on a plan of how we can steal the jewels. I think we can really do it."

To his surprise, Granny looked intrigued. "Pull the curtains and keep your voice down," hissed the old lady, flicking the switch on her hearing aid to full power.

Ben quickly pulled the curtains around Granny's bed, and then sat down next to her.

"So, at the stroke of midnight we swim across the Thames in scuba-diving gear, and locate the ancient sewage pipe, here," whispered Ben, showing her the detailed diagram in the back issue of *Plumbing Weekly*.

"We have to swim up a sewage pipe?! At my age!" said Granny. "Don't be daft, boy!"

"Shush, keep your voice down," said Ben.

"Sorry," whispered Granny.

"And it's not daft. It's brilliant. The pipe is just wide enough, look here…"

Granny lifted herself up from her pillows and moved closer to the page in *Plumbing Weekly*. She studied the diagram. It did indeed look wide enough.

"Now, if we swim up the pipe we can get inside the Tower undetected," continued Ben. "Everywhere else around the perimeter of the building there are armed guards and security cameras and laser sensors. Take any other route in and we wouldn't stand a chance."

"Yes yes yes, but then how the blazes do we get into Jewel House where the jewels are kept?" she whispered.

"The sewage pipe ends here at the privy."

"I beg your pardon?"

"The privy. It's an old word for toilet."

"Oh yes, so it is."

"From the privy it's a short run—"

"Ahem!"

"Er, I mean a short *walk* across the courtyard to Jewel House. At night the door to the house is of course locked and double locked."

"Probably triple locked!" Granny didn't seem

that convinced. Well, Ben would just have to convince her!

"The door is solid steel, so we'll drill out the locks to open it—"

"But the crowns and the sceptres and all that gubbins must surely be kept behind bulletproof glass, Ben," said Granny.

"Yes, but the glass isn't bomb proof. We'll set off a small explosive device to shatter the glass."

"An explosive device?!" spluttered Granny. "Where on earth are we going to get that from?"

"I swiped a few chemicals from Science class," replied Ben with a smirk. "I am pretty sure I can create an explosion big enough to get through that glass."

"But the guards will hear the explosion, Ben. No, no, no. I'm sorry, that's never going to work!" exclaimed Granny as quietly as she could.

"Well, I thought of that," said Ben, momentarily delighted with his own ingenuity. "You need to board a train to London earlier that day, posing as a sweet old lady—"

"I *am* a sweet old lady!" protested Granny.

"You know what I mean," continued Ben with a smile. "From the station you take the number seventy-eight bus, all the way to the Tower of London. Then you give the Beefeater guards chocolate cake with something in it to make them sleep."

"Oh, I could use my special herbal sleeping tonic!" said Granny.

"Er, yes, fantastic," said Ben. "So, the guards eat the chocolate cake, and by night-time they will be fast asleep."

"Chocolate cake?" protested Granny. "Surely the guards would prefer some of my delicious homemade cabbage cake*."

*Granny's recipe for CABBAGE CAKE:

Take six large mouldy cabbages

Mash up the cabbages with your

potato masher

Put the cabbage mush into a baking tray

Bake in the oven until your whole house

smells of cabbage

Wait a month for the cake to go stale

Slice and serve (sick bucket optional)

"Erm," Ben squirmed.

He didn't want to upset Granny, but there was no way anyone would eat a piece of Granny's cabbage cake unless they were intimately related to her, and even then they would probably spit it out when she wasn't looking.

"I think a chocolate cake from the supermarket would be better."

"Well, you seem to have thought of everything. I'm very impressed, you know. The idea of using that old pipe is genius."

Ben flushed with pride. "Thanks."

"But how did you know about it? They don't teach you that stuff at school do they, about sewage pipes and that?"

"No," said Ben. "It's just... I've always loved plumbing. I remembered the old pipes being in my favourite magazine." He held up *Plumbing Weekly*. "It's my dream to be a plumber one day."

He looked down, expecting Granny to tell him off or mock him.

"Why are you looking at the ground?" asked Granny.

"Um… Well, I know it's silly and boring to want to be a plumber. I know I should want to do something more interesting." Ben felt his face turn burning red.

Granny put a hand on his chin and gently tilted his head up. "Nothing you did could ever be silly or boring, Ben," she said. "If you want to be a plumber, and it's your dream, then no one can take it away from you. Do you understand? All you can do in this life is follow your dreams. Otherwise you're just wasting your time."

"I… I guess."

"I should hope so. Honestly! You say that plumbing is boring, but here you are, planning to steal the Crown Jewels, for goodness sake… and it's all down to plumbing!"

Ben smiled. Maybe Granny was right.

"But I have a question for you, Ben."

"Yes?"

"How do we escape? A plan like this is no good if you are going to get caught red-handed, my lad."

"I know that, Granny, so I thought we should go out the way we came in, through the sewage pipe, and swim back across the Thames. It's only fifty metres wide, and I've got my hundred-metre swimming badge. It will be a doddle."

Granny bit her lip. She obviously wasn't sure that any of this would be a doddle, not least swimming across a fast flowing river at night.

Ben looked at her with hope in his eyes.

"Well Granny, are you in? Are you still a gangsta?"

She looked deep in thought for quite a while.

"Please?" pleaded Ben. "I've loved hearing all about your adventures, and I really want to go on a heist with you. And this would be the ultimate: stealing the Crown Jewels. You said yourself it was every great thief's dream. Well, Granny? Are you in?"

Granny looked at her grandson's glowing face. After a while she murmured, "Yes."

Ben leaped from his chair and hugged her. "Brilliant!"

Granny lifted her weak arms and embraced him. It was the first time in years she had really hugged him.

"But I have one condition," said the old lady with a deadly serious look in her eyes.

"What?" whispered Ben.

"We put them back the next night."

20

Boom Boom Boom

Ben couldn't believe what Granny had just said. There was no way he would risk stealing the Crown Jewels only to put them back the very next night.

"But they are worth millions, billions even…" he complained.

"I know. So we'd definitely get caught if we tried to sell them," replied Granny.

"But…!"

"No 'buts', boy. We put them back the next night. Do you know how I evaded prison all these years? I never sold a thing. I just did it for the buzz."

"But you kept them, though," said Ben. "Even if you didn't sell them. You've got all those jewels in your biscuit tin."

Granny blinked. "Yes, well, I was young and foolish then," she said. "I have learned since that it is wrong to steal. And you need to understand that too." She gave him a fierce look.

Ben squirmed. "I do, of course I do…"

"It's a brilliant plan you've put together, Ben, honestly it is. But those jewels don't belong to us, do they?"

"No," said Ben. "No, they don't." He felt a tiny bit ashamed now that he'd been so horrified at the idea of giving back the jewels.

"And don't forget that every policeman in the country, maybe even the world will be looking for the Crown Jewels. They'll have all of Scotland Yard after us. If we were found with them we'd be thrown into prison for the rest of our lives. That might not be so long for me, but for you it could be seventy or eighty years."

"You're right," said Ben.

"And the Queen seems like such a nice old dear. We are around the same age actually. I would hate to upset her."

"Me too," murmured Ben. He had seen the Queen on the news loads of times and she seemed like a nice old lady, smiling and waving at everybody from the back of her giant pram.

"Let's just do it for the thrill. Agreed?"

"Agreed!" said Ben. "When can we do it? It will have to be a Friday night when Mum and Dad take me to stay at yours. Did the doctor say when you'll be out of hospital?"

"Erm, oh yes, he did, he said I could leave any time."

"Fantastic!"

"But we need to do it very soon. How about next Friday?"

"Isn't that too soon?"

"Not at all, your plan seems very well thought out, Ben."

"Thank you," said Ben beaming. It was the first time ever that he felt like he had made a grown-up proud of him.

"When I get out of here I'll get on to pinching the equipment we need. Now run along, Ben, and I will see you next Friday night at the usual time."

Ben pulled back the curtain. Mr Parker, Granny's nosy neighbour, was standing right there!

Startled, Ben took a couple of steps back towards the bed, and quickly shoved *Plumbing Weekly* up the back of his jumper.

"What are *you* doing here?" asked Ben.

"Hoping to see me take a bed-bath, no doubt!" said Granny.

Ben chuckled.

Mr Parker scrambled for words. "No, no, I..."

"Matron! MATRON!" hollered Granny.

"Wait!" said Mr Parker, panicking. "I'm sure I heard one of you talking about the Crown Jewels..."

It was too late. The matron, who was an unusually tall lady with very big feet, clomped down the ward at speed.

"Yes?" asked the matron. "Is something the matter?"

"This man was spying at me through the curtains!" said Granny.

"Were you?" demanded Matron, eyeballing Mr Parker.

"Well, er, I heard that they were..." whined Mr Parker.

"Last week he spied on my granny doing her naked yoga," offered Ben.

Matron's face turned puce with horror. "Get out of my ward at once, you filthy little swine!" she screamed.

Humiliated, Mr Parker backed away from the terrifying matron and scuttled out of the ward. He paused at the swing doors and yelled back to Granny and Ben, "YOU HAVEN'T SEEN THE LAST OF ME!" before rushing out.

"Please let me know if that man comes back," said Matron, her face returning to a more normal shade.

"I will," replied Granny, before Matron returned to her duties.

"He could have heard everything!" hissed Ben.

"Maybe," replied Granny. "But I think

Matron scared him off for good!"

"I hope so." Ben was very worried about this unfortunate development.

"Do you still want to go through with it?" asked the old lady.

Ben had that feeling you have when you are on a rollercoaster and it's slowly making its way up the track. You want to get off and you want to stay on. Dread and delight all rolled into one.

"Yes!" he said.

"Hurrah!" said Granny, giving Ben a big smile.

Ben turned to leave, then turned around. "I… I love you, Granny," he said.

"And I love you too, little Benny," said Granny with a wink.

Ben winced. He had a gangsta granny now, and that was great – but he was going to have to teach her just to call him Ben!

✻

Ben ran along the corridors, his heart beating incredibly fast.

Boom boom boom.

He was electrified with excitement. This eleven-year-old boy, who had never done anything notable in his life except once been sick on his friend's head on the big wheel at the local funfair, was going to take part in the most daring robbery the world has ever known.

He ran outside the hospital, and began fumbling with the keys to unlock his bike from the railing. Then, looking up, he saw something unbelievable.

It was his granny.

That, in itself, was not unusual.

But this was:

Granny was abseiling down the side of the hospital.

She had tied a number of bed sheets together and was lowering herself at speed down the side of the building.

Ben couldn't believe his eyes. He knew his granny was a proper gangsta, but this was off the scale!

"Granny, what on earth are you doing?!" shouted Ben across the car park.

"The lift wasn't working, dear! See you next Friday. Don't be late!" she shouted as she reached the ground, leaped on her mobility scooter and roared off... well, *whirred* off home.

∗

Never had a week passed so slowly.

Ben spent all week waiting for Friday to come. Every minute, every hour, every day seemed like an eternity.

It was strange having to pretend he was just another ordinary boy when really he was one of the greatest criminal masterminds of all time.

Finally, Friday evening came. There was a knock on Ben's bedroom door.

RAT-TAT-TAT.

"Well, are you ready, son?" said Dad.

"Yeah," said Ben, trying to act as innocent as possible, which is actually quite hard when you are feeling extremely guilty. "You don't need to pick me up too early in the morning tomorrow, Granny and I normally play Scrabble until quite late."

"You won't be playing Scrabble, son," said Dad.

"No?"

"No, son. You won't be going to Granny's tonight at all."

"Oh no!" said Ben. "Is she back in hospital?"

"No, she's not."

Ben sighed with relief then felt a prickle of anxiety. "So, why am I not going to her house?"

The plan was in place, and there was no time to lose!

"Because," said Dad, "tonight it's the under-twelve dancing championships. At last it's your big moment to shine!"

21

A Tap-Shoe

Ben sat silently in the back of the little brown car in his Love Bomb outfit.

"I hope you didn't forget about the competition, Ben," said Mum, as she fixed her make-up in the passenger seat, her lipstick accidentally scrawling across her face as they went round a corner.

"No, of course not, Mum."

"Don't worry, son," continued Dad, as he proudly drove his son to dance competition immortality. "You've done so much training up in your bedroom, I know you'll get top marks from all the judges. Straight tens!"

"What about Granny? Won't she be expecting me?" said Ben anxiously.

Tonight was supposed to be the night that they stole the Crown Jewels, but instead he was on his way to take part in a dance competition, despite never having danced a step in his life.

For the last two weeks, he had avoided thinking about the dance competition, but now the time had come.

It was really going to happen.

He was going to have to dance a solo number.

Which he hadn't prepared.

In front of an entire theatre full of people…

"Oh, don't worry about Granny," said Mum. "She doesn't know what day it is!" She laughed, as the car stopped suddenly at a red light and mascara splattered over her forehead.

They arrived at the town hall. Ben saw a

rushing river of multi-coloured Lycra making its way into the building.

If anyone at school found out he'd entered, he would never live this down. The bullies would have all the ammunition they would need to make his life hell for ever. And what's more, he hadn't rehearsed his dance. Not even once. He didn't have a clue what he was going to do on stage.

This was a competition to find the best junior dancers in the local area. There was a prize for best couple, best solo female and best solo male.

If you won here, you would get the chance to compete for your county, and if you won there, for your country.

This was the first step on the road to international dance superstardom. And the host for the evening was none other than *Strictly Stars Dancing* heartthrob and his mum's favourite, Flavio Flavioli.

"It's wonderful to see so many beautiful ladies here tonight," he purred in his Italian accent.

Flavio looked even more shiny in real life. His hair was slicked back, his teeth were dazzlingly white and his outfit was as tight as clingfilm. "Now, are we all ready to rumba?"

The crowd all screamed, "Yes!"

"Flavio can't hear you, I said 'are you ready to rumba?'"

"YES!" they all screamed again, a little louder than before.

Ben was listening nervously backstage. He heard one woman's voice screech, "I love you, Flavio!" It sounded suspiciously like his mum.

Ben looked around the dressing room. It might as well have been a convention of the most annoying children in the world. They looked so unbearably precocious, adorned in these ridiculously garish Lycra outfits, smeared in fake tan, and with pearly white teeth so bright they could be seen from outer space.

Ben looked anxiously at his watch, knowing he was going to be terribly late to meet his granny. He waited and waited as the over made-up quickstepped, jived, waltzed, Viennese waltzed, tangoed, foxtrotted and cha-cha-cha-ed.

Finally, Ben's turn came. He stood in the wings as Flavio announced him.

"Now it's time for a local boy who is going to delight us all tonight with a solo dance piece. Please welcome Ben!"

Flavio glided off the stage as Ben plodded on, his Lycra Love Bomb outfit riding uncomfortably up his bottom.

Ben stood alone in the middle of the dance floor. A spotlight shone on him. The music started up. He was praying for some sort of escape from this. He would have been happy with anything at all, including:

A fire alarm

An earthquake

World War III

Another Ice Age

A deadly swarm of killer bees

A meteor from outer space hitting the earth and spinning it off its axis

A tidal wave

Flavio Flavioli being attacked by hundreds of flesh-eating zombies

A hurricane or tornado (Ben didn't really know the difference, but either would do)

Ben being abducted by aliens, and not returning to the earth for a thousand years

Dinosaurs returning to the earth through

some kind of time/space portal, and smashing through the roof, devouring everyone inside

A volcano erupting, though annoyingly there didn't seem to be any volcanoes nearby

An attack of giant slugs

Even an attack of medium sized slugs would do.

Ben wasn't fussy. Any of the above would have sufficed.

The music played for a while and Ben realised he hadn't moved his body yet. He looked over at his parents, who beamed with pride seeing their only child centre stage at last.

He looked to the wings where the ever-smiling Flavio was giving him an encouraging grin.

Please, make the ground open up now...

It didn't.

There was no choice but to do something. Anything.

Ben started moving his legs, then his arms, then his head. None of these parts of his body moved in time or sequence, and for the next five minutes he threw his body around the dance floor in a style that can only be called unforgettable: as much as you might want to forget it, you can't.

Ben tried a jump at the end, just as the music stopped, and he fell to the floor with a thud.

There was silence.

Deafening silence.

194

Then Ben could hear the sound of one pair of hands clapping. He looked up.

It was his mum.

Then another pair of hands joined in.

It was his dad.

For a few seconds he thought it might be one of these moments you see in a film when the underdog triumphs against all the odds: that soon everyone in the hall would be on their feet cheering and applauding this local boy who had at last made his loved ones proud and at the same time re-invented dancing for ever.

The end.

Well, no. That's not what happened.

After a few moments, his parents felt embarrassed to be the only people applauding, and stopped.

Flavio returned to the stage.

"Well that was, that was…" For the first time

the Italian heartthrob seemed lost for words. "Judges, can we have your scores for Ben please?"

"Zero," said the first.

"Zero."

"Zero."

Only one more judge to go. Could Ben make it four zeros?

But the final judge must have felt sorry for the sweaty little boy in front of her who had shamed his family for generations with his epic display of talentlessness. She shuffled her scoring paddles under the desk. "One," she announced.

There were loud boos and jeers from the audience so she corrected her score. "I am sorry, I mean zero," she said holding up her original choice of paddle.

"Slightly disappointing scores from the judges, there," said Flavio still trying hard to smile. "But, young Ben, all is not lost. As the only boy who entered the solo male category tonight, you are therefore the winner. May I present you with this solid plastic statuette."

Flavio picked up a cheap-looking trophy of a dancing boy, and presented it to Ben.

"Ladies and gentlemen, boys and girls, a round of applause for Ben!"

There was silence again. Even Mum and Dad didn't dare to clap.

Then boos started, and then jeers and catcalls: shouts of "SHAME ON YOU!" "NO!" and "FIX!"

Flavio's perfect smile began to crack. He leaned down to Ben and whispered in his ear, "You'd better get out of here before you get lynched."

At that exact moment a tap-shoe was thrown from the back of the audience. It flew at speed

through the air. It was probably aimed at Ben, but instead it hit Flavio right between the eyes, and he fell to the ground unconscious.

Time to make my excuses and leave, thought Ben.

22

Lycra Lynch Mob

An angry mob of ballroom-dancing enthusiasts chased the little brown car down the street. Looking out of the back window, Ben thought this would perhaps be the only time in history a lynch mob was dressed entirely in Lycra.

Dad put his foot down on the accelerator

VVVVVVVRRRRRRRRRRR RRRRROOOOOOOOOO OOOOOMMMMMMMM MMM!

...and they turned a corner and lost them.

"Thank goodness I was there to give Flavio the kiss of life!" said Mum from the front seat.

"He was just unconscious. He hadn't stopped breathing, Mum," said Ben from the back.

"You can't be too careful," said Mum, re-applying her lipstick. Most of it was now smeared over Flavio's face and neck.

"Your performance was, in a word, dreadful and embarrassing," pronounced Dad.

"That's two words," corrected Ben with a chuckle. "Three if you count the 'and'."

"Don't get funny with me, young lad," snapped Dad. "This is no laughing matter. I was ashamed of you. Ashamed."

"Yes ashamed," grumbled Mum in agreement.

Ben felt like he would give anything to disappear. He would give all of his past and all of his future, just so he didn't have to be sitting in the backseat of his mum and dad's car right now.

"I'm sorry, Mum," said Ben. "I want to make you proud, I really do." It was true: making his parents ashamed, well, that was the absolute last thing he wanted, however stupid he thought they were sometimes.

"Well, you have a funny way of showing it," said Mum.

"I just don't like dancing, that's all."

"That's not the point. Your mother spent hours making your costume," said Dad.

It's strange how parents always refer to each other as 'Mother' or 'Father' rather than 'Mum' or 'Dad' when you are in trouble.

"You made no effort up there on the stage whatsoever," Dad continued. "I don't think you even rehearsed once. Not once. Me and your mother work night and day to give you the opportunities we never had, and this is how you treat us…"

"With contempt," said Mum.

"Contempt," echoed Dad.

A single tear ran down Ben's cheek. He caught it with his tongue. It tasted bitter. The three sat in silence as the car rumbled home.

No words were spoken as they got out of the car, and went into the house. As soon as Dad opened the front door, Ben bounded up to his room and slammed the door. He sat on his bed, still in his Love Bomb outfit.

Ben had never felt more alone. He was hours late to meet Granny. Not only had he let down his mum and dad, he had let down the one person he had grown to love more than anyone, his granny.

They were never going to steal the Crown Jewels now.

Just at that moment, there was a quiet tap on his window.

It was Granny.

Dressed in her scuba-diving gear the old lady had climbed a ladder to reach her grandson's bedroom window.

"Let me in!" she mouthed theatrically.

Ben couldn't help but smile. He opened the window and hauled the old lady inside, like a fisherman might haul a particularly big fish on to his boat.

"You are very late," admonished Granny as Ben helped her over to the bed.

"I know, I'm sorry," said Ben.

"We said seven o'clock. It's half-past ten. The sleeping tonic I gave the guards at the Tower will be wearing off soon. "

"I'm really sorry, it's a long story," said Ben.

Granny sat on Ben's bed and looked him up

and down. "And why are you dressed like a demented Valentine's card?" she demanded.

"As I said it's a long story…"

It was a bit rich for Granny to criticise what he had on considering she was dressed in a wetsuit and scuba-diving mask, but there wasn't time to get into that now.

"Quick boy, put on this wetsuit, and follow me down the ladder. I'll start up the mobility scooter."

"Are we really going to steal the Crown Jewels, Granny?"

"Well, we are going to have a go!" said the old lady with a smile.

23

Caught by the Fuzz

They whirred through the town: Granny driving, Ben clinging on behind her. Both in wetsuits and diving masks, with Granny's handbag wrapped in miles of clingfilm sitting in the basket at the front.

Granny spotted Raj closing up his newsagent's shop.

"Hello Raj, dear, don't forget to save me some Murray Mints for Monday!" she shouted.

Raj looked at the two of them, open mouthed in shock.

"I don't know what's got into him, he's

normally so chatty!"

It was a long way to London, especially on a motorised scooter with a top speed of three miles per hour (with two passengers).

After a while Ben noticed the roads getting

wider and wider; two lanes, then three lanes.

"Bums! We are on the motorway!" shouted Ben from the back as ten-ton lorries whooshed past, nearly wrenching the scooter off the road with the force of their slipstream.

"You know, you really shouldn't swear, young man," said Granny. "Now, I'm going to step on it so hold on tight!"

A moment later, a particularly big petrol tanker thundered by, inches from their heads, beeping its horn.

"Big hairy bums!" said Granny.

"Granny!" said Ben, shocked.

"Whoops, that one just slipped out!" said Granny. Grown-ups *never* lead by example.

"I'm sorry, Granny, but I am not sure this thing is built for a motorway," said Ben. Just then an even bigger lorry blustered past. Ben could feel the wheels of the scooter lift off the road for a second, as the slipstream dragged it in the lorry's wake.

"I'll take the next exit," said Granny. But before she could, flashing blue lights began to spin behind them. "Oh no, it's the fuzz! Let's see if I can outrun them." She slammed her foot on the accelerator, and the scooter leapt from three miles per hour to three and a half miles per hour.

The police car drove alongside them, and the officer inside gestured angrily for them to pull over.

"Granny, you'd better pull over," said Ben. "We're done for."

"Let me handle this, my boy."

Granny stopped the mobility scooter on the hard shoulder as the police car parked in front of them, blocking any chance of escape.

"Is this your vehicle, Madam?" said the police officer. He was fat and had a small moustache, which made his fat face look even fatter. He also had a smug expression on his face that suggested telling people off was his favourite thing in the world. Or maybe second favourite, after doughnuts. His name tag said that he was called PC Fudge.

"Is there a problem, Officer?" said Granny innocently, her diving mask a little steamed up from all the excitement.

"Yes there is a problem. The use of motorised mobility scooters on motorways is strictly prohibited," said the police officer in a patronising tone.

(Other modes of transport not permitted on a motorway are:

Skateboard
Canoe
Roller skates
Donkey
Shopping trolley
Unicycle
Sledge

Rickshaw

Camel

Magic carpet

Comedy ostrich)

"Well, thank you so much for pointing that out, Officer. We'll remember for next time. Now if you'll excuse us we are running a little late. Goodbye!" said Granny cheerily, as she restarted the mobility scooter.

"Have you been drinking, Madam?"

"I had some cabbage soup before I came out."

"Alcohol, I mean," he sighed.

"I had a brandy liqueur chocolate on Tuesday night. Does that count?"

Ben couldn't help but chuckle.

PC Fudge's eyes narrowed. "Then would you care to explain to me why you are dressed in scuba-diving gear with your handbag wrapped in clingfilm?"

This was going to take some explaining.

"Because, because, erm…" Granny was stumbling over her words.

They were done for.

"Because we are from the Clingfilm Appreciation Society," said Ben with authority.

"I've never heard of that!" said PC Fudge dismissively.

"We are very new," said Ben.

"Just two members so far," added Granny, continuing the lie. "And we like to keep the society low key, so we have our meetings underwater, hence the wetsuits."

The policeman looked utterly baffled. Granny didn't stop talking, apparently in the hope that she might baffle him further.

"Now, if you'll excuse us, we are in rather a

hurry. We have to get to London for an important meeting with the Bubble Wrap Appreciation Society. We are thinking of merging the two organisations."

PC Fudge was all but lost for words. "How many members have they got?"

"Just one," said Granny. "But if we join forces we can save money on teabags and photocopying and paperclips and the like. Goodbye!"

Granny put her foot down on the accelerator and the mobility scooter lurched off.

"STOP RIGHT THERE!" said PC Fudge, holding his podgy hand out straight in front of him.

Ben froze in terror. He wasn't even twelve yet, and he was going to spend the rest of his life in jail.

PC Fudge leaned over and put his face next to Granny's.

"I'll give you a lift."

24

Dark Waters

"Just here, please," said Granny directing from the backseat of the police car. "Just opposite the Tower. Thank you so much."

PC Fudge strained as he unloaded the scooter out of his boot. "Well, next time, please remember that mobility scooters are meant only for pavements, not main roads, and certainly not motorways."

"Yes, Officer," replied Granny with a smile.

"Well, good luck you two, with the whole… erm… clingfilm-bubble wrap alliance thing."

And with that, PC Fudge sped off into

the night, leaving Granny and Ben gazing at the magnificent thousand-year-old Tower of London on the opposite bank of the river. It was particularly spectacular at night, its four domed towers lit up, its reflection shimmering on the cold dark River Thames below.

The Tower was once a prison, with an illustrious list of former inmates (including the future Queen Elizabeth I, the adventurer Sir Walter Raleigh, the terrorist Guy Fawkes, the senior Nazi Rudolf Hess, and my mother*). Now, though, the Tower is a museum, and home to the priceless Crown Jewels, housed in

---

*I lied about that last one: my mother was never locked up in the Tower of London. But she should be because she puts coffee in banoffee pie. She says the "offee" in "banoffee" is for coffee when actually it should be toffee.

their own special building, Jewel House.

The unlikely pair of gangstas stood at the riverbank. "Are you ready?" asked Granny, her mask completely steamed up from sitting in the back of a police car for over an hour.

"Yes," said Ben, trembling with excitement. "I'm ready."

Granny reached out to hold Ben's hand, and then she counted, "Three, two, one" and on one they leapt into the dark waters below.

The water was freezing cold even with the

wetsuits on, and for a few moments all Ben could see was black. It was terrifying and exhilarating in equal measure.

When their heads bobbed out of the water, Ben took the snorkel out of his mouth for a moment.

"Are you OK, Granny?"

"I have never felt more alive."

They doggy-paddled across the river. Ben had never been a great swimmer and lagged behind a little. Secretly he wished he had brought his armbands or at least a lilo.

A huge party cruiser, with music blaring and young people shouting, chugged down the river. Granny had swum ahead, and Ben had lost sight of her.

Oh no!

Had she been crushed by the cruiser?

Was Granny in a watery grave at the bottom of the Thames?

"Come on, slowcoach!" shouted Granny as the party boat passed and they caught sight of each other again. Ben sighed with relief, and continued doggy-paddling across the deep dark dirty water.

According to the diagram in *Plumbing Weekly*, the sewage pipe was situated just to the left of Traitors' Gate. (This was an entrance to the Tower only accessible from the river, where many prisoners would be taken to be locked up for the rest of their lives or beheaded. Nowadays

Traitors' Gate had been bricked up, so the pipe was the only way into the Tower from the river.)

Then, with a rush of relief, Ben found the pipe. It was partly submerged under the water. It was dark and eerie, and he could hear the echoes of lapping waves reverberating inside it.

Suddenly Ben began to have second thoughts about the whole adventure. As much as he liked plumbing, he didn't want to have to crawl up an ancient sewage pipe.

"Come on, Ben," said Granny, as she bobbed up and down in the water. "We haven't come this far to give up now."

Well, thought Ben. *If a little old lady can do it, then I certainly can.*

Ben took a deep breath and propelled himself into the pipe. Granny followed close behind.

It was blacker than black in there, and after he travelled a few metres he could feel something crawling across his head. He heard an *eek-eek* noise, and could sense something scratching his scalp.

It felt like claws.

He put his hand on his head.

He touched something big and furry.

Then he realised the awful truth.

IT WAS A RAT!

A giant rat was clinging to the top of his head.

"AAAAHHHHHHHHH!"

screamed Ben.

25

Haunted by Ghosts

The sound of Ben's scream echoed through the length of the pipe. He whacked the rat off his head and it landed on top of Granny, who was crawling up the pipe just behind him.

"Poor little rat," she said. "Be gentle with it, dear."

"But—"

"He was here first, now come on, we have to hurry. The sleeping-tonic chocolate cake I gave the guards will be wearing off very soon."

The pair crawled further up the pipe. It was wet and slippery, and it smelled awful.

(Unfortunately for Ben and Granny, it turns out that ancient poo does still pong.)

After a while, Ben could see a shaft of grey in all the black. It was the end of the tunnel, at last!

He hauled himself out of the ancient stone privy, and then reached down the pipe to help his granny clamber out. They were covered from head to toe in disgustingly stinky black slime.

Standing inside the cold dark toilet, Ben spied a glassless window in the wall. They clambered through this and landed on the cold wet grass of the Tower's courtyard below.

For a few moments they lay there, gazing up at the moon and the stars. Ben reached out and held Granny's hand. She squeezed it tight.

"This is amazing," said Ben.

"Come on, dear," she whispered. "We've barely started yet!"

Ben stood up and helped Granny to her feet.

The old lady immediately started unwrapping the clingfilm that she had waterproofed her handbag with.

This took several minutes.

"I think I may have overdone the clingfilm. Still, better safe than sorry."

Eventually the mile-long roll of clingfilm was off, and Granny took out a map Ben had cut out of a book in the school library, so the two unlikely thieves could locate Jewel House.

It was eerie being inside the Tower of London courtyard at night.

The Tower is said to be haunted by the ghosts of people who died there. Over the years, several guards have run away in terror, claiming that at the dead of night they had seen the ghosts of various historical figures who had died there.

Now, though, there was something even

stranger roaming the courtyard.

Granny in a wetsuit!

"This way," hissed Granny, and Ben followed her down a walled passage. Ben's heart was beating so fast he thought he was going to explode.

After a few minutes they were standing outside Jewel House, overlooking Tower Green and the monument to those who were beheaded or hanged there. Ben wondered if he and Granny would be executed if they were caught stealing the Crown Jewels, and a shiver ran down his spine.

Two Beefeaters were lying on the ground, snoring loudly. Their immaculate black and red uniforms emblazoned with 'ER' were becoming soiled on the wet ground. Granny's herbal sleeping tonic in the chocolate cake had worked.

But for how long?

As she hurried past them, Granny let out a
familiar quacking sound from her bum. One of
the guards' noses crinkled at the smell.

Ben held his breath – not just because of the smell – but because he was afraid.

Was Granny's bottom burp going to wake the guard up and ruin everything?

An eternal moment passed…

Then the guard opened one eye.

Oh no!

Granny pushed Ben back, and raised her handbag, as if to clobber the Beefeater with it.

This is it, thought Ben. *We'll be hanged!*

But then the guard closed his eye again, and continued snoring.

"Granny, please try to control your bottom," hissed Ben.

"I didn't do a thing," said Granny, innocently. "It must have been you."

They tiptoed to the huge steel door at the front of Jewel House.

"Right, I just need your dad's power drill…"

said Granny, reaching inside her handbag. With a juddering whirr, she started drilling through the series of locks on the door. One by one the metal locks crumbled to the ground.

All of a sudden the guards snored extremely loudly.

ZZZZZZZZZZZZZZZZZZ

ZZZZZZZZZZZZZZZZZZZZZ

ZZZZZZZZZZZZZZZZZZZZZ!

Ben froze and Granny nearly dropped the power drill. But the guards slept on and, after a few nerve-racking minutes, the door was finally unlocked.

Granny looked exhausted. Sweat was dripping down her forehead. She sat down on a low wall for a moment, and then pulled out a thermos flask.

"Cabbage soup?" she offered.

"No, thank you, Granny," replied Ben. He shifted uneasily. "We'd better get going before the guards wake up."

"Rush, rush, rush, that's all you kids do these days. Patience is a virtue." She poured the last of her cabbage soup down her throat, and rose to her feet.

"Delicious! Right, let's do this!" she said.

The huge steel door creaked as it opened, and Ben and Granny entered Jewel House.

Out of the dark, came a flurry of black feathers, hitting Ben and Granny in the face. Ben was so startled he screamed again.

"Shush!" said Granny.

"What were they?" said Ben, as he saw the winged creatures disappear off into the black sky. "Bats?"

"No, dear, ravens. There are dozens of

them here. Ravens have lived at the Tower for hundreds of years."

"This place is spooky," said Ben, his stomach knotted in fear.

"Especially at night," agreed Granny. "Now stay close to me, boy, because it's about to get a whole lot spookier…"

26

A Figure in the Dark

A long winding corridor stretched out ahead of them. This was where tourists from around the world queue for hours to see the Crown Jewels. The old lady and her grandson tiptoed their way silently along it, dripping smelly icy water from the Thames in their wake.

Finally they turned a corner, into the main room where all the jewels were kept. Like the sun bursting through the clouds on a grey day, the jewels illuminated Ben and Granny's faces.

The pair of thieves stopped in awe. Their mouths fell open as they looked at the treasures laid out before them. They were more magnificent than anyone could imagine. It truly was the most superb collection of precious objects in the world.

Dear reader, not only were they beautiful and priceless, they symbolised hundreds of years of history. There were a number of royal crowns:

- St Edward's Crown, with which the new king or queen is crowned by the Archbishop of Canterbury during the coronation ceremony. It's made of gold and decorated with sapphires and topazes. Proper bling!
- The Imperial State Crown, in which were set an incredible three thousand gems, including the Second Star of Africa (the second largest stone cut from the largest diamond ever found. No, I don't know where the First Star is).

- The breathtaking Imperial Crown of India, set with around six thousand diamonds and magnificent rubies and emeralds. Unfortunately not in my size.

- The twelfth century gold Anointing Spoon, used to anoint the king or queen with holy oil. Not to be used for eating Coco Pops.

- Not forgetting the Ampulla, the gold flask in the form of an eagle which contains that holy oil. Like a really posh thermos flask.

- And finally, the famous Orb and Sceptres. That's a lot of gear.

If the Crown Jewels were featured in the Argos catalogue, they would probably look like this:

Granny took out the rolled-up supermarket carrier bag she'd kept in her handbag, ready to put the Crown Jewels in.

"Right, we just need to break through this

glass," she whispered.

Ben looked at her with disbelief. "I'm not sure we are going to get all of these jewels in there."

"Well, sorry, dear," she whispered back. "You have to pay five pence for plastic bags at the shops these days, so I only bought the one."

The glass was inches thick.

Bulletproof.

Ben had smuggled a few compound chemicals out of his Science class, and combined them to go…

KKKKKKKAAAAAAAAAAA BBBBBBBBBOOOOOOOOO MMMMMMMMMM!!!!!!!!!!!!!!!!!!!!!!!!

… if set alight.

They stuck the chemicals to the glass with some BluTack. Then Granny attached one end of a ball of pink wool to the BluTack. (Wool would be the perfect fuse.) Then she produced some matches. They just needed to make sure they were far enough away from the explosion. Otherwise they might be blown up too.

"Right, Ben," whispered Granny. "Let's get as far away from the glass as we can."

The pair retreated around a wall, unravelling the pink wool as they went.

"Do you want to light the fuse?" said Granny.

Ben nodded. He really wanted to, but his hands were trembling so much with excitement he didn't know if he could.

Ben opened the matchbox. There were only two matches inside.

He went to strike the first, but his hands were

shaking so much that it broke in two when he did.

"Oh dear," whispered Granny. "Have another go."

Ben picked up the second match.

He tried to strike it but nothing happened. Some river water must have leaked out of the sleeve of his wetsuit. Now both the match and the matchbox were soaking wet.

"Noooo!" cried Ben in desperation. "Mum and Dad were right. I am useless. I can't even light a match!"

Granny put her arms around her grandson.

As they cuddled, their wetsuits squeaked a little.

"Don't talk like that, Ben. You are an amazing young man. You really are. Since we have been spending so much time together I am a hundred times happier than I could ever say."

"Really?" said Ben.

"Really!" replied Granny. "And you are so very clever. You planned this whole extraordinary heist yourself and you're only eleven years old."

"I'm nearly twelve," said Ben.

Granny chuckled. "But you get my point, dear. How many other children your age could plan something as daring as this?"

"But we aren't going to steal the Crown Jewels now, so it's all been a massive waste of time."

"It's not over yet," said Granny, as she pulled out a tin of cabbage soup from her handbag. "We can always try some good old-fashioned brute force!"

Granny handed the tin to her grandson. Ben took it with a smile, and then walked over to the cabinet.

"Here goes!" said Ben, as he swung back the tin to strike the glass.

"Please don't," said a voice from the shadows.

Ben and Granny froze in terror.

Was it a ghost?

"Who's there?" Ben called out.

The figure stepped out into the light.

It was the Queen.

27

An Audience with the Queen

"What on earth are you doing here?" asked Ben. "Er… I mean, what on earth are you doing here, Your Majesty?"

"I like to come here when I can't sleep," replied the Queen. She spoke in that instantly familiar posh voice of hers. Ben and Granny were surprised to see she was wearing a nightgown and little furry Corgi slippers. She was also wearing the coronation crown on her head. It was the most magnificent of all the Crown Jewels. The Archbishop of Canterbury placed it on her head when she was crowned Queen in 1953. The crown, which dates back to 1661, is made of gold, encrusted with diamonds, rubies, pearls, emeralds and sapphires.

It was an impressive look, even for the Queen!

"I come here to think," the Queen went on. "I got my chauffeur to bring me over from Buckingham Palace in the Bentley. I have my Christmas address to the nation in a few weeks, and I need to think carefully about what I want to say. One always finds it easier to think with one's crown on. The question is, what on earth are you two doing here?"

Ben and Granny looked at each other, ashamed.

Being told off was bad enough at the best of times, but being told off by the Queen was on a whole other level of being-told-offness, as this simple graph demonstrates:

TOLD-OFFNESS

A PARENT | TEACHER | HEAD TEACHER | AIR HOSTESS | LIBRARIAN | POSTMAN | SCOUT MASTER | TRAFFIC WARDEN | PARK KEEPER | VICAR | POLICE MAN | JUDGE | THE QUEEN

"And why do the pair of you smell like poo-poo? Well?" pushed Her Majesty. "I am waiting."

"I am solely to blame, Your Majesty," said Granny, bowing her head.

"No, she's not," said Ben. "It was me who said we should steal the Crown Jewels. I talked her into it."

"That's true," said Granny, "but it's not what I meant. I started this whole thing, when I pretended to be an international jewel thief."

"*What*?" exclaimed Ben.

"Pardon?" said the Queen. "One is terribly confused."

"My grandson hated staying with me on Friday nights," said Granny. "I heard him one night, calling his parents and complaining about how boring I was—"

"But Granny, I don't think that any more!" protested Ben.

"It's all right, Ben, I know things have changed since then. And in truth I *was* boring. I just liked to eat cabbage and play Scrabble, and I knew deep down that you hated those things. So I made up stories from the books I read to entertain you. I told you I was an infamous jewel thief called 'The Black Cat'…"

"But what about those diamonds you showed me?" said Ben, feeling shocked and angry that he'd been deceived.

"All worthless, dear," replied Granny. "Made of glass. I found them in an old ice-cream tub at the local charity shop."

Ben stared at her. He couldn't believe it. The whole thing, the whole incredible story, was made up.

"I can't believe you lied to me!" he said.

"I— I mean…" said Granny, falteringly.

Ben turned to glare at her. "You're not my gangsta granny after all," he said.

Then there was a deafening silence in Jewel House.

Followed by a rather loud and rather posh cough. "Ahem," said an imperious voice.

28

Hung, Drawn and Quartered

"I'm terribly sorry to interrupt," said the Queen, in her clipped tones, "but might we get back to the important matter at hand? I still don't understand why the two of you are here in the Tower of London in the middle of the night, smelling of poo-poo, and attempting to steal my jewels."

"Well, once I had started, the lie grew and grew, Your Majesty," continued Granny, avoiding Ben's eyes. "I didn't mean for it to happen. I just got carried away I suppose. It was so nice to spend that extra time with my grandson, to have fun with him. It reminded me of when I used to read him bedtime stories. That was in the days when he didn't find me boring."

Ben fidgeted. He was starting to feel guilty, too. Granny had lied to him, and that was horrible – but she'd only done it because she was upset that he thought she was dull.

"I had fun too," he whispered.

Granny smiled at him. "I'm glad, little Benny. I'm so sorry, I really—"

"Ahem," interrupted the Queen.

"Oh yes," said Granny. "Well, before I knew it, things had snowballed, and we were planning to take on the most daring robbery of all time. We climbed up the sewage pipe, by the way. We don't usually smell like this, Your Majesty."

"I should hope not.

"PPPPPPOOOOOOOOOOEEEEEE

EEEEEEEEEEYYYYYYYYYYYY YYYYYYYYY!!!!!!!!!!!!!"

Ben was feeling *really* guilty now. Even if Granny had never been an international jewel thief, she certainly wasn't boring. She had helped plan this robbery with him, and now here they were in the Tower of London at midnight, talking to the Queen!

I have to do something to help her, Ben realised.

"The robbery was my idea, Your Majesty," he said. "I am so sorry."

"Please let my grandson go," interjected Granny. "I don't want his young life ruined. Please, I beg you. We were going to return the Crown Jewels tomorrow night. I promise."

"A likely story," murmured the Queen.

"It's true!" exclaimed Ben.

"Please do what you want with me, Your Majesty," continued Granny. "Have me locked up here in the Tower for ever, if you like, but I beg you, let the boy go."

The Queen looked lost in thought.

"I really don't know what to do," said the Queen eventually. "I am touched by your story. As you know, I too am a grandmother, and my grandchildren find me dull sometimes."

"Really?" asked Ben. "But you are the Queen!"

"I know," the Queen chuckled.

Ben was stunned. He had never seen the Queen laugh before. She was usually so serious, and never cracked a smile when giving her speech on TV at Christmas, or opening Parliament, or even watching comedians at the Royal Variety Show.

"But to them I'm just their boring old

granny," she continued. "They forget that I was young once."

"And that they too will be old one day," added Granny, with a meaningful look to Ben.

"Exactly, my dear!" agreed the Queen. "I think the younger generation need to have a bit more time for the elderly."

"I'm sorry, Your Majesty," said Ben. "If I hadn't been so selfish and moaned about old people being boring none of this would have ever happened."

There was an uncomfortable silence.

Granny rummaged in her handbag and offered the Queen a bag of sweets. "Murray Mint, Your Majesty?"

"Yes please," said the Queen. She unwrapped it and popped it into her mouth. "Gosh, I haven't had one of these for years."

"They're my favourite," said Granny.

"And they last so long," added the Queen as she sucked it, before composing herself again.

"Do you know what happened to the last man who attempted to steal the Crown Jewels?" enquired the Queen.

"Was he hung, drawn and quartered?" asked Ben excitedly.

"Believe it or not he was pardoned," said the

Queen with a wry smile.

"Pardoned, Your Majesty?" said Granny.

"In 1671, an Irishman by the name of Colonel Blood tried to steal them, but was caught by guards as he tried to escape. He hid this very crown I am wearing now under his cloak and dropped it on the ground just outside. King Charles II was so amused by Colonel Blood's daring attempt that he set him free."

"I must Google him," said Ben.

"I don't know what Googling is," said Granny.

"Nor me," chuckled the Queen. "So, in royal tradition, that's what I am going to do. Pardon you both."

"Oh thank you, Your Majesty," said Granny, kissing her hand.

Ben fell to his knees. "Thank you, thank you, thank you so much, Your Majesty..."

"Yes yes, don't grovel," said the Queen, haughtily. "I cannot abide grovelling. I have met far too many grovellers during my reign."

"I am so sorry, Your Majestical Royal Majesty," said Granny.

"That's exactly what I mean! You're grovelling now!" replied the Queen.

Ben and Granny looked at each other in fear. It was hard not to speak to Her Majesty without grovelling at least a little bit.

"Now jolly along quickly, please," said the Queen, "before this whole place is overrun with guards. And don't forget to watch me on the telly on Christmas Day…"

29

Armed Police

It was dawn by the time they trundled back into Grey Close. This time there was no police car to give them a lift. It was a very long way home from London on a mobility scooter. Over the speed bumps they went, bump bump bump, and whirred into Granny's drive.

"What a night!" sighed Ben.

"My word, yes, good golly I do feel rather stiff from sitting on that thing for so long," said Granny, as she eased her old and tired body off the scooter. "I am sorry, you know, Ben," she said after a pause. "I really didn't mean to hurt you. It was just so nice spending time with you, I didn't want it to stop."

Ben smiled. "It's OK," he said. "I understand why you did it. And don't worry. You're still my gangsta granny!"

"Thank you," said Granny softly. "Anyway, I think that's quite enough excitement to last a lifetime. I want you to go home, be a good boy, and concentrate on your plumbing…"

"I will, I promise. No more heists for me," chuckled Ben.

Suddenly Granny froze.

She looked up.

Ben could hear a helicopter whirring overhead.

"Granny?"

"Shush…!" Granny adjusted her hearing aid and listened intently. "That's more than one helicopter. It sounds like a fleet."

WOOO-WOOO-WOOO-WOOO-WOOO!

The sound of police-car sirens screeched from all around, and within moments heavily armed police surrounded them from every angle. Granny and Ben couldn't see any of the bungalows in the close any more because they were trapped behind a wall of policemen in bulletproof vests. The whirr of police helicopters overhead was so deafening that Granny had to turn her hearing aid down.

A voice came over a megaphone from one of the helicopters. "You are surrounded. Put down your weapons. I repeat, put down your weapons or we will shoot."

"We haven't got any weapons!" shouted Ben. His voice hadn't broken yet and it came out a bit girly.

"Don't argue with them, Ben. Just put your hands in the air!" shouted Granny over the noise.

The gangsta pair put their hands up. A number of especially brave policemen surged forward, pointing their guns right at Ben and Granny. They pushed them over and pinned them to the ground.

"Don't move!" Came the voice from the helicopter. Ben thought, *How could I move with a great big policeman kneeling on my back?*

A flurry of leather-gloved hands made their way up and down their bodies and fumbled through Granny's handbag, presumably searching for guns. If they had been searching for used tissues they would be in luck, but they didn't find any weapons.

Ben and Granny were then handcuffed and brought to their feet. Out from behind the wall of policemen stepped an old man with a very big nose wearing a pork-pie hat.

It was Mr Parker.

Granny's nosy neighbour.

30

A Packet of Sugar

"Thought you could get away with stealing the Crown Jewels, did you?" whined Mr Parker. "I know all about your wicked plan. Well, it's over. Officers, take them away. And lock them up and throw away the key!"

The policemen pulled the captives in the direction of two waiting police cars.

"Hang on a sec," shouted Ben. "If we stole the Crown Jewels, where are they?"

"Yes of course! The evidence. All we need to put you two gangstas behind bars for ever. Search the basket of the scooter. At once!"

said Mr Parker.

One of the policemen went through the basket. He found a large package wrapped in soggy clingfilm.

"Ah, yes, that must be the jewels," said Mr Parker confidently. "Give it here."

Mr Parker shot Granny and Ben a smug look. He started unwrapping the package.

Quite a few minutes passed until the big package was a little package. Finally, Mr Parker reached the end of the clingfilm.

"Ah, yes, here we are!" he announced, as a tin of cabbage soup fell to the ground.

"Could I have that please, Mr Parker?" said Granny. "It's my lunch."

"Search her bungalow!" barked Mr Parker.

A few policemen tried to bash open the front door by charging at it with their shoulders. Granny looked on, amused, before venturing,

"I've got the key right here, if you'd rather use that!"

One of the policemen approached her and rather sheepishly took the key.

"Thank you, Madam," he said politely.

Granny and Ben shared a smile.

He then opened the door, and what seemed like hundreds of policemen charged inside. They frantically searched the bungalow, but after a short while they re-emerged, empty handed.

"There's no Crown Jewels in there, I'm afraid, sir," said one of the policemen. "Just a Scrabble set and quite a few more tins of cabbage soup."

Mr Parker's face went red with fury. He had called out half the police officers in the country, all for nothing.

"Now, Mr Parker," said one of the policemen to him. "You are very lucky we aren't arresting you for wasting police time..."

"Wait!" said Mr Parker. "Just because the jewels aren't on them or in the house, doesn't mean they don't have them. I know what I heard. Search… the garden! Yes! Dig it up!"

The policeman put up a calming hand. "Mr Parker, we can't just—"

Suddenly, a light of triumph lit up in Mr Parker's eyes. "Hang on. You haven't asked them where they were this evening. I *know* they went to steal the Crown Jewels. And I bet they don't have an alibi for tonight!"

The policeman turned to Ben and Granny, frowning. "Actually, that's not a bad point," he said. "Would you mind telling me where you were tonight?" Mr Parker was positively beaming now.

Just then, another policeman waddled over to them. There was something familiar about him, and when Ben saw his moustache, he knew why.

"Boss, we've just had a call through for you on—" PC Fudge began, holding up a walkie-talkie. He stopped suddenly, staring at Ben and Granny. "Well!" he said. "If it isn't the clingfilm people!"

"PC Pear!" said Ben.

"Fudge!" corrected Fudge.

"Sorry, yes, Fudge. Nice to see you again."

The superior officer looked confused. "Sorry?"

"The lad and his granny. They're the Clingfilm Appreciation Society. They went to their annual meeting in London tonight. I dropped them off, in fact."

"So they weren't stealing the Crown Jewels?" asked his boss.

"No!" laughed PC Fudge. "They were merging with the Bubble Wrap Society. Stealing the Crown Jewels indeed!" He smiled at Ben and Granny. "What an idea!"

Mr Parker had gone red in the face. "But… but… They did it! They're villains, I'm telling you!"

While he was spluttering, the superior officer took the walkie-talkie from PC Fudge. "Yep. Uh-huh. Right. Thank you," he said. He turned to Ben and Granny. "That was Special Branch. I asked them to check if the Crown Jewels were still there. Turns out they are. I'm sorry, Ma'am. And boy. We'll have those handcuffs off you in a jiffy."

Mr Parker slumped, looking utterly dejected. "No, it can't be—"

"If I hear one more peep out of you, Mr Parker," said the policeman, "I will throw you in the cells for the night!" He turned smartly on his heel and walked over to one of the patrol cars, followed by PC Fudge, who waved at Ben and Granny as he left.

Ben and Granny approached Mr Parker, their hands still cuffed together.

"What you heard were just stories," said Ben. "Just my granny telling me stories. Mr Parker, I think you may have let your imagination run away with you."

"But, but, but…!" blustered Mr Parker.

"Me? An international jewel thief?!" Granny chuckled.

The policemen all started chuckling too.

"You'd have to be a bit daft to believe a thing

like that!" she said. "Sorry, Ben," she whispered to her grandson.

"That's OK!" Ben whispered back.

The policemen unlocked the handcuffs, and hastily retreated into their cars and vans and sped off out of Grey Close.

"Sorry to disturb you, Madam," said one of the departing officers. "Have a good day."

The helicopters disappeared up into the dawn sky. As the blades got faster, Mr Parker's precious pork-pie hat flew off his head and into a puddle.

Granny approached Mr Parker, who was standing hatless in her drive.

"If ever you need to borrow a packet of sugar…" she said kindly.

"Yes…" said Mr Parker.

"Don't knock on my door or I will shove that bag of sugar up your backside," said Granny with a sweet smile.

31

Golden Light

The sun had risen, and Grey Close was bathed in golden light. There was dew on the ground, and an unearthly mist made the little row of bungalows look somehow magical.

"Ah well," said Granny with a sigh. "You'd better run home now, young Ben, before your parents wake up."

"They don't care about me," said Ben.

"Oh yes they do," said Granny, tentatively putting her arm around her grandson. "They just don't know how to show it."

"Maybe."

Ben yawned the biggest yawn he had ever yawned in his life. "Gosh, I'm so tired. Tonight was amazing!"

"It was the most thrilling night of my life, Ben. I wouldn't have missed it for the world," said Granny with a twinkling smile. She took a deep breath.

"Oh, the joy of being alive."

Then her eyes filled with tears.

"Are you all right, Granny?" said Ben softly.

Granny hid her face from her grandson. "I'm fine, child, I really am." Her voice wavered with emotion as she spoke.

Suddenly, Ben knew something was very wrong.

"Granny, please, you can tell me."

He held her hand in his. Her skin was soft but worn. Fragile.

"Well…" said Granny hesitantly. "There is one other thing I lied to you about, dear."

Ben had a sinking feeling.

"What's that?" he asked and he squeezed her hand reassuringly.

"Well, the doctor gave me my test results last week, and I told you I was fine. That was a lie. I'm not fine." Granny paused for a moment. "The truth is, I have cancer."

"No, no…" said Ben with tears in his eyes. He had heard about cancer, enough to know it could be deadly serious.

"Just before you ran into him at the hospital the doctor told me the cancer, well, it's very advanced."

"How long have you got left?" spluttered Ben. "Did he say?"

"He said I wouldn't make Christmas."

Ben hugged his granny, as tight as he could, willing his body to share its life force with hers.

Tears were running down his cheeks. It was

so unfair – he'd only really got to know Granny in the last few weeks, and now he was going to lose her.

"I don't want you to die."

Granny looked at Ben for a moment.

"None of us are going to live for ever, my boy. But I hope you never forget me. Your boring old granny!"

"You're not boring at all. You're a proper gangsta! We very nearly stole the Crown Jewels, remember!"

Granny chuckled.

"Yes, but not a word of that to anyone, please. You could still get in a whole heap of trouble. It will have to remain our little secret."

"And the Queen's!" said Ben.

"Oh yes! What a nice old dear she was."

"I will never forget you, Granny," said Ben. "You will for ever be in my heart."

"That's the nicest thing anyone has ever said to me," said the old lady.

"I love you so much, Granny."

"I love you too, Ben. But you'd better be running along now."

"I don't want to leave you."

"That's very sweet of you, dear, but if your mummy and daddy wake up and find you gone, they are going to be extremely worried about you."

"They won't."

"Oh, yes, they will. Now Ben, please be a good boy."

Ben reluctantly rose to his feet. He helped his granny up off the step.

Then he held her close and kissed her on the cheek. He didn't mind her hairy chin. In fact, he loved it.

He loved the whistle of her hearing aid. He

loved that she smelled of cabbage. And most of all, he loved that she blew off without even knowing it.

He loved everything about her.

"Goodbye," he said softly.

"Goodbye, Ben."

32

A Family Sandwich

When he finally arrived home, Ben noticed the little brown car was missing from the drive. It was still very early in the morning.

Where could his parents have gone at this hour?

Nevertheless, he climbed up the drainpipe, through the window, and back into his bedroom.

All that clambering was hard work; he was tired after staying up all night and the wetsuit made him heavier than usual. Ben moved his *Plumbing Weeklys* aside so he could hide the wetsuit under his bed. Then, as quietly as he could, he put on his pyjamas and climbed into bed.

Just as he was about to shut his eyes, he heard the car speed up the drive, and the front door open, and then the sound of his mum and dad sobbing uncontrollably.

"We've looked everywhere for him," said Dad, sniffing. "I don't know what to do."

"It was my own stupid fault," added Mum, through her tears. "We should never have entered him for that dance competition. He must have run away from home…"

"I'll call the police."

"Yes, yes, we must, we should have done that hours ago."

"We have to get the whole country out looking for him… Hello, hello, I need the police, please… It's my son. I can't find my son…"

Ben felt so wretchedly guilty. His parents *did*

care about him after all.

Massively.

He leapt out of bed, burst open his bedroom door, and ran down the stairs into their arms. Dad dropped the telephone.

"Oh my boy! My boy!" said Dad.

He hugged Ben tighter than he had ever hugged him before. Mum put her arms around her son too, until they were one big family sandwich, with Ben as the filling.

"Oh Ben, thank goodness you came back!" wailed Mum. "Where have you been?"

"With Granny," replied Ben, not quite telling the whole truth. "She's… well, she's very ill," he said, sadly. But he could see from his parents' faces that it wasn't a surprise to them.

"Yes…" said his dad, uncomfortably. "I'm afraid that she's—"

"I know," said Ben. "I just can't believe you

didn't tell me. She's my granny!"

"I know," said Dad. "And she's my mum too. I'm sorry I didn't tell you, son. I didn't want to upset you…"

Suddenly, Ben could see the pain in his dad's eyes. "That's OK, Dad," he said.

"Me and your mum have been up all night looking everywhere for you," added Dad, as he squeezed his son even tighter. "We never would have thought to look for you at your granny's. You always said she was boring."

"Well, she's not. She's the best granny in the world."

Dad smiled. "That's sweet, son. But you could still have told us where you were."

"I'm sorry. After I let you down so badly at the dancing competition, I didn't think you cared about me."

"Care about you?" said Dad, a shocked expression on his face. "We love you!"

"We love you so much, Ben!" added Mum. "You must never think differently. Who cares about a silly dancing competition hosted by TV's Flavio Flavioli? I am so proud of you, whatever you do."

"We both are," said Dad.

They were all crying and smiling now, and it was hard to know if the tears were happy or sad ones. It didn't really matter, they were probably a mixture of both.

"Shall we go to Granny's for a cup of tea?" said Mum.

"Yes," said Ben. "That would be nice."

"And me and your dad have been talking," said Mum, taking her son's hand in hers. "I found the plumbing magazines."

"But—" said Ben.

"It's all right," continued Mum. "You don't have to be embarrassed. If that's your dream, go for it!"

"Really?" said Ben.

"Yes!" chimed in Dad. "We just want you to be happy."

"Only…" continued Mum, "…me and your dad think if the plumbing doesn't work out as a career, it's very important you have something to fall back on…"

"Fall back on?" asked Ben. He really didn't understand his parents at the best of times, let alone now.

"Yes," said Dad. "And we know ballroom dancing isn't your thing…"

"No," agreed Ben, relieved.

"So, how do you feel about ice dancing?" asked Mum.

Ben stared at her.

For a long moment Mum just looked straight back at him, then finally her face cracked and she burst out laughing. And then Dad was laughing too, and even though there were tears still on his face, Ben couldn't help joining in.

33

Silence

After that, things were much better between Ben and his parents. His dad even went to the hardware shop with him and bought him some plumbing tools, and they spent an extremely enjoyable afternoon together taking apart a U-bend.

Then, a week before Christmas, the three of them received a late night phone call.

A couple of hours later, Ben, Mum and Dad were gathered around Granny's bed. She was in a hospice, which is where people go when the hospital can't treat them any more. She didn't have long left to live. Hours maybe. The nurses said she could go any time.

Ben was sitting anxiously by Granny's bed. Even though she had her eyes closed and didn't seem able to speak, sitting in that room with her was an incredibly intense experience.

Dad paced up and down at the foot of the bed, unsure of what to do or say.

Mum sat looking on, feeling helpless.

Ben simply held Granny's hand.

He didn't want her to slip away into the darkness alone.

They listened to her raspy breathing. It was a horrible sound. But there was only one sound that was worse.

Silence.

That would mean she was gone.

Then, to everyone's surprise, Granny blinked and opened her eyes. She smiled when she saw the three of them. "I'm… famished," she said in a weak voice. She reached under her sheets and took out something wrapped in clingfilm, which she started unpeeling.

"What's that?" asked Ben.

"It's just a slice of cabbage cake," wheezed Granny. "Honestly, the food in here is *ghastly*."

A little later, Mum and Dad went out to get a coffee from the vending machine. Ben didn't want to leave Granny's side for one second. He reached out and took her hand. It was dry, and so light.

Slowly, Granny turned to look at him. She was running out of time, Ben could see that. She winked. "You'll always be my little Benny," she whispered.

Ben thought how he used to hate that name. Now he loved it. "I know," he said, with a smile. "And you'll always be my Gangsta Granny."

❋

Later, after Granny had finally gone, Ben sat quietly in the backseat of his mum and dad's car as they drove home from the hospice. They were all tired from crying. Meanwhile, loads of people were out Christmas shopping, the roads were full of cars, and there was a long queue outside the cinema. Ben couldn't believe life was going on as normal when something so momentous had just happened.

The car turned a corner and approached the little parade of shops.

"Can I pop into the newsagent, please?" said Ben. "I won't be long."

Dad parked the car, and as a light snow was falling, Ben made his way alone into Raj's shop.

DING! went the bell as the door opened.

"Aah, young Ben!" exclaimed Raj. The newsagent seemed to notice the sad look on

Ben's face. "Is something the matter?"

"Yes, Raj…" spluttered Ben. "My granny just died." Somehow saying that made him start crying again.

Raj rushed out from behind the counter and gave Ben a big hug.

"Oh, Ben, I am so so sorry. I hadn't seen her for a while, and I guessed she wasn't well."

"No. And I just wanted to say, Raj," said Ben between sniffs, "thank you so much for telling me off that time. You were right, she wasn't boring at all. She was amazing."

"I wasn't trying to tell you off, young man. I just thought you had probably never taken the time to get to know your granny."

"You were right. There was so much more to her than I ever imagined." Ben wiped the tears away with his sleeve.

Raj began searching his shop. "Now… I have

a packet of tissues somewhere. Where are they? Oh, yes, just underneath the football stickers. Here you go."

The newsagent opened the packet and passed them to Ben. The boy wiped his eyes.

"Thank you, Raj. Is it ten packets of tissues for the price of nine?" he said with a smile.

"No no no!" chuckled Raj.

"Fifteen packets for the price of fourteen?"

Raj put a hand on Ben's shoulder. "You don't understand," he said. "They are on the house."

Ben stared. In all the history of the world, Raj had never been known to give anything away for free. It was unheard of. It was madness. It was… it was going to make Ben cry if he wasn't careful. "Thank you so much, Raj," he said, quickly, choking up a little. "I'd better get back to my parents. They are waiting outside."

"Yes, yes, but just one moment," said Raj.

"I have a Christmas present somewhere here for you, Ben." He started rummaging around his cluttered little shop again. "Now, where is it?"

Ben's eyes lit up. He loved presents.

"Yes, yes, it's right here behind the Easter Eggs. Found it!" exclaimed Raj, as he produced a bag of Murray Mints.

Ben was a tiny bit disappointed but he did his best to hide it.

"Wow! Thank you, Raj," said Ben, doing his best school-play acting. "A whole packet of Murray Mints."

"No, just one mint," said Raj, opening the bag, and taking a single Murray Mint out before handing it to Ben. "They were your granny's absolute favourite."

"I know," said Ben, with a smile.

34

Zimmer Frame

The funeral was on Christmas Eve. Ben had never been to a funeral before. He thought it was bizarre. As the coffin lay at the front of the church, the mourners mumbled their way through unfamiliar hymns, and a vicar who had never met Granny made a tedious speech about her.

It wasn't the vicar's fault, but he could have been waffling on about any old lady who had just died. He went on in a dreary monotone about how she liked visiting old churches and was always kind to animals.

Ben wanted to shout out. He wanted to tell everyone, his mum and dad, his uncles and aunts, everyone there about what an incredible granny she was. How she told the most amazing stories.

And most of all he wanted to tell them about the marvellous adventure he had shared with her, how they had nearly stolen the Crown Jewels and met the Queen.

But no one would have believed him. He was only eleven. They would assume he had made the whole thing up.

When they arrived home, most of the people who were at the church descended on the house. They drank cup after cup of tea, and ate plate after plate of sandwiches and sausage rolls. It seemed weird having the Christmas decorations up at such a sad time. At first people chatted about Granny, but soon they were gossiping about other things.

Ben sat alone on the sofa, and listened to the adults talking. Granny had left him all her books, and they were now cluttering up his bedroom in great piles. He was tempted to hide away in his room with them.

After a while a kindly-looking old lady moved slowly across the room with her Zimmer frame and eased herself down next to him on the sofa.

"You must be Ben. You don't remember me, do you?" said the old lady.

Ben looked at her for a moment.

She was right.

"Last time I saw you, was your first birthday," she said.

No wonder I don't remember! thought Ben.

"I am Granny's cousin, Edna," she said. "Me

and your granny used to play together as girls, when we were just about your age. I had a fall a few years ago, and I couldn't cope on my own, so I was put into an old folk's home. Your granny was the only person who would come and visit."

"Really? We didn't think she ever went out," said Ben.

"Well, she came to see me once a month. It wasn't easy for her. She had to get four different buses. I was extremely grateful."

"She was a very special lady."

"She was indeed. Incredibly kind and thoughtful. I don't have any children or grandchildren of my own, you see, so me and your granny would sit in the lounge of the old folk's home and play Scrabble for hours together."

"Scrabble?" said Ben.

"Yes. She told me how much you liked playing it too," said Edna.

Ben couldn't help but smile.

"Yes, I loved it," said Ben.

And to his surprise, he realised he wasn't lying. Looking back, he had loved it. Now his granny was gone, every moment he had spent with her seemed precious. More precious even than the Crown Jewels.

"She never stopped talking about you," said Edna. "Your dear old granny said you were the light of her life. She said she would really look forward to you coming to stay on a Friday. It was the best part of her week."

"It was the best part of my week too," said Ben.

"Well, if you like Scrabble you must pop over to the old folk's home one day for a game," said Edna. "I need a new partner now your granny's gone."

"That would be great," said Ben.

Later that evening, as his parents watched the *Strictly Stars Dancing* Christmas Special, Ben climbed out of his bedroom window and slid down the drainpipe. Without making a sound, he took his bike out of the garage, and cycled to Granny's house one last time.

Snow was falling. It crunched under the wheels of his bike. Ben watched it come down, landing softly on the ground, barely paying attention to his route. He knew the journey off by heart now. He had cycled to the old lady's so many times over the last few months he knew every bump and crack in the road.

He stopped his bike outside Granny's little bungalow. There was a scattering of snow on the roof. Post was piled up outside, the lights were all off and there was a 'For Sale' sign with icicles hanging off it standing outside.

Even so, Ben was half expecting to see Granny at the window.

Looking at him with that hopeful little smile of hers.

But of course she wasn't there. She was gone for ever.

But she wasn't gone from his heart.

Ben wiped away a tear, took a deep breath, and cycled off home.

He sure had an amazing story to tell his grandchildren one day.

Postscript

"Christmas is a special time of year," said the Queen. She was her usual serious self, seated majestically on an antique chair in Buckingham Palace. Once again delivering her annual message to the nation.

Mum, Dad and Ben had just finished their Christmas lunch, and were slumped together on the sofa with mugs of tea watching the Queen on TV, as they did every year.

"A time for families to get together and celebrate," Her Majesty went on.

"However, let's not forget the elderly. A few weeks ago, I met a lady around my age and her grandson, at the Tower of London."

Ben squirmed uncomfortably in his seat.

He glanced at his parents, but they were watching the TV, oblivious.

"It made me think how the young need to show a little more kindness to the elderly. If you are a young person watching this, perhaps give up your seat for an elderly person on the bus. Or help them carry their shopping. Share a game of Scrabble with us. Why not bring us a nice bag of Murray Mints, once in a while? We old folk do love a nice chomp on a mint. And most of all, young people of this country, I want you to remember this, we old people are certainly not boring. You never know, one day we might even shock you."

Then, with a mischievous grin, the Queen lifted up her skirt to the entire country and flashed her Union Jack knickers.

Mum and Dad spat out their tea all over the carpet in astonishment.

But Ben just smiled.

The Queen's a proper gangsta, he thought. *Just like my granny.*

Jack's grandpa wears his slippers to the supermarket, serves up Spam à la Custard for dinner and often doesn't remember Jack's name, but he can still take to the skies in a speeding Spitfire and save the day…

When Tom gets hit on the head by a cricket ball, he finds himself at Lord Funt Hospital, and is greeted by a terrifying-looking porter. Things go from bad to worse when he meets the wicked matron in charge of the children's ward… But Tom is about to embark on the journey of a lifetime!

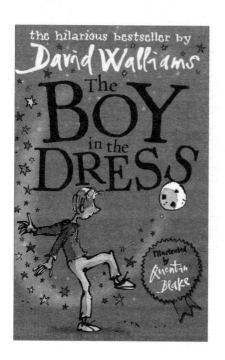

Dennis lives in a boring house in a boring street in a boring town. But he's about to find out that when you open your mind, life becomes anything but boring!

When Chloe makes friends with Mr Stink, the local tramp, she soon learns that some secrets have a way of leading to disaster. And that there just might be more to Mr Stink than meets the eye... or the nose.

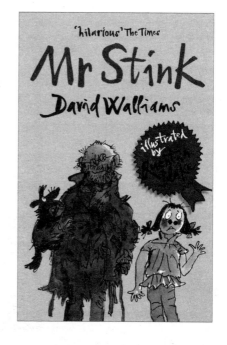

Meet Joe Spud, the richest twelve-year-old in the world. Joe has absolutely everything he could possibly want. But there's one thing he still really needs: a friend...

Ben's grandma is the boringest grandma ever: all she wants to do is to play Scrabble, and eat cabbage soup. But then he discovers she has a dark secret… She was once an international jewel thief!

Join Ben on the adventure of a lifetime – you'll never think of grannies in the same way again…

Zoe's got a lot of things to be unhappy about... Her stepmother's so lazy she gets Zoe to pick her nose for her. And the school bully loves flobbing on her head. Worst of all, the dastardly Burt has terrible plans for her pet rat. And guess what he's going to do with it? The clue is in the title.

Stella Saxby is the sole heir to Saxby Hall. But awful Aunt Alberta and her giant owl will stop at nothing to get it from her. Luckily Stella has a secret – and slightly spooky – weapon up her sleeve...